Scylla & The Monsters of the Enneagram

by

E. E. Whitaker

WWW.OAKLEAPRESS.COM

CONTENTS

Dedication

For my inner Child.
You make me brave.

Prologue: Death

I cradle her in my arms, wrapping her stone-cold flesh in the ravaged black clergy robe. Tears burn like fire from hell as they stream down my frozen face. I stare down at the woman I love. Lips blue, body limp. She's gone. For God's sake, Maria is dead.

1 - Anger

Christmas Eve is chilly every year, although last year was an exception. It was cold—the temperature dropped into the low twenties. Not this year. The air feels almost refreshing as we step into the night—it's only slightly below freezing. We quickly realize, however, that we need to watch where we put our feet—the pavement is slippery in spots. Remnants of the afternoon drizzle must have turned to ice when darkness fell.

Maria descends briskly down the stairs, and waits for me by the iron gate. I shut the ten-foot-high wooden sanctuary doors and lock them. I glance up at the church—its front wall ascends high into the night sky. Built in the mid nineteenth century, the gothic architecture of St Luke's Catholic Church gives it a hint of romantic whimsy juxtaposed by the tingly, slightly creepy feeling of a haunted history. The dark walls climb eight stories high on the west wing where a small tower houses a large bronze bell that rings three times a day—at dawn, midday, and dusk.

I hurry to catch up with Maria, my long legs descend the steps two at a time. Maria opens the rod iron gate, which groans ungratefully in the cold. She pulls at a newspaper that has been wedged between the bars by the winter wind. She scans it for a moment or two, tosses it into a recycling bin, and then remarks with exasperation in her voice, "A house caught fire and of course it was across the street from the Braden house." She crosses her arms and continues. "A young black couple—both of them killed. They're blaming it on a space heater. What a load of bullshit. I bet this is another one of those hate crimes made to look like an accident."

Maria has been following news reports over the past six months that have to do with accidental and unexplained deaths—specifically the deaths of minorities and marginalized people in the poor west end of our city. Her theory is that these deaths are not accidents—that somehow they are all connected by a large evil system—a cabal that plagues the city of Louisville. Personally, I think she's paranoid, but nevertheless, I do find their deaths appalling.

I reply with frustration, "Makes me sick. Shit like this shouldn't happen."

I shut the gate behind us, latching it back into place so that it reconnects to the three-foot high rod iron fence that surrounds the property.

We walk together on the sidewalk—I gaze up at the small cathedral. Her sanctuary only sits a couple hundred parishioners, but her presence is fierce and beautiful in this neighborhood of 19th century Victorian homes.

Our footsteps echo off the walls of the building—the downtown streets are nearly abandoned this late hour. We turn down fourth street, and I hear my colleague black boots click on the cement at a slightly quicker pace than mine. She's half a foot shorter even in her three-inch heeled boots. Barefooted and side by side, my narrow hips end up at the bottom of her robust chest.

I catch a glimpse of our reflection in the storefront windows that we pass by. We're opposites in almost every way, drawn together by difference, complementing one another in both skill and personality. I'm larger in physique with broad shoulders that never fit right in anything with sleeves, and I have a long narrow waist that sits on top of thick, muscular legs. Standing at a height taller than the average man, I naturally take up space. The streetlights turn my fiery, red tangles into dark crimson locks that end at my shoulder, which causes my pasty skin to glow.

My name is Alex. An abbreviated name I gave myself in early childhood to mask deep layers of a shameful, dysfunctional family history. I'm a therapy case for the best psychologist, but I'd rather work my shit out with a spiritual director—a catholic nun in her nineties named Sister Agatha. After twelve years, she's at least helped me name and claim a small truth—I've got anger issues.

We cross over Broadway Boulevard, and our pace slows as Maria and I cautiously navigate ice patches on black asphalt. I glance over at her—she zips up her large, puffy, purple coat, pulls the hood over her head, and tucks in the scarf that's wrapped around her face—you'd think we were in the middle of a blizzard. This brings to mind that Maria grew up in central Texas and that she often reminds me Kentucky is closer to Canada than it is to Texas. These thoughts make me grin.

I put my gloved hands in the pocket of my black, leather jacket. I've owned this jacket for five years now—a gift given to me the day I took my first set of vows. If the temperature doesn't drop into the teens, it keeps me warm enough. I wrap my red scarf twice around my neck, and the sheep's wool gloves given to me by my Scottish friend keep my hands cozy from the cold, damp air.

We step onto the sidewalk just as two police officers patrolling on foot cross over to the other side of the street. I can only see their backs—cannot make out their faces, nor am I willing to stop for conversation considering the late hour and our narrow window of time. Maria picks up the pace and walks ahead of me as we move closer to our destination.

The presence of cops causes my heart rate to quicken. I wonder, "Why would police be patrolling these abandoned streets at this late hour?" Then I think, "Maybe they're looking for someone. Two young people walking the streets on Christmas Eve—we probably look suspicious, or worse—like easy prey."

I gaze protectively at Maria who is now about five feet ahead of me. A gust of wind blows her hood back, exposing her face and hair. It pulls her dark, wavy hair away from her face so that it cascades gracefully down the middle of her back. Deep, green eyes compliment her high cheekbones and chestnut skin. She's attractive, with curves in all the right places. I can see why both men and women desire her. I think I would too if I were sexually attracted to women. "Why" is a question I've often asked myself, "Why not women?" I have come to the conclusion that not all women are attracted to other women—even those as luscious as Maria—because I often find myself coming to the realization that I'm only sexually attracted to men. Anyway, it doesn't matter now. Having taken our vows, neither men nor women are options for either of us.

My defensive instinct quickens my steps. I catch up with her and walk close beside my petite friend and colleague. Maria is twenty-six years old and has been my associate for the past year. At the end of next year, she'll take her final vows to become a full Catholic Priest. For now, her title is Sister Maria, and my job is to guide her, train her and watch over her. From the moment I met her, I've felt a strange impulse, a deep pull in my gut to protect her from only God knows what. I'm responsible for her as her supervisor and Mother Superior. But my protective posture toward her comes not only from the desire to help her prepare for ordination, but also because I've noticed how people look at her—and the look I see unsettles me.

When Maria enters a room full of people, something strange

occurs. If you watch closely, you will see people naturally shift towards her. She may be short and petite but her presence always instantly becomes known. She has the qualities of a seductive chameleon, changing herself often unconsciously in order to pull people towards her. I call this trademark of hers, "woo" power. She has an unnatural ability to win over others.

I, on the other hand, have "shoo" power. I naturally shove others away. My intensity, often unspoken, is felt by any person within a ten-foot radiance of my presence. It's partly why I prefer the company of non-human beings. The stature of my body doesn't help my intimidating nature—but it isn't the primary cause. I've known for a while now that my intense presence isn't why people move away—not why they give me a wide berth.

Sister Agatha says I have a gift, but most of the time it feels like some sort of medieval witch's curse. And I don't mean one of those curses that superheroes complain about. I'm not whining about x-ray vision, superhuman strength or the ability to fly—no. I have the not-so-cool ability to see the darkness in people. If I lock eyes with someone long enough, inner monsters emerge like shadowy creatures oozing out of that person's body. Sister Agatha says I have the spiritual nose of a bloodhound, sniffing around in the dark to find foul pieces of the human soul. Most people aren't consciously aware of what I see and sense in and around them, but that doesn't keep their bodies from instinctively pulling away the moment we meet.

I'm jostled out of my thoughts when Maria and I turn a corner, and my feet wobble on the icy concrete. My black oxford shoes with leather soles start to slide, but I stabilize myself and am able to keep my hands in my jacket pockets.

We pass under a large sign that arches across the street that welcomes us to Louisville's downtown entertainment area. The words in neon red letters buzz with electricity and light up the street, "Fourth Street Live."

It's ten o'clock on Christmas Eve. All the shops are closed and the windows of restaurants dark, making the evening seem haunting—certainly not holiday jolly.

I notice the same two cops from moments ago circling back to the other end of fourth street. One of them, a tall, well-built man, stares in our direction. We turn down another street, and when he spots us, I see a broad smile spread across his face. An icy shiver ascends my spine, but I keep walking and attempt to shake off the tingling chill created by his Cheshire grin. Marie and I pause as a car passes by. Then we cross Fifth Street and turn down a familiar dark alleyway towards our favorite bar. I peek down at my watch and see that it's five after ten.

We're stuck in the gap between two Christmas Eve masses. Last year, we tried waiting to eat until after midnight mass, but I found myself drooling over the body of Christ. That night I was grateful that our Catholic tradition obligates us to eat every last crumb of the Eucharist or we would have looked insane scarfing down the body of Christ like rabid dogs huddling in the robe room.

Maria and I are part of the first generation of female Catholic priests, or rather, perhaps I should say, "Catholic priestesses." But everyone, even the Pope, still uses the word "priest" for both male and female. It seems that patriarchy is always harder to let go in word than in deed, and yet, here we are, two female priests running our own parish.

Five years ago, the Catholic church opened up the role of priest, bishop and even cardinal to women. Women are now allowed to lead the Church—as if they hadn't been doing so for two thousand of years. Five years ago, I was one of ten women world-wide to become an official priest of the Roman Catholic Church. The formalities of these changes are irritatingly late but necessary for the survival of the Institution of the Roman Catholic Church.

This new rule came about when the Vatican realized that male priests, especially in western countries like the United States, were dying out quicker than men were replacing them. As happened during the World Wars, women stepped into male positions that had been denied them for centuries. They quite naturally rose to the occasion. But such a massive change did not come without concessions.

The two biggest compromises included forbidding opposite gender priests to work together in the same parish. And, no surprise—sadly, the rule of celibacy didn't change. The Church still speaks of sexuality with a stick shoved up their ass. God forbid that we priests should embrace our whole bodies, or even acknowledge the spirit of God moving in areas below our bellies. This is not to mention the absurd rule of segregating parish leadership by gender. The Church doesn't want any priests succumbing to the temptation of procreation—not to mention that its leaders are still avoiding any conversation concerning same-sex attractions.

We don't have a female pope yet but I believe it's only one generation away. Maria says I'm an idealist, but deep down I'm just a stubborn and controlling feminist who wants to redeem centuries of misogyny with a female pope. I've told her countless times that whatever it takes, I will push the rivers of religious patriarchy to flow in this direction—even if it kills me.

Maria, a third generation Mexican American, who was raised by a strong mother and grandmother, shares my passion for empowering women. The day we met back in seminary, she said to me, "We forget that women have always had that power. We give life, co-creating with God in ways that men can only grasp in theory. I believe men envy women, which is why they create artificial systems and rules that put them in charge, which makes them feel superior—such as the Church and the nuclear family. It gives them the illusion of being the Creator."

I'm snapped out of my thoughts when Maria and I finally arrive, chilled and famished, at our favorite bar and secular sanctuary. I look up at the neon sign. A few of the red letters have bulbs burned out but the outline of each letter can still be seen. TONY'S GAY BAR & DANCING.

We climb six concrete steps to a large metal door. Pop music seeps through the cracks of the door frame. Maria reaches for the door handle. Without warning, the door flings open and a wave of Adele crashes into us along with a two-hundred-pound drunk. The force of the intoxicated human knocks Maria backward causing a domino effect of a melodramatic proportion.

I'm knocked back by Maria's flaring arms as my hands try desperately to grab onto her puffy sleeves. Her jacket rips under my fingertips and I tumble backwards over the railing into a large dumpster. I land on a cushion of God—knows-what.

Stuck inside this damp metal box, I hear Maria groaning and shouting curse words in Spanish. The noisy commotion and Adele bellowing out the ballade, "Hello," fill the otherwise silent night.

I hear a deep voice yell down the alley as I heave my body up, popping my head out of the dumpster. The same two cops from earlier are walking towards us with flashlights in hand.

One cop yells with his a hand on his holster, ".LCPD , what's going on down there?"

"Of course," I mumble to myself. "The Louisville City Police just happen to be walking by at this very moment."

The cop yells something I can't make out. He flashes his light on the drunk body sprawled face down on top of Maria.

She grunts urgently, apparently trying to answer and somehow free herself. Her hundred and twenty-five-pound petite frame is trapped face up on the ground—the full weight of a two-hundred-pound sack of potatoes pinning her down, crushing her. She struggles to push the human lump onto the cobblestoned ground; her ankle-length, black skirt slides up her knees, revealing her bare calves and far too much flesh of an upper thigh.

The cops grin wide, casually walk towards the two of them, and pull handcuffs from their belts.

The taller one chuckles and says, "Alright, alright—at least you two coulda found a better place for this illegal Christmas intercourse."

The trash below me is swishy, hindering my ability to move as quickly as I would like to the edge of the large dumpster, but I get to the metal side and hoist my body up and out of the stinking place.

"Wait!" I bark out. "She's with me."

I breathe heavily and bring one long leg over the dumpster edge. I remind myself this is why I always wear pants. I don't want to imagine what sort of hogwash would have slipped its way between my legs if I had a skirt on.

Poor Maria was not so lucky.

My second leg swings over the edge and one of my black oxford shoes slips off and sinks beneath the quicksand of disgusting debris. No time to search for it now, I hop down and land gracefully on two feet—one shoeless.

I stand tall and speak clearly as I catch my breath. Then I inhale and say calmly, "Officers, we were just coming from the parish a few blocks down for a quick bite to eat before midnight mass."

The tall cop keeps his eyes on the burlesque show entitled in my mind, "Ava Maria and the Drunk."

The shorter cop says sarcastically, "Yeah, yeah. Sure you were, and we're male strippers on our way to a bachelorette party."

He continues his mocking monologue, and I realize I know this guy. His name is Wendell Thompson. He's one of our parishioners at St. Luke.

I decide words are not necessary and remove my red scarf and filthy jacket, drape them over my arm, and face him with a glare of irritation and indignation on my face.

Wendell glances over at me and the white mark centered on my neckline, and immediately stops his snickering. I feel my white clergy collar glowing, bright and obvious, tucked into the neck of my black long sleeve button down shirt.

Wendell's eyes grow wide. His horrified gaze moves from my collar to Maria struggling on the ground. He sobers up and says in an apologetic tone, "Forgive me, Mother. I didn't recognize you or sister Maria." Then he darts over to help Maria who is still pushing and shoving in an attempt to get the drunk man off her body.

The taller officer, whom I do not recognize, helps Wendell remove the drunk and pull her up off the ground. Then Wendell makes an effort to bring the drunk man back to consciousness. Maria stands slightly hunched over a bit dazed and confused as she begins straightening her skirt, which is twisted halfway around her waist. The other officer, whom I still don't recognize, watchers her in a way that instinctively bothers me. She removes her jacket, which has been torn on the left arm and examines the damages. The officer intensifies his scrutiny of her body with each of her movements.

She looks over at me, her ponytail pulled to one side, and holds up her torn jacket. In a frustrated tone she says, "Alex, this is what happens when we try to eat between services. I knew we should've stayed behind and prayed. But no, you said 'this year we eat, pray, sleep.'"

I half smile at Maria's surprisingly accurate impersonation of my voice and hand her my jacket knowing that her southern blood is already starting to freeze solid. She graciously puts it on and her body is swallowed up—the leather sleeves drooping like curtains over her arms. I turn to Wendell who now has the drunk man slumped up against the dumpster from which I just escaped.

Wendell is a stocky man, standing at what I generously judge to be five foot seven. A few strands of dark brown, curly hair pop out beneath his wool police hat. He is a few years older than me with a wife of ten years and two children under two. I know his family well and believe Wendell to be a kind man who would rather follow another's lead. He certainly has no desire to be in any position that requires making decisions. His family has been faithful members of St Luke's for three generations.

I smile warmly at him and ask, "How's your mom doing, Wendell?"

He freezes not expecting casual pleasantries from his priest he thought was a prostitute up until a few moments ago, particularly not in a dark alley outside of a gay bar. He looks hesitantly at his partner—I glance at him as well and it occurs to me with a twinge of certainty that I've seen somewhere before.

Wendell replies anxiously, "Mom's doing okay—thanks for asking."

Three months ago, Wendell's father, John was diagnosed with stage four prostate cancer. I'd recently been giving him and his wife marriage counseling after a one-night fling he had with a female co-worker six weeks after the diagnosis. I decide to keep the awkwardness going with another question.

"Will you be able to celebrate Christmas in the morning with Brene and the kids?"

Wendell's glances over at his partner as his face turns red. It's clear to me he does not want to expose his religious life to his partner. He puts his handcuffs away and appears to think for a moment before answering.

"Uh. Yes. I'll meet them at the parish for midnight mass when I get off at eleven."

Maria speaks up. "Wonderful! We look forward to seeing y'all there." She appears to have regained her cheerful demeanor. "Hopefully your father will feel well enough to come with your mother. Maybe your partner would also like to come."

Maria walks over to the dumpster and bends down to inspect the unconscious man lying against it. I figure she feels compelled to help him.

I also catch another unsettling look from the other officer who grins a predatory smile as he watches Maria's derriere rise into the air. He moves quickly, bends down beside her and appears to check the man's vital signs.

Wendell says, "My partner? Oh, right." He turns and looks over at him. "Officer Laine, are you free this evening for midnight mass?"

My attention sharpens, and I look in the direction of Officer Laine—intrigued to hear his answer. My gaze drifts to the man slumped up across the metal grime of the dumpster. His dark face contrasts greatly next to the pale hands of Officer Laine who seems to be gripping the man's shoulder extra firmly with his other hand. To my relief, the unconscious man is breathing heavily, but when Office Laine releases his hold, the man's head falls to one side like that of a rag doll. Apparently unfazed by this, the dark-skinned man begins to snore so loudly that it drowns out the music wafting from the wide open bar door. Without Officer Laine's hand on the black man's neck, I can see a mark of some sort, a white scar or tattoo just below his ear. I squint hoping to make out the shape or symbol. From where I stand, I can tell they're letters—two to be exact, the letter "A" and something else.

My view is blocked when Officer Laine stands up and smoothly guides Maria towards us like true southern gentlemen—one hand on her lower back and the other grasping her left hand.

With a sympathetic grin, he looks straight at Maria and says, "No miss, I'm afraid I'm not available to attend mass tonight."

She smiles back graciously.

My stomach rolls.

Seeing the strange hands on my partner I growl under my breath. "Well, now, that's just too bad."

Officer Laine scowls at me and says in a frigid tone, "I'm not Catholic anyway. We Baptists don't do midnight mass."

I glance at my watch and notice that it's already a quarter past ten so I push aside the temptation to make a snide comment about Baptist and Catholics.

"Well," I say in an overly friendly voice. "We're in a bit of a hurry. Sister Maria and I need to eat before service so we'll just leave you two with him. I know you both realize this, but I feel compelled to say it nonetheless. It's far too cold to leave a man in his condition outside. I trust you'll fulfill your duties as servants of the people and make sure he finds a warm place to sleep."

Then, with a nod, I say, "Peace to you both," grab Maria's other hand and turn towards the blaring vocals of Celine Dion singing "I will always love you."

I take one step up the concrete stairs when a feeling hits me that I'm forgetting something very important. The thought vanishes when Officer Laine speaks, behind us.

"You know the Waffle House over off Eighth street is open. Wouldn't that be a safer place to eat? You obviously see what kind of filthy fags come and go from this place."

I crane my head to the side in time to witness Officer Laine kick the foot of the dark-skinned man sleeping helplessly on the ground, and my grip on the handrail tightens. Hearing his words stirs up my internal hornet's nest of suppressed anger and rage pulses like wildfire through my veins. "Really?" I say to myself. "Did he just spew those homophobic, racist, wise ass words to two priests?"

My heart thumps heavily in my ears. I turn slowly around and stare directly at Officer Laine. He stands tall with the confidence of a male of the species privileged from birth. The rage builds as words begin forming in my mouth.

I tell myself, "Breathe, just breathe."

Ten years ago, I'd have spewed cursed words no human, let alone a priest, should ever utter, and my fist would have broken his nose before he could take hold of his police baton. Now, after a decade of anger management, a few nights in jail and long hours of soul work with Sister Agatha, I have learned the ancient art of breathing and counting to ten in my head—all of which is easier said than done.

I breathe in through my nose and search Officer Laine's baby, blue eyes. This is the first time I have really looked at him. He's taller than me, but I stand one step above him, and so we are currently eye-to-eye. His skin is golden—as though he had just stepped out of the California sun. Unlike Office Thompson, he does not have on a wool hat. His blonde hair is cut short on the sides, and it is longer on top in trendy hipster style. By the outline of his thick police coat, and the way he carries his body, I can tell he is muscular and athletic. He must be somewhere in his early forties—an attractive man with a confident stature and a charming smile that makes me dislike him even more.

We gaze at one another for a long moment—eyes glaring. Intensity growing. Then I see it, a dark shadow flickering in the whites of his eyes. The smell hits me—an aroma of decay, burnt flesh roasting in fire. When I first started seeing others' shadow creatures, or as I call them, "Scylla," I didn't connect the smell with the creature right away. But now I know the odor well—it always accompanies the Scylla.

Maybe it was the dumpster debris clinging to me that kept me from smelling Officer Laine's Scylla before its scent began emanating from his body. Either way, his Scylla has emerged like smoke rising from a cigar. A murky haze hovers around his figure creating an eerie halo. The air around me shrinks. My senses sharpen and the whiff of human decay lingers in my nostrils.

I step down and close the gap between us. I watch the shadow creature outline his body in a black misty cloud. The hairs on my neck stand erect—I now see the creature wrap its tentacle-like arms over Officer Laine's shoulders, around his waist and between his legs. Then Scylla tightens, squeezing his body. I peer into Laine's smoldering eyes and watch fear dilate his pupils. Paralysist outwardly sets in—his right-hand twitches and he tries unsuccessfully to grab the gun from the holster attached to the belt around his waist.

My concentration is broken when I feel a hand gently touch my shoulder. Maria speaks with a firm but soft tone. "Mother Alex and I prefer to eat here."

The sound of her voice and the warmth of her hand cause me to blink, and I release the eye lock. The world reopens. Scylla disappears instantly and Officer Laine smoothly places his right hand in his pocket.

Maria's hand tightens on my shoulder and she continues in a scornful motherly tone. "We don't mind eating with those children of God discarded by the rest of the world." Then, with a nod and a half smile, she says, "Now, y'all both have a very Merry Christmas."

My eyes are still focused on Officer Laine as my lips curl into a slight, satisfying smirk. He glowers at me—shock combined with rage boiling in his eyes.

I watch his mouth move, silently calling me a name I haven't heard since I was convicted of attempted murder thirteen years ago. The word "Witch" forms around his lips and a wide smirk spreads across his face. As I turn to follow Maria up the stairs, Officer Laine winks wickedly at me. My intestines twist as I walk through the open door to Tony's Gay Bar and Dancing.

2 - Pride

Maria slams the heavy metal door. No doubt she wants to be sure it shuts all the way. I pass by and hear her take a deep breath. She releases it in a long sigh of relief. I know she prefers to avoid any and all conflict and is fully aware of my anger issues. Nevertheless, she doesn't appear to know about my strange abilities to see the monsters that inhabit and can come forth from people. Come to think of it, I've only told one person about Scylla, Sister Agatha.

I look at Maria and shake my body like a dog that's just emerged from a bath, flicking off the excess water. "Well, that could have been worse." I say with a hint of sarcasm.

I walk in front of her along the dimly lit, narrow hallway. The fleeting thought that left me moments earlier comes to me due to the freezing, wet sock on my limping left foot.

Apparently Maria notices it too and in a loud voice says, "Alex, where is your shoe?"

Over my shoulder, I begrudgingly yell out, "It's in the dumpster! I'll get it later. My stomach is getting the best of me. Let's go ahead and order food."

The thought of seeing Officer Laine again ignites anger in me that's so intense it radiates out of my bones and heats up my body. Sister Agatha once told me that standing within a five-foot radius of my fury is like standing at the edge of an erupting volcano.

I hear Maria stifle a laugh and know good and well she knows that my ridiculous logic about hunger isn't the only reason I don't want to go back outside. We both silently acknowledge that I want to give the cops time to leave the alley before I embarrass myself in front of two white men by rummaging through a dumpster.

Maria's been privy to very little about my past but she does know about my deep grudge against men, particularly white, Baptist men. I've only given her a few glimpses into my ugly past and that happened only after I'd consumed three double bourbons on the rocks.

We walk down the long passageway and a dark memory comes to mind. It happened nine months ago, following our Good Friday service.

* * *

We'd been working together for about two months, and she felt it was time to give me an honest read concerning our relationship. Maria's always been good about expressing her feelings in real time, and she expresses herself well, even though she prefers to avoid any tension in relationships. We were here at Tony's recovering from another night of lynching Jesus when the conversation turned to my childhood. I told her how my mother died when I was ten years old, and I followed that cheery story with the one about how I defaced a Baptist pastor with a letter opener after catching him with a naked teenage girl in his office. I'd been going on and on about why on God's green earth I would end up becoming a priest with my asshole personality and the capacity for empathy that mirrors that of a serial killer. She was laughing in kindness, I believe, realizing that I was for the most part being accurate in my self assessment.

Then her face became serious, the look in her eyes pierced my soul, and she spoke words I will never forget, "Alex, I liked you the first moment we met back in seminary. You're certainly bristly, cold and complicated—a no bull kind of gal. You say what you think, not giving a damn who is on the receiving end of your intensity. But the power you hold captivates and draws me like an insect to light. Five years ago, I was terrified of the future unfolding before me and even more worried about the world I was leaving behind. But Alex, you never seemed to feel any ounce of fear or weakness. Your confidence is intoxicating. From the moment our hands shook that first day of class, I knew I would follow you anywhere, even into the darkness."

The shock of hearing her sobering, sweet words silenced my usual snarky remarks. My soul was shocked by her kindness, and I was stunned speechless. I raised my glass in appreciation and sealed the moment with the last gulp of whiskey.

* * *

Back to the current moment and the long passageway, Maria has apparently decided to drop the subject of my missing shoe.

We step out of the dark hallway and into a large turn of the century converted ballroom. I glance around the room and admire the charming architecture that adorns our haven from ministry. Worn art deco with columns spaced every fifteen feet support several floors of the building above. It occurs to me that my favorite thing about Louisville is its underrated architecture and the design of the city. Most people outside of Kentucky couldn't tell you where Louisville is located on a map much less that Fredrick Olmsted, the great 19th century landscape artist who designed Central Park in New York City crafted the multi-facet park system of Louisville. Five beautiful parks are connected across the entire city. They wind around buildings like this little gem that now houses Tony's Gay Bar and Dancing.

Maria has only been in Louisville for a little over a year, and we go back and forth on our love for our home states. Maria says Texas is quite different from the rest of the country. She often tells me about the lovely mesquite trees in the hill country of Texas, but they always seem less enchanting than the vibrant oaks and maples of Kentucky that turn incredible shades during autumn. However, she makes a good point about Texas not having bitter, gray winters.

We pause and look to see if our usual table is available. Maria stands beside me, scanning the place. I notice her body shivers as she clutches my leather jacket. I wonder how in the world Maria will survive another Kentucky winter.

"Come on," I say, motioning to the table across the room. "Let's get you some bourbon and hot food before you shiver yourself back to San Antonio."

We glide over to our usual corner booth that's adjacent to the bar. Maria takes my coat off her shoulders and hands it to me saying, "I know—it's pathetic. Sometimes I wish my blood boiled like yours."

She twists her skirt slightly to the right, adjusts her bra and blouse, then sits. "Thanks again for letting me wear your jacket," she says. She looks at her torn winter coat and sighs. "At least my underwear and my ego are better off than this mangled thing."

She tosses the torn jacket to the other end of the booth before scooting her petite frame across the worn leather seat.

Still standing, I smile wide and let out a hardy laugh. She looks up at me with disapproval, shakes her head, and then returns my laughter. We both cackle together recalling the ridiculous series of events.

She says, "I still can't believe you lost your shoe." She smiles and stares down at my feet.

I nod. "What a series of unfortunate events. I'll go look for it in a bit."

Her eyes move from my feet to the tangled, flames of hair around my head.

"You should probably take a look at yourself in the bathroom before you do anything. Something green and horribly gross will sprout legs in your hair if you don't remove it soon."

She grabs my left hand and looks at the blood around the two middle knuckles, and I recall that I scraped on the inside of the dumpster.

"Maybe you should get a tetanus shot, too. Are these cuts from the dumpster or from a fist fight you had with that cop while I was too busy playing the prostitute?"

We laugh again, and I pull my hand away playfully. "If I get a tetanus shot, then you're getting a pregnancy test."

She winks. "Touché."

"Want me to order our usual from Tony?"

She agrees, still giggling. I head back around the booth towards the bathrooms making a pit stop at the bar. I make eye contact with the bartender who is also the owner. Tony is a tall, lean yet strong man from Scotland. He's probably close to six and a half feet in height and carries himself with a gentle grace, especially for a man his size. He must be somewhere in his early forties; his thick, dark brown hair is cut close to his scalp, and his five o'clock shadow is speckled with gray hair.

I joyfully greet him with a wide grin and a bit of residual laughter, "Merry Christmas, Tony."

He smiles back at me with a surprised expression growing on his face. "Aye, yeu're in a jolly mood. In the past fives yers I've known yeu I've never seen yeu laugh like this before."

"Well, I—"

His response makes me self-conscious, and I feel my body tighten. But I remember it's only Tony. He's a good friend, and so I ease down my guard.

I say, "It's Christmas, you know. If you only knew half the story of my evening, you'd probably have a good laugh, too."

His charming smile broadens, and I feel the tension in my shoulders ease. Five years ago, when I met Tony, he'd just taken over the bar after relocating here from Edinburgh, Scotland. In the time I've known him, he has disclosed the same amount of personal information with me as I have with him, which is little to none. Tony's not a religious person but from a few conversations I gathered he most likely grew up Catholic or Presbyterian. To my knowledge, he's not married, and I'm not sure whether he's gay or straight. All I know is that he's in town working on a PhD at the University of Louisville.

I met Tony at the bar the night after I took my priestly vows. The ceremony was at Saint Luke's where I served as associate and now serve as senior priest. After all was said and done, I searched my phone for bars nearby. Tony's Gay Bar and Dancing showed up. Coming here made sense. No way was I going to break my vows of celibacy if I spent my first night out as Mother Alex drinking at a gay bar.

Over the last five years, Tony's place has been a sanctuary for me. I come here regularly—whenever I need a strong drink and a respite from the rigors of clergy life. For some reason, my clergy collar doesn't cling as tightly when I'm with Tony. I feel a closeness with him, a deep connection I'm not able to explain. When everyone else seems to pull away from me—or rather, is pushed away, Tony stands his ground. He somehow is able to withstand the tension others apparently feel due to the intense presence I exude.

Thinking about our connection causes me to grin, and it draws my gaze into his kind, emerald eyes. We stare at each other for longer than we've done before. Heat grows between my thighs, and my heart beats rapidly in my chest. My cheeks flush, which forces my eyes to dart to the shelves of bourbon above his head.

I swallow slowly as I feel his gaze still resting over me.

He breaks the awkward silence. "Since Christmas is tomorrow, after all, may I offer yeu a flatterin' word from a friend?"

My eyes return to his, and my face contorts as if I just ate sour grapes.

"Consider it an early Christmas gift."

I tilt my head to one side, questioningly. "Alright, but just this once."

He leans in close to me, forearms resting on the bar top. The masculine musk of his body wafts over me, and I swallow again.

He pauses for a few seconds before speaking.

"Alex, yeu're a bonnie lass... especially when yeu're laughin', which is far too rare, in my opinion."

My face grows hot and I can feel blots of redness swarming my pale face. I start to say something witty but Tony holds up his hand.

"Hold on, now. I'm not finished. I know yeur coldness protects yeur heart like a vulnerable chamber hidden inside an ice castle, but when yeu smile, if only for a moment, the ice begins to melt and warm lovely lines form around yeur mouth—rippling softly across yeur pale face. Yeu... yeur beautiful."

My lips pressed firmly together along with my legs. I can tell by his reaction to the expression on my face that my warm heart has hardened back into the ice castle. Suddenly, daggers of intensity fly out from my mouth, words that will certainly wound.

"Fuck, Tony. Where did that come from? I literally just climbed out of the rubbish in your alley dumpster, and you throw that shit at me."

He stands up straight and adverts his eyes from mine, grabbing two glasses nearby. I can tell he's upset by my response as he mumbles to himself in a mixture of Gaelic and English.

I make out a few words of his rant. "God forbid anyone give yeu a compliment... yeur an attractive woman... clenching yeur fist... punchin' me in the balls."

Then he starts aggressively drying glasses with an off-white dish towel. I officially feel like an ass and try to recover the moment.

"Tony, I'm sorry." I stumble miserably over words. "I know... It's just that."

"Stop."

He interrupts me, slamming his towel down on the counter. His eyes stab me in return, penetrating my soul. I feel his intensity in my gut and blood pumps hard through my veins, my pulses thumping in my ears.

Then a familiar sour smell wafts up my nose.

"Not now. Not with Tony," I say in protest to myself, but I can't seem to advert my gaze. Then a shadow begins to shift around his green eyes, growing in strength, enlarging his pupils. I feel his shame and anger all at once as I watch the haze of darkness move out from behind him.

Then something strange happens. Instead of breaking away in the middle of an eye-lock, he leans in closer to me. Our faces are now less than an inch apart. His Scylla continues to grow stronger reaching out towards me, touching me. Electricity shoots across my skin as six large tentacles wrap around me. My body tenses, bracing itself for pain but then a peace that passes beyond understanding begins pulsing through my veins. My heartbeat quickens and my breathing becomes heavy as Tony holds my gaze for what seemed like forever.

A broad smile spreads across his face and his Scylla disappears. Tony leans back across the bar and returns to drying off the glasses as if nothing happened. I stare at him bewildered for several long moments until he breaks the silence.

"Thank yeu," he says in a lighter tone. "That's all yeu had to say. But no, that's impossible for yeu with yeur filthy sailor's mouth. With that temper yeu'd be better off saving people in a Scottish pub than a catholic parish."

I smirk, grinning at him, refusing to give him a gratifying full laugh that he recently disclosed as beautiful. With my mind unsure of how to process the last few moments of my life, I go with my gut.

"So, uh, any chance the kitchen is still open?" He nods smiling with the same charm from earlier. "Great. We'd like the usual, two chicken salad sandwiches and two old fashions."

With another nod, he turns and grabs a bottle of Weller's, my favorite Kentucky bourbon, on a nearby shelf. Tony may be from Scotland, but he knows his bourbon, and he somehow has mastered the southern delicacy of a chicken salad sandwich—halved red grapes, diced green onions and more chicken than mayo. In my opinion, chicken salad is never complete without a homemade crescent—too bad Tony will not give out his recipe, nor will he tell me where he gets his flaky crescents.

Tony prepares our drinks, and I move towards the bathroom. Along the way, I watch a lone dancer across the room swaying with an imaginary partner. He—at least I think "he" is the right pronoun—holds his right arm up, hand grasping the air with his left arm curved out in front of him. His dancing is surprisingly peppy under the circumstances, but how can you dance with glum, even alone, when "All I Want for Christmas" is blaring in the background.

I walk back down the dark hallway we came in through earlier and stop at the bathroom on the right. It's marked by a gender-neutral stick figure with half a triangle dress and half a straight leg. The figure is positioned above the word "whichever."

I smile and push open the door. The bathroom has two stalls with doors and a single urinal along one wall. Two pedestal sinks stand together adjacent to the stalls. The bathroom is several decades in need of updating but Tony keeps it clean. The first stall is occupied so I move towards the second one trying hard not to touch too much of my shoeless foot on the bathroom floor.

I hobble into the first stall and squat down with one foot off the ground. I lower myself down with the help of the handicap rails and glance down to the floor to check the bottom of my filthy sock. I catch a glimpse under the opening of the stall, and I see the navy, masculine shoes of the person in the stall next to me. Pants aren't gathered loosely around this person's feet, so I assume whomever it is has already finished their business. I half expect to meet them as I flush and step out. However, when I get to the sink and look in the mirror, I see the door of the first stall still closed behind me.

Using the mirror in front of me, I try to make out the figure I sense peering back at me through the cracks of the door. I shake off the weird vibes and rationalize to myself that this person just needs privacy to cry out their Christmas blues. Looking at myself in the mirror, Tony's words buzz back into my head as I clean up one section of my neck that's covered with black smudges.

Pulling out a few bits of debris from my hair, I try helplessly to smooth the waves poking out in all directions. My thoughts swirl around Tony's words. I can't believe he called me beautiful. Even more so, I can't believe he leaned into the eye-lock with me. It's as if he knew what I was seeing deep within him and cared less—or worse, cared more.

Seeing my face in the mirror, I examine my skin, pasty and blotchy in the dim light of the bathroom. Dark swells sit below my gunmetal, gray eyes. I, unlike Maria, choose not to wear any makeup. Currently the Catholic Church has no hard rules for priests and make-up. According to Maria, that might be a deal breaker for her when it comes to taking the priestly vows.

She once said to me with pride, "I believe it's possible to be poor, celibate and pretty. There is no vow of ugliness so why shouldn't I be allowed to highlight my God-given facial features."

I wash the grime off my hands with soap and glance back toward the occupied bathroom stall. I turn off the water and almost say something like, "You okay in there?" But I think it better not to impose on some poor soul obviously trying to hide from the world.

I exit the bathroom. When I see Tony place two orange peels in our old fashions on the bar top, the stranger in the stall completely exits my mind. I smoothly place two cocktail straws in our much-needed bourbon, and Tony winks at me.

I return to our booth with our drinks and sit across from Maria. We clink our glasses in the air.

"Here's to Christmas adventures."

She giggles again as we each both take large sips. The bourbon warms my belly, and I decide to remove the cold wet sock from my left foot. My wrinkled toes wiggle free. Maria stares down at the tattoo on the inside of my left foot where blood red words are painted across my pale skin. She shakes her head trying to pronounce the phrase.

"Yippee...ki...yay? Remind me again what the tattoo means."

"It's only a quote from the best Christmas movie ever." I smile, remove the straw and take a gulp. She gives me a confused look.

"*Die Hard*. Classic Bruce Willis," I reply slightly annoyed. "You should watch it with me tomorrow. It'll get you into the Christmas spirit." I take another big sip and my glass is suddenly half empty.

"I make no promises. Anyway, a real Christmas classic is *Love, Actually* and I've got baby Jesus to get me into the Christmas spirit."

I give her a sour look. "I completely disagree with you, not on the baby Jesus part but on the movie. Now, I'm totally forcing you to watch *Die Hard* with me tomorrow. Consider it a learning experience from your mother superior on how to better pastor people like me."

She takes a small sip of her old fashion and replies in a sarcastic, dry tone. "You're right, I do need to brush up on my pastoral care abilities for adolescent teenage boys desperately trying to suppress their sexuality with violence and machismo."

I snort with laughter and raise my glass. "Touché, Maria. I have to say, your wit has grown sharper under my guidance."

We sit, both of us smiling in silent contentment. I nurse my drink a bit more slowly, hoping our meal comes out soon so that I can continue to stall long enough for the cops to have left the alley.

I inspect the basement ballroom and notice a handful of people scattered about. It is Christmas Eve, after all. My heart feels twinges of sadness for the outcasts in the room—those individuals shamefully abandoned by their families because of their sexuality or their gender choice.

A man wearing a red Louisville cardinal sweat suit nurses a martini. He slouches on a stool at the century-old bar all the way at the far end from the one Tony is wiping down. A heavyset woman with short, buzzed hair sits at one of the small bistro tables to the right of the hallway. She's watching the lone dancer doing his thing in the middle of the ten-by-ten dance floor. I turn my eyes back to Maria and notice her staring intently at the lone dancer swaying under the lights of the disco ball. A tear slides slowly down her saddened face.

I'm taken back by the sudden change in mood and ask with concern in my voice, "Maria, you okay over there?"

"I'm okay," she says as though crying is the natural response for anyone who happens to be in the midst of misfits. She sniffles and adds, "It's just the way the disco ball scatters light across the walls of the room. It reminds me of my Quinceanera." She turns and faces me. "The day I became a woman ironically was the day I told my father I was a lesbian."

"Oh," I respond. I hold back as much shock in my voice as possible. "How'd that go down?"

Another large tear forms in the corner of her eye, and she takes a deep breath. Then she tells me a story that seems to have taken place a lifetime long ago.

"I was fifteen years old, standing in the middle of the dance floor looking up at the disco ball turning slowly above me—scattering light fragments across the grand ballroom. I was wearing a soft pink ball gown with jewel beading covering every inch of the sweetheart neckline and corset waist. Layers of satin and tulle bubbled out and down to the floor covering my four-inch, hot pink, peep-toe heels. Beaming with pride, I watched friends and family sitting at the beautifully decorated tables adorned with purple, pink and white roses. I'd been helping my mother clean an office building for three years, saving every penny for this one moment. Most Quinceaneras in our Mexican heritage are traditionally held in makeshift spaces like neighborhood alleys, backyards or converted gymnasiums. But I'd known ever since I was a little girl that I wanted a really elegant ballroom, with crystal chandeliers, fine china resting on white satin tablecloths and a large dance floor with a disco ball.

"Soon the music changed and I knew it's time for the father daughter dance. So my father gently took my hand and guided me closer to him. His name is Daniel, but everyone calls him Danny. Being the only girl between two brothers, I was a daddy's girl. He would say how he always loved me more than my brothers, Miguel and Samuel. If anyone was more excited about this day, it was my father who wanted more than anything in the world for me to be a good Catholic girl, marry a good Catholic boy and have lots of good Catholic babies. I was not opposed to any of his desires, except the part about marrying a boy. You'd think, the year same-sex marriage was legalized across the country that this wouldn't be an issue, but some traditions will never be redeemed.

"I remember my father squeezed my hands and looked down at me continuing the same ole conversation we'd been having for the past few months. He listed the names of all the eligible bachelors now present at the party whom he would approve of me dating, if not later marrying. I had no intention of telling him at that moment that I was gay. I was actually planning on avoiding the whole conversation until I was eighteen or maybe even eighty. But as we swayed alone on the dance floor, his intensity increased, his tone almost forceful. I remember he even started pointing at a few of the teen boys who were sitting nearby. Some of the teenagers started laughing at us. Everyone knew I was gay, even my own mother did, although she would never speak the words aloud."

Tony walks up to the booth with two large plates of food, and Maria stops talking. The aroma of hot fries and chicken salad hits my empty gut that's growling with longing for food. We grab our plates, and I see Tony looking at Maria's teary eyes, concern on his face. He glances over to me, and I shake my head and purse my lips to indicate that now is not a good time to ask. He nods and gives me a small smile. He reaches over and gives Maria a sympathetic squeeze on her shoulder before returning to the bar.

I look down at my food and make a painful yet sensitive decision to wait until she finishes her story before I gobble up my food. I take another large drink of bourbon and nod for her to continue her story.

"Something must've happened that night because my father never spoke to me like this in public. His face was stern, even angry. I could hear more laughter in the room. Then all of sudden my embarrassment turned to anger. I stopped dancing and froze, holding my father's hand in the air. I took a deep breath and braced myself. Then I summoned the words I had packed away deep inside me. I said to him with as much courage as I could muster, 'I love you, daddy, but it's time you knew. I'm not attracted to boys and will never marry a man. Daddy, I'm going to marry a woman.'"

I smile at Maria with pride. I've never heard her say anything about her sexuality. Actually, we rarely say anything about our own sexuality to one another. She closes her eyes and another tear falls down the side of her cheek. When she opens her eyes again her mascara is smudged on one eye. With one finger she blots the next incoming tear from her eye and continues her story.

"My dad stares at me with a blank expression, impossible to read. He drops my hand so forcefully it snaps against my dress. The music stops. I feel every eye in the room gazing in our direction. His face turns red with rage, eyes grow narrow, his lips purse. Out of nowhere—never had he ever done this before—he slapped me. His large hand slams across my cheek, and I fall to the ground.

"I look up at him with tears of embarrassment filling my eyes. He says in a low voice. 'Estoy avergonzado de ti. Ya no te amo.'

Then he turned and stormed off the dance floor, passing by the tables full of snickering teenagers and out the back exit door. That was the last time my father ever spoke to me."

Maria rubs the right side of her face as Mariah Carey's Christmas album fades out and Britney Spears begins singing "Jingle Bell Rock." I stay silent for a long moment and then drain the last of my bourbon from the class.

"Maria, I'm so sorry. Families can be real shits sometimes."

She smiles and wipes the grief residue from her cheek. "I know, you of all people understand."

Looking at my watch, I realize twenty-minutes have passed since we left the alley, and I desperately want to get my shoe and give Maria space and time to recover. I stand up, turn to her, and say in my best Arnold Schwarzenegger impersonation, "I'll be back."

Her eyebrows lift, and she gives me a questioning look. I stare blankly at her, lean over the table and take a big bite of chicken salad.

With a mouthful of food, I say, "Good God, didn't you grow up with brothers. No time to educate you, I need to go fish my shoe out of the garbage before she's lost forever in Dante's dumpster inferno."

I take another big bite.

She rolls her eyes and says in a dry tone, "I see what you did there."

I swallow quickly and laugh a little. "Come on, it was funny. No? Not even a chuckle. Okay, okay. Don't eat my fries while I'm gone."

I put on my leather jacket and walk as casually and confidently as possible with one naked foot down the dark hallway and out the door.

3 - Deceit

I push the exit door harder than intended, it flings it open and makes a loud bang when it hits the metal handrail. I wince at the startling crash and the rush of wintry air, then hurry down the steps and over to the dumpster's edge. The cops and the drunk are gone and both lids over the top of the dumpster are closed.

"How strange," I say to myself.

I decide not to dwell too much on the shut lids and tug the flimsy black rubber up and over the other side creating a whoosh of foul odor. Coughing and pressing my hand over my mouth, I hold my breath and stick my head inside. The dumpster is about three-quarters full.

I sigh, saying to myself, *"The only way to rescue my Beatrice is to dive down into the seven layers of human hell."*

I find my courage and take the plunge. My foot finds a protruding piece of metal attached to the side of the dumpster to use as a step, and I climb up and over the edge and descend back down into heaps of trash. I dig around, excavating through papers, bottles, and nasty wet things I dare not look at too closely. After a few minutes I feel a large piece of wool fabric and pull hard hoping to unearth my shoe. I yank and a thick limb flares up out of the trash and hits me in the shoulder.

I shriek, "Holy Mary and Joseph!"

Before I can scream again an expressionless face emerges in the trash. Dark brown eyes—open and lifeless. I scramble to the opposite end of the dumpster and cling to the side. I'm in shock—my mind is blank. An eternity goes by. I shake my head and breathe deeply, then reach over and poke the thick limb. No question—it is indeed a human arm. The dark brown face tilts unresponsive to one side, and a familiar, two letter, white mark is revealed. This is the same drunk man, the drunk who tackled Maria!

Cautiously, I call out, "Hello? Sir? Can you hear me?"

No answer. No movement. Then I see blood covering his upper chest, drenching the collar of his coat. A large slit beneath his chin has created a nasty, and apparently fatal wound across his throat. My body quivers and I know I need to get out of the dumpster but I can't move an inch.

My mind races, *Get out of the dumpster! Get out of the dumpster!* But I cannot move.

At last, my body responds, and I scramble to the edge while trying not to disturb anything around me. I throw one leg up onto the side, hoist my body up and over, and land hard on the cold cobblestones—hands and forearms first. Pain zips through my naked frozen left foot. I hunch over on the ground and suck in air. Then noises down the alley penetrate my consciousness.

A familiar voice calls out, "What's going on down there?"

Déjà vu hits hard, and my head swirls along with my intestines. Nausea sets in. I look up to see two sets of lights rushing towards me.

"Mother Alex, is that you?"

Officer Thompson's voice echoes in my ears. I shake my head again, my vision is blurred as they run towards me.

"Yes. Come quick."

I pull myself to my feet and use the stair rail for balance. Gagging and pointing to the dumpster, I say, "There's a person in the trash bin. I think they might be dead."

Officer Thompson and Officer Laine stand in the same place they stood less than half an hour ago. They stare at me as I settle myself getting a grip on both reality and my body. I speak clearer this time looking directly at both of them.

"There's a person in the dumpster who isn't moving or breathing or anything. I think whoever it is, is dead."

Officer Laine's reaction is less shock and more one of curiosity as he moves towards the dumpster.

He passes by, sniffs the air in front of my face, and gives me a sour look.

Under his breath he says, "Already drunk I see."

I remain silent, now regretting drinking my old fashion so quickly. I'm not drunk by any means, but I can see how it looks from his perspective. When they saw me, I was on the ground, appearing to be on the edge of vomiting, which is true, and then I stumbled to my feet out of breath.

Could this night get any worse?

Officer Laine steps over to the dumpster and shines a light inside.

"Yeah, there's a man in here. Looks like the same drunk from earlier." He speaks into the dumpster half-heartedly. "Hello? Can you hear me?"

Taking his police baton, Officer Laine pokes around inside

the bin and then grunts with little sympathy. "Yep, he's dead alright."

Officer Thompson steps over to the dumpster speaking with grave concern. He says, "How can you be sure?"

"I'm no expert, but there's a slit across his throat Jesus Christ couldn't heal." Officer Laine glances over at me, and with a condescending sneer says, "No offense, Mother. But he probably had it coming."

My eyes narrow as rage builds once again in my gut. I clench my fists, take a step closer to the dumpster, and stop short when Officer Thompson pulls out his radio.

He calls dispatch. The words "homicide" and "murder" jolt me out of my fury.

I want to leave the scene for several reasons, and turn in the direction of the club door. First, I'm about to pick up a fight with a police officer. In my not-so-long-ago adolescent years I've learned that fights with police officers never end well, especially for me. Second, I need to inform Maria and Tony about my grim discovery. Third, the cold-hearted, empty portion of my being is still very hungry.

The sisters at Sacred Heart often referred to me as 'food motivated.'

My stomach settles and I say, as casually and sympathetically as possible. "Well, I'm not of any help here. I'll head back inside and not get in your way. Let me know if you find my shoe."

I point down at my pale frozen foot covered with dirt and grime. By the look of Officer Thompson's face, my words and my nasty foot come across as being more insensitive than I intend. I climb the first step but am halted by the voice of Officer Laine.

"Wait now. You discovered the body. You're a witness."

I sigh to myself and keep my back turned towards him.

He continues, "Actually come to think of it, mother, you're a suspect."

I whip my head around so fast that my neck makes a cracking noise.

"What?!"

Moving to intervene, Officer Thompson steps between us. "Come on," he says, "she's a priest. There's no way she's the murderer." He turns and looks sympathetically at me. "But he's right, Mother. You're the only witness we have right now. The detectives will need to take a statement. They'll be here shortly."

I take another deep breath letting it out slowly. "Can I at least run inside and let Sister Maria know what's happening?"

"No, you can't," Office Laine replies sharply. "We have to keep you in our sight and at the scene of the crime."

I frown at Wendell with frustration smeared across my face. He gives an annoyed look to Office Laine and speaks in a polite but serious tone. "What Officer Thompson means to say is that one of us should go inside and inform everyone to stay put for their safety."

Officer Laine chimes in. "Yeah, the killer is probably inside as we speak. You never know what kind of fu—" He trails off catching the anger in my eyes and turns to Wendell with his back towards me but I can still hear his voice even though they are doing their best to whisper.

"Wendell, I would prefer not to go inside that rat hole. How about I stay out here and wait for backup?"

I fold my arms across my chest mainly for warmth but also to make clear my irritation. Wendell swivels back towards me and the door to the club. He says, "Officer Laine will stay out here with you, and you both will wait for the ME and the detectives to arrive. I'll go inside and check everything out."

Wendell walks up the steps, and as he passes by, he says softly, "Thank you for your patience. I'll send Sister Maria out as quickly as possible."

He opens the heavy metal door. Christmas pop music fades as the door closes behind him.

I put my hands in my jacket pockets and sit on the stairs with my bare foot wrapped around my right ankle. I watch Officer Laine closely but intentionally, careful to avoid any direct eye contact. I've already seen enough of his monster tonight—this isn't the moment to poke around his nasty wounds. Sensing my desire to evade interaction, he moves several steps down the alley towards the main street. He shines his flashlight around the cobble path and stops on pieces of trash here and there.

The cold begins to seep through my thin leather jacket. I exhale and meditate to clear my mind as I wait. Against my best efforts, however, the cold alley brings a haunting memory to mind from thirteen years ago.

* * *

I was seventeen years old, shivering and coatless on a bitter January evening, waiting outside the doors of the Southern Baptist Church, which my aunt and uncle dragged me to every Sunday morning and evening. I could still hear the hymn of invitation, or as I like to call it, the hymn of obligation, being played on the keys of the old church organ. A moment earlier, I was inside, I but thought it best to leave before I murdered someone.

During the sermon, the red-face pastor brought a word from the Bible on sex, which naturally made every man say "amen," and

45

every woman fold their hands over the laps like a chastity belt. Having already engaged in heathen intercourse, I slouched in my pew with my long legs falling wide open in protest. I shut out the yelling voice of the preacher until he brought up a teenage girl in front of everyone.

She was a peer I knew vaguely from school. I recognized her as the senior varsity cheerleader whose name was Hannah, and she had some second first name like "grace," "faith" or "hope." Her parents sat in the front pew several rows ahead of me. The father's arm wrapped around his crying wife. Propped up in my pew, fully attentive now, I wondered what was about to unfold. I could feel the tension in the room rising and my gut churned anxiously as I stared wide-eyed at the eighteen-year-old standing on display in the clutches of the preacher. Her face displayed shame and terror, which ignited anger inside me that began to boil. It was like watching a witch trial in real life.

Then the preacher said in a booming baritone voice, "Miss Hannah Grace has confessed to me this week—" He took a long dramatic pause, "in the privacy of my pastor's office she has been sexually active in the wicked ways of her youth."

The lack of pause between the words "office" and "she" was unfortunate, and perhaps even unconsciously timed because it made it sound as though she'd been sexually active in his office.

I smirked to myself but sobered up when he spoke again.

"Now, her sins have led to an appalling revelation—" He glanced down at her and raised his left arm in the air. "Pregnancy!"

The crowd gasped and groaned. Hannah Grace dipped her head down low, tears fell like rain to the floor. She clutched her arms self consciously around her waist. I leaned forward, rage pulsing, palms gripping the pew in front of me. I wanted to scream, run down the aisle, and smack a hymnal across the face of this arrogant, evil man. I glared at the preacher whose eyes swept the crowd slowly and eventually landed on me.

Our eyes locked. That's when I saw something I had never seen before, a darkness emerging in the whites of his eyes. A shadow began to grow out of him as he stared back at me. He stopped speaking to the congregation and held my gaze. Horror and curiosity sealed a trance I did not wish to break. I sensed his hatred, his anger, and his lust. The shadow slowly seeped out of his eyes forming a haze around the back of his body. I leaned in closer trying to comprehend logically what I was seeing. The world around me narrowed, my heart pounded in my ears, and then the odor of rotting eggs filled my nostrils.

Suddenly, like an alarm, the organist played a loud chord and the monster once wrapped around the preacher's sweaty body disappeared into thin air. For a second, a sly grin passed over the preacher's face as he combed his hands through his smooth, graying, red hair. He turned back to the teenage girl and started his fire and brimstone altar call. He extended the hymn of obligation and asked all members to come and lay healing hands over this allegedly wicked girl who had been sucked into a life a sin.

I looked down at my white knuckles, nails digging into the back of the pew. Beads of sweat fell from my forehead. My breath was heavy as I glanced around to see if anyone else saw what I saw. But no, everyone seemed mesmerized, too deceived by the preacher's performance. Many stood up and made their way down the aisle.

I stood, too, shaking and nauseous. My first instinct was to rescue the poor girl from the grips of Satan. But if I had, the witch trial would have turned to me and I would've burned as well. Instead of walking down the aisle, I went the other way up the aisle and out the glass doors—escaping into the cold, winter night.

* * *

A shiver from the cold snaps me out of my reverie. I'm back on the steps of the damp alley. My eyes focus on Officer Laine. Apparently, he is searching the crime scene for clues. I hear sirens in the distance and sigh a breath of relief. It isn't long before an ambulance and several police cars pull into the alley.

I stand and watch officers and detectives get out of patrol cars and make their way towards us. A tall black man in a suit and tie goes in the direction of Officer Laine. His face is stern as he exchanges a few words with Officer Laine before heading towards me and the dumpster.

He stretches out a wide hand towards me and says, "Hello, Mother. My name is Detective Clay."

I reach out, shake his hand, and notice he's several inches taller than I am. His hands are worn and I can feel his strength and sense his confidence in his grip. His soft brown eyes tell me he is kind but serious about his work and about the world.

I reply warmly, "You can call me Alex unless, that is, you start coming to my church."

"Thank you. I know you've had a long night and probably need to return to your parish as soon as possible."

"Yes, we do have mass at midnight. I must return to St. Luke's as soon as possible."

Detective Clay releases my hand and moves towards the nearby dumpster.

"Well, we will do our best to get you back."

I watch him search around the dumpster, as well as the steps and along the wall. Then he returns to me.

He says, "Can you tell me the details of your evening?"

I recall the events as best I can, starting when we first arrived at Tony's and ending my account when Sister Maria and I entered the bar. He listens attentively but I notice he's scanning my eyes and body language for any disconnect—for any false truths.

I finish and Detective Clay shines a light at my cold, white foot and then over into the dumpster he replies causally, "I see you're still missing your shoe."

"Nice catch detective," I say sarcastically.

He stares at me, and I Immediately regret what I just said.

He chuckles. "You're an unusual priest," he says playfully.

"Yeah, I get that a lot often before I put my foot in my mouth. Yes, I came back out here to look for my shoe, and that's when I discovered the body."

In a serious tone he says, "Why did it take you so long to come back out? I imagine your foot was quite cold."

"Well—" I hesitate. I want to formulate a response that makes sense concerning both my pride and hunger. "You see, I was hungry and in a hurry, and I wanted to get my associate settled inside with our food before I came back out."

"Hmm," he mutters, clearly not satisfied with my answer.

It occurs to me that silence is now the best course to follow.

I turn my attention to the officers marking off sections of the alley with caution tape. They set out barriers to keep pedestrians out. My gaze returns to Detective Clay who is now squatting behind the dumpster.

"No signs of struggle," he says into a small recorder in his right hand. "No signs of the murder weapon either. The killer might have dumped it, or it still could be on them."

He stands up and turns to me saying, "Alex, let me give you a straightforward assessment of the current situation."

I search him questioningly and prepare myself for the worst.

"Right now, things do not look good for you. You seem to be telling me the truth but some pieces aren't adding up. Mainly the fact that you came back out here by yourself to look for a missing shoe that could've been found earlier in the evening. It also doesn't help that your DNA is probably all over the dumpster and on the dead body. I'm afraid, tonight, you will be coming back to the precinct with me."

Before I can protest, the metal door behind us swings open. It slams hard again against the railing. Officer Thompson chases a coatless, worried Maria down the steps, followed to my surprise by Tony.

"Alex!" Maria exclaims. "I'm so glad you're okay." She hugs me tight, enfolding her small arms around my torso. "When Officer Thompson came in with a terrifying look on his face. I thought the worst."

Tony stands behind Maria, and she continues to squeeze the life out of me. He nods at me with a worried expression before turning his attention to Officer Laine who is all the way at the other end of the alley.

Officer Thompson and Detective Clay walk off to the side talking to one another at a volume too low for me to hear.

"Maria, I'm okay. You can let go of me." I stare down at her face and whisper with concern in my voice. "What did you tell Officer Thompson when he came in?"

She steps back and says, "I told him the truth. You and I went inside to Tony's for food and a drink. You ordered at the bar before going to the bathroom for a few minutes to get cleaned up and then we sat and ate for a while before you came out here to find your shoe."

"You told him, I went to the bathroom for a few minutes?" I snap, knowing that Maria's trying to help me but that piece of information is certainly not going to help my case.

"Yes, because you did go to the bathroom." Seeing my alarm, she tries to encourage me. "Alex, you didn't kill this man. We know that. They know that. The truth will set you free."

Maria glances back at Tony who seems to not be listening at all. She pokes him in the side. "Right Tony?"

Tony's focus quickly returns to us. He steps beside Maria and grabs my right hand. A wave of electricity jolts through my body. By the look on Tony's face, he seems to have experienced something similar. He speaks to me, but seemingly for the benefit of Maria.

"Alex, everythin' will be alright. Don't worry."

Tony's thumbs caress my skin with a soothing touch I haven't felt for years. My eyes close for a moment and my breath stops short. Then he suddenly releases my hand. My eyes open, and I follow his gaze to Officer Laine who is walking in our direction. Toney leans his head down beside my ear and whispers, "Don't trust him, Alex."

Tony straightens up, turns to Maria and me and says, "I need to get back to the bar. Let me know if you need me." Then he hurries up the steps and back into the building.

Maria looks at me and says, "He's acting strange. But he's right. Everything will be alright."

I'm not at all sure, but before I can respond, Officer Laine walks past us towards the dumpster, and Officer Thompson and Detective Clay return.

Detective Clay says to Maria, "Sister Maria, you are free to leave. According to your account of the evening, and the other patrons of the bar, there is no way you could've possibly been involved in this crime."

He turns to me with his kind eyes, but I already know what he is about to say.

"Mother Alex, I regret that you still have to come with me. More information has come to light that doesn't help your case in any way."

I put on my best poker face and nod silently. At this point making a big scene about my innocence is not going to help.

I turn to Maria and grab her shaking hand. "Maria, I need you to go back to St Luke's right away." I glance down at my watch and see that it's already half past eleven. With urgency I say, "You must conduct midnight mass without me. I know you know what to do. Then, as soon as you can, call Bishop Anderson and let him know what's going on."

She gives me a look that says her gut is wrenching, and her eyes are now watering.

"Don't worry. I'll be back later. Do me a favor. Don't watch *Die Hard* without me." I wink at her. "Office Thompson, can you give Sister Maria a ride to St. Luke's. It's cold and she doesn't have her jacket or time to walk back."

"Yes, of course." Officer Thompson squeezes my shoulder with reassurance and he and Maria make their way down the alley towards his LCPD patrol car.

Detective Clay and I stand next to one another.

He speaks first. "Well, I was expecting a little more protest from you about the situation but you seem to already know that making a scene at a crime scene doesn't help the innocent... or the guilty for that matter."

I give him a half grin. "The sooner we get to the precinct for the interrogation the sooner I can get back to my parish. Do y'all water board priests or stick with the simple good cop, bad cop routine?"

Detective Clay laughs with a wide smile. He starts to reply but Officer Laine walks up to me with handcuffs in hand, and screams, "Why is she not under arrest?"

He reaches for my right wrist, and I pull back looking at Detective Clay for support.

My voice shouts with equal intensity as Officer Laine reaches out again towards me. "What do you mean, under arrest? I've already agreed to go down to the precinct with you."

"Everybody calm down," Detective Clay says, grabbing Officer Laine's shoulder.

Officer Laine says, "Sir, she's no longer a witness. The current evidence and timeline now make her a prime suspect—currently the only suspect. You know as well as I do, according to the law, she must be placed under custody. Just because she's a priest doesn't mean she's not held to the same laws."

Officer Laine maneuvers out of the grip of Detective Clay and grabs hold of my arm. He twists it around behind my back. I know from experience that the more you struggle while being placed in handcuffs the more painful it can become for your wrists and your shoulders, and so I surrender to the claws of Officer Laine and keep my mouth shut. My eyes burn with anger as he slaps cold metal cuffs around both my wrists.

Detective Clay looks at me with concern and caution in his eyes. He intervenes, diplomatically. "Officer Laine, since Office Thompson has taken your patrol car to return Sister Maria to the parish, I will take Mother Alex to the precinct. I need you to stay here and help secure the crime scene."

Detective Clay takes hold of my elbow like he's my escort to a banquet. Officer Laine tugs me back causing the cuffs to dig further into my wrist.

I wince as he says, "Sir, I don't mind taking her. I can borrow another patrol and let you finish your detective duties here."

"No," Detective Clay replies forcefully. "As you pointed out, she's now a murder suspect and therefore as the LCPD Homicide Detective, I'm responsible for her."

Detective Clay steps forward and forces himself between us. He places one hand on my shoulder and the other on my lower back and pulls me away from Officer Laine.

Officer Laine clenches his teeth and replies, "Fine, sir. As you wish."

It's obvious Officer Laine is seething. He slowly steps back, crosses his arms over his chest in silent defiance, pouting as Detective Clay guides me down the alley at a fairly quick pace. The large hand on my back stabilizes me as I limp along.

A dozen steps away from Officer Laine, Detective Clay speaks into my ear. "Now I wonder, why on earth would Officer Laine behave so aggressively towards a lovely, Catholic priest?"

I turn my head towards him, keeping our pace. "Only God knows why, but then again she always does, doesn't she?"

A subtle smile spreads across his face.

"Detective Clay, you seem like a cop with integrity who follows the rules. One who rights the wrongs and who would usually step in with more ...uh... confidence when a fellow police officer handles a woman in the manner Officer Laine did just now."

We suddenly come to halt, and I have his full attention.

I continue, "Now I wonder—why on earth would you let Officer Laine's behavior slide with little reprimand in front of, as you said, 'a lovely Catholic Priest?'"

Detective Clay's expression remains neutral. I suspect he's wearing his poker face.

"You have an interesting way of reading the world. I should call you, Detective Alex instead of Mother Alex. But as to your question, only God knows why, doesn't she?"

A smirk twitches in the corner of his mouth as he pivots towards the police car at the end of the alley. He adds, "How about we get to the precinct before you have to change professions."

We arrive at his unmarked black Dodge Charger, and he opens the rear door behind the driver's seat.

"Thank you for getting the door for me. That's very kind of you." I say with a facetious tone of gratitude.

Detective Clay smiles with a brilliant set of pearly straight teeth. He opens his mouth to speak, but to the shock of both of us, a camera flashes behind us. It takes a couple of seconds for my eyes to adjust. That's when I see a reporter standing six feet away, behind the caution tape. He's taking photos of me, a priest, handcuffed and getting into a .LCPD car.

Detective Clay pushes me into the back of the car as gently as possible before another round of the camera flashes. He jumps into the driver's seat, and we accelerate quickly out onto Main Street.

"Alex. I had no idea the media was here already. I would've been more cautious if I'd known. With that said, I need to read you your Miranda rights. You have the right to remain silent—"

Detective Clay continues the criminal creed as I sit back, resting my head against the seat. I say to myself, "I was wrong. This night certainly could get worse."

4 - Envy

Thirty or so minutes later, I sit alone at a table surrounded by three empty chairs in a small, sterile room. I stare in a large two-way mirror on the wall in front of me. Luckily for my wrist, the handcuffs were taken off by Detective Clay as soon as we got to the precinct, and he was also kind enough to bring me some coffee. I tuck my hands comfortably into the pockets of my leather jacket and glance at the clock on the wall above the one and only door to the interrogation room. Both clock hands point straight up to the heavens. Midnight. Right now, Maria is beginning mass, reciting the sacred words of greeting and peace to our parishioners on this high holy Christmas day. Sighing to myself, I wonder why I can't be accused of murder on some other day—like, for instance, All Saints Day or Pentecost?

Glaring into the looking glass, my thoughts wander. They return to memories of my childhood—memories of my mother. I can hear her voice, as she reads to me every night before tucking me snug as a bug in bed. I remember our reflection in the mirror on the dresser across from my bed. She laid beside me and in the dim light of a nearby lamp, we traveled far away to new worlds, journeyed across time together, just she and me. On Christmas Eve, we discovered the ghosts of Dickens. Around Easter, we explored Dante and his inferno, and on ordinary, everyday night, we wrestled with monsters from the great heroic adventure of Odysseus to the great hunt of Moby Dick. Greek mythology was my mother's favorite, especially when it came to the monsters like Scylla, the six headed monster who lived in the waters across from Charybdis, the giant whirlpool monster that sucked ships into the deep.

I close my eyes, my heart warming at memories from long ago, and my mind returns to the night my mother told me the full story of Scylla. I was curled up under the covers, cradled against the warmth of her body. Her silky, black curls cascaded down her slender shoulder as she rested on her elbow. The bedside lamp behind casted a shadow over me as she read the story of sailors who sailed beside the shoreline, and were devoured by a monstrous six headed beast. I shivered and closed my eyes. I confessed to her my fear of monsters eating me in the night.

She closed the old leather-bound book with the words "The Odyssey" etched in gold along the spine. With her index finger, she twirled a loose red spiral of hair that jetted uncontrollably from my scalp. We sat in silence for a moment, her cool breath fell over me. Then she spoke, her voice in a low whisper.

"Isobel, you do not need to be afraid of monsters. Let me tell you about Scylla. Scylla was born a beautiful nymph but fell victim to lust and power. The envious sorceress Circe used Scylla as a means of vengeance against the sea god, Glaucus, who would not return her love. The sea god loved the beautiful nymph but was tricked by the grief and anger of the sorceress. It was a bath of poison that transformed Scylla into a monstrous creature with six dragon heads, each one filled with sharp, dagger-like teeth. Isobel, my darling child, monsters are simple people who have been victims of broken love."

Then she pulled me into her chest, wrapping her long, strong arms around my small frame. A melody from her motherland of Scotland flowed from her. Words from a language I did not know. Music from the ancient past. She sang a song of her people. She sang to me every night until she disappeared from my life forever.

* * *

My mother's voice wakes me from my trance. My eyes open searching for her presence but I realize it's not my mother's singing but my own that fills the sterile, interrogation room.

I find it interesting and perhaps not coincidental, that Scylla is the shadow creature I see in others on a regular basis. A few months after I first began seeing the Scylla monsters in others, I wondered if I had a Scylla living inside me. For years, I've felt her presence within me, and anytime I'm alone in front of a mirror, I look for her. I try to enter into an intimate eye lock with myself. But for thirteen years now, nothing has emerged—no shadow creature, no Scylla.

I peer across the room at my reflection in the large mirror, and stare for a long moment, wondering if and when Scylla would reveal herself. I take a sip of hot coffee, and the images of Scylla float away as the interrogation door opens.

Detective Clay walks in accompanied by an older white man who is a few inches shorter than myself and more than twice my age. He nods and grins warmly at me as he closes the door behind them.

"Mother Alex, let me introduce you to my partner, Detective Phelps. We've been assigned to this case. We also need to ask if you would like to have a lawyer present while you're being questioned."

Before I can answer, there's a knock at the door. Officer Phelps pulls the door and a familiar face walks in wearing black pants and a black button down shirt with a white, clergy collar. He's a short, stocky pale-skinned man in his late seventies with little hair left on his shiny, round head. He bounces into the room with the energy of a teenage boy on his way to a theme park. It's Bishop Anderson, my boss, mentor, and friend who is also a damn good lawyer.

"Sorry I'm late. I just got word about the situation about ten minutes ago. My name is Bishop Anderson." He shakes the hands of both detectives who stare at him with looks of confusion. "Before you ask, it's true. I am both a priest and a lawyer. It's a long story, but in moments like this I've found it fruitful to keep my lawyer credentials up to date. Have you all begun?"

But before the detectives can answer, Bishop Anderson turns, smiles at me, and takes the empty seat beside me in a swift movement that shows his grace. I wish this was the first time Bishop Anderson has had to put on his lawyer hat for me, but it is not. I watch him remove a large leather binder from his briefcase as the detectives sit down across the table.

Detective Clay clears his throat, and with what seems slight irritation, responds, "Welcome Bishop Anderson. No, we were just beginning when you arrived so divinely."

I half smirk at Bishop Anderson from the corner of my eyes.

"Now then." Detective Clay holds his fist to his mouth and coughs. "Mother Alex, can you recount the evening from beginning to end once again for us?"

I nod and begin. This time I start from when Maria and I left the parish.

Detective Phelps repeats. "So you arrive at Tony's Gay Bar and

Dancing at around ten fifteen?"

I confirm and add more to the account. "Yes, I remember looking at my watch after the series of events with the drunk, now deceased man, and the two police officers. It was about ten twenty-five by the time it all went down."

Detective Phelps asks, "Was that your first time meeting Officers Laine and Thompson?"

"I have known Officer Thompson for several years now. He and his family are members at St. Luke's. Tonight was the first night I had met Officer Laine."

"Detective Clay informs me that it appears that Officer Laine and you don't like one another. Did something happen this evening that would explain Officer Laine's behavior towards you?"

I glance over at Bishop Anderson and take a drink of my coffee, which is now cold.

"Officer Laine said a few homophobic words about the deceased and other patrons of Tony's. This upset me, and I made this clear to Officer Laine."

Detective Clay says, "You made it clear? How so?"

"Well... we exchanged a few intense glares, and I established that I was not going to tolerate that type of dehumanizing language."

"So... you looked at each other?" Detective Phelps shoots a quick look over at Detective Clay. "No words or aggressive actions were taken?"

I respond with hints of sarcasm. "Well, you see... I've been told I can give a rather unpleasant stare."

I feel Bishop Anderson next to me tense up, but he gives no outward signs of alarm.

* * *

Bishop Anderson has known me since I was in high school when I was handed over to my aunt and uncle by my abusive father. It was a few years after my mother died, and I started rebelling more openly and more often against any authority figure in my life. This brought about a series of periods spent in and out of juvenile detention centers. It was around that time that I ran into Bishop Anderson at the courthouse. And by "ran," I mean I literally ran into him. I had recently experienced my second uncomfortable eye lock in the hallway with the creepy, pervert of a prosecutor who was on my case. I bolted the moment his Scylla seeped out of him and came towards me. I was moving so fast around the corner, and at the same time peeking behind me, that I smacked right into Bishop Anderson, tackling him like a linebacker. He fell back, the wind knocked out of him, and he landed hard against the wall. I recall seeing him clutching his briefcase, a surprised expression on his face. I was on the ground catching my own breath, trying to think of a way to get out of that place. But before I could move, Bishop Anderson reached out to me with an open hand. He wasn't angry, not even upset. He was amused, and laughing to himself. I extended my hand to him and he pulled me up.

With a respectful tone, he says, "You should go out for the Chicago Bears next season."

With my usual quick, dry wit, I said, "Well, you see that's why I'm here. The courts are trying to decide whether men are ready for women to beat them at their little games."

He tilted his head to one side. At first, I was nervous that I had taken the joke too far, but he just laughed again and said, "What's your name, child?"

From that day forward, Bishop Anderson has been my friend, a friend who keeps reaching out to me.

* * *

I'm jolted out of my blast from the past when Detective Phelps waves at me and says, "Mother Alex, please. Please continue."

I walk them step by step through the event leaving out only minor details, like my intimate conversation with Tony. I regrettably get to part about me going to the bathroom, which is located by the alley door in a spot where no one could see me from inside the bar.

Detective Phelps chimes in again, "So you were in the bathroom cleaning yourself up for roughly three to five minutes. Was there anyone else in the bathroom with you?"

To my delight I answer with relief. "Yes! Yes, there was someone else in the bathroom. They were in one of the stalls. I didn't get a good look at them but I know for sure that someone saw me in the bathroom for that entire time."

"That's good news," Detective Clay says with a little too much enthusiasm. "So what did this person look like? Did you speak to them?"

"No, I didn't speak with them, nor did I get a good look. I actually cannot tell you much at all." I sigh frustrated with myself for not engaging the stranger in the stall earlier.

"I do know that whoever it was was wearing pants. They had to be over six feet by the height of their head in comparison to the height of the bathroom stall. Oh, and the person was wearing large navy men's shoes."

Detective Clay turns to Detective Phelps and says, "Okay. At least that's something, not much but something."

Detective Phelps adds, "Yes, if there was indeed a person to verify that you were in the bathroom during this time it helps your case. But we need to find this person and get a statement. And there's still the matter of you going back to the dumpster by yourself. No one was with you when you returned to the alley, correct?"

Taking another sip of sludge, I parse through those horrible moments alone in the dumpster with the dead man. I get to the point in the story when the officers find me on the ground in shock.

Detective Phelps jumps in. "Officer Laine said, and these are his words not mine, 'She was drunk and sloppy when we found her by the dumpster.' Any comments?"

"Drunk!" I bark back in fury. "I wasn't even tipsy. I had one drink. That lying son of—" But before I can continue my rant, Bishop Anderson interrupts me.

"Unless there is documented proof of my client's alcohol levels that statement is slanderous against her."

Detective Clay nods graciously and cautiously says, "Forgive us. Detective Phelps is merely recounting the perspective of one of the only two other people present at the murder scene. In the small window of time, you were in the bar and with the testimony of Sister Maria, I am positive Detective Laine was mistaken. We didn't mean to upset you, Mother Alex."

The soft chestnut eyes of Detective Clay lingering on mine. I hold his gaze, sensing a strange protectionism pulsing towards me. Several moments pass, and I feel Bishop Anderson shift before he clears his throat.

My eyes move away from Detective Clay, and I calmly say. "I did think it strange that they were still so close to the alley. It was my understanding when Sister Maria and I left them with the drunk man that they would make sure he found shelter. What did the officers do to help this man after we went inside Tony's?

The question immediately turns the tables. Detective Clay and Detective Phelps give each other a look that says a thousand words. I'd asked a question they had neither thought about, nor did they know the answer too, but could not say aloud.

The room is silent for a long moment, then Bishop Anderson speaks, "Yes, perhaps, my client has a point here. I believe Mother Alex has given you all she knows about the evening. Unless you are going to press charges, or keep her based upon better evidence, I think it is time for us to leave."

Bishop Anderson puts his leather notebook into his briefcase, pushes himself back in his chair, and stands up.

Detective Phelps speaks up, "Yes, it appears that Mother Alex has indeed given us all she knows." He turns to me and says, "Thank you for your honesty and cooperation. However, I must ask you not to leave town anytime soon. We may need to bring you back to answer more questions. We will actually be coming by later today to speak with Sister Maria."

I stand. I'm too tired to argue about them coming to our cottage on Christmas Day—the short hand on the clock above the door is over the Latin numeral one. My thoughts turn to Maria and feelings of envy fill my heart. At this moment, she is most likely cleaning up the crumbs of bread from the Eucharist table, securing all the sacred elements before locking up the church and taking the path to the small sanctuary we call home.

Detective Clay opens the door, and Bishop Anderson and I make an exit. As I walk towards the door, all three of them stop and stare down at my feet.

Bishop Anderson speaks first, "Goodness, Mother, your toes are practically blue."

"Well, the poor little girl was taken down into Dante's dumpster inferno. By now I imagine she's probably being examined by some low level intern in forensics."

Bishop Anderson grins, clearly amused by my sarcasm. I eyeball the detectives waiting for their confirmation.

"You're right." Detective Clay says, sympathetically. "Your shoe is here but it won't be returned to you anytime soon. Sorry, you have to go home Christmas morning shoeless."

I nod and add, "Well then, just tell the wise men around here to fill it with gold before you return it."

Detective Clay's face breaks into a full smile. Bishop Anderson gives me a wink then turns to ask Detective Phelps to discuss further details about my involvement in the case. I sidestep out of the way to allow them both to walk into the open room full of office cubicles where they continue their conversation. Then Detective Clay and I both try to move through the door at the same time, and we bump into each other.

We both stop abruptly—slightly embarrassed. He smoothly shifts to the side and holds the door. He gestures for me to exit the room first. "After you, Alex."

I walk past him and feel his hand press against the small of my back guiding me out the door. It's a strange feeling—I have no impulse to pull away. His hand is soft and stabilizing, a comfortable strength after a long night of intensity. A peace floods my spirit causing my mouth to turn up.

Detective Clay leans in close to my ear and says corner of his mouth, "Does the tattoo on the outside of your foot really say,

'Mother Fucker?'"

My smile widens to full pearly white as he asks, "Does you other foot say,' Yippee Ki Yay?'"

I lean in closer and whisper into his whisper. "Now, that's between me and God herself." He chuckles.

I can feel his eye on me as I follow Bishop Anderson who is walking confidently, as I limp along with a lopsided grin.

5 - Greed

My head lands on the soft pillow and my aching body wraps around the warm down comforter. Sleep consumes me—I'm officially dead to the world.

Dreams come to me almost every night, vivid and real, as if each day I live two different lives and exist in two separate worlds. Often, the next morning, I can piece together my subconscious as I try to decipher the code my mind works through when it's in another realm.

Tonight, my dreams come in a rush of intensity. Some deep place in me seems to register when a dream is about to turn into a nightmare. It's as if I can see it coming, and I yet am helpless to stop it as the dream warps into terrifying scenes. I land back in the alley alone and shivering, and I instantly know my dream is well on its way to becoming overwhelmingly dreadful.

* * *

I head straight for the dumpster, still shoeless but hoping to recover the unreconciled pieces of the night before. I get there and look inside. Empty. No trash. No body. No shoe. I slam the lid close, angry and confused. Then I hear footsteps behind me, I turn and see Officer Laine running fast—at superhuman speed—towards me. My feet stick to the ground like I'm glued permanently to the cobblestones. Five feet from me now, Officer

Laine leaps into the air and rams into me. We land hard on the ground and roll down the alley scratching and pulling at one another. When we finally come to a stop, he's on top of me. My arms and legs are pinned under his weight. One of his hands is clamping around my throat. I feel the cold earth piercing my body as breath leaves my lungs.

My right hand reaches out into the alley for anything to use as a weapon. My legs kicking, eyes blurring. I feel something in the dark. A piece of smooth wood. I grab hold and bring it into my line of sight. It's a dagger, a knife with a wooden handle. Without hesitation, I grip the knife tightly and slash Officer Laine's throat. A look of shock and horror fills his face. His hand releases my throat, and his body falls limp against mine. I feel his warm blood spill out of him and onto my chest. I push him off of my body, keeping a tight hold on the dagger. I get to my feet and take a close look at the knife. The blade is bloody. It's about four inches long and has one straight side. The other is curved, and it ends in a deadly sharp point. The handle is a quality wood, like mahogany. It looks and feels old and worn, and yet it's been properly maintained with oils and sharpening tools. I notice a mark branded by fire into the wood. Two letters that form a symbol. A distant memory tickles my mind but the thought is interrupted by church bells ringing in the distance.

* * *

I wake up to the noonday bells of St. Luke's ringing out to the neighborhood. The sun is peeping through the curtains casting beams of light across my bedroom. I curl up tight in the blankets and clutch for warmth. Bits of that dreadful dream come to mind. I stare across my room. My small wooden desk holds a lamp, a few candles, a bible, a rosary and my laptop. A few feet from it is my wardrobe. It's made of heavy oak, and carved with beautiful, simple details around the edges. The wood brings the last moments of my dream into focus.

"The wood of the wardrobe." I say to myself. "The wood of the dagger. Okay. You remember. Now what's the connection?"

I hear noises in the next room. Maria is in the kitchen most likely making her delicious breakfast tacos. My stomach growls in protest and all thoughts of the dream and daggers dissipate to my most basic desire: Food.

I slowly crawl out of bed, snatch wool socks from my night-stand and quickly cover my bare feet before placing them on the cold, hardwood floor. I take the comforter from my bed and drape it around my shoulders like a large, bohemian shawl. I open the bedroom door and my senses are flooded with the delightful aroma of fresh tortillas, chorizo and eggs. I breathe in deeply the smells of Christmas morning from my Mexican American colleague.

Maria is across the room at the small kitchenette. She wears an apron over her thick robe. Her hair is in a high messy bun and her feet are covered by two layers of wool socks. I move to the worn leather couch a few feet away from the kitchen and greet her as I plop down into the soft, sofa cushions.

"Hail Maria, full of grace and delicious breakfast. The Lord is with thee."

She laughs without turning to look at me. "You know I hate it when you refer to me as our blessed Mother Mary. It feels blasphemous... especially on Christmas morning."

Maria takes the bacon off the burner and reaches for the coffee. I respond in the same playful tone.

"It's just so easy to do. I can't help it."

She pours two cups of coffee and sits beside me on the couch. I reach out for the saving cup of life sustaining sustenance. Against my physician's advice, I still believe I can live on coffee and bourbon alone.

"What time did you get in last night?" I ask before indulging my morning vice.

"I came in around one forty-five after cleaning up and seeing everyone out. You were already asleep snoring like an old man. You even left your bedroom light on." She gives me a wry smile and adds, "Also, when I came in to close your door and turn off the light I heard you talking in your sleep. Something about "Tony" and "monsters." Any chance you want to elaborate? You and Tony did look pretty intimate at the bar last night."

I'm caught off guard by her question and choke on the hot coffee. I was expecting her to ask about the interrogations at the precinct, but she jumped right into a conversation I'm trying more so to forget. From her accounts of my sleep talking, my subconscious mind is trying to make sense of that dismal moment. I respond as casually as possible even though I know Maria can see right through my evasiveness.

"Well, Tony and I have known each other for a while now. I suppose he has learned how to push my buttons—that's all."

"Yeah, right. Sure enough—that's all. Since it's Christmas, I'll let you be greedy with your dreams. But I expect you to come to confession tomorrow."

She winks at me before hopping off the couch and heading towards the oven.

I reply with a dramatic tone. "Anyway, here's what I'm thinking about for Christmas Day festivities. We eat your delicious traditional tacos while you tell me about mass last night. We watch *Die Hard* and pray about whether 'Love Actually' would enhance Christmas Day or ruin it. Then we walk over to St James Square and check out all the beautiful Christmas lights."

Maria gives a big cheer in agreement, and I take another swallow of coffee. I soon peel myself off the couch and sit with Maria at the small dinette where I inhale her cooking like a hungry orphan child. For the next hour she tells me about mass and which families were present. We laugh together when she confesses to spilling the blood of Christ when she raised the cup to bless it.

She giggles and says, "I was so nervous doing it by myself. My hands were shaking in front of all those folks watching me. I felt like Martin Luther, but luckily my guilt radar isn't as high, or we'd have another reformation."

I fold my pinky and thumb into my right palm, straightening the first three fingers and motion in the air the shape of a cross and say, "Child, your sins are forgiven."

We both burst into laughter, again. Then Maria asks about my interrogation with the detectives. I tell her about Bishop Anderson showing up so divinely, and the line of questions asked. I leave out the moments between Detective Clay and myself but do, however, tell her about my dream last night—the one concerning Officer Laine.

She says with a look of concern on her face, "So, in your dream you kill Officer Laine, slicing his throat with an old dagger? Yep, I think we should keep your dreams between us. I don't think that one would help the case against you as the murdering sociopathic priest."

I chuckle, push my empty plate away and take a sip from my third cup of coffee. Then I hear a knock on the door. I look over at the clock. One thirty. I turn to Maria who is already on her feet moving to the front door of our little cottage.

She opens the wooden arched door and greets the visitors cheerfully, "Merry Christmas. What a surprise to see you again Detective Clay and... I'm sorry but I don't believe we've met."

I sit up straight and hear Detective Clay's voice. "Merry Christmas, Sister Maria. This is my partner Detective Phelps. We're sorry to intrude on your Christmas but we need to ask you a few questions."

I quickly and silently move from the table across the room to my bedroom before Maria is able to invite them in for coffee and conversation.

I hear her say to the detectives. "Please excuse our messy home. As you know, it was a busy night. Please take a seat at the table. I'll get some hot coffee for you both."

I close my bedroom door as both detectives walk in. I have no interest in further dialogue with the detectives, and they are clearly here for Maria—not for me. It's a good time to blow off some steam from last night, and so I decide to go for a run around the neighborhood. I put on my winter leggings, long sleeve thermals, and lace up my running shoes. Then I grab my wireless earbuds and walk out of my bedroom.

I glance briefly across the living room and see the detectives and Maria, who appear to be engaged in conversation. Before anyone can invite me to the table, I announce, "Maria, I'm going out for a run. Be back in a bit. Good to see you again, detectives."

The detectives sit, drinking coffee at the table Maria has miraculously cleared of our breakfast feast. Maria waves me on but Detective Clay looks at me with disappointment. Detective

Phelps is the only one who comments. He says flippantly, "Oh, darn. We were hoping you would join us."

I respond briskly. "I know you came for Maria's perspective on the evening. I don't wish to interfere."

I hurry out the front door, close it behind me and inhale the cold, crisp air. The frost from the night before clings to the trees and shrubbery around the cottage that sits snuggled up against the main building of St Luke's. To my joy, the neighborhood is silent, enhancing the enchantment of creation glistening in the sunshine of Christmas day.

Moving through the garden of dewy icicles, I push open the rod iron gate to the sidewalk. I can feel the presence of the tall stone cathedral above me. Her beauty and stature rise majestically up into the clear blue heavens. I stretch my legs taking in more deep breaths before jogging down the sidewalk.

I run for the next thirty minutes to clear my mind. The brisk air singes my lungs, sharpening my thoughts. My aching muscles slowly warm up and ease into a rhythm of gratitude. The burning intensity in my bones, which at times seems never ending, finally is released from my body.

* * *

Running along, my thoughts turn to a spiritual direction session a few years back when Sister Agatha informed me that physical work was good for my personality. She explained that physical exertion is one avenue for my constant aggression to express itself. I agreed with her and gave her a brief glimpse into the early aggressive years of my childhood.

I said, "For a child who grew way too fast for my age, I was surprisingly coordinated. When your forced antisocial childhood is spent on the margins of the playgrounds, you learn to harness and develop your strengths. I spent many days alone, leaping and flipping around on jungle gyms, which helped me escape into my mind where I was able to create imaginary worlds where I fought the monsters of the universe."

* * *

The memory of that moment fades a mile into the run and the dream of Officer Laine and the dagger enters my mind. The image of the engraved mark on the wooden handle dogs my thoughts—the letters "AM" weave together in a circle like a cattle brand. I make a wide loop around Old Louisville and it hits me. That's the same mark I saw on the neck of the black man in the dumpster. I look up, and the steeple of St. Luke's comes into view. I pick up the pace for the last quarter mile. I arrive at the edge of the church property and end the run out of breath. Stretching my arms around my body, I think aloud.

"What a strange connection? The dream dagger and real-life tattoo. What does that mark mean?"

I gingerly stroll towards the rod iron entrance to the cottage. At the gate, I see the detectives head out of the front door and grunt in dismay because I hoped they'd be gone by now.

I try to be gracious, after all it is Christmas, hold the gate open for them and say, "I hope you all enjoy the rest of your Christmas Day."

Detective Clay smiles wide at me. "Thanks. How was your run?"

Detective Phelps, clearly not interested in small talk, moves past me appearing to be slightly annoyed as he makes his way towards their car across the street.

Still panting and dabbing the sweat off my forehead with my sleeve I reply to Detective Clay, "Actually, it was rather breath-taking."

"I can see that. You know, you continually surprise me, Mother Alex."

"As I said last night, you can call me Ale—that is, unless you start attending St. Luke's."

"Since I'm still a Baptist, I guess I'll stick with Alex." He leans against the opposite side of the gate. "Alex, you're a very unusual priest. You and Maria are not what I would expect from the Catholic church."

"Well, thanks—I think." I grip the gate and pull my right foot up towards my butt stretching my quad muscle.

Detective Clay looks down at the ground. "It's good to see you have both shoes today. I hope we can return the other in a day or two."

"I'd really appreciate that. She's one of my few but favorite personal items. I hope your conversation with Maria was fruitful, but by the look on your partner's face, I'm guessing it may not have been what you came to hear."

Detective Clay leans closer to me. His face changing to a more serious expression. "It's been a difficult case, or should I say cases. What happened last night was one of several murders this year that have the same MO, but each crime scene has come up cold. It's been frustrating. Last night's situation was a little different. Not just because two catholic priests were involved—but because we had a witness."

"Sorry to hear this. I didn't realize those other murders around town were connected. Is that why Officer Laine was so on edge?

If I was a less grace-filled person, I might file a complaint the way he put me in cuffs."

"Sorry again about that. I should've stepped in sooner as you said to me last night. But your instincts were right, I have other concerns about Officer Laine and did not want to tip him off."

I tilt my head questioningly. "That's okay. I can keep confidence pretty well as a priest. Though I would like to ask you about something I saw last night that I just remembered this morning."

He smiles back, the serious tone leaving his voice, "Sure. What is it?"

"I remembered an image, a brand of sorts I saw on the neck just behind the ear of the deceased before and after he died. It came to me in a dream this morning. I'm sure it's not relevant, but I think at the very least I should get it off my mind."

The smile on his face dissolves and his voice sharpens, "What did you see, Alex?"

His tone alarms me, and I decide the best way to describe it was to outline the image on the palm of his hand.

"Let me see your hand."

He lays his large brown hand face up in my pinkish, pale palm. His hand is warm as I stretch my fingers to hold it steady. I take my right index finger and trace the image "AM" in the artful circle I remembered seeing.

Looking up at him I ask, "Mean anything to you?"

Eyes wide, he nods, and I can sense his resistance to give up more knowledge about the case. He evades my question with another question.

"Did you see this image anywhere else besides on the body?"

"Well, not exactly. I saw it in a dream I had last night, but in the dream, it wasn't on the body."

"Where was it?" He asks with urgency.

"Remember this was only a dream. In it, I was back in the alley last night and I discovered a knife several yards down from the dumpsters."

I think it best not to say much more about me slitting the throat of Officer Laine in that same ally.

"The symbol was engraved on a knife."

Distressed by my words he interrupts me. "Was it a wooden dagger? Old and worn like it was from another century?"

I let go of his hand and stare at him. "Yes, but how would you know that?"

"I can't say, but I know that dagger. I have to go now."

"Ok. Please, let me know if I can be of any further help."

I move around the gate towards the cottage. As I brush past Detective Clay, he grabs my arm gently but firmly.

He whispers in my ear, "Be careful, Alex." His breath is warm on my neck as I peer into his compassionate, yet anxious eyes. "You need to know something. You are a person of interest, and I am not just talking about the LCPD."

I nod slowly—he lets go of my arm. I walk to the front door, turn and gaze back at Detective Clay as he crosses the street and gets into the passenger seat of the car. They drive away.

My thoughts linger on Detective Clay's warning as I scan the neighborhood.

I go inside the warm cottage, and call out, "Maria?"

She's standing over the sink washing dishes. "Yeah? What's up?"

I enter the kitchen area and ask, "Did you tell the detectives about my dream?"

"No, I said earlier that would be a bad idea. And it was only a dream. It wasn't real."

"Okay. Good. Thanks."

My chest tightens as I turn and move towards the bathroom. I want a hot shower and a reprieve from my paranoid thoughts.

Maria and I spend the rest of the day enjoying the last bits of Christmas joy without burdening ourselves with more discussion about the events of the previous night.

6 - Fear

Christmastide has always been my favorite season. The commercial and cultural pressures of parties, gifts and all the pomp and circumstance fade away, followed by a quiet, relaxing period of twelve days. People aren't hurrying to buy things they and no one really needs. Schools closed. Children playing in the snow. For the most part people seem to experience joy. The only truth we clergy have to remember is that people who are on the edge of death, often pass away right after Christmas. It's as if they hold on for the one last holiday hoorah, and then let go. Others squeeze in surgeries after Christmas and before New Year's Day because they've already met their annual deductible.

These two realities nip my Christmastide enthusiasm in the bud. This morning, the day after Christmas, Mr. Thompson, a sixty-nine year old member and father of Officer Wendell Thompson, passed away from cancer. Maria is currently sitting with a family whose loved one is in surgery, and so the pastoral moment falls to me.

The call from the Thompson family prompts me to put down my two morning indulgences—coffee and philosophy. I look over at my bedside table full of books stacked high in no particular order that are surrounded by several dirty coffee mugs. A side table full of literature is one the few good things I remember from my childhood.

Reading has always satisfied a deep longing. I love to learn about and imagine worlds beyond the wreckage of my current reality. Growing up, when I was not physically exerting myself in sports, I was reading just about anything and everything. Science, fiction and philosophy were my preferred topics, but I would devour any book that kept me in my head and my thoughts far from my broken heart.

Now, as an adult, I've developed a steady rhythm of reading. In the morning I'm into a variety of books—philosophy, science, religion. Then, in the evening, I go to bed with a wizard, who will one day die doing the right thing.

Begrudgingly, I change out of my warm loungewear and put on my black wool dress pants and black long sleeve shirt. I fold in the white collar around my black neckline and instinctively reach for my oxford shoes but end up disappointed.

I say to one lonely shoe in the closet, "No worries my friend, If I have time this afternoon I'll swing by the precinct and see if we can rescue your sister."

My thoughts turn to Detective Clay and wonder whether he will be at the precinct this afternoon. I put on an old pair of black boots with two-inch heels, throw on my leather jacket, and look briefly at myself in the floor-length mirror by the front door. I'm more than six feet tall in these boots—my head touches the top of the mirror edge. I notice the tangles of hair around my face and run my fingers through the fiery waves. I reach over to the entrance table, pick up a bobby pin and pull the loose hairs hanging around my face behind my ear. Then I wrap the red scarf around my neck and leave the toasty cottage.

Maria needed our only car, a twenty-year old blue mini cooper, for the hospital visit across town, and Barley Brother's Funeral home is about five blocks North of the church. So, I'm left with three options: reliable but slow public transit, my road bike, or a brisk walk through the neighborhood. I decide to walk to the funeral home, and if time allows, take the bus to the precinct.

The sidewalks are busier than yesterday. People are out and about, doing this and that around their homes, and to my dismay, there aren't many children playing outside. I imagine them all imprisoned indoors playing with new technological toys that require a screen and little or no physical exertion. Maria and I share the same frustration with contemporary culture. She once preached on the false gods of Egypt, comparing them to the false gods of consumerism and smartphones. In the pulpit that Sunday morning, she spoke with conviction:

"Technology, like gold and fine jewels, is not evil, but how we warp them and shape them into gods breaks the first two of the ten commandments. Thou shalt have no gods before me, and thou shalt not create any graven image."

I remember her homily explicitly because it kept being interrupted by a phone ringing in the massive handbag of an elderly woman, who, bless her heart, couldn't hear the phone, let alone the sermon.

My journey across the neighborhood leads me to the Barley Brother's funeral home quicker than I expect. I walk in the main entrance, and I'm greeted by Mr. Barley, himself, the youngest and only living Barley brother. He is a bald-headed, tall, thin white man in his mid-eighties. Hunched over his cane, he stretches out a shaky hand to me.

I take his hand and say warmly, "Merry Christmas, Frank. I hope you had a peaceful Christmas yesterday."

He shakes my hand firmly and replies, "Yes, you know how it is. Folks try and hold on till after the holidays. I know that Mr. Thompson was a beloved parishioner in your church, and that he will be missed."

"Yes, I was fond of him. I knew his passing would come before long and was able to give last rights three nights ago when hospice informed the end was imminent. He was a pillar of our parish, a member for more than fifty years. Has the family arrived?"

"No, they were still wrapping up a few details at the home when we picked him up. They've already decided on cremation. That being the case, would you like to come see him before they arrive?"

"Yes, thank you. I'd like that."

We walk slowly side by side, his cane clicking on the old, hardwood floors with every other step. We make our way through the large open foyer where a large fireplace burns bright in the middle of the room warming grieving souls when they enter. I look up at the large painting hanging above the wooden mantle—a landscape scene of the rolling bluegrass hills of Kentucky farmland. Horses gallop in the distance as the sun fades on the horizon, creating beautiful shades of oranges, yellows and reds streaking across the spring sky. The painting always brings back the positive memories of my past—the few years I spent living with the Franciscan sisters across the river in Indiana.

Having officiated at a least a dozen funerals over the last two years, it's hard to tell who, if anyone, is leading as we walk down the halls. On the way toward the basement, Frank turns to me and picks up conversation.

"Mother Alex," he begins, speaking slowly. "Did you know that this funeral home was converted from a home built back in

1845? During that time the deceased would remain in the home for three days. The priest or pastor was required to stay with the body throughout the night, keeping watch over the dead."

"Interesting. I did *not* know that. It does seem a strange sort of vigil that gives a rather creepy vibe to our postmodern priestly perspective. Was this your family's home or did you purchase the property with your brothers?"

"My great, great grandfather built this home." His shaky voice replies with pride.

We come to the stairs leading down to the basement where the bodies are kept and prepared for cremation or burial. I walk down the dark, narrow stairs gripping on the handrail. Frank follows cautiously behind and continues educating me on his family history.

"Back then, this neighborhood was brand new. Victorian homes such as this were being built, courtyards were developed, and families like we Barley's were taking up residence. It wasn't until 1950 that my older brothers Bill and James converted her into a funeral home."

I wait at the bottom of the stairs to make sure Frank makes it down safely. I give him no indication that my standing there is not to listen, but for the sole intent of catching him if he falls. I subtly turn my gaze to the walls and floor of the concrete basement.

I say, "So, I would imagine that most of the material such as the floors and architectural details are original to home."

"Yes, you are correct." He's out of breath but arrives safely at the bottom of the stairs.

He leads me through a damp, musty basement, I follow him

into a room where I see the back of a tall man working over a dead body.

Frank introduces me, "Mother Alex, this is my great nephew-in-law, Keith Laine. He is married to the granddaughter of my late brother Bill and has agreed to take over the funeral home."

The young man turns around and I'm disturbed to see the stark resemblance of Officer Laine, a face I will never forget. Keith Laine couldn't be any older than me, and with his tall, muscular stature and piercing blue eyes, he has to be the younger brother of Officer Laine.

He removes a white glove from his right hand and smiles at me with the same family charm I saw two nights before. He shakes my hand and speaks to me in a surprisingly gracious tone. "Hello, it's nice to meet you. It's always good to see young people like us take up occupations that seem to be dead or dying."

I return the smile with a hint of caution. "Hi. Yes, it's strange but refreshing to meet someone else my age in a traditional role such as this. I believe I've recently run into a member of your family. Are you in any way related to an Officer Laine of the LCPD?"

His smile fades slightly, and his mouth stiffens. "Yes, he happens to be one of my older brothers." Abruptly, he changes the subject, awkwardly asking, "So, uh... you're Mr. Thompson's priest?"

I'm startled that he clearly does not wish to speak about his brother, or his family in any way. Most folks around Louisville leap on any social moment to speak about their family and describe in great detail who is related to whom, and how we're all connected in some weird way. These moments always become unbearable and awkward when they ask about my family connections to Louisville, and so out of respect for Keith's response, I do not push the matter. Instead, I say, "Yes, he's been a part of St. Luke's for half a century."

Feeling small pains of sadness, I look down at the cold, stiff body of Mr. Thompson, covered to his face by a white sheet. I rest my hand on his shoulder.

"He was one of my favorite old men at the church. He loved science and faith and was always open minded to understanding how they complement one another. Up until about four months ago, he was active, still riding his bike, but then he was diagnosed with stage four prostate cancer. Mr. Thompson would invite me over to his home once a month and make us his favorite bourbon drink—Manhattans. He wanted to talk to his priest about his fighting days in WWII, about science and philosophy, and most importantly, how it all connected with his faith. At times he even wanted to confess his sins. I loved that his confessions came not in a booth at the back of the sanctuary but on his living room couch, with pimento cheese and strong bourbon. I secretly wish my other parishioners would confess with the same hospitality."

I walk around the table as Frank and Keith join me looking over Mr. Thompson and continue reminiscing about my time with him. "I remember the first time I went to his house for drinks and confession. His wife was out shopping for groceries, and he leaned across the couch and whispered to me, 'Do you think the neighbors are going to talk?' I said to him, 'John, who cares if they do. I'm not worried about it."

Frank and Keith crack up with laughter.

Frank looks at me and says, "I would've been nervous too. Not every day your priest is an attractive, young woman. I could certainly imagine what the neighbors might have thought with you calling on him once a month and staying for a few hours while his wife was away."

I chuckle and say playfully, "Well I never thought of it like that, but thank you, Frank, for making me feel like some temple prostitute."

"Now," Frank replies blushing with embarrassment, "you know I was just giving you a hard time. I didn't mean to offend you."

"Frank, I've been called worse, and I know you were kidding."

Frank smiles at me and looks at Keith who is listening to the exchange of friendly banter between us with a look of curiosity and astonishment.

"Well," Keith interjects. "It appears that I'll be filling some big shoes when you leave the place to me Uncle Frank. It'll take some time before I'm brave enough to call the catholic priest a prostitute to her face."

We all laugh, and I silently wonder, *Maybe Keith is not like his older brother.* But the thought vanishes when Keith's phone buzzes on the table nearby.

He answers it and informs us that the Thompson family has arrived.

The three of us make our way back upstairs to greet them. Keith and I meet with the Thompson family in a small conference room nearby. An elderly woman, Shirley, the wife of John, hugs me tight with tears streaming down her face. Her two sons, Rick and Wendell, who is wearing his officer's uniform, greet with me with outstretched arms. Shaking Wendell's hand, I address him casually, trying to separate his role as LCPD officer from the grieving son of my dead parishioner.

My efforts go in vain when Wendell's embarrassment and guilt regurgitate out of his mouth. He squeezes my hands, shaking it wildly, saying, "Mother Alex, I'm still so sorry about the confusion a few nights ago. I'd never think you would be prostituting yourself in an alleyway on Christmas Eve."

Everyone looks at me—clearly stunned. Keith grins wide, placing a hand over his mouth to hold back his laughter.

Wendell continues his apologetic speech. "Please tell sister Maria how sorry I am. I had no idea things would escalate like that and then my partner, well he can get hyper sometimes. Officer Laine's a—"

I interrupt him trying to smooth out the awkwardness before Wendell puts his foot in his mouth any further. "Thank you, Wendell, and yes, this is Officer Laine's brother, who is working with me on your father's service."

Wendell's face turns red when I turn and introduce him to Keith, who is standing next me. As Keith graciously introduces himself to the sons as I shake hands with another woman, John's sister, Maggie.

Keith leads us to the family conference room and we discuss details about the memorial service and other arrangements for about forty-five minutes. As we conclude the meeting Maggie expresses her gratitude to me.

"Thank you Mother Alex. I know my brother was dear to you. Keith, it was nice meeting you, too. Our older sister, Brenda, was cremated here five years ago. I trust you all will take the same care for John as you did Brenda. Soon, we'll all eventually be standing at the gates of glory."

I stand up quickly, not wanting to continue the "I'll fly away oh glory" banter that people jibber jabber about at funerals. Keith rises to his feet as well, and we both shake the hands of both brothers, Shirley and Margaret.

With sympathy and assurance, I address the family. "John was dear to me. He will be missed. Wendell, Rick, you let me know what I can do for you all during this time. Shirley, say 'hello' to the family for me. I know this wasn't what everyone was expecting the morning after Christmas."

We all leave the conference room and make our way back to the large foyer. Along the way, Wendell pulls me to the back of the group.

In the hallway, waiting for Keith and the other to move onto the foyer, Wendell finally speaks in a low voice. "Mother Alex, thanks for stopping me earlier. I almost said too much, and in front of Keith."

I reply with a smile, "No problem. That happens to me more than I'd like to admit. Wendell, I do have some questions about the events of last night. What did you and Office Laine do when we went inside?" Wendell's face hardens into stone as his eyes grow wide. In a whisper he says, "I'm sorry but I cannot talk to you about the murder case. I wish I could but—"

"I'm just curious." I interrupt him, impatiently. "Did you all have to go to get help, or the car? Did you leave him alone for a while?"

"Yes, sort of. I went to get the car and when I came back Officer Laine said he woke up and went home."

My head dips towards the floor as I rub the back of my neck

trying not to look overly annoyed with Wendell's naivety. I stare at the ground for a long moment and notice the navy shoes Wendell is wearing.

"Wendell, are those shoes a part of all LCPD officers' uniforms?"

"Uh, yes, everyone is issued these standard shoes, why?"

His eyes glance down the hallway at Keith standing with the family. "I'm sorry but I've got to go."

Without further word, Wendell hurries down the hallway. As the family say goodbye to Keith, I walk them to the door and say, "Please call me if you need anything. Here's my card with my cell phone and Sister Maria's cell phone number."

Tears in her eyes, Shirley hugs me tight. I hold her petite frame, reassuringly.

"We shall celebrate his life together and give his memory honor on Saturday."

With a soft squeeze, I release her to her sons who help her outside and into the car. Then I turn around and grin wide at Keith.

"Was that your first formal family consultation? If so, I couldn't tell for the most part." I say with a slight playful tone of sarcasm.

"Uh, thanks." Keith replies with a shy smile. "And yes, it was my first. For someone our age, you have lots of experience with this. How did you know it was my first consultation?"

"When you called the service a funeral service and not a memorial service."

"Crap. I knew better, too. I am cremating the body after all."

Frank chuckles from behind us and chimes in on the conversation. "I told you she was good. Yes, the body will not, and should not be present on Saturday and therefore the service is a memorial."

He winks at us both before walking carefully, cane in hand, out of the room and into the side office.

"Well, Keith, it's a pleasure working with you." I look down at my watch and it see that it's only one fifteen. "I need to run a few errands this afternoon and hope that you'll be able to spend more time with family today."

"Yes, I'll wait and cremate Mr. Thompson tomorrow so I can get back home to the family. I have a little girl named Eva. As of October, she's two years old. It's so much fun around the holidays with little children. Do you have any children? Uh... wait." He steps back and his left hand combs through his thick blond hair that hangs just above his ears. "That was a stupid question wasn't it?"

"Well, no. There was at one point priests who could enter the priesthood with a spouse and children. They amended that rule about ten years ago when they allowed women the opportunity to become Catholic priests. But there are still a few priests with families serving the church today."

"Wow, really. They let married men become catholic priests?"

"Yes. But it only lasted a few years until the Vatican realized that along with married priests come children and family obligations that pull priests away from serving the church twenty-four seven." My curiosity was getting the best of me—I had to ask about his brother Officer Laine. "Were you able to see your brothers yesterday?"

Clearly caught off guard he shifts his weight to his heels before replying, "Uh, no. We're not exactly on good terms. He along with my other older brothers weren't too thrilled when I married a Catholic girl."

"Oh. I see you. You must've grown up Baptist."

"Yes. How d'ya know?"

"Well, I grew up Baptist—southern Baptist, that is. I get it. Baptists fear that other groups of religious folk might have more answers about their God. Therefore, all of them, especially Catholics, are going to hell."

"Ha! Very true. Yes, well, no. I don't believe that anymore than you do at this point." He smiles. Apparently, he feels he's finally met someone who understands why he married a catholic heathen. With excitement and relief in his voice he says, "Salvation to me has always been confusing. The whole God-saves-some-and-leaves-others-behind thing is so disturbing. I also hated walking down that stupid aisle. Why did salvation have to rest upon me—as if we get the key to open heaven gates by accepting Jesus Christ into our hearts? Wouldn't that imply, then, that we are the agents of our own salvation?"

I laugh lightly at his enthusiasm. I realize he probably has never been able to share this piece of himself with someone who might understand.

I say, "I certainly get it. I still wrestle with the whole salvation piece of God. All I know is that God has to be bigger than one group of folks who make up their own thoughts about how God should and shouldn't save the world."

"Yes, exactly. Well, I know you need to go." He says reluctantly. "Thanks—my wife and I might even come to St Luke's sometime soon."

We shake hands, and I say to my own surprise, "Great. We'd love to have you. Oh, and I look forward to working with you."

I leave the funeral home and check my watch to see if I can still make the next bus heading downtown. To my good fortune, I arrive just as the bus is pulling in. I scan my card and take my seat. In the open seat next to me, I see a copy of today's Louisville Tribune. I pick it up, glance at the front page and see the most dreadful image. A large photograph with me—unmistakably me—in the forefront.

MURDER SUSPECT: CATHOLIC PRIEST ARRESTED XMAS EVE.

The photos are of course the one and only image of me taken two nights ago. Looking like a deer in headlights, handcuffed and confused I'm climbing into the backseat of Detective Clay's police car. The black and white photo highlights the whiteness of my clergy collar and the glaring tattoo on the outside of my white left foot. Luckily the first word was the only visible part. To my fortune, the city of Louisville only saw the word "Mother." As I continue my journey toward the precinct, I pray to God, hoping that those who read today's paper simply believe I'm a narcissist who had "Mother Alex" tattooed on my foot and not "Mother Fucker."

7 - Gluttony

I arrive at the fourth street precinct a bit hesistant as the result of the newspaper headline and slightly paranoid about being seen walking inside the police station. To my relief, no news crews or media photographers are waiting outside. I pull open the heavy metal doors and immediately find a heavyset, white woman in her late sixties with large hair pinned on top of her head sitting at the reception desk.

She greets me with a cheery smile and a light eastern Kentucky accent. "Merry Christmas Ma'am. How can I help ya?"

Without any additional holiday greeting, I cut straight to the point. "I'm hoping to speak with someone about retrieving a personal item found at a recent crime scene. Who do I need to talk to?"

"Well, you would need to go downstairs to the record department and put in a request."

"Okay. How long does it normally take to return an item?"

"Well, it depends but most likely somewhere between two weeks or maybe even a month. Lots of folks are takin' time off this time of year."

"Wow. Really?" I try to not come across as being as annoyed as I feel. "In that case, I'd like speak with Detective Clay."

She gives me a look like I'm asking her to call Santa Claus the day after Christmas. Her tone shifts from Cindy Whoo to grumpy Grinch.

"He's probably not in, like I said, most people get to take time off for the holidays. He, like everyone else, is most likely home with his family."

Her not-so-subtle envy made me realize the sudden change of mood had nothing to do with me and everything to do with the fact she has to work the holiday shift. I try to harness my inner Maria and woo this woman to help me. I take off my scarf and jacket, revealing my white clergy collar, and take notice of the nameplate on the counter which reads, "Mary Ann Sprier."

I give her a sympathetic look and say, "Yea, Mary Ann, I wish all of us could have gotten off for the holidays." I leaned against the counter. "I just came from the funeral home. One of my parishioners passed early this morning. I feel bad for the family who now has to remember Christmas like this from now on."

The tension in the woman's shoulder slacks and her face saddens. Her eyes move from my clergy collar to my pale, blue eyes.

With a heavy voice she replies, "Yes, I understand their pain. My Aunt Susan recently passed over on Thanksgiving—my mother's older sister. When my mother died ten years ago, Aunt Susan was there for me. Especially two Christmases ago when I got this strange rash on the back of my thighs. I thought I had cancer, you would, too, if you saw how it was spreading. So, Aunt Susan took me to the ER on Christmas day, and we sat in the waiting room singin' carols as we waited. We spent all the holidays together, Thanksgiving, Christmas, Derby. She made the most delicious derby pie. You see, I'm divorced with no children. I grew up here in Louisville but it's—"

I stare at her as sympathetically as possible as she rambles on about rashes and dead family members. I think to myself, *Sweet baby Jesus, I have no soul. I just don't know how Maria lives like this all the time while people ooze excessive details about their personal lives.* I give Shirley a slight smile to indicate I'm still listening.

Shirley gasps for air and then to my horror, starts weeping. Then she finally comes to the end of her story. "... and that's why I now work during the holidays."

"Oh goodness." I sigh with relief but hope it comes across as compassionate. "How miserable. I'm just so sorry."

She dabs the tiny tears with a tissue that are swelling up in the corners of her eyes. She sniffles and says, "Thank you so much for listening. Everyone's always in a hurry these days, but you, you're such a kind woman of God." With the Kleenex crunched in her fist, she grabs the phone and dials. "At the very least, if he's not in, we can leave Detective Clay a voice message."

I put both elbows on the counter and rest my head in the palm of my hands. "Thank you, Mary Ann, for taking the time." I give her a generous grin and hand her another Kleenex through the small opening in the bullet proof glass. My inner voice sends a message to my soul, "Yep, you're officially a sociopath."

I can hear the phone ringing on the other end and a male voice answers.

"Praise Mary, there is a God." I utter under my breath.

"Oh, good afternoon Detective, I was expecting your voice-mail. There is a priest here looking for you." She presses the phone down against her large bosom. "I'm so sorry. I was carrying on like a mad woman and didn't even ask your name."

"Mother Alex." I answer hastily.

"Detective, Mother Alex is down here at the reception... Yes, I can send her up to the third floor. No problem." She winks at me, beaming as she gives me a big thumbs up.

I now know for sure I would be the worst receptionist in the world.

She says, "Thank you so much Detective. Merry Christmas to you, too," and hangs up the phone. She looks at me and says, "Okay. He'll meet you upstairs on the third floor just outside the large office space."

She stands up and starts directing me like a flight attendant. "Now, you need to go to your right, my left, followin' the hallway to the staircase. You'll pass several offices and a men's restroom. Once you get to the stairs, you can take... Oh wait. Silly me, you might rather use the elevators. If you want to use elevator then you—"

Unable to stand any longer the excessive social details, I interrupt her as politely as possible. "I'm so grateful for your help but I happened to have been here just a few nights ago. I think I remember how to get back up to the third floor."

She laughs like we're old friends, "Well, why didn't you say sooner. Mother Alex, it was so nice to meet you. I hope you have a very Merry Christmas."

"Now, you do the same, Mary Ann." I grin back at her, give her a very awkward wink and a patronizing thumbs up. I turn to the right and move swiftly down the hall, hearing her call out behind me, "Thanks again for listening. Bye, now."

As I make my way to the stairs, Mary Ann's squealing voice is still ringing in my ears. At that point, I decide for my wellbeing to grab a bourbon at Tony's after I leave the precinct.

With my jacket and scarf under my arm, I ascend the stairs two at a time increasing my pace at each step, my leg muscles enjoy the stretch and exertion along the way. My eyes focus downward, careful not to miss a step. I reach the top landing on the way to the third floor and smack into a large, solid figure. I fall against the rail dropping my jacket and scarf.

"Excuse me. I'm so sor—" I start to say, but I stop my apology when I look up at the large solid figure. Officer Laine stands two steps above me wearing civilian clothes, brown leather shoes, pressed khakis, a white collared shirt beneath a tailored navy, sports coat that fits his toned, six-foot two frame perfectly. He smirks down at me as I stand up tall and step up the last few steps. My two-inch, heeled boots nearly bring us eye-to-eye.

"Well, hello again," he says in a charming tone and a flash of white, pearly teeth. He takes a few steps to the side, looking me up and down. "Isobel Alexandria Wayland. What an interesting name you have."

The last time my full name was said out loud was at my ordination service ten years ago. I have a feeling Officer Laine was not using it in the same divinely ordained way.

He moves back in front of me, stands two arm lengths away, and continues in the same smug tone. "I'm surprised to see you here. Actually I'm surprised they released you yesterday. I was hoping to find you downstairs in one of the cells this afternoon."

I return the wide smile and say, "You know we still have this thing called, 'innocent until proven guilty.'" I add, "I know the law is challenging for you to follow but there are still servants of the people around here who possess the virtue of integrity."

Officer Laine's dimples drop from his face and an expression of rage fills his eyes. I stare into the deep, dark sea of madness brewing beneath his pupils. Unlike Christmas Eve, this time he doesn't retreat backwards, rather, he moves towards me. The intensity grows between us as he moves within arms reach. The hairs on my neck stand up and send a pulse of electricity through my veins. The smell of sewage fills my nostrils and the shadows around his eyes seem to come to life and emerge rapidly around his body.

Less than a foot apart now, our eyes lock. Officer Laine growls and licks his lips. He says, "How is Maria doing? It was such a treat for me to meet her that night."

Rage boils my blood and my body tightens as his scylla begins to breed six long tentacles. They grow out of his shoulders and hips like weeds and move quickly towards me. Panic swells in my chest as they wrap around my body and squeeze my spirit like a rope, strangling my limbs.

"Don't be a fool Alexandria," he warns. "Whatever witch's curse you used on me before won't work now."

Unwilling to concede I shove aside the fear inside me and keep my eyes locked on his. I push my own rage back into him, but the Scylla arms dig deeper into me. The pain, not physical but psychological, begins sucking life from my soul. A terrifying coldness freezes over my anger like a fire extinguisher. Then a numbness starts settling in my spirit and for the first time ever during an eye lock, I am helpless and afraid.

Somewhere in the distance I hear a voice call out. "Officer Laine, it's time for you to go home."

Officer Laine breaks eye contact. I immediately retreat against the wall behind me, out of breath and dizzy. I tilt my head and see Detective Clay twenty yards away walking towards us. I glance over at Officer Laine who is standing tall, seemingly unaffected by the moment. He stares back at me with a hungry gaze and speaks at a level only I can hear. "Witches, like niggers burn. Oh, and say hi to Maria—or maybe, I might just do it myself."

With a wicked grin, he hurries down the stairs.

By the time Detective Clay reaches me, the sour smell of decay has vanished and the dizziness has left me.

He places both hands on the sides of my shoulders, steadies my balance, and says, "Alex, are you alright?"

I respond, more intensely than I intend. "Yes–Jesus Christ—I'm fine."

He promptly releases me and steps back.

"Uh, sorry." I say, still frustrated and out of breath. "That wasn't meant for you. Thanks, Detective, I'm glad you're here."

"You're welcome." He says with little enthusiasm as he picks up my jacket and scarf from the stairs. He hands them to me. "But I'm not quite sure what just happened between you and Officer Laine. You both seem to be gluttons for intense situations. It looks as though you were about to kiss, or fight, or something that was not going to turn out well."

"Kissing Officer Laine would be like kissing a copperhead."

He laughs and retorts, "For him, or for you?"

"Hah—both of us, probably. All I can say is I believe he's a real piece of shit." I stand up straight and move away from the wall. "I could use a cup of coffee—if not something stronger."

"Come to my office and we'll see what we can find."

I follow behind him and the bitter cold begins to lift from my spirit. A few deep inhales and I'm back to normal by the time we reach his office.

Detective Clay takes a seat in a large faux leather swivel chair behind his old oak desk. He gestures to the chair alongside the desk, and I plop down and realize I'm more exhausted than I thought.

He takes two mugs from the left bottom drawer of his desk, glances up at me and says, "Something stronger you said. Will this work?" He holds up a tiny bottle of Elijah Craig.

I smile wryly. "Yes. A drink made from the only Baptist pastor I trust."

He pours a healthy portion of bourbon into each mug and hands one to me. I lift my cup in gratitude, and we both take a swig. Sighing, he reclines back into his chair.

"Now tell me please," he begins. "Since I got to see it again in today's newspaper, how on earth does a quote from *Die Hard* end up tattooed on the foot of a priest?

I chuckle in surprise, expecting the conversation to begin with Officer Laine or the murder case.

"Well since you have inquired twice now, I guess I'll have to tell you." I take another drink of bourbon before continuing on. "When I turned sixteen, I decided that it was time for my first tattoo. Back then, I was hanging out with a few older college kids from U of L who took me out for my birthday, which just so happens to be the day after Christmas. I couldn't afford a car but a cheap tattoo would suffice. The tattoo artist asked me what I wanted and the first thing to come to mind was a line from my favorite Christmas movie that I had just watched the day before, *Die Hard*. When I got older and took my vows, I figured there was no need to get it removed. Who would see it anyway? My foot would be covered all the time." I laugh, and add, "Well, as you know, that theory has proven incorrect."

I finish off my bourbon and place the mug on the desk. Detective Clay gives me a curious look staring silently at me.

"What?" I respond to his silence. "Have you never made a decision as a kid that you regret?"

"Oh, yes, of course. But that's not what I'm thinking about. Today is your birthday?" He says with a tone of surprise.

"Ya. So what? Everyone's got a birthday," I say, and then realize I just sounded more like a teenage girl than a grown woman.

"Well, yes, that's true," he says, apparently trying to recover the moment. "So, what've you done to celebrate?"

"Well, I got to catch up on a fascinating philosophy book on the importance of shining things in culture. Then I went to the funeral home to meet a dead parishioner and his family. Oh, I got my photo in the paper. I'm pretty sure now half of Louisville thinks I'm a murderer, and I just had a lovely social exchange with a homophobic, racist cop. You know, your typical birthday festivities."

Detective Clay gawks at me again before reaching back into his bottom drawer, pulling out the bottle of bourbon again. I push my mug across his desk as if it were a bar top.

Grinning at me he says with a small hint of sadness in his voice, "I think you deserve another drink." He pours another round for both of us and hands me the mug.

"Here's to another year. Happy Birthday, Alex."

We clink our mugs together and take a drink.

"Thank you Detective Clay. Birthdays aren't really my thing. I guess the whole baby Jesus part has always overshadowed it."

Glancing around his office I notice a few diplomas on the wall beside a bookshelf overflowing with hardback editions. I get out of the chair holding my mug of bourbon and walk over to the shelf to get a better look at the titles.

"You know," Detective Clay continues, "if I don't need to call you mother you don't need to call me detective."

"Alright, Mr. Clay." I reply, searching the titles on the spines of the hardback books wedged tightly in the narrow bookcase. "I see you got the gang all here, Dick, Dante, and Odysseus. Which one is your favorite?"

Without hesitating he replies, "Moby Dick and please, call me Marcus."

"Oh, and I was hoping your first name was Ishmael."

He laughs and says with a smile, "I see you're a Melvin fan, too."

"Yes, I like them all. It would be hard for me to pick out of the three. I'm partial to Dante though. Something about descending into hell has always intrigued me." I pull his copy of *The Divine Comedy* from the shelf. "Though, I didn't care for the ending."

"You didn't like Dante simply letting go of Beatrice and staring for all eternity at God?"

"No, actually, I didn't." I flip through the pages of the book. "But he didn't know any better. A distant God was all they knew in the Middle Ages and any form of human, earthly love, was never recognized as agape love for centuries to come. That's why the ending is disappointing to me. I was hoping Dante would lead us away from the Greek mystical experience and possibly offer a prophetic way out of our nihilism, but instead the ending simply wipes out the possibility of Jesus being an embodiment of love in exchange for a passive relationship with a distant Zeus-like God."

Silence falls over the room causing me to pause my lecture

and glance up from the book, only to see a strange expression on Marcus' face.

I break the silent awkwardness. "I guess you weren't looking for a sermon. Sorry about that." I snap the book close and put it back on the shelf.

He leans forward in his chair. "If what you said was anything like your Sunday sermons, I might just have to start coming. But then, I guess I'll have to call you Mother Alex after all. Are you sure you're a Catholic Priest?"

"Yep," I reply, and take another drink of bourbon. "I've got a decade of poverty and a shiny chastity belt to prove it."

With that last comment, Marcus laughed hard—his deep baritone voice booming throughout the small office. After a few moments, he catches his breath and says, "Alex, I want to be your friend.".

"Sorry but I'm going to need to pray about it first. And second, isn't there the matter of you being the detective on the case I'm a suspect for murder."

"Um. Right. Concerning your second point, some evidence has come to light. DNA was found on the body that matched some DNA we found at one of the other crime scenes. Lucky for you, that DNA didn't match the DNA we got off your shoe."

"Well that's certainly the best birthday gift I could ask for. Thanks."

"So can we be friends now?"

"Give me a second." I close my eyes and bow my head whispering to myself. After a few seconds I cross my chest and say, "Yes, by the grace of God, we can be friends."

He stands up from his chair and lifts his mug in the air. "Cheers to friendship."

"Cheers." We clink our cups together once again and finish our bourbons.

"With all this said," Marcus makes his way to the door. "I have a birthday gift for you."

"I hope her name is Beatrice."

He laughs and I follow him out the door. We walk down the hallway towards the stairwell and he asks me, "So if your left shoe is Beatrice what do you call your right shoe?"

"Moby." I answer as we descend the three flights of stairs into the basement.

"So, are you Dante or Ahab?" He asks, curiously.

"I fear I'm more like Captain Ahab."

"But you led me to believe you weren't a fan of Nietzsche's nihilism, and you certainly don't come across as a mad man to me."

I retort in my best drunken sailor's voice, "Dissect him how I may, then, I but go skin deep."

He laughs and says with a smile, "That was Ishmael not Captain Ahab. But I see your point."

We both step down into the basement at the same time. The heels of my boot pound loudly on the stained cement floor. There are two hallways. The one on the right has a sign labeled "Holding Cells." The sign over the left hallway is labeled "Records & Evidence."

Marcus leads me to the left, and I shudder when I think how I might have ended up somewhere down the right hallway on Christmas Eve. We arrive at the records room where a short elderly black man who looks to be in his seventies sits behind a desk reading a paperback book through cheap reading glasses.

"Good Afternoon, Mike. Do you have that piece of evidence

I sent a request for earlier?"

The man called Mike puts down his book with a shaky hand and looks up at us confused. "No, I don't Detective Clay. Officer Laine came by earlier and got it. He said you sent him down here."

"What?!" Marcus cried out. "You gave it to Officer Laine?"

"Yes, I'm sorry." Mike replies. He's obviously taken back by the sudden outburst from Marcus. He adds, sheepishly, "He said he got orders from you to get it."

It takes a moment but Marcus recovers his stoic demeanor. "It's ok. You didn't know. I'll give him a call. No worries."

"I'm sorry again, sir. I should've called you to double check."

"It's alright, Mike."

Marcus pulls me aside and speaks, worry on his face—anger returning to his voice. "Now, why would Officer Laine come get your shoe? What would he want with evidence that is no longer applicable to the case?"

Apparently, he realizes he's asking himself more so than me, he stops and thinks in silence for a few seconds. Then it hits me. I grab his arm tightly and say one word. "Maria!"

His eyes widen, urgency fills his voice. "Come on. I'll drive. You call Maria."

8 - Lust

Scrambling to get a hold of Maria, I slam the passenger car door and press "call" again on my cell phone as Marcus starts the engine. The phone rings and rings as he zooms out of the parking garage, wheels screeching around each turn. I try her several more times before I make a decision.

"She went to the hospital around nine this morning. The surgery was at ten. It's two thirty now so she's most likely home. We need to get to the cottage asap."

Marcus takes a sharp left turn out of the garage onto Broadway Blvd. He turns on his police lights and sirens while swerving around cars, passing them somewhere around sixty miles an hour. I text Maria, urging her to pick up the phone. The church office is closed all week for the holidays, and we had the landline disconnected to the cottage last year when we both decided to carry our cell phones day and night. My gut churns when Marcus takes a hard right and the car drifts several seconds before he gains control again. My thoughts race as we speed onto the highway. Maria always answers her phone unless she's in the confession booth or in a worship service. Worry floods my mind as we rapidly exit highway sixty-five towards the neighborhood of Old Louisville.

My thoughts search for answers. "Where could she be? What on earth is Officer Laine capable of if he reaches her before us?"

"No luck?" Marcus asks, both hands gripping the steering wheel.

"No, no answer." My hands and forearms cling to the window and console as he wheels the Dodge Charger down another street. "Marcus, I don't have a good feeling. I saw the lust in his eyes a few nights ago when he first met Maria. Please," I urge him. "Tell me what you know about Office Laine."

He gives me a are-you-sure-you-what-to-know look before his eyes return to the road. After a long inhale he informs me about Officer Laine.

"I've been suspicious about Officer Laine for about a year now. We even opened a private internal investigation. We, being mainly myself and Chief Mason, believe he's involved with an underground white nationalist group that has been targeting minorities since the presidential elections a year and half ago." Marcus turns to look at me for a brief moment and says, "These are hate crimes that have ended with murder and in some cases rape."

I punch the window with the side of my fist, adrenaline pumping through my body.

"Shit." I cry out, my voice filling with rage. "Maria is Mexican American. Her grandparents immigrated to the US so I'm assuming this makes her an easy target for him and his group, right?"

Marcus remains silent. I shout at him. "Marcus! Is she in danger?"

He speaks in a flat, neutral tone. "Yes, I believe she is."

I clench my fist and to my brief relief see the steeple of St Luke's. We screech to a halt by the rod iron gate leading to the cottage. I jump out of the car while noticing our mini cooper parked across the street. We race to the front door of the cottage, and I try the handle before pulling out my keys. The door is unlocked.

I whisper to myself, "Maria never leaves it unlocked even when she's home."

Marcus gives me a grave look of concern and motions for me to step behind him. He pulls a side arm from his shoulder holster and opens the door slowly with his left hand.

I step into the cottage behind Marcus whose handgun is raised and ready. Maria's purse rests on the entrance table with her cell phone beside it. The main living space and kitchen are empty.

I call out to her. "Maria. Maria, are you home?"

Marcus quickly checks the two bedrooms and informs me with a head shake that they're empty. I hear the shower running in the one and only bathroom. We both make our way to the bathroom door that sits slightly ajar.

I shout through the door, my voice shaking. "Maria? Maria?"

Marcus pushes open the door slowly. Fear grows in my gut, wrenching my insides. Haunting visions plague my mind. Maria naked, helpless, vulnerable and possibly dead.

As the bathroom door creeks open, I plead from the pits of my soul. "God of all grace please, please..." To our surprise and relief the bathroom is empty, curtain pulled back, steaming water rushing out of the shower head. I look anxiously into the tub terrified I'd find Maria's bloody body. But instead, I find a shoe. A black, size nine oxford shoe in a pool of water.

"Shit. Shit! Sweet Mary mother of Jesus." My heart racing out of my chest, I slump down onto the toilet knowing good and well Maria was taken. "Of all people. Why Maria? Why not me? I'm the one who pissed him off."

I look at Marcus who's leaning against the sink with equal frustration and anger. He puts a hand on my shoulder trying to console me. Rage and salty tears begin burning my eyes.

Then I glance behind him. "What's that behind you?" I say, looking at the mirror above the sink.

Marcus quickly turns around and sees the words written in what appears to be one of Maria's shades of red lipstick.

"Witches like niggers burn." Marcus reads the mirror message allowed. "Well, I'm assuming this is for you and me."

He walks through the bathroom doorway and then turns around. I see him staring at me out of the corner of my eye, but my eyes are focused solely on the written message.

"Marcus, Officer Laine said something to me in the hallway before he left." Rising to my feet, I move closer to the mirror. "I don't know why I wasn't concerned about it before. Maybe I just thought it was another racist man spouting off again. But this message." I continue to stare at the mirror. I finally turn and look at him. "I should've said something sooner."

Marcus, returns his gun to his side holster and asks, "Alex, what did he say to you in the hallway?"

I gaze into his eyes seeing his mind swirl with so many unanswered questions. "He said, 'witches, like niggers burn.'"

His right-hand swipes across the thick black hair cut short across his scalp. "Alex, I don't get why he's after you and Maria. What happened in the alley two nights ago? Was that truly the first time you met Officer Laine?"

I respond sharply. "I didn't lie to you. I'm just not sure. He looks familiar but I can't place how I know him. I also didn't know how to explain—"

I pause to think how in the world I can articulate the reality of Scylla without sounding mad or much less like a witch.

"It's complicated." I finally say. "And I fear it'll take much longer to explain at the moment. Right now, I'm more concerned about Maria." I take two steps towards him and stretch out my right hand. "Marcus, I promise I'll tell you soon. You have my word. But first, can we find Maria?"

Stretching out his arms, his right hands clasp into mine. "Yes, alright." He replies in a serious, yet kind tone. "We will find Maria. That I promise you."

Marcus releases my hand and immediately pulls out his phone. I hear him speak with dispatch and then call his partner, Detective Phelps. While he talks, I turn off the shower and retrieve my shoe from the undignified baptism and place it on a towel to dry. I leave the bathroom and go to the living room where Marcus is pacing back and forth near the kitchenette. I hang up my jacket and scarf by the front door, and turn around. The cottage feels strange, like I've landed on an alien planet. I grab Maria's cell phone and purse and return to her bedroom.

I sit on her twin mattress and search her things for something, anything that might give me hope. I come up with nothing but her wallet, car keys and some makeup. I glance around her bedroom. The layout and furniture are identical to mine—bedside table with lamp, old desk and chair, large wooden armoire. Our two rooms reveal our opposite nature once again. Maria's room is neat and tidy as if she had magical elves cleaning the nooks and crannies of every square inch. At night, the dust bunnies of my room come out to snuggle in my bed and the spiders do web design along the window seals. Maria's bed is always made, sheets and quilt tucked neatly under the mattress in what she calls, "An act of daily spiritual discipline."

My bed was hell in comparison—messy sheets, crumpled quilts and forsaken socks like castaways in unkempt layers of bedding. I still don't know when a person is supposed to wash their bed sheets. Is it every few months, or when they smell? Ever so often Maria would sneak into my bedroom while I was out and wash them for me, returning them to my bed folded neatly with a little note on top that read, *Grace abounds but so does the smell. M.*

Thinking about Maria and how much she truly means to me causes tears to well in my eyes. Not many, perhaps no one in my thirty years of living, has chosen to stay with me. Sister Agatha tells me I fear betrayal most of all—being discarded like trash left in a dumpster. The idea of being left behind, broken and vulnerable, by another human terrifies me the most about relationships. However, Maria has never once hinted that she would betray me, and now I feel as though I have done the very thing to her I feared would happen to me. My head falls back on the wall behind me as my thoughts grow grim. I betrayed her. I left her alone and vulnerable to attack by my enemy.

The phone in my hand buzzes and startles me out of my pity party. A text message pops up on the screen. The number is from Louisville, but I don't recognize it. I swipe my thumb to open the phone and see the ten missed calls from my earlier efforts. Clicking on the text message app, I see the recent text pull up onto the screen. My eyes freeze on the words. There's a knock at the bedroom door.

"Alex," I look up as Marcus walks into the room. "LCPD should be arriving any minute to sweep the place and set up a makeshift office."

Tossing the phone at him, I say with hostility in my voice, "Read the text that was just sent to Maria's phone."

With a smooth glide of his hand, Marcus catches the phone and peers into the screen. His eyes widen as he reads the words out loud. "William Oaks Distillery. Tomorrow. 7PM. Witch and Nigger ONLY."

A loud banging on the front door springs me to my feet. Marcus puts a calming hand on my shoulder and says, "It's okay. That'll be the other officers."

He turns and walks into the living room, leaving me alone in Maria's room. The conversation outside the bedroom seems miles away as my heart continues to thump like a jackhammer. Dizziness washes over my body, forcing me to sit down on the desk chair. I close my eyes and take deep breaths. Beads of sweat form on my brow, and I feel my blood sugar dropping. I realize now, the only nourishment I've taken in today was coffee and bourbon. After several minutes, I feel the adrenaline in my bloodstream settling down and decide it's time to leave the room.

I walk into the living room and a dozen pairs of eyes turn to look at me. The chatter stops, and sudden silence takes over the tiny space. I feel claustrophobic. I see Marcus staring at me with deep concern before making his way around the loveseat in my direction. At his movement, everyone returns their attention elsewhere and conversation picks up once again.

"Hey, you okay?" He says to me in a low troubled voice.

"Yaa, I'm fine. What's the plan?" I respond, self-consciously rubbing my neck.

Ignoring my question he adds, "You're really pale, Alex."

"Thanks. I know—I'm Scottish." I retort, trying to lighten the mood.

"Seriously," Marcus grabs my hand. "Your hands are clammy, and your face is sweating."

Using the sleeve of my black shirt, I dab my face. "I just have low blood sugar. I haven't had a chance to eat today. This happens all the time. It's nothin' to worry about."

He looks at me for a moment before releasing my hand. "Okay. Well, we're going to be here awhile. The situation is officially a kidnapping case, so this will be ground zero. But you need to eat and rest. Is there a place you can go for a bit? Maybe to the church or a friend's house?"

I stifle a laugh when he says "friend's house" as if I'm some social butterfly who can call up folks out of the blue and have a slumber party. Maria's my only friend and I prefer it that way. My theory is that the odds of betrayal lessen, the lower the number of relationships one maintains.

Marcus' next suggestion surprises me. "What about Tony? The owner of the bar downtown."

Tony? I hadn't thought about him. He's currently the only other soul in this world I'd call my friend. Tony, a man whose last name I don't know, but he would certainly let me crash at the bar for a while.

"Yaa, he's an option I guess, but how did you know we're friends?"

"Uh." He hesitates, shifting his weight slightly. "I had to get a statement from him yesterday. He mentioned he had known you for several years. If anything, it's better than being stuck in the church next door. You also look like you could use a good hot meal."

I glance down at the floor. My stomach rumbles loudly as if to argue in favor of his position on Tony's.

Marcus urges me one last time. "Just go and eat something. Wait there until I come by with more information about Maria and our plan for tomorrow."

We walk to the front door and Marcus hands me my jacket and scarf from the coat rack.

"Let me drive you there." He says paternally while glancing around the bustling living room. "I know it's close but...uh... I don't think you should be walking by yourself."

"Thanks." I respond while grabbing a set of keys from my pocket. "But Merida will take me."

"Okay. I'm assuming Merida is the mini cooper parked outside." I smile at him and he adds, "Keep your cell on. I should be by there in a few hours. And whatever you do, don't fall back into the dumpster."

I laugh at his teasing and reach for the door, but Marcus grabs the door knob first, opening it for me. He follows me down the sidewalk. When we reach the iron gate we stop. He places a large, warm palm on my shoulder.

"Alex," I turn as he speaks, his tone is serious, again. "Tony is a good guy. You can trust him."

Nodding slowly, I begin to wonder what he means when he says I can trust Tony. My thoughts then shift to Christmas Eve.

"Marcus, I'm sort of embarrassed that it's taken me this long to ask you, but who exactly was the man murdered and dumped in the trash?"

"His name was Kevin. He was a student and athlete at Springtown College near Lebanon. He was here visiting family for the holidays. His parents thought he was at his girlfriend's house. They were shocked to hear the news of his murder and where he was when it happened."

I start to feel sick again imagining his parents viewing their dead son's body in the morgue. "God, how terrible. Why are the papers not calling this a hate crime, and what about the mark on his neck?"

Marcus leans against the gate and answers. "Well, Kentucky has very loose, and pardon my French, really shitty legal policies on what is deemed a hate crime. And considering we don't know who the murderer is yet, we can't make that claim. As far as the mark on his neck, I'm still looking into it, but I do know that the tool that created it was a cattle brand farmers use to mark their livestock."

Hearing the words cattle brand and livestock applied to a human being brings the taste of bile into my mouth.

"Christ. I can't imagine that in the twenty-first century human beings are still being treated like animals—as if we were trading slaves again like livestock."

Marcus opens the gate, shakes his head, and says, solemnly, "We live in the United States of amnesia. Sadly, I'm not surprised at all. I'll be by in a bit. Drive safe, Alex."

I say goodbye and make my way to the mini cooper across the street. I get into the car—another vehicle pulls up, and parks along the same side of the street. A tall white man who looks like he's nearing seventy climbs out of the full size sedan. He's wearing a dark, blue suit and long dress coat that probably cost more than three months of my salary. His hand combs through thick gray hair as he walks confidently across the street. It looks as though his body was once that of a very fit athlete. I recognize him from a recent news clip—he's Chief Mason.

Still sitting in my car, I watch him walk up to Detective Clay and greet him with a handshake. I turn the key to start the car—they both turn their heads and watch me, lips moving. Chief Mason gives me a wave and I nod back before pulling out onto the street making my way toward Tony's Gay Bar and Dancing.

9 - Sloth

I park along fourth street and stroll down the sidewalk toward the infamous alleyway. My Christmas morning dream comes flashing back and I instinctively peek over my shoulder every few steps to see if Officer Laine is running up behind me. My paranoia gets the best of me when I come to the dumpster just outside of Tony's alleyway entry. I lift the rubber lid and glimpse inside. To my relief, the dumpster is full of trash and rubbish from the previous two days. I climb the stairs, take hold of the large metal handle and pull it toward me. I half expect to be tackled by a drunk patron but the doorway is empty.

I trudge down the dark hallway, hyper aware that Maria is not with me. The large open ballroom is practically empty tonight—no patrons sitting at the bar and no lonely transgender person dancing under the disco ball.

The lights shining across the barren dance floor remind me of the story Maria told me on Christmas Eve. My heart grows heavy at the thought and guilt sinks further down in my belly. I sit down on the bar stool, look around for Tony and notice two men sitting at the same booth Maria and I usually occupy. I glance at my watch—fifteen after six. My head droops down further, as I look at my phone anxiously, hoping that Marcus will call soon with a plan to save Maria.

Time seems to come and go as it pleases today, and right now, as I sit still, I feel like a sailing ship stuck out on the ocean and the wind nowhere to be found. After two or three minutes, Tony emerges from the back with two baskets of hot food. He walks around the bar to the men sitting at the nearby booth. The scent of deep-fried potatoes and crispy wings causes the empty cavern of my stomach to grumble.

Tony makes his way back around the bar and catches my eye. His smile is wide, but I can't help but wear the long day of disappointment on my face. He notices my sadness straight away, and quickly begins making me a drink.

"Hi Alex. Looks like t'was a long day." The warmth of his voice is comforting, like sitting in an old leather chair that has become contorted to your body.

"T'was indeed, m' friend, t'was indeed." I echo with a poor mimic of his Scottish accent.

Tony's eyes keep watch over me as he finishes my old fashioned with a smear of orange around the glass rim. He glides it across the bar to me, and I reach out and grab hold. His hand lingers on the glass under my own hand. The touch of his warm flesh sends a quick pulse of energy through my veins. I shrug it off as static energy, but his skin under my fingertips somehow softens the agony of the day.

He releases his grip on the glass, and I glance up at him through watery eyes. He says in low voice, "Whatever 'tis, lass, know that it all be a'right."

A lump the size of walnut fills my throat. Willing back the grief, I give a nod in silent gratitude before averting my eyes. Tony busies himself around the bar a few feet away, giving me space to collect myself. I take in a few deep breaths and two large gulps of bourbon—hoping the burn will ease me into a numb, slothful state of apathy.

After a few minutes, Tony hollers at me over the music, "Alex, yeu look famished." He glides back over to me. "Let me make yeu some food."

Finishing my drink, I give him a nod and raise my glass signaling for another drink.

"Food first m' dear. Be back in a few."

To my annoyance, he quickly moves back to the kitchen before I can protest. Knowing that it'll be at least five minutes before he returns, I decide to go wash my face in the bathroom.

I make my way back down the hallway and into the bathroom—deja vu follows close behind. Both stalls are empty tonight and regrets return to mind about the mystery man in the bathroom two nights prior.

"Alex, you stupid fool. Why didn't you at least speak with them?" I utter in frustration. "When Marcus comes by later, I can't forget to tell him about the navy shoes.

I use the bathroom, return to the mirror to wash my hands and see a few red blotches around my gray, stormy eyes. It's been years—over a decade—since I've cried, and just the hint of tears causes my skin to swell. I splash water over my face and dab a paper towel around my eyes, hoping to sop up the redness with water. My head spins with thoughts of Maria and soon with the memory of the last time tears filled my eyes. The memory becomes so intense that sorrow begins to spew over me with vomit on its way up and out.

Gripping the sink's edges, I stretch my arms out and bend over taking in deep breaths through my nose. I close my eyes and tell myself, "It's in the past. It's in the past. Let it go, Alex. Just let it go."

The helpless face of the pregnant teen in the church consumes me. Her sobbing cries echo in my ears as though I was walking out of that Baptist church all over again. I inhale deeply again and push back the guilty purge lingering in my throat. My eyes open and I stare down at my feet. A thought flickers in my mind that gives my unsettled stomach a reprieve.

"My shoes," I say aloud. "Why am I now thinking about my shoes? Probably because I wish I would've changed into my oxfords before leaving the cottage."

Still bent over, I look up at my reflection in the mirror. The thought about my shoes fades as Tony's voice enters my mind. Two nights ago, he said I was beautiful. I wonder what he thinks now with my blotchy, teary-eyed face. Poking and prodding my face, I ponder at my appearance for a moment.

But then, standing back up to my full height, I return to reality. "Get hold of yourself. You're a priest, Alex." I say to women in the mirror. "You no longer have to spend energy on the opinion of men concerning how you should or shouldn't look."

I move closer to the mirror and stare into the black pupils of the woman looking back at me. I hold the gaze of my twin, and feel my heart rate pick up speed. Then a shadow flickers in my pupils. Slowly, it grows in the gray sky around the eyes, and then expands to become larger and larger. The shadow emerges like dark storm clouds, and my right hand reaches out towards the mirror in an attempt to touch the emerging monster. A familiar rotten smell turns my stomach over. Electricity fills the room, causing the tiny hairs on my arms and neck to stand erect. My body freezes in fear and awe. Scylla—never before seen by my own eyes—extends six dragon like arms. A battlefield of feelings in me goes to war. Grief, guilt, power, lust, rage and revenge stretch like serpents out of my body and snake wildly across the room. I stand paralyzed, watching the shadow creature consume the space with darkness. Then I hear the bathroom door swing open and bang hard against the outside wall. I jump at the noise and turn to see two men walk in—their conversation cut short at the sight of me. I glance back into the mirror and realize Scylla is gone—vanished into thin air. In the mirror's reflection, I see the two men stare at me.

I say dryly, "Well, I was just finishing up."

I grab a paper towel and act as though I had been washing my hands. I move towards the door, hoping to avoid conversation.

I walk past the men without looking at them. I put my hand on the door, and one of the men, a white male in his early sixties wearing jeans and sweatshirt speaks up.

"Wait. I know you."

I sigh, dreading the next moments to come.

He continues. "Billy, look, it's her. She's got to be the priest from the paper, the murder suspect."

To his credit, at least he uses the word "suspect."

I turn around to look at them both.

The man on the right, called Billy, hits his potbelly friend in the arm playfully adding, "You're right, Greg. This is why I said it'd be worth coming here t'night. We got to see the crime scene and the murderer!"

They both laugh and my intestines clench as the rest of my body stiffens. Billy, a short, overweight, white man in his early fifties, also wearing blue jeans, boots and U of L sweatshirt, steps within a foot of me. I'm now grateful for the extra two inches on my shoes, because I tower over him, his head only reaching my shoulders.

I've learned that men respond in two ways to taller women. The first group welcomes the taller woman with equal grace and confidence, maintaining their power in the moment while acknowledging the power of the woman. The second group projects their insecurities back onto the woman by either using sexual dominance through means of language and touch or by completely submitting to the power of the woman's stature.

The stocky man stinks with insecurity. I assume he and his friend fall into group two and in this situation, two shorter men against one taller woman confined in a small space will most likely place them both into the sexual dominance section.

I hold my ground, squaring my shoulders, giving him a clear look that says, "Go fuck yourself."

Billy glares at me with contempt and remarks while looking me up and down.

"Ya, Greg, this is the bitch that murdered that black man. I hope the pope kicks·you out of the church. This is why women can't be in positions of power. They're too emotional. Can't keep it together under pressure."

Greg steps forward parallel to Billy and adds, "Besides, you're too pretty, anyway, to be a priest. You'd make more money as a stripper or something."

He reaches up to touch my face and I instinctively swat his hand away like a fly buzzing around my head. They both laugh at me.

Fire burns in my bones but I maintain control of body and mind as I reply passively, "You boys better be getting on your way, or you'll miss the game tonight."

I take a chance that the only reason these two men are even downtown tonight is because the men's U of L basketball game is taking place a few blocks over at the YUM Center.

"You're lucky we've got someplace to be." Bill says in a sweet voice, as if it would have been my pleasure to pleasure him.

They both step back giving me space to turn and push open the door. But the moment I turn my back and push open the door only to feel a large hand grab my ass and squeeze.

Instinctively, I swing around with a right hook, slamming my fist hard against Billy's left, chubby cheek. Greg catches his friend who, to my pleasure, would've fallen onto the ground from the impact. The door begins to close behind me but I think it best not to linger any longer. With a swift motion, I slide through the door opening and exit the bathroom.

In the hallway, I grab a nearby broom and wedge it between the door handle and wall. I run down the hallway towards the bar, knowing good and well that otherwise Billy and Greg would not be far behind.

I glance over my shoulder and hear them call out as they slam their bodies against the door, "We'll get you bitch."

Racing across the dance floor, I see Tony at the bar.

"Alex," he calls out. "What's going on?"

I hastily move to the bar and say, "Well, it's a long story, but I may have just punched a pervert in the bathroom."

Tony turns his head, now hearing the shouts of the men who will burst through the bathroom barricade at any moment. He looks at me and says, "Come 'round the bar to the back room. Quickly, now."

I waste no time racing around the bar. He opens a door to a back room I had never noticed before until now and pushes me inside the dark room. I stumble over what appears to be a chair and desk.

"Wait here," he says. "I'll send them away. Keep the lights off."

Tony closes the door behind me, and I'm left in the cold, pitch black space—no windows or other light source except for the crack between the door and the floor. I move close to the door, put the side of my head and my ear flat against the wood, hoping to hear. Multiple voices confirm that Billy and Johnny have escaped and are now on the hunt. I can't make out specific words over the music.

Several moments pass by and my anxiety grows—my heart beats rapidly in my chest. I stand still and quiet until something large brushes against my leg causing me to jump against the door. Stumbling back against a wall, a wave of fear ripples through my body.

I yelp as quietly as possible. "Shit, what's in here?"

Before the creature engages again, the door opens, and I hear Tony's voice speak in the distance.

"Ah, it's just my wee cat, Sam."

As the door crack opens, I see a shadowy creature dart out of the dark room and into the bar.

"See I told yeu, that woman isn't here. She must've gone out the back door to the alley."

The door closes again. I sigh in relief, lean back against the wall, and slink down until my bottom rests on the floor. I breathe deeply.

A few minutes pass before Tony cracks the door open again. "Alex?" He looks down at me, huddled on the ground. "It's okay. Yeu're safe. The men are gone."

I can't seem to get up. The comfort of sitting in the dark is just too good. I stare into the dark room and say, "I think I'll just stay here for just a bit longer."

Tony opens the door all the way and steps into the room. The light from outside fills the room—I look around. It's a large space, bigger than I had imagined in the darkness. The back part of the room has a twin-size bed with an old wooden headboard. There's a dresser and a makeshift closet with a rod dangling from the ceiling where a few flannel shirts and a jacket hang. The front of the room has a desk pushed up against the wall with a small cushion on the floor underneath the chair opening.

I glance back up at Tony, who says in a cheery tone, "Welcome to my flat."

As if on cue, the shadow creature that scared me moments before strides into the room again and curls up on the cushion under the desk. A cat, with a coat the color of a moonless night, wears an expression of annoyance, or agitation, or maybe just a regular feline glare—who knows. Whatever look it is, I can tell that our first greeting in the dark put our relationship on rocky footing.

Tony moves to the desk and bends over to stroke the fur behind the cat's head. "This is Sam."

I say, "Ah, like Samwise Gamgee."

"No, like Samantha from Bewitched." Tony corrects me with a crooked smile. "Sorry, she gave yeu a fright earlier. She was probably just sayin' 'ello."

I smile at the cat, and say, "I probably terrified her more than she did me," and add, sympathetically, "Sorry my friend. I didn't mean to scare you either. I hope you can forgive me."

Tony raises his hand and Sammy, as if responding to my apology, gets up, stretches and comes over to me, and nestles her head against my leg. I reach out and return the gesture with the same ear strokes I saw Tony give her. Then she climbs into my lap and flips over onto her back with nonverbal demand for a belly rub.

Tony laughs and sits beside us on the floor. "She likes yeu."

I grunt a retort, "I'm just glad something breathing does today."

He gives me a woeful look before asking about the men chasing after me. Massaging the fur of Sam's belly with my left hand, I explain the situation in the bathroom giving details about the comments from the men and the grabbing of my ass.

"Well, if it's any consolation," he says smiling wide, "the fat man's eye was swellin' shut and his face was bleedin'."

I hold up the red, bloody knuckles of my right hand and reply, "Honestly,

I've never punched a man not worth the pain of a swollen hand."

"Well, that's good to know. I hope I'm never on the receivin' end of yeur right hook."

He takes my right hand into his, begins to examine the damage, and I have to make efforts to will my hand relax in his care. Poking at the knuckles and stretchin' out my fingers he finally says, "You're lucky nothin's broken. Now, yeu wanna tell me about the rest of yeur day?"

Hesitating, I reply, "Uh, that's only if the second round's on you."

Tony tilts his head with a smirk. "Why not? But yeu must promise me yeu'll eat some food with that drink."

He rises to his feet, Sammy moves instinctively off my lap, and returns to her bed beneath the desk. I move to get up and reach up the wall for leverage with my left hand. I'm unsteady because my legs are slightly numb from sitting crossed legged on the floor. Tony seems to notice this and squats down, placing a large shoulder under my left armpit. He wraps a strong hand around my waist, and carefully brings me to my feet. I feel the dizziness I felt in Maria's room earlier and am grateful for the help. I close my eyes, my face contorting in concentration as I try not to pass out. Tony's arm and hand tightens their grip around my waist, holding me steady.

"Woe now. Take it easy. Yeu've gone ghost white."

My right palm prs against my forehead as my head begins to ache.

"Shit." I sigh in exasperation. "I'll be ok. I've just got low blood sugar."

My hand pulls away from my head and my eyes meet Tony's as he looks down gravely at me.

"Alex, yeu're not okay. Yeur legs are shakin' and yeur face is sweatin'."

Then in one smooth motion, using the leverage of his arms around my torso and placing his right arm under my legs, Tony lifts me off the ground, cradling my body against his chest. The motion not only catches me off guard but sends my head swimming again.

"Tony, I'm okay." I exclaim with heavy breath. "This isn't necessary.

Seriously, I can walk."

Without a word, he responds to my plea by carrying me over to the twin size bed and gently lowering me onto it. I feel the muscles of his arms and chest flex through the fabric of his flannel shirt. My upper back and head are placed against the headboard as he removes his arms from my waist and legs.

Tony places a hand on my shoulder and looks down at me—his deep, green eyes are soft and kind. He gives a shy smile and says with concern, "Rest. I'll bring you some food."

I watch him rise, standing like a statue above me, and the dizziness returns. I sigh, closing my eyes again, pinching two fingers on the bridge of my nose.

My left hand rises into the air, and I call out with a shaky voice, "Don't forget the drink you promised me."

He chuckles and turns on the lamp that sits on the bedside table.

"Alex," he says quietly. "My father would've liked yeu a lot." I hear his footsteps leave the room and the sound of the door closing shut behind him. Before my grumbling stomach can protest, my mind slips away into a deep sleep.

10: Head

Dreams flicker in my subconscious. Visions of Maria chained, beaten and raped by angry white men. She's shackled, naked and shivering, next to a radiator in a dark, damp basement. Her long hair is wet and wild, clinging to her body like a matted mane. I feel my legs twitch as though a piece of me is trying to arouse my mind and bring me back to reality. But I do not wake up. Instead, more nightmares come.

I'm back in the alley fighting Officer Laine with a dagger but this time he pulls out his gun and fires at me. One bullet hits me in the leg. I fall and fall and fall, descending deep into the alley dumpster. My body lies in the same place where the dead, black man lay. I see the faces of Billy and Greg gawking over the dumpster, cackling at my helpless form. They grab my body—squeeze my tits, slap my face, stroke my crotch. They rip the white collar from my neck and hand it over to Officer Laine who lights in on fire and tosses it into the dumpster. I watch in horror as the trash around me begins to blaze. I'm unable to move my body, and I cry out as the flames grow larger. I look around frantically. A shoe near my shoulder catches my attention—my black oxford shoe, still sopping and wet from the shower. Water drips out of the heel and sizzles in the flames growing around it. I glance up and watch Officer Laine pull his body halfway over the edge of the dumpster.

He reaches out and grabs the shoe with one hand and then leans over me, clutching me by the throat with his other hand. Then he kisses me hard on the mouth. I bite his lip and he pulls back laughing. He releases my throat and whispers into my ear, "Witches, like niggers burn."

The flames spread faster and faster throughout the dumpster. Officer Laine pulls his torso out of the burning coffin and the lid slams shut, closing me inside, sealing my fate to the inferno. I scream again and again as I feel the scalding heat pressing into my flesh.

Then I hear a voice call out in the distance, "Isobel! Isobel!" The voice seems familiar and yet so far away. The fire consumes me, burning deep into my bones. I feel my skin turning to ash and the rotting smell of burning flesh churns my stomach. Again, the voice calls out to me somewhere in my head. "Isobel! Wake up." The dumpster begins to shake, the rubber lid swings open and a large pair of dark, green eyes stare down at me.

11: Heart

The dark eyes send terror through my body and my self-defense instincts kick in. My right fist swings through the air at the face before me. But a strong, firm hand catches my wrist. I squirm in frustration as my arm is pulled tightly against a hairy chest. Another hand rests firmly on my legs, keeping me from kicking the monster holding me down. The large eyes move closer to my face and a familiar voice pierces my ears.

"Isobel. Wake up, lass." My hearing finally connects to my consciousness and the voice comes through more clearly. "Alex. Alex! It's me, Tony."

I close my eyes tight, body still, the tension slowly leaving my muscles. After a moment, I blink my eyes open and see Tony sitting beside me on the tiny twin mattress. My body pressed up against the wall with my right hand tucked securely against his body. I feel Tony's large, warm palm pressing on my right thigh. My breath is heavy and quick. The pillow under my head is damp with cold sweat.

Tony speaks softly, close to face. "Alex. You're safe. You're a'right."

His soothing voice calms the remnants of fear still lingering from my night terror. I keep my head on the soggy pillow and smile gratefully up at him. His hand moves off my thigh and gently swipes a strand of wet hair to one side of my sticky brow. I open the fist of my right hand and place my palm through the opening of his partially unbuttoned, shirt. His skin is warm, muscles tensing at my cold touch. The steady beating of his heart slows the racing rhythm in my chest. He places his hand against mine causing me to wince as the dried blood on my knuckles is pulled away from my skin. Tony's face contorts seeing my pain and he tenderly takes my right hand away from his chest. But then my eyes, still blurry from sleep, see a large figure move behind Tony. Startled, I sit up quickly in alarm.

Tony's hands grab hold of my shoulders to steady me as he tries to calm me down. "It's okay. It's Detective Clay. He's come to see you."

I move my head around Tony's broad shoulders and my eyes focus on the figure. I blink a few times, letting the blood that rushed to my head drain back into my body. Marcus sits in the desk chair a few feet away observing me sympathetically. I smile, trying to reassure both Marcus, Tony and possibly myself that I'm alright.

"Hi Marcus. What took you so long?" I say sarcastically through a scratchy throat.

Tony releases his hold on me, gets up from the bed, and leans back against the nearby wall. I grab a glass of water that was placed on the bedside table while I was asleep and guzzle the entire glass in three gulps.

Marcus waits for me to finish, then says, "Well, it's only been a few hours since you left, but by the looks of things, it appears as though it's been a very long night for you."

I look down at the watch on my left wrist which to my surprise reads only nine fifteen in the evening. My deep sleep gave the illusion of a full night.

Marcus continues, "I arrived about thirty minutes ago. Tony informed me that you had fallen asleep, and I figured you needed the rest so I decided to let you sleep."

"That was noble of you." I remark matter-of-factly. "Well, we've got work to do."

I swing my legs over the edge of the bed and place the empty glass on the table. I begin to rise to my feet, but before I know it, Tony and Marcus promptly move to help as though I'm their grandmother getting out of bed after hip replacement.

My voice lashes out at them. "Sweet Jesus, I'm not a cripple—nor am I your elderly grandmother. Back off boys!"

I wave my bloody right hand, shooing them away. Both stop in their tracks. Tony crosses his arms and Marcus puts his hands on his hips. To my frustration, I'm moving slower than I expected, but I manage to stand up all by myself, no assistance from men required.

I raise my head in satisfaction and say, "See, I got this."

To my shame, however, as I step forward, I stomp on something thick and squishy. Sam, the cat, is lying partly under the bed unnoticed by me. She meows in shock when her tail is squashed beneath my foot. She leaps up from her slumber and tangles herself between my feet. Cut off just above the roots, I stumble forward and my body is well on its way to crashing to the earth below like an old oak tree. Marcus moves quickly, flinging a strong arm around my waist and snags me in mid descent.

He pulls me back up to my feet and laughs. "My grandma may be old but she ain't blind with pride like you."

"Good point." I reply with an ounce of humility. I look down at my sock covered feet and realize my shoes have been removed. "Uh, Tony? Where are my boots?"

Marcus releases his grip on my waist as Tony walks up behind us with two black, heeled boots in his hand.

I turn and take the boots and give him a look of serious frustration. "Please tell me this is the only article of clothing you thought necessary to remove while I slept."

Tony smiles wide, a full set of gleaming white teeth. "Aye, but I guess yeu'll have to confirm that for yeurself."

He answers with too much pleasure for my liking. Then he winks at me and walks confidently out of the room. I sit in the desk chair, put on my shoes and mumble to myself about the pride of Scottish men.

Marcus turns to me and says, "You know. I kinda like him." Then, with a tilt of his head towards the door, "We can catch up at the bar when you're ready." He walks out of the room, leaving me alone with Sam. I look over at the black cat now sitting on the desk cleaning her right paw.

"You just had to lay right where I was stepping. Made me look like a fool." She looks at me and replies with a soft meow. I scratch behind her ears and she purrs.

"Sorry about your tail. Lucky for you, Tony took off my boots."

Standing up more confidently this time, I make my way to the bar. I come out of the room and see Marcus sitting on a bar stool nursing a half pour of bourbon. I take a seat on the stool next to him and grab his glass. Throwing my head back, I gulp down the rest of his bourbon.

He turns to me and remarks, "Help yourself."

I place the empty glass back in front of him. "I figure you owed one for not waking me up when you first arrived."

"Yes, I do regret that now." A look of guilt flashes across his face. "After hearing your screams, I now realize I could've saved you from whatever nightmare you were having."

I wince, closing my eyes as the images of the dreams flash in my mind. My right hand forms a tight fist and pounds against the bar top. I feel the dried blood over one knuckle break open and warm blood ooze between my fingers.

I look at it, raise my hand in the air and say, "Well isn't that great. Now I need to go wash the blood off my hand in the bathroom. Be right back."

I move to get off the stool, but Marcus puts a hand on my leg.

"I don't think that's a good idea." He says, quickly removing his hand from my thigh. "While you were sleeping, Tony told me how your knuckles got that way." He looks at me with a hint of respect in his eyes while adding, "Let me find something to clean that up for you right here."

Marcus moves back around the bar and pulls out a first aid kit from under the fire hydrant on the back wall. He comes back around to me, unfastens the kit and takes my hand, placing it palm down on the bar top. He dabs the cuts with alcohol wipes, I try hard to conceal the sharp twinges of pain.

Perhaps to take my mind off the moment, Marcus picks up conversation. "So, you and Tony, huh?" He remarks playfully, glancing up at me only to receive a flat stare that clearly states my opinion on the subject. He concedes. "Okay. Okay. I won't push."

I grunt and exclaim, "Maria. Officer Laine. What's the plan?"

His face turns serious as he wraps an ace bandage around my hand.

"Nothing knew as of the moment. We tried his cell phone but no answer. My team is running a trace on it but I'm not hopeful. It's probably turned off. We have officers searching the distillery to see if that's where he's hiding. But that's probably just an exchange location where he wants us to meet him. At the very least, the officers can search the building for any traps, or for clues that might explain why he's using that site. I plan on going over there when I finish here with you."

"I'll come with you. I may be able to help in some way."

"No, I don't think that's a good idea. You, uh... " He hesitates. "Not in your condition," he says, cautiously.

I snap back. "My condition. What does that mean?"

Before I can press any further Tony emerges from the kitchen, a plate of food in hand.

I say, with a sigh, "Let me eat something and I'll feel better."

"Condition was the wrong word." Marcus says in frustration. "However, the situation is too dangerous, and keep in mind, you're not a police officer."

Tony chimes in, "Alex, yeu're a priest. Let them do their job."

My irritation is growing with the feeling of being cornered against my will. "Okay. So, what the fuck am I supposed to do then? Go back to the church and pray all night?"

"I just need you to wait." Marcus replies coolly. "Tony says you'd be safe here and since the cottage is full of noisy cops, I think this is the only place for you to get any rest."

In silent protest, I lift my hand with the bandaged knuckles.

Tony speaks up from across the bar. "Don't worry 'bout that, I've closed the bar for the night."

I look at him—closing the bar will eat into his already affected revenue for the evening. "Tony, I'm sorry. I didn't mean to cause you this much trouble, but I can't stay here. It isn't fair to you."

Getting up off the bar stool, I search the bar area for where I last left my leather jacket and red scarf. I see both hanging on the coat rack near the hallway that leads to the exit door out to the alleyway.

I move towards the hallway, Marcus calls out to me, "Alex, where are you going to go?"

I holler back in defiance without turning around, "I'll figure it out."

Tony races ahead and cuts me off. He turns to face me, petitioning me with his hands raised in a peace offering position. "Please. I know you feel helpless. But Detective Clay seems like a good man. Let him work. Please, please, don't leave."

I can't seem to bring myself to look him in the eyes. My blood is boiling, and I stare off in the direction of the dance floor. I noticed for the first time, there is no music playing and the room is silent. I think about Maria, helpless and alone somewhere out there. Her voice echoes in my head, giving me advice I don't want to hear. Too tired and hungry to fight with him or the voices, I let out a long sigh of defeat.

"Okay, I'll stay." I turn around and head back to the bar.

Marcus stands up and puts on his jacket.

"Alex, I promise I'll call you as soon as I have more information." He reaches into his coat and pulls out a card. "Here's my card with my cell phone number. Don't hesitate to contact me any time, day or night."

He squeezes my shoulder and gives me a reassuring smile.

I watch him walk away, down the hallway. I hear the metal door open and slam shut. I turn to Tony who is already back behind the bar.

He says, "Eat. Pray. Share whatever yeu want to while I make yeu that drink I promised."

For the next ten minutes, I eat in silence, sipping on my old fashion and cramming down the same meal I was forced to leave behind two nights ago - chicken salad and hot seasoned fries. I feel strength returning to me, and look up at Tony who is busying himself, cleaning around the bar.

"Tony. Thank you for helping me." I say with less enthusiasm than intended.

He looks over at me, a towel draped over his shoulder.

I add, "I know I'm not the easiest person to be friends with so thanks."

"Yeu certainly got that right. But lucky for yeu, I don't have many friends to compare yeu with."

He walks over to me, face beaming and leans over the bar resting his upper body on his forearms. Our eyes lock for a long moment. The image of his scylla from two nights ago jogs my memory. I finish the scraps of food on my plate and ask him flat out.

"Tony, what happened two nights ago, here at the bar, when you locked eyes with me?"

His head tilts to one side, like a curious puppy. He leans in closer as he did before and stares into my eyes. "I believe you know what happened and you know how hard it is to explain. It be best, perhaps, if I show yeu again."

I hesitate, averting my eyes from his gaze. "Yes, I do know, and you're right, it's difficult to put into words... Scylla that is."

Tony pulls back away from the bar and asks in a tone of surprise. "What do you call it?"

"The shadow creature, the six headed monster that pops out of people like that movie, Aliens—when you stare into their eyes."

He laughs hard and long before responding. "Yes, I guess so. Sorry to laugh but I've never heard it described that way before. A six headed monster."

He crosses his arm, and his eyebrows tighten as if he was examining the image in his head. "'Tis a fairly accurate description now that I think about it. I'm assumin' that's where yeu got the name Scylla?"

I laugh, then say, "Tony, no offense, but I didn't take you for a fan of ancient Greek literature."

A smirk forms on his face and he makes his way around the bar, and speaks in a dignified tone. "The Odyssey happens to be one of my favorite pieces of literature. I find it quite engaging— especially in the original Greek." He sits down next to me and swivels me on my stool to face him. "Isobel, explain this to me, if yeu please. How in God's green earth does a woman like yeu, with the talent yeu have and the blood in yeur genes, become a priest in this forgotten corner of the world?"

My eyes narrow, and I stare at him for a long while. Suddenly remembering the name he used to rouse me from my sleep, fear grips me. I stand up, take a step back and raise my hand at him. "Tony, how do you know my first name? For that matter, I have no idea exactly who you are."

Obviously alarmed, he gets to his feet and comes towards me.

I move instinctively around a nearby table and spew another series of questions. "Why did you insist on me staying here? What did Marcus tell you about me? Who are you, Tony? Tell me now." I grip onto the closest chair preparing myself to use anything as a weapon.

Tony replies in his usual calm tone. "Alex, I didn't mean to frighten yeu. Yeu've know reason to fear me. Sit down please, and I'll answer yeur questions."

He pulls a chair out from the table and gestures for me to sit.

I keep my distance but decide to sit down in the chair I'm already holding.

"Fine. You've given me no reason at this point not to at least hear you out."

Tony sits down across the table in the chair he pulled out for me.

"First," I begin in a demanding tone, "clearly, you're not some run of the mill bartender. Who are you?"

He takes a deep breath and answers. "My name is William Anthony Wallace."

His name causes an eruption of laughter from me. "Seriously," I say with my arms crossed. "I thought you were going to tell me the truth."

"I am. That is m' name." He says it as if not understanding why I wouldn't believe him right away.

"Your name is William Wallace, like the famous Scott they made a movie about decades ago."

"Oh ya, I forgot 'bout that movie. I nev'r saw it, but yes, he's my great, great something ancestor. Lots of men in my family are named after him. That's why we all go by our middle names, kinda like you goin' by yeur middle name, Isobel Alexandria Wayland."

I glare at him. "You couldn't possibly understand why I go by my middle name. But that's beside the point. Next question. How do you know my full name?"

He looks at me and pauses for a long moment. I see a small spasm of pain flash across his face.

"I knew yeur mother. Her name was Sophia Charlotte Wayland. She too went by her middle name. She once told me her friends called her Charlie."

The sound of my mother's name crushes my heart, like bricks dropping on me from the sky. I stand up, chest aching and turn away from Tony. Breathing hard I place my hands over my heart, keeping it from leaping out at any moment. Another lump fills my throat. After a few seconds, I turn back around, tears in my eyes once again. My voice is shaky but determined, "How did you know my mother? She's dead. She died over twenty years ago."

Tony gets up out of his chair and moves towards me.

Wordlessly waving my hand, I signal for him not to come any closer.

"Yes, I know she's dead." His face turns down to the floor as his voice fills with regret, "I was there when she died."

"What do you mean you were there? She died of ovarian cancer that was caused by her pregnancy with me."

His face distorts with anger, and he says in a low growl. "No, she didn't. Who told yeu that lie?"

"My father." I say and the lump in my throat dissolves at the memory of him. Instantly, I'm filled with rage. "That son of bitch told me. He told me that story often, often enough with a belt in his hand."

Tony shakes his head and gasps out. "That lying piece of shit."

My hands shake, forcing my fingers to clench around the chair as anger overwhelms me. I quickly pick the chair off the ground and slam it down with a loud grunt. One wooden leg breaks off and I clench my fist tightly. Tony, ignoring my desire for him to stay back, moves towards me and smoothly wraps his arms around my body to steady me. I scream out in rage, fury flooding my eyes, salty water streaming down my face. He holds me tight against his chest like a straight jacket. My breath is heavy, my chest rises and falls rapidly against his firm grip.

He speaks, grief in his voice. "Alex, I'll tell yeu what happened. I'll tell yeu the truth 'bout yeur mother's death."

My breath begins to slow, and I feel his heart beating against my back. I calm down, he releases his arms, and I slump over the nearest table with my back to him.

After several moments, I respond in a clear demanding voice. "Yes, you will tell me the truth, the whole truth. But first, I'm going to need a drink before I break another one of your chairs."

He responds with no argument. "Ya, I need one too."

Tony marches back around the bar and pours two bourbons neat. He comes back around, places the drinks on the table where we were sitting before I turned into Moby Dick and raged against the wooden planks of his bar. We both sit and sip the bourbon for a bit before he speaks again.

"Yeu know, yeu look like yer mother. Tall and pale skinned, eyes the color of storm clouds. Her hair was not red though, hers was the color of coal. Dark, black hair, curly from the roots."

Taking a deep breath, I say. "I was so young, and it's hard for me to remember what she looked like. All I remember was the black curls of her hair that always smelled of lavender." My heart warms at the memory of her scent. "After she died, my father tore up any and every photo of her in the house. He told me it grieved him too much to see her face."

Tony's forehead furrows as he takes a large drink of bourbon.

He continues, "I met her fourteen years ago in Scotland. I was a bartender while I was finishing my master's degree at the University of Edinburgh. I worked at a pub that she came into every week. She told me she was on an extended vacation in Scotland visitin' family. I was twenty-four years old, single and consumed with my studies. At the time, I didn't think how strange it was that she'd come by ev'ry Thursday night for a year without anyone with her. She would sit on the same stool at the bar and drink whisky all night. Her liver must've been Scottish at the rate she drank."

He grins at me and lifts his glass in my direction.

"Some nights if we weren't busy, she'd bring in a book to read and talk to me about it. We both loved readin' about philosophy and religion. Often, I'd close the pub and walk her back to a flat where she was staying nearby. The only time I questioned her about her life was when I noticed her wedding ring and asked about her husband. When I did, her face went ghost white and fear seemed to freeze her in time. I didn't push her to answer. Then one night, the day after Christmas, she finally mentioned her daughter, Isobel, who had just turned seventeen years old."

A hot tear rolls down my left cheek. I take a swig bourbon, and the lump in my throat slides back down. I wipe my cheek and say, "Ten years she was alive while I was led to believe she was dead."

Tony shakes his head. "Isobel, I'm truly sorry."

"Tell me. I need to know. How did she die?" Conflicted, part of me wants to know, but a piece of me doesn't want to hear the truth.

"One night it was very busy in the pub."

Tony pauses to finish his drink. I study his face and notice the familiar look of regret—long sighs, stoned eyes, guilt-stricken face. Tony continues his story.

"I didn't notice the two men sittin' nearby watching her until they came up to the bar and sat beside her and then started to give her a hard time. I could tell by their thick accents, they were Americans, somewhere from down south. I told the two men to fuck off and leave her alone. But they claimed to know her, said something about her daughter's father, that they were sent to clean up his mess. I didn't make much of their words then, knowin' they were both drunk and shootin' off at the mouth. It wasn't until she didn't return from the toilet that I became concerned. I was tendin' to so many folks that night that I didn't see her leave, nor did I see the two men follow her out. By the time I noticed, I ran back to the toilets and the space was empty, all except for her purse. I thought about tellin' the authorities, but I had nothing real to go on. I kept her bag for days, until I heard on the news that a woman was murdered nearby. They were askin' for anyone to come forward to identify the body."

Keeping my eyes glued on him, I take a gulp of bourbon and then ask same question again but this time in a low growl. "Tony, how did she die?"

He stares into my eyes summoning his courage. Then speaking so low that I can barely hear him. He says, "They burned her."

My breath grows heavy. I sit up straight and slam my hands on the table. My head spins, refusing to believe his words. I cry out. "How do you know for sure it was her? She could still be alive living in Scotland. How do you know for sure?"

"Isobel, I saw the body. It was her. They, whoever those men were, were interrupted in the middle of burnin' her. She was far too gone by the time police put out the fire. I knew it was her by her hair and her tall figure. Trust me, I didn't want it to be her. But they did a DNA match with the DNA from items in her purse. She's dead, Isobel. They killed her."

My heart is heavy with the few memories I have of my mother, plus the weight of her death all over again, and my head falls into my hands. Silent tears gush forth and fall from my face onto my black trousers. I weep for what seems an eternity until the rage returns and pulls me back to reality. I look up at Tony and see the residue of tear streaks on his face.

The next word that leaves out of my mouth comes with fumes. "Why?"

"Why?" He repeats as though the question has haunted him for years.

My voice fills once again with anger. "Why did they burn her? Why? Why did you wait five fuckin' years to telL me?"

I finish my drink, push myself up onto my feet, and pace back and forth.

"Why have you been keeping this from me? Why, tell me why, Tony?"

He stares at me, eyes filling again with tears. His voice trembling. "Isobel, I'm sorry. I didn't tell yeu because I didn't know how or where to begin. I loved Charlie, like she was my own mum.

I came to Louisville not only for my PhD but to solve yeur mum's murder and, and, well, to find yeu. When yeu came into the bar five years ago, I thought about tellin' yeu then, when yeu introduced yeurself. But I couldn't find the words and yeu had just taken yeur vows as a priest. As time went on, and I got to know yeu more, it became harder for me and, and I lost m' courage."

My fury builds listening to his betrayal. I bark back like a raging dog. "Why now, why tell me this all now?"

Obviously overwhelmed by the moment, he rises to his feet and answers me in a strained voice. "About a year ago, some evidence from yeur mum's murder led me to Detective Clay who's been chasing down clues to several murders across town. We've been working together ever since. We thought it best to wait up until now because Marcus believes yeu're now a target by the same group that murdered yeur mum. Alex, I'm sorry about Maria. I'm sorry about yeur mum. I'm sorry I didn't tell you sooner."

Grabbing my empty glass, I storm around the bar, my heels hammering hard on the wooden floors. I pour myself a shot of bourbon and swig it back letting it burn all the way down. Pouring another round, I raise my glass and say loudly to no one in particular, "Cheers! Cheers to all men being fucking liars."

My head tilts back and bourbon burns once again down my throat, sizzling in my chest, brewing in my belly. I slam the glass against the counter and it shatters in my right hand. Tony swiftly makes his way around the counter to help. Tears fill my eyes again, and I fall to the floor sobbing, blood streaming down my hand. Tony grabs a towel and lowers his large physique down to the ground, kneeling on one knee.

He speaks to me in a soft voice. "Isobel. Let me look at yeur hand. There might glass stuck in there."

Once again, I release my right hand to his care. He places it palm up, resting it on his bent knee to inspect it closer. Due to the amount of blood already covering my hand I decide not to watch and turn my head to the side.

He soon takes one hand, places it under my chin, and swivels my face to his. I look up at him as he tells me about the wound.

"There's one large piece of glass at the bottom of your palm just below the other bandage. I need to pull out."

I nod in acknowledgement, and feel the numbness caused by bourbon and adrenaline wash over me.

He stands up and I hear him searching through the first aid kit still open on the bar. I compose myself as I wait, wiping my face with the sleeve of my other arm, embarrassed by my lack of emotional control.

Tony returns to the floor with tweezers, alcohol wipes and another sterile bandage. He takes my right hand once again and places it on his knee. With the tiny tweezers held by his large fingers, he grabs hold of the shard of glass and pulls it out with one smooth motion. I wince, mainly at the sight of blood oozing out after the piece pulls away from my flesh. Tony takes the towel and presses it firmly in my palm.

Removing the towel, he uses the alcohol wipes to clean the cut. To my shock it burns worse than the bourbon and startles me out of my apathetic state.

After the cut has been cleaned, he wraps my hand delicately with the long bandage. I study his face as he finishes and can see the worry in the wrinkles at the corners of his eyes. His jaw is stiff, lips rolling into his mouth. I can tell he's upset with himself. Taking my left hand, I touch the short, briskly hairs on the side of his face. His face turns to me and green eyes stare into mine.

Calming myself, I say to him in a whisper, "The last person to call me Isobel was my mother." He smiles at me as I add, "Sorry, I shouldn't have lost it like that."

"Yeu got nothin' to be sorry 'bout. I must also confess another truth to yeu. When I first met you five years ago here at m' bar, I fell hard for yeu. Just the thought of yeu coming to the bar on a regular basis, made me purchase the bar from the owner. These past few years, yeu've enchanted me like Glaucus, the sea god who falls in love with the beautiful nymph. But for whatever reason, she cannot return his love."

His eyes fill with tears, and he dips his head down. His voice fills with grief and shame. "I didn't tell yeu about yeur mum because I didn't want you to hate me, hate me like I've hated myself for lettin' her die that night. Can yeu ever forgive me?"

My left hand takes his chin and pulls his eyes back up to mine. Staring into his watery gaze, I whisper, "There's nothing to forgive."

Taking my left hand, Tony places it over his mouth and kisses my palm and then pulls me up to my feet. Wobbling a bit, I lean back against the counter. He looks down at me, and I look up at him. Our eyes are heavy with grief and fatigue. A yawn takes over me, and I realize I'm at the sleepy stage of my drunkenness.

Tony recognizes it too and says, "Yeu take the bed, I'll sleep out here in one of the booths."

I give him a wry look, "Don't be ridiculous. You're taller than me, I'd fit better in the booth."

His eyes tighten, as though this topic is now non-negotiable. "No, yeu'll not be sleepin' out here in the open where I can't see yeu."

I decide not to push it and walk back to the bedroom/office space to grab a pillow off the bed and one of the blankets. I take both back to the large room as Tony walks around, turning off the lights and straightening furniture. The room feels peaceful with all but one exit light illuminating the room. A calm presence fills the space in the dim light. Tony works his way around the bar and back into the room in which I'll be sleeping. Choosing the booth nearest the room, I put together a makeshift bed.

As I lay the pillow at the back of the leather booth, I realize the impossibility of Tony's six- and half-foot frame fitting on the narrow five-foot-long bench. I decide to pull three chairs together alongside one end of the booth. At the very least, he can lay on his side and stretch out his legs. As I pull the third chair into position, Tony comes out of the back room wearing sweatpants and to my surprise, nothing on top. I pause for a moment and watch him wander barefoot across the room to grab his cell phone plugged in an outlet at the far end of the bar counter. His upper body is toned, but not overly muscular. In the dim light, shadows ripple across his stomach, accentuating the lines of his abs. When he reaches for his phone, I study the muscles of his back and how his arms flex with every movement. He looks down at his phone and types into the screen before strolling over to me.

We now stand only a foot apart and my heart picks up speed. He says, "I got a message from Marcus. The location was clear, no signs of Maria or Officer Laine. He'll be by in the mornin' with a plan for the meet up at seven tomorrow night."

I clear my throat before speaking. "Yeah. Okay. Thanks for letting me know."

Straightening the chairs tightly together I try to distract my hormones from the half-naked man before me. With my eyes still turned away from him, I say sympathetically.

"I hope this will be okay for one night."

He looks down at the makeshift bed—then at me with a lopsided grin. "Thanks, I've slept in worse places."

He moves to position himself in front of me and appears to start to say something but then stops himself. I hand him the blanket from the bed and say as casually as possible. "It's pretty chilly out here. Are you going to be warm enough?"

Stepping closer to me, he drapes the blanket around his shoulder. With his muscles still exposed and only inches away, I can't help but stare at his bare chest.

In a low voice he says, "Isobel, are you worried about me?"

Consciously averting my eyes from his naked flesh, my answer surprises both of us. "Yes. Yes, I am."

He grins, blushing a bit at my honesty and drawing nearer to me. "I must say, when I first found out Charlie's daughter had become a catholic priest, I was a bit disappointed. But then again, I've never followed religious rules very well."

His words cause my face to flush with embarrassment as my gaze focuses on the wall at the back of the room. But then I feel his calloused hand under my chin, gently guiding my face back in front of him. Our eyes lock and I feel my heart leap into my ears. The hairs on my arm stand up. My face flushes with heat, and I know the skin around my cheeks must be roused with red.

Tony smiles wide, his hand still under my chin. I linger in his eyes—the color of spring grass on the rolling hills of Kentucky farmland. My lips spread across my face as his hand moves around my jawline and his thumbs glides over my cheekbones.

"Like I said before, yeu're a bonnie lass."

My left hand moves at his words and touches the cavity between his bulging chest. His heartbeat penetrates my skin, sending the rhythm of flesh and blood through my fingertips. My heart skips with anticipation, as he pulls me even closer. His face is so close now that I can see glistening shades of blue, green and yellow in his eyes. Our lips are millimeters apart when a wave of electricity shoots through my body, and I see for an instant my six-headed Scylla shove Tony in the chest.

As if he had touched the inside of a wall outlet, Tony's body jolts back ten feet and smashes against a nearby table. Now, on the ground, he looks up at me in disbelief and to my surprise starts chuckling.

He comments haphazardly, "Well, that's what I get for trying to kiss a priest."

I stare at him less amused and slightly winded. "Uh oops. I forgot to tell you my monster has recently come out of the closet."

He stands up slowly still laughing. "Ya, I was worried that might happen."

I retort between breaths, "Excuse me? You knew Scylla might strike if you kissed me."

"Well no. I was worried about kissing a person with this kinda power, especially a person who doesn't know how to use it. This is why we Scotts call it, *créachta scáth*, the shadow wound. Our wounds can be quite defensive if not vicious in intimate moments."

Reaching out to Tony, I grab his hand and help him to his feet. Releasing his hand, I touch my clergy collar which now feels like an electric dog collar that zaps when boundaries are crossed.

I say with regret, "Sorry. I guess we shouldn't do that again."

He gives me a look of disappointment. "It's okay. For now anyway."

Embarrassment and confusion cause me awkwardly and hastily to leave with an abrupt, "Good night."

I hurry back to my sleeping quarters and quickly shut the door. I lean against the wooden door and smack my forehead on it in frustration. "Alex, get your shit together," I say to myself. "Sweet Jesus, what has gotten into you?"

I shake the last few moments out of my head and make my way to the bed. Sam is sleeping peacefully on the quilt, curled up tight at the far corner by the headboard. I pull the covers back and realize I have nothing to sleep in. Not wanting to sleep in my collar or slacks and blouse, I decide the best option is to keep my undergarments on and hope the fire alarm doesn't go off in the middle of the night.

Down to my bra, panties and argyle socks, I slip my body into bed and turn off the lights. I close my eyes and pray for sweet dreams, but my body tosses to and fro like a ship at sea. This goes on for hours until my bladder has shaken itself to bursting. I check the time on my phone—five past one.

Reluctantly getting out of bed, I turn the lamp on and strategize the best method of covering myself for a quick bathroom trip. I see several of Tony's button-down shirts hanging nearby. Dancing in place with agony, I quickly pull one of his shirts over my head. It falls past my butt at a semi comfortable length at my thighs. I tiptoe out of the room, trying with all my might not to wake Tony.

I open and close the bedroom door silently, gliding across the dance floor to the hallway leading to the bathroom. A few snores from the direction that Tony is sleeping reassures me. Slipping inside the bathroom, I turn on the bright light which suddenly blinds me with tiny stars hovering over my vision. I make it to the toilet and sit, sighing in relief, as the several drinks from hours earlier leave my body.

After a long while, I make my way to the sink, wash my hands and splash water on my face. Then I hear a noise outside, turn off the water, and freeze in place. I hear someone pulling on the metal door down the hallway. I turn off the light, silently push the bathroom door open and peer out into the darkness. The contrast of the dark hallway causes my eyes to adjust, slowly. I step out of the doorway, a large hand covers my mouth, and someone forces me against the wall. I fight to free myself, but before I decide to kick my assailant, Tony's voice whispers in my ear. "Isobel, it's me." I freeze under his weight. "Shhh. There's someone at the door."

The noise of someone pulling at the locked metal door echoes down the hallway. Tony pulls his hand away from my mouth, and I lean into him, separating myself from the wall. The person at the door shakes the handle again and Tony sweeps my body behind him putting himself between me and the exit door.

My eyes adjust to darkness and the red light from the exit door allows me to see the outline of a gun in Tony's hand, stretched out towards the noise at the door. Silence lingers in the air for several minutes. After a long while no new noises come from the metal door.

Tony turns to me and says in low murmur. "What are yeu doin' up?"

I cannot see his face clearly, but his tight grip on my hand gives me a good idea of his facial expression.

I reply in a low voice, "I had to pee. What are you doing up and with a gun?"

"It's America, everyone has a gun. I'm up because I heard someone at the door. I thought it was just a patron of bar, but then I heard the water runnin' in the bathroom."

"Ya, it was me. I was trying not to wake you." I pause for a second and then ask the obvious, "Do you really think that was a bar patron at the door?"

I feel Tony take a deep breath before answering me. "No, I don't."

He guides me back down the hallway and out into the large room. I make my way around the bar and pour myself a glass of water. As I drink, I see Tony looking down at his phone.

He turns to me and says, "I have no messages from Marcus. The person at the door wouldn't have been him. If that wasn't him, or someone he sent, it means either yeu or Marcus were followed here."

He walks around the bar and pours himself a glass of water before adding, "But if they were followin' Marcus, they would've known he had left hours ago. Which means the person at the door was here for yeu."

Chiming in, I downplay his paranoia. "First of all, we can't be sure who exactly was at the door, and second, I'm not that paranoid yet.

Tony gulps down the entire glass of water before giving me an odd look.

"Are yeu wearin' my shirt?" He asks with a flash of teeth.

"Uh… yes." I stammer, self-consciously. I look down and realize the top four buttons are undone and a deep, bare-skinned "V" is exposed down my chest past my bra line. I clasp shut the opening with my right, wounded hand. "Sorry. I just didn't have anything to wear other than my clergy clothes."

He leans in so close, the warmth of his breath tickles my skin.

He whispers in my ear, "I dunna mind at t'all."

Then his lips press gently against my cheek, and I freeze in place as he says, "Happy Birthday, Isobel, m' bonnie lass."

Tony leaves me at the bar with the gift of goosebumps crawling over my skin. My paralysis disappears and my body moves again. I head straight to bed, beaming like a teenage girl.

Sleep comes swiftly and to my great relief, it's a dreamless sleep.

12: Gut

The aroma of coffee awakens me. Eyes still shut; I feel a ball of fur wedged against the small of my back cuddling for warmth under the several layers of blankets. My body is heavy, and my eyelids refuse to open. I try not to move and keep the heat of the bed tucked in tightly. The sound of fingers clicking on a keyboard forces the opening of my one eye not smashed against the pillow. I see a soft neon light from a laptop screen shining brightly in the darkness of the room.

Tony's voice greets me with over-the-top Scottish cheer, "Good mornin'."

I grunt and pull the blankets over my head and turn my body over toward the wall. Sam shifts her feline form, and snuggles deeper into the curve of my gut. I stroke her fur in the oven of our cocoon. After a while, I peep my head out of the blanket—the allure of freshly brewed coffee intensifies. I look across the bed, and the light of the computer reveals a large cup of steaming java resting on the bedside table. My long arm reaches out and pulls the mug close to my lips. The taste of heaven brings me back to earth. I sit up and, luckily, I remember I'm wearing only two small undergarments, and so I secure the quilts over my body—everything except one arm to hold the coffee in the chilly, cave-like room.

Tony still has on his sleeping attire—sweatpants and no shirt. He is typing intensely in the shadows at the nearby desk. He shuts the laptop screen, darkness consumes the room. I hear the click of the desk lamp, and intense light forces my eyes to snap shut. Before I can bear opening my eyes again, I feel the wait shift in the bed. I squint my eyes and see Tony sitting beside me.

"Uh, hi," I say, and then take another sip of coffee, doing my best not to stare at his sculpted upper body.

He grins at me and says, "I have somethin' for yeu. A late birthday gift."

"Tony," my eyes widen, "I'm not really into birthdays, so you really don't—"

Tony interrupts me, and in a playful tone says, "Will you just shut up?"

He reaches into his pants pocket, pulls out a small piece of paper, and puts it down on the blanket that covers my lap and chest. I gasp in shock. My other arm flings itself from the covers to take hold of the slip of paper. I bring it close to my face and stare long and hard at an image of a woman with pale skin, dark, curly hair, holding the hand of a nine-year-old, redheaded girl. My mother wears an A-line navy dress, nude pumps and a green scarf fluttering in the wind. I stand beside her in a burgundy, corduroy jumper, and tennis shoes. We're standing on the sanctuary steps, outside the Baptist church my father pastored for ten years in the East End of Louisville. I remember the grand steeple, the white-washed building, and the colonial columns at the front of the sanctuary. Good, sweet memories flood my mind. My father took this photo during the last fall that the three of us were still to-gether.

"Tony," I react, keeping my eyes glued on the photo. "Where did you get this?"

"I found it in her purse the night she disappeared. For whatever reason, I kept it from the police. It's been in my wallet ever since."

I look up at him—eyes watery, my heart swelling. Pulling the photo to my chest, I exclaim, "Thank you so much."

Before he can respond, there's a knock at the door and Marcus walks in. He stops short, looking surprised and slightly embarrassed. I realize at that point the blankets have slid down to my waist exposing my bra and chest. Marcus gives us both a quizzical look as Tony stands to greet him with a handshake that blocks his view from me so I can cover myself. I try hard not to look guilty over something that didn't happen, sip my coffee, and listen to Tony and Marcus discuss the latest news about Maria.

Marcus briefs us. "I watched Officer's Laine's house all night, but no one was there. He has no wife or children, and as Chief Mason pointed out to me last night, all we really have to go on is Alex's shoe from the evidence in the room."

Marcus and Tony both turn and glance over at me as I continue to sip my coffee in bed. Tony speaks to Marcus as if I wasn't in the room.

"I told her everything last night. Alex will be helpful not only in this case with Maria but in the case of the murders I've been consulting with you on."

I stare back at them and say in a facetious tone, "Well, yes, I'd love to be the helpful priest and amateur private eye who cracks this case wide open, but first I'd need to put on my clothes."

My annoyed expression causes them both to avert their eyes to the floor and make their way out of the room. I dress quickly, jump into my black slacks, pull my black blouse over my head and tuck it into my pants. I slip the clergy collar in place over my neck and reach for my boots. Sam hops off the bed and brushes against my hands knocking my grip off my left boot.

I sit down and pat her on the head. "Hey girl, I had a good time last night, too. Sorry, I can't stay longer."

I stroke her fur for a while and then reach for my shoe. Again, Sam nudges my hand away with a quiet, "Meow."

"Sam, I'll come back later I promise." I say and give her another pat on the head. Sam ignores my affections and drapes her body across the left shoe.

I say, "What's going on?"

She lets me put on the right boot, but will not budge her position with the left. My irritation is growing as she glares at me with her blue, beady eyes. Then suddenly it hits me. Like light piercing the darkness, a sharp revelation slams to the forefront of my mind. My response seems to satisfy Sam, and she steps gingerly off the shoe and sits nearby cleaning her paws again. I grab the boot and hobble my way out of the room to inform the guys of my recent revelation.

Interrupting their conversation at a table, I declare with confidence, "My shoe!"

Marcus and Tony turn and look at me confused.

Tony stands and responds with sarcasm. "Aye, that's yeur shoe a'right. Maybe we need to get yeu some more coffee."

"No! I mean, yes, please, to coffee. But no, you don't understand. My shoe, the oxford shoe that fell in the dumpster, the one taken into evidence. It was my left shoe. Marcus, the one we found in the shower yesterday, that was my right shoe."

Marcus flashes a look of shock. Hesitantly, he says, "Are you sure, Alex?"

"The only way to be sure is to see for ourselves. Let's go." I move hastily towards my jacket and scarf at the entrance to the back hallway. Moving along, I turn to Tony and ask in all seriousness, "Any chance I can get a cup of coffee to-go?"

Tony replies, "Yes, as long as we talk about yeur vices along the way."

Marcus and Tony spring into action—fling on their coats and grab their keys along with my cup of coffee. They catch up with me down the hallway by the exit door to the back alley.

I push open the metal door, the morning chill slaps my face along with brisk, winter wind. The three of us descend the steps and hurry to the cars parked out on the street.

Along the way, Tony exclaims, "Marcus, I'll ride with Alex, and we'll meet you at the cottage."

I unlock the mini cooper, and Tony and I crawl inside. His long legs fold into the narrow passenger seat. He holds my coffee, his body slightly hunched towards the dashboard. The engine turns over, and I stomp on the gas pedal. Close behind is Marcus who puts on his police sirens. Tony grips onto the window as we take a sharp turn somehow managing to not spill my coffee.

Seeing his discomfort, I say sympathetically, "Sorry, it's a bit tight in here. At least if we wreck, the air brag won't break your nose."

He snorts and replies, "Ya, m' nose won't break but m' legs will and this hot coffee will most likely scald my face fer all eternity."

I grab the coffee from him, and take a large sip, keeping my left hand on the steering wheel. "Ah, but it be a noble sacrifice."

Tony chuckles and uses both hands to steady himself in the car. We both go quiet when the steeple of St. Luke's comes into view. Tony hops out of the car before I park. Marcus and I follow directly behind him through the rod iron gate towards the front door of the cottage. I pull out my keys, and reach to unlock the door, but a young black male police officer swings it open before my key touches the lock.

"Good Morning, sir," he says, addressing Marcus, "here's the shoe that you requested from the first bedroom. The other was nowhere to be found."

The three of us step into the warm cottage, and I take the shoe from the officer. My instincts were correct, this is the right, black oxford.

I glance up at Marcus, and Tony asks the obvious question. "So, if this is not the shoe from evidence, what is Officer Laine up to?"

At that moment, Marcus' cell phone rings. Following the second ring, he answers, "Good morning, Chief." He looks at me and his expression shifts from confused to horror. He turns away from us, but is still in hearing distance.

"What?! Sir, that's not possible. I know, I'm here at the cottage looking at it."

Pulling both Tony and me into my bedroom, he continues his conversation with the Chief. "Yes, sir. I'm on my way. Yes, I'll bring Mother Alex with me." Marcus closes the door behind us and hangs up the phone. He paces back and forth, his face contorted with anger.

Impatient, I ask, "Marcus, what's going on?"

"Well," he begins with a sigh, "seems as though Officer Laine has not only found Sister Maria but has rescued her and delivered her safe and unharmed to the precinct."

"What?!" my voice screams in disbelief.

"SHHH!, keep it down," Marcus demands. "We three, along with Chief Mason are the only ones who know about Officer Laine. Here in a minute, I'll give the good news to the officers outside this room, and I need you both, as friends of Maria, to look relieved if not enthused. Then, Alex, you and I will go the precinct and thank Officer Laine for his fine work and see that Maria is indeed unharmed."

"Shit," I say under my breath. "I can't do that. I can't in good conscience look that evil, son of bitch in the face without punching him!" My voice intensifies, but I keep it at a whisper. "I can't. I won't. He's up to something. He's used us as pawns to position himself as a hero."

Tony reaches out to me, but I'm too hot with rage. I shift my body before his hand reaches my shoulder. Scowling at Marcus, I see my own anger mirrored back at me. His brown eyes are wild but deep down, we both know he's right.

Tony speaks in a calm, rational tone, "Marcus, I'd like to go to the precinct with yeu both. Yeu need another set of eyes right now. I'll come as a friend to Alex and Maria. Officer Laine doesn't suspect me being involved in anyway."

Marcus tightens his lips as he gives the plan some thought.

A few moments pass, and he says, "Yes, it's okay. But I need you both smiling when we leave this room—look relieved if not downright joyful. Alex, collect some clothes for Maria, and then both of you meet me at the precinct."

Tony and I nod, following Marcus out of the bedroom. The rouse of my smile feels funny on my face, but I hold the grin, and walk across the tiny cottage as Marcus informs everyone of the good news. Cheers erupt and the officers pat one another on the back. I collect some warm, casual wear from Maria's dresser and put it in a small duffle bag. Tony meets me at the front door with my car keys and my coffee in hand.

He greets me dryly, "I'll drive, yeu drink."

Still angry, I decide not to waste my energy protesting about feminism and driving roles. I take my place in the passenger seat of my own car, sip my coffee, and think to myself, "No, I'll save my rage for someone else."

13: Patience

Tony parallel parks Merida with ease along the curb across from the Fourth Street Police Precinct. I walk into the three-story building, trash my empty coffee cup in a nearby receptacle, and swing the bag full of Maria's clothes across my shoulder. The chatty receptionist from yesterday sits in the same desk chair behind the bullet proof glass. Mary Ann Sprier sees Tony and me approach, and her face breaks into a rosy smile.

With the cheer of a child seeing Santa on Christmas she cries out, "Mother Alex!"

Then to my horror rambles on as though we are now old friends.

"It's good to see you again. You just made my day yesterday. I went home and had a good cry for a couple hours, and then went to visit my aunt Susan at Cave Cemetery. Next time you'll have to join me."

Tony observes me with a snicker, which causes me to groan before beaming wide back at her. Mirroring her enthusiasm, I cry back, "Hi, Mary Ann! It's good to see you, too."

Seeing Tony next to me, Mary Ann rises from her seat and awkwardly slides open the window to shake our hands.

She takes mine, then Tony's. Blushing, she asks, "Now, Mother Alex, who do we have here?"

I turn my head to watch Toney, who intentionally keeps his hold on Mary Ann's hand while simultaneously flashing his Scottish charm. He then introduces himself with the thickest accent I've ever heard him use.

""'Ello lassie, m' name is William Anthony Wallace. 'Tis m' pleasure to meet yeu."

Mary Ann's face blossoms like a pink tulip. Letting out a short giggle, her shoulders scrunch into her ears as her extended arms fall limp. Tony, noticing my chagrin, gently returns her hand. My overly dramatic disposition returns quickly when I ask her about Detective Clay.

"Well, Mary Ann, did Detective Clay happen to come in this morning?"

"Yes, Mother Alex. Detective Clay just walked in a few minutes ago. He told me to tell you to meet him in his office when you arrive. Now, you remember where that is. It's down the hall to your left, passed the—"

I interrupt her but trying to keep my smile, "Yes, thank you, I do remember. Again, thank you so much, Mary Ann, for all your wonderful help."

"You are quite welcome, Mother. Let me know when you'd like to visit my aunt with me."

I give her a nod and cheeky grin while pushing Tony in the ribs in the direction we need to go. He cranes his head back towards Mary Ann and flashes his pearly smile at her one more time.

Several steps down the hallway, I can hear Mary Ann giving us more goodbyes, "It was nice meeting you William. You both have a wonderful day! God bless!"

I exhale dramatically, letting out my relief and irritation. Tony laughs while mocking me.

"Mother Alex, I didn't know yeu and Mary Ann were best friends? When yeu goin' to see her dead aunt?"

I give him a playful jab in the shoulder with my right fist and instantly regret it. Pain shoots through my swollen hand, and I can't help but blame Tony.

"AHH! Curse you, you Scottish flirt. Look what you made me do."

He laughs again and adds, "I've noticed, Isobel, that yeu always seem to run out of leniency for me."

I shrug my shoulders and give him a lopsided grin.

We ascend the two flights of stairs up to the third floor. Tony beats me to the top, not even winded, and glances back at me as though to see if I need help.

I hold my breath and try to look as though I'm in equal physical shape as I lead him to Marcus' office. Along the way, I glance to my left and right, and peer around open cubicles wondering where Maria might be waiting.

We arrive at a closed door with a nameplate along the door frame that reads, "Detective Marcus Clay." I hear two sets of voices inside, knock twice, and wait. After a few moments, the door opens, and Chief Mason stands in the doorway. His soft green eyes look weary, surrounded by wrinkles—yet his face wears the pleasant grin of a politician.

"Mother Alex, Tony." He steps back and opens the door wide. "Come in, please. We don't have much time."

Tony and I enter the small office, and I see Marcus leaning against the front of his wooden desk. He's clutching a large clear evidence bag with a black, oxford, left shoe. Chief Mason closes the door behind us as Marcus begins the briefing.

"This was sitting on my desk when I arrived a few minutes ago. When asked, Officer Laine claims he returned the shoe immediately after retrieving it from the evidence room yesterday afternoon, not long after Alex got physical with him in the hallway."

Tony gives me a wry look. I cross my arms over my chest and reply, defensively, "Physical! I didn't even touch him."

"Well," Marcus says flatly. "He claims you intentionally rammed him coming up the stairs and knocked him over."

"Well, yes, I did run into him, but that was an accident. I didn't see him at the top of the stairs."

Chief Mason chimes in, "Whatever happened, we know that Officer Laine is building a case against you. It was no coincidence that there was a reporter waiting with a camera at the end of the alley the night of the murder. We, Marcus and I, that is, believe Officer Laine contacted a photographer to somehow use the media to try to discredit you."

Marcus adds, "That's why he was so adamant to arrest you and bring you in himself. He wanted to be the cop in the photo taking you down to the precinct. Now, with the shoe situation and rescuing Maria, he's now the obvious hero."

I plop down on a leather chair beside the bookshelf and rub my face with my hands. I look up at the three tall men towering over me and ask, "What do we do now?"

After a long pause, Chief Mason answers my question. "For now, we need you to lay low, patience is a virtue in this case. Give Officer Laine the gratification as if he has beaten you." He steps towards me. "Alex, you need to look weak, vulnerable. We think

Officer Laine has pinpointed you as an adversary, you're someone strong he wants to crush. His desire is to dominate you, and for him this means framing you for murder, ruining your reputation and possibly hurting those you love." The Chief looks over at Marcus and adds confidently. "But we, we believe we can use you against him."

"Okay," I say with a long sigh. "I get the whole psychopath thing, but what I can't understand is why he took Maria and not me? Why not hurt me or just kill me and get me out of the way?"

At this point Tony steps closer to me and says, "My private investigation has led me to Officer Laine but not for the same reasons as Marcus and the Chief. I believe he's a link in yeur mother's murder. He's connected somehow to the men I saw thirteen yers ago in that pub. I believe he might not be allowed to kill you."

So many questions race through my mind. How is Officer Laine connected to my mother's murder? Who gave the order not to kill me? Who's at the end of this long noose of killings? But right now, I have to set aside my need for answers for Maria's sake, for my mother's sake. I rise to my feet and instantly feel the blood rush to my head. I place my good hand on the desk and look each of them in the eye, my voice unwavering.

"I'll do whatever it takes to punish Officer Laine for Maria and for my mother. You want me to look weak and vulnerable, I'll do it. You want me to lay low, fine. You want to use me as sheep for the slaughter, alright. But what I ask in return is that I become a part of this investigation. Any and all information get's relayed to me, no questions asked."

Tony looks across the room at Marcus who glances over at Chief Mason. The Chief takes two more steps towards me and extends his right hand and says, "I believe we have an agreement."

I reach out with my injured right hand and firmly grasp his withholding any sign of pain from the wounds I incurred last night. Chief Mason stares into my eyes and I give him a nod. Chief Mason releases his grip and steps back.

Marcus picks up a folder from his desk and says, "Now, that we are all on the same page. Maria is currently down in the basement with two officers we trust, along with officer Laine who is also down there finishing up some paperwork concerning the kidnapping. We haven't spoken to Maria yet, but here is Officer Laine's report."

Marcus hands the report to Tony who opens it as Marcus continues verbally detailing the written account inside.

"Officer Laine is claiming he overheard a conversation by two black men in a local bar last night bragging about kidnapping a hot, Latino priest. He says they mentioned something about holding her in an apartment complex across the street from a rundown distillery in the West End. This distillery being William Oaks, the only distillery on that side of town. So Officer Laine takes it upon himself to investigate the situation. He stakes out the apartment complex all night until he sees one of the men enter the building early this morning. Officer Laine said he followed the man to the fourth floor, and he claims that he heard a woman scream from inside one of the apartments. He kicked open the door to find a naked, Latino woman shackled, head covered and chained against the heater in the bathroom. When the two black men see Officer Laine, they reach for their weapons, which forces Officer Laine to shoot and kill them. He then rescues Maria and calls for backup."

Tony glances up from reading the material in the folder and asks, "Other witnesses? Anyone see or hear anything?"

"None so far. But I have no doubt we'll find something or someone that discredits this story. Such as, how is it that my men didn't see Officer Laine last night staking out the apartment as we were searching for the abandoned distillery next door? Or, how is it that the two black men shot by Officer Laine have the same mark as the murdered man in the dumpster?"

Tony closes the folder and adds, "I'll stay up here while yeu three go down to Maria. I want to take a deeper look into this report, and I don't want Officer Laine to see me. Alex, come get me when yeu and Maria are ready to go."

I follow behind Marcus and Chief Mason who are already halfway out the door, but Tony tenderly takes hold of my left bicep and brings his lips close to my ear.

He whispers a word of encouragement. "Isobel. Yeu can do this. Don't let him use yeur power against yeu."

Seeing the backs of both Marcus and the Chief, I turn my head to give a witty reply but stop short as the sensation of Tony's rough stubble presses against my face. He turns slightly into me, and his lips softly brush up against the skin of my cheek. Goosebumps lift the hairs on my neck. I'm unsure whether the act was intentional, or if his lips were just so close to my face that when I turned, they happened to touch my cheek. Either way, out of the corner of my eye, I see a lopsided grin on Tony's face. He releases his hold, and I step through the doorway, close the door, and a smile flashes over my face. I pick up my pace to catch up with Marcus and the Chief.

We descend four sets of stairs to the basement, which gives

me several minutes to sober up and focus myself on the task at hand.

Be weak. Be vulnerable. Be weak. Be vulnerable. I repeat internally over and over with each step I take.

Thoughts of my childhood creep into my head—the days after my father told me my mother died and about the consequence that followed. The blame, the burden, the beatings I endured as a helpless little girl for six years. Feelings of sorrow for that child long ago clump into my throat. I feel my eyes burn, and tears begin to form.

I step onto the cement floor of the basement. As I continue to move along, my heels echo with each stride.

Marcus glances over at me and asks, "Alex, you ready?"

Without looking at him, I nod, sensing the red blotches covering my cheeks and swelling around my eyes.

"Good. Follow me. I'll take you to Maria, and Officer Laine who's sitting with her.

This time I follow Marcus down the right side of the hallway. As we pass the prisoner holding cells, I begin to wonder why Maria is being held in this section of the precinct. Chief Meyers answers my question as if he heard my thoughts.

He says in a low voice beside me. "We thought it best to keep Maria and Officer Laine down here in a section of the precinct where media and reporters would not be passing by unannounced."

We stop at a door with a sign that says, "Viewing Room." Marcus opens the door and enters the small space, which is filled with recording devices, television screens and a large one-way mirror in the middle. My eyes dart to the window where I see Maria sitting cross legged in a metal chair wearing oversized sweatpants and an LCPD sweatshirt. She holds her grace and beauty, even with bare feet and tangled waves falling down her back, giving the impression of a princess recently rescued from the wild woodlands. My heart eases a bit at the sight of her but then I notice the tall, blonde, man leaning against the wall nearby.

Officer Laine wears the same clothes he had on yesterday, but now his white collared shirt is dirty and torn across the chest, revealing a portion of his bare chest. His khakis are filthy as well with blood splattered across one thigh, and his golden locks are tucked neatly underneath a LCPD ball cap. My body tightens as though I could smell the stench of his arrogance through the glass.

Marcus steps up behind me and places a calming hand on my shoulder. Repeating almost verbatim the same pep talk from Tony.

"Alex, you can do this. Don't let him use his power against you."

The words pierce my rage, and I look Marcus in the face, unsure if he knew of the power Officer Laine possessed. No matter what, in the next few moments, I need to make Officer Laine believe he's gotten the best of me. I close my eyes, take several deep breaths, and bring forth the thoughts of the scrawny little redhead I keep hidden in a remote region of my soul.

My eyes open, and I say, "I'm ready."

Marcus leads me out of the viewing room and around the side to the door that leads to Maria. I inhale through my nose and exhale through my mouth.

He grabs the doorknob and says, "You'll go in alone, but know, if you need help, we'll be watching." A tear rolls down my cheek, signaling Marcus to open the door.

I step into the room and focus my sight on Maria, who to my delight leaps out of the chair and hugs me tightly. Letting her joy surround me as tears pour down my face. I feel Officer Laine's eyes on us as I pull Maria's petite frame up and off the ground, embracing her for a long moment.

Choking out a few sentimental phrases that were true but said in a manner I would not usually articulate, I squeal out, "Maria! I was so very worried about you."

I place Maria back down on her feet, releasing her from my grip. Taking both her hands in mine I speak again with distress. "Ever since you were taken, I've felt so helpless. Please tell me those men didn't hurt you!"

She looks into my eyes, tears and mucus streaming down her face. Grateful that her back is turned to Officer Laine, I see Maria's face suddenly contort with confusion most likely seeing through my melodramatic performance.

I hug her again and whisper in her ear. "Play along."

Getting the message she whimpers and says, "Alex, I was so scared. I'm so glad Steve found me."

"Steve?" Screams a voice inside of me. "She's calling him by his first name?"

At the sound of his name, I watch Officer Laine, also known as Steve, move towards us. I release my arms around Maria and speak to him as politely as possible.

"Officer Laine, thank you so much. I'm so glad you were there in time to save Sister Maria."

A boyish grin spread across his face, as if my gratitude has embarrassed him. He replies in a tone from an old John Wayne film.

"Oh, I was just doing my duty. I'm just glad I got her back safely."

He looks down at Maria, touches her shoulder, and gives her a nod.

Maria graciously smiles up at him. I decide that hugging him would be overkill, most likely killing me. I force another tear down my face and extend my right hand to Officer Laine. My words are warm and tender, "Truly, thank you, Officer Laine. I thought I had lost Maria forever."

He glances down at my bandaged hand and takes hold of it, squeezing my tender knuckles tightly. I feel the wound on my palm pull open as pain shoots through my arm. His blue eyes search mine for signs of defiance. I turn my face down like a whipped dog and wipe my nose with the sleeve of my jacket. Still crushing my hand, he conveys his sentiments with the charm of a sociopathic salesman.

"I know how helpless you feel, that is, losing someone so valuable to you. I'm so glad I could be of service to you both."

With one more squeeze, he releases my hand and I quickly slip it into my coat pocket before Maria can notice anything. At that moment, Marcus opens the door and walks into the room, casually, with a cup of coffee in his hand.

"Thank you, Officer Laine, for staying this long. I know Sister Maria is grateful for your presence while she waited for Mother Alex." Marcus shakes Officer Laine's hand and adds his sentiments, "We all appreciate your thorough account of the past twelve hours. You have certainly earned some time off."

"Just doing my duty. I want to keep all God's children safe."

Officer Laine winks over at Maria. "If you don't mind, Detective, I'll just wait in the next room in case you need me."

Tapping the bill of his hat with one hand he excuses himself from the interrogation room. He closes the door and I turn my back to the one-way mirror, my eyes shooting a fierce dagger at Marcus.

Seeing my expression, he politely asks. "Mother Alex, Sister Maria, will you both please take a seat?"

All three of us take a seat, me to the right of Maria and Marcus across the table from us.

Marcus continues, "Sister Maria, I know you must be exhausted and overwhelmed so I don't wish to keep you any longer than necessary. But we need to take a statement from you. Will you please let us know what happened from beginning to end?"

Maria sits up straight and brushes her long hair back behind her head. She looks at me, and I give her a serious look that translates, "It's okay. I trust him."

She nods and turns back to Marcus, beginning her account of the last eighteen hours. "Around two o'clock yesterday, I returned home from visiting a parishioner downtown at U of L hospital. I got Mother Alex's text message about the death of a member in our church, and didn't expect her to be home from the funeral home for a while. So I decided to straighten up the cottage and get a few chores done. I did the dishes and some laundry knowing our beds sheets needed washing. When I went to get the sheets off Mother Alex's bed, I saw her lone, black oxford shoe. At that moment, I decided to take a shower and then head to the precinct to see if I could get the missing shoe as a birthday gift for her. I took the shoe and placed it by the front door so I would not forget it. I figured that I might need proof I knew Alex when I went to retrieve the shoe. Then I went to the bathroom, undressed and turned on the shower. That's when I heard a knock at the door. I put on my robe and went to see who it was. But when I opened the door, no one was there. I was not about to look around the cottage in this freezing weather with only a robe on, so I quickly shut the door and hopped back in the hot shower.

It must've been the sound of the shower that kept me from hearing the men enter the bathroom. Two men in masks pulled me out of the shower. It happened so quickly I couldn't process anything, and then everything went dark. Hours, minutes, days went by, I don't know but then I woke up, I was naked and cold, lying on the floor. Everything was still black, and I felt a thick fabric against my face. I started screaming and a few minutes later, I heard gunshots and the voice of Officer Laine telling me I was safe."

I reach over and squeeze her hand, giving a tearful look of concern in full view of the mirror. Maria hugs me again and then asks the question I was hoping we could avoid.

"I'm assuming those men followed me home from the hospital. But, Detective, why was I targeted? Why me?"

Marcus takes a sip of coffee. Holding his poker face, he puts the cup down and says, "Well, we aren't sure yet. But you're right, they must've followed you home. We think they might've been connected to the murder that took place a few nights ago. We aren't sure if they were involved in the killing, or if they were friends of the victim who were trying to get vengeance. They may have been looking for Alex, who as you might have seen in the papers yesterday, was broadcasted as the suspected murderer. But all of this is speculation, now."

Marcus shifts topics and begins to ask Maria follow up questions. "Thank you for sharing your account, Sister Maria. I can only imagine how you must feel. I do need to ask you a few follow up questions. Can you think of anything, any details from when they first grabbed you? The color of their eyes, a strange mark? Anything at all would help."

Shaking her head in dismay, she answers, "I really don't remember much. They wore black masks that covered their eyes. I know they were taller than me, but everyone's taller than me. I'm truly sorry I'm not more help."

"It's okay. Maybe something will come to you in the next few days. If so, please contact me."

Marcus rises out of his chair, and we follow behind him as he opens the door for us. Marcus shakes his hand and walks out into the hallway. As I pass him, I speak in a low voice keeping my eyes forward.

"Remember our agreement. Keep me posted."

Marcus places his hand on my lower back guiding me out of the room while giving a quiet reply, "Will do. Stay out of trouble."

We make our way down the hallway to the elevators and inform Maria that I have a bag of warm clothes, shoes and coat for her upstairs in Marcus' office. She hugs me in gratitude and speaks as we enter the elevator.

"I also expect you'll be filling me in as to why you suddenly turned into Meryl Streep when you came into the room."

My face breaks into a wide smile as the elevator doors close.

"Well, I did mean everything I said, but the point of all that was not intended to try and convince you."

Maria turns and looks at me with a serious face. "Alex, I know you're suspicious of him, but Steve's given me no reason to think otherwise. When he found me naked on that floor, he covered me up immediately with his coat and then wrapped a blanket around me in the car. If anything, Steve made me feel safe and secure in a rather horrible situation that any bad person might take advantage of."

Rage foams in my mouth, and I snap back at her, "For god's sake Maria, don't call him Steve like y'all were out on date last night!"

Maria's face goes cold. The elevator doors open to the third floor and she stomps out into the hallway. I follow her trying to find the right words to apologize, but they don't come, and I know Maria too well by now. She'll avoid any conflict with me until she calms down. Passing ahead of her, I arrive at Marcus' office door, and open it for her, hoping the gesture might be of some consolation. She ignores me all together and would have remained in her silent aggression mode if Tony had not been waiting inside. Her temperament changes immediately seeing his familiar face.

She cries, "Tony! What are you doing here?"

"Hi Maria! I came for moral support. It's so good to see yeu."

Maria gives him a big hug and says, "Thanks so much. I'm so glad you're here to rescue me from the big bully behind me."

My body tightens at the label Maria knows I hate being called: "Bully." A name I loathe more than "bitch." Bully is a term used only for those insecure, wounded victims of the world who can't control their emotions and use them as weapons to victimize others. But in that moment, I know full well that I deserve the name.

Tony lets go of Maria and looks at me. His eyes linger on my blotchy face, and I can tell he's worried.

I hand Maria the bag of clothes, and she takes it without a word or even a glance up at me.

She turns to Tony and says, "Any chance we can grab some food at the bar before we go home? I'm famished and not quite ready to get back to the cottage."

He smiles and nods enthusiastically.

She says, "Great. Let me change. I'll be right back."

Maria leaves the room. Tony closes the door and turns to me. "So," he begins slowly. "Should I even ask how it t'all went?"

I plop down in a nearby chair feeling defeated on several accounts. "Well," I say, pulling my right hand out of my jacket. "I definitely played the weak and vulnerable card." I stare at the crimson stains emerging on the cloth around my right palm. Seeing the bloody bandages, Tony pulls a chair in front of me and sits.

"Let me see that." He says softly. He takes my hand into his as he pulls back the bandage.

Wincing I say, "It's my fault. I offered my hand to him, and he took the bait."

"Isobel, there had to of been another way to look weak other than offering yeur wounded hand to the devil."

He unwraps the bandages and lays my ravaged palm open and exposed on top of his thick thigh. I glance down at the blood around the cuts that are just shallow enough not to need stitches.

"I knew tears would only be an appetizer to him." I say defending my actions. "It had taken flesh and blood to seal the deal. So, when he squeezed my hand, I cowardly played the victim. Officer Laine left that room feeling strong and in control."

"I can see why. I take it Maria didn't notice, or she wouldn't be so angry with yeu."

"No, she didn't, and don't you tell, either. I said something shitty in the elevator. That's why she's mad. Help me get it wrapped back up before she returns."

He gives me a look of disapproval before wrapping the wound. We stand, and I slip my hand back into my pocket just as Maria opens the doors wearing clean clothes that now fit her petit, curvy frame.

"Let's go." She says with a refreshed demeanor. "I'm starving, and—is it too early for a drink?"

I glance at my watch. The hands tick just past the twelve. I respond playfully, "Oh, I think not. It's past noon, after all—I think we ought to celebrate."

To my delight, Maria turns towards me and smiles. The pain in my hand lessens, and my heart lightens. Tony announces that he'll run down to the car and put on the heat for Maria. Maria and I ride the elevator down and make our way out of the building. My spirits lift higher when I see a sign on the glass reception window that indicates Mary Ann is out taking her lunch.

But our enthusiasm is cut short the moment we step outside, and a mob of news crews swarm us. Camera lights shine in our eyes and news reporters shout questions at Maria. I take her by the hand and force our way through the crowd. I bark orders like a sea captain to the mutiny of salty dog news crews. "Everyone, back up! Let us through! We have nothing to say."

Before I get my bearings, Officer Laine swoops out of nowhere, pulls Maria close to him and wraps an arm around her.

My hand breaks away from Maria and the mob forces me out of the inner circle. I hear Officer Laine, politely asking the reporters to give Sister Maria space. Cameras flash all around them. After a few moments in this photo opt, Officer Laine leads her safely to our car. I follow as fast as I can behind the mob and watch Officer Laine open the passenger door and help Maria inside. My teeth grit together as cameras move from Maria to Officer Laine who proceeds to answer the reporters' questions. I race around the two-door mini cooper to the drivers side. Tony manually rolls down the window—I must shout to hear my own voice over the mob.

"Get out of here, Tony! I'll meet you at the bar in ten minutes!" He protests, but I insist—waving him on. "Tony, go! Get Maria out of here!"

Tony's green eyes blaze back at me before he puts the car in gear and drives away. I stand in the street for a second, contemplating my next move. Should I take the high road or the low road?

A few feet away I notice a scrawny reporter stuck at the back of the mob that's interviewing Officer Laine. He pivots and stares at me for a second before calling out, "There's the priest suspected of murder!"

The reporter's declaration distracts a number of others around him. Their attention moves away from Officer Laine and onto me. My next move is decided for me.

Run!

14: Humility

I wheel around on the heels of my boots and speed walk my way across the street, hoping not to call any more attention to myself. I step up onto the sidewalk, veer left and see a bunch of reporters and cameras following me. My discreet stroll breaks out into an all out run as I take a sharp turn down an alleyway. I hear a few voices hollering behind me as I approach a small, gated park. I leap over the four-foot, rod iron fence, sprint left, and to my relief I see a church at the far end of the park.

I look over my shoulder. The three reporters and their camera people are stuck behind the fence, and so I slow down. I ascend the flight of stone steps, praying the church is open, and pull at the large red door. The doors open, I sigh in relief, and swiftly slip inside.

The narthex is empty, except for a welcome table at the entrance of the sanctuary. I move quietly through the sanctuary doors and to my horror immediately notice a large baptistery behind the chancel. A vision of the last time I stood in a Baptist church comes to mind. Flashbacks from thirteen years ago paralyze me in the center aisle. It was the night I left the poor pregnant girl to burn at the stakes of that wicked Baptist pastor. The horror of his face, blazing with god's wrath—a god I'll never worship. My ears start to ring—like a train in my head—then the sound of the front doors opening startles me back to reality. I immediately duck in-between two pews and crouch down on my knees. One of the sanctuary doors swings wide and the voice of the scrawny reporter shouts into the room.

"No, I don't see her. Maybe she went out the side door back there."

The moment I hear the sanctuary doors close behind him, I release the breath I've been holding. I peek over the top of the pew and focus all my senses towards the narthex. Then I hear a man's voice behind me and almost leap out of my collar.

"Strange place for a Catholic Priest."

I freeze, still kneeling and bending over the wooden seat of the pew.

He chuckles and says in a tone that seems to suggest we've met before, "My, my, I thought Catholics had their own prayer benches."

I turn towards the voice and see a familiar face.

"Keith!" I exclaim. "Uh, it's good to see you."

With the help of the pew, I push myself off the floor, reach out to shake his hand.

He looks down at it, bloody and bandaged, then back up at me.

He smiles.

Embarrassed, I put my wounded hand back in my coat pocket.

Keith graciously ignores the awkward moment and says, "Yes, Mother Alex, it's good to see you, too. Welcome to my church, Third Street Baptist."

I ask with a quizzical look, "Your church?"

"Yes, I've been the pastor here for almost two years."

"But I thought you were taking over the family funeral home."

"It's true, I am. But I will also remain the pastor here. The congregation has diminished greatly over the years. When they hired me two years ago, they moved the position down to part time. That was about the time my wife Sara's grandfather offered to train me to take over the family business. So here I am."

"Wow, I never dreamed the day I'd meet a Baptist pastor who was married to a Catholic."

He laughs, and says with deference, "Well, that makes two of us. It's a story I need to tell you at some point. But right now, I must ask," he glances in the direction of the narthex, "What are you doing here?"

"That's an interesting story as well. But for another time. I'm in a bit of a hurry. Is there a backdoor I could leave from without being seen?"

Keith turns serious and asks abruptly, "Does this have anything to do with my brother, Steve?"

His question catches me off guard, and I respond with a look of anger and surprise that seems to satisfy his question.

Keith turns and says, "Follow me. I'll make sure you get out of here safely."

We walk down the aisle, take a left at the communion table, and out the door next to the organ. I follow him down a long narrow hallway that grows darker with each step. The odor of mothballs and Clorox bleach brings to mind more childhood memories of old Baptist churches.

My curiosity gets the best of me and I break the silence, "Keith, why are you helping me?"

He stops short at a large metal door with a green exit sign above it, the only light source in the dark hallway. Without looking at me he responds with another question.

"Did you know that the average Baptist still believes Catholics are going to hell?"

I laugh unsure of where he's going with his statement. "Yes, I know that. My own father was a Baptist preacher."

He turns around and stares intensely into my eyes. Keith has his older brother's blue eyes, but his are not filled with hate. Keith's eyes hold flickers of light, glimmers of hope, a soul filled with humility.

He grabs my shoulder and says in a strong but gracious tone, "Alex, there's much you don't know about me or my family, but for now, know this. The friend of my enemy is still my friend." With that, he pushes the metal door open with his back and pulls me into the afternoon light.

He looks me in the eyes and says, "Go now, my friend. We will speak again."

It takes a moment to get my bearings concerning what street Keith has released me on, but before long I do. Then I trek several blocks to Tony's bar. Fortunately, there are no reporters and no cameras. My only followers are my weighty thoughts and ever-growing questions.

Who was my mother? Why is her death still haunting me? Why is Officer Laine involved and why is his baby brother Keith estranged from the family?

How do all these pieces and people fit together?

15: Honesty

In desperate need of a stiff drink, I plop down winded at the familiar bar, and I call out, "Tony, make me a double, please."

Maria sits next to me chowing down on extra spicy wings and seasoned fries. She turns to me, her lips and fingers covered with buffalo sauce, and once again asks about the events of the last hour.

Annoyed, I say, "I told you, when y'all left, I was standing in the street, not making a scene, or doing anything at all. Then a reporter recognized me, and he and others started coming after me. I ran down the sidewalk and got rid of them in the park on third street."

Maria says, "Hmmm. Is that so?" One eyebrow raised, she looks at Tony who is leaning on an elbow listening in on her interrogation. "So you're telling us it took more than forty-five minutes for you to walk four blocks and with those long legs of yours."

She slaps my leg and takes a sip from her third bottle of Dos Equis.

Tony chimes in, "Alright, we won't push yeu." He slides my double bourbon on the rocks across the bar. "We're just curious, that's all."

I'd been avoiding the part in the story about the Baptist church scene for two reasons. One, I didn't want to dredge up old memories again. And two, I'm still processing everything about my mother, Tony and the Laine brothers. Plus, I didn't want to turn the drama of the day away from Maria and onto me. But they both stare at me begrudgingly. Taking a swig, I cave to their curiosities.

I mumble under my breath. "Okay, so I might have taken refuge in a Baptist church on the way."

"What?!" Maria chokes out with a mouth full of food and holds her buffalo fingers in the air like a surgeon in mid operation. "You were in a *Baptist* Church?"

I take a sip of my drink, sigh, and brace myself for reason number three, Maria's gift of sermonizing any situation.

"You haven't stepped foot in a Baptist church for over a decade. Suddenly, you find salvation in the very place you met Satan thirteen years ago. I'd've thought you choose the camera crews over those backstabbing Baptists, but hey, I've been wrong before. Wow! Now, that's exactly the kind of redemptive story I needed today. Praise the Lord. My suffering has been redeemed!"

Tony's eyebrows rise with Maria's cheering, and he gives me a strange stare of confusion as he watches Maria flaring her hands above her head.

I wave her down, and try to ease the moment. "Okay now, Joyce Meyer, calm down."

Tony raises his hand towards Maria. "Question. What d'yeu mean, the very place she met Satan?"

Maria replies with a slightly tipsy slur, "Alex, you haven't told him that story?"

Maria turns to Tony and begins the story—my forehead plops into my left palm.

"When Alex was seventeen, she caught a Baptist pastor molesting a teenage girl in his office. Well, you know Alex well enough to know she wasn't just going to walk away and do nothing. So what do you think she does?"

Tony's eyes move back and forth between the narrative Maria is spewing and my attempt to downplay it with a roll of my eyes and a shake of my head.

Maria pauses, and Tony lips curl up the side of his face as he stares at me. His posture straightens; the look of interest grows in his eyes.

Maria continues, "Oh, I'll tell you what she does when she catches the bloated Baptist with his britches below his belly—holding down a helpless, half naked minor across his desk. Well, Alex calmly walks back out to the receptionist desk, grabs a large, bronze letter opener, and returns to the pastor's study. At this point the girl is off his desk, putting on her clothes in the corner."

I take a large gulp as Tony's eyes grow wider.

"Holding the dagger behind her back, Alex makes sure the girl leaves before she turns her attention to the pastor who is now leaning back in his office chair pantless and dripping with pride. A smirk smears across his face as if he is the one with the power. Grasping the six-inch dagger, Alex lunges across his desk and knocks the pastor down to the ground. Caught off guard, the pastor starts screaming and throwing his fist into her sides. But Alex holds him down just long enough to carve the letter "A" into the flesh of his forehead."

Feeling no shame or guilt, a wide grin spreads across my face. I finish my drink and carefully place it on the bar.

Tony stands before me with a bewildered look.

I look him in the eye and say, "Well, there you have it. Now, you know everything you need to know about me."

Maria laughs and swivels around in her stool. "Well, I certainly do feel better. Alex, take me home, but first, I'll use the lady's room, or the human room. Oh, never mind, I'm going to the *bano*."

Maria slides off the seat and makes her way rather slowly and wobbly to the bathrooms down the hallway. I watch to make sure she makes it to the hallway without stumbling over a table.

Tony turns to me and says with devilish grin, "Tis strange that my first reaction to hearin' that story about yeu is a desire to kiss yeu."

I'm grateful that my eyes are elsewhere for they'd give me away. Slowly turning my sight from the hallway to my empty glass, I feel Tony's presence towering over me.

"Isobel, yeur mother would've been proud to hear that story."

Keeping my eyes down I reply, "Maybe now, but not at that time. The consequences of my actions were severe enough to make any mother ashamed of her child."

"Isobel, tell me what happened after yeu disfigured Satan?"

Lifting my chin into the air, I hold his gaze and finish the story.

"It only took a few moments to etch into his skull and only a few moments after that for the deacons to find me on top of their pantless pastor with blood on my hands. Well, you can imagine the story they saw. 'Crazy, troubled teen tries to murder helpless, beloved pastor praying in his office.' The police were called. I was arrested and convicted of attempted murder—but luckily as a minor. The teenage girl I found him with never came forward. He denied everything and concocted some story about the devil possessing me and the rumor about me being a witch caught fire around town. The juvenile center found a loophole to keep me out. My aunt and uncle wouldn't take me back—especially under house arrest. The only place that opened their doors to me was the Benedictine Convent over in Indiana. I never saw that man ever again nor have I been in a Baptist church since... well, until today."

I bite my lip, wait for Tony to speak, and for Maria to return so I can leave this moment and this memory. To my surprise, Tony doesn't say a word. Silently, he opens his left hand, signaling for my right hand, the wounded one still tucked away in my jacket. I give in, grateful, that he doesn't want to pry any deeper into the memory.

My hand bandaged and bloodied lies helplessly in his left palm. I half expected him to remove the worn, dirty cloth and tend to my wound as he did the night before, but this time he doesn't unwrap the bandage, nor does he make efforts to clean the hand. Instead, he gently lifts my crumpled hand up to his mouth and kisses the exposed skin of my fingers. My eyes close as his lips press against my flesh. Heart pounding, stomach fluttering. His kisses soon move to my bruised knuckles, as I feel his fingers stroke the inside of my forearm my eyes open to his emerald gaze.

Swiftly, I watch his shadow creature emerge from his pupils, extend out of his back and six long arms expand around him, making their way towards me. My body is paralyzed by his touch. I feel all my senses intensify, but he keeps his lips pressed against my skin. Out of the corner of my eye, I see one tentacle inches away from me.

Then right before his Scylla contacts me, the bathroom door slams shut with a loud bang. I quickly rip my hand back and pull my body away from Tony. His face falls forlorn at my reaction but quickly recovers his cheerful demeanor as Maria walks back up to the bar.

Maria speaks casually to us both, obviously unaware of the last few intense moments. "Well, I certainly look like a hot mess. First order of business is to find the courage to take another shower. Alex, you will probably need to sit on the toilet while I shower. I probably already have PTSD." She turns and smiles at me.

I give her a half grin as I do my best to shake off the lingering feelings between Tony and me.

Maria looks at my face and then down at my right hand, which is resting on my leg under the bar. She squeals in horror and immediately grabs my right hand. "Alex, what in the name of all that is good and holy happened to your hand?"

I shrug my shoulders. "Oh, just a wee bit of an accident, last night. It's no big deal."

She gives Tony a look of determination and says, demandingly, "Tony, she won't tell me what actually happened, so you must—and I mean everything." She clenches my wrist and holds my right hand in the air. "Start with why there are two different bandages—one wrapped around her knuckles, and another around her palm."

Tony pours me another round of bourbon, pulls out another Dos Equis for Maria, and then downs a shot of scotch. He clears his throat and then describes the events of the evening, from the fist fight in the bathroom to the broken glass at the bar. He conveniently leaves out details about the conversation we had about my mother, and the rather intimate moment where we almost kissed.

"Well," Maria responds in a surprisingly calm tone at the end of his account. "Alex, I was expecting worse. I even feel slightly bad for snapping at you in the elevator. You are always honest with me, and your hand must've been in a lot of pain from the hand shake you gave Ste...uh...Officer Laine."

I put my hand back in my jacket pocket and say, sincerely, "Don't feel bad. I shouldn't have said those things. You had every right to be pissed."

Maria touches my face and smiles. "All is forgiven, my friend."

We sip our drinks and embrace the silence for several long moments. Maria checks the messages and emails on her phone, as I watch Tony cleaning up around the bar. He glances up at me a few times, grinning wide. I can't help but smile back, knowing full well that this thing between us, whatever it is, is outside my orders as a Catholic Priest. He doesn't seem to care about any of that. Neither is Tony bothered by my past, my wounds, my personality—and certainly not Scylla.

He's a handsome man, with strength and stature. The powerful physique of his body makes me feel secure, but not in a helpless, co-dependent sort of way. Rather his might and vigor allow me to feel at ease and strong at the same time. His thick, dark hair is cut short, slightly longer on top than on the sides, and the small gray flecks that pepper his unshaven face give him an air of wisdom to accompany his strength. I begin to wonder what life with him would be like, but my thoughts end abruptly when Maria interrupts my internal fantasy.

"Alex, I was thinking earlier in the bathroom, do you remember the name of that pastor you defaced?"

I chuckle to myself watching Tony perk up from across the bar awaiting my answer.

"Well, I'm not sure. It's been so long. I think it was Alan. Alan something. Sammy... Swammy. Oh, Samsonite, I was way off." I laugh out loud at my own joke as both Tony and Maria give me blank stares.

I gasp, "Really, neither of you ever saw *Dumb and Dumber?*"

Maria shakes her head and asks again, "Alex, seriously, what was his name?"

"Okay. Okay. Let me think."

I take a swig of bourbon, close my eyes, visualize the church, then the office area, and then the pastor's study. A nameplate on the outside of the door appears in my vision. In white letters the first line reads, "Senior Pastor." Then the line underneath spells out his name, "Rev. Alan Laine."

My eyes pop open with the horrifying revelation.

I turn to Maria and ask with urgency, "Why would you ask me about that? You've known that story for a while, why the sudden curiosity?"

"Well, the reason I ask is that Officer Laine said something in the room while we were waiting for you to come. He mentioned something about the men in his family being a bunch of pastors, so I asked him why he became a cop. He said his father was almost murdered in his office by a puck teenager who got off easy. For some reason, it made me think about your story."

The name takes shape in my mouth but only comes out in a whisper. I take another drink and try to calm the rage rattling the glass in my hand. I say it louder to make sure they hear me this time.

"His name was Reverend Alan Laine."

Maria freezes. Tony looks at me, and then pulls out his phone. I finish my drink in one burning gulp—the rest of the afternoon and evening are likely to be a distant blur.

Tony races over to Marcus at the police department to begin a whole new avenue of research on the Laine family, making phone calls, looking up old records and searching the internet for anything and everything that might provide clues to the murders around town, the murder of my mother, and Maria's recent kidnapping.

Maria wants to go back to the cottage to shower and recover from the recent traumatic events by binge watching sappy romance films. I have no desire to leave her alone and feel obligated to join her in watching mind-numbing flicks for the rest of the evening.

The whole night is spent in the living room eating junk food, drinking bourbon in front of overrated Christmas films.

16: Equanimity

I lie restless in bed—awake, staring into the darkness. The door across the room opens, and a tall figure with broad shoulders steps into the room. My body stiffens as my name is said in a low raspy whisper.

"Isobel."

Tony's presence eases my anxiety.

My stomach flutters, and I call out to him, "I was hoping that was you."

The door closes, and I hear him cross the room in darkness. He stops at the bed. The sounds of clothing dropping to the floor creates butterflies in my belly. The mattress dips. He crawls across the bed, under the sheet and layers of blankets, to hover over my warm flesh. I shift under his weight. His lips find my neck and begin pressing firmly against my skin. Goosebumps spring across my skin as Tony's lips move from my neck, cross my collar bone and slowly down to my breast. He slips one hand around my back and pops the clasp of my bra. The other lifts it from my bosom, and his lips continue their journey downward. He hovers over a nipple—a moan exits my mouth. My back arches slightly as Tony caresses my flesh, deeper, ever deeper.

Tony slides even further down as my hands cling against the muscles of his biceps as his tongue journeys past my navel. My chest rising and falling, I dig my fingers into his flesh as his teeth pull away the last cotton article. With one smooth motion the small garment glides down my legs, out of his way. Soft lips advance across the bones of my hips and my body clinches with anticipation. My wounded hand grips the bed sheets and the other wraps my fingers around Tony's head, weaving through long, thick, wavy locks.

The texture of his hair suddenly sharpens my senses, and I realize Tony is not the man in my bed. My body convulses. I try to push the imposter away, reach out into the darkness and turn on the bedside lamp.

The light burns my eyes, and my heart stops as a familiar, menacing laugh shrieks beneath the blankets. The covers rise—a horrifying face emerges. Officer Laine grins wide, hovered over my naked body.

I fight to get away—he pins me down with both hands and stares into my eyes. His scylla darts out of his back—its dragon jaws come after me. My body freezes, helpless and vulnerable, unable to move. The tentacles thrash around me—he raises a sharp wooden dagger above my head—a deadly blade. His eyes wild with lust, he squeezes the dagger tightly in his fist.

I shriek in terror.

He cries out in a deep, devilish voice, "You will pay for your sins, witch!"

He places the tip of the dagger against my forehead and begins carving my flesh. I scream again and again with every slice and penetration of the blade. Blood and tears stream down my face as he howls with laughter.

Then two small hands grip my shoulders, and my body begins

to shake. The room suddenly becomes dark again, and I hear Maria's voice. I'm pulled into conscious awareness—I leave that terrifying realm—and open my eyes.

17: Generosity

Maria stands over me, the morning light from a nearby window creates an angelic glow around her. I look about our cottage and reorient myself. I'm in the living room, curled up with a blanket over me in our oversized armchair. I must've fallen asleep during one of the inane movies we were watching last night.

Maria removes her hands from my shoulders and says, "You were having one of your night terrors." She moves to and sits down on the sofa a few feet away. "Was it your father again?"

I shake my head side to side and notice a large cup of fresh coffee on the small table next to me. I sit up, take the cup, drink, and look over at Maria, waiting patiently for my response. The coffee rejuvenates me and clears my mind.

After another sip, I respond. "No, I wasn't dreaming about my father this time. It was different people. Officer Laine and Tony—well, maybe not Tony, actually." I pause, trying to recall the specifics of the dream.

Maria kindly changes the topic giving me time to think. "Well, our little living room slumber party ended around eight last night when you fell asleep in the first five minutes of *Love Actually*. It didn't bother me until you started snoring during the last romantic scenes."

"Uh, sorry. I know you wanted me to stay up with you in case you couldn't sleep. I've always been lousy at slumber parties."

"It's okay. I slept surprisingly well last night. The couch definitely had to be more comfortable than that chair."

I stretch out my legs, and my knees make crackling noises. "Oh it was fine. Glad one of us slept well."

"You know Alex, it's probably time to go see Sister Agatha. How long has it been since your last session?"

I think for a moment. With Thanksgiving and the Advent season, it must've been at least eight weeks since I had gone to spiritual direction. Considering my dreams lately and the amount of stress I'd been under, Maria's right. It's time to visit Agatha. I look up at the clock ticking above the fireplace and respond to Maria's suggestion.

"It's only seven right now. I'll give her a call in about an hour and see if I can come by later today. This morning I need to work on John Thompson's eulogy for tomorrow's service. What are you going to do today?"

Maria takes a deep breath, and lets it out slowly. "Well, since Fridays are my usual Sabbath, I think I will embrace the discipline of doing nothing. I've got a juicy, romance novel I'd like to start, so maybe I'll hang by the fire today."

"That sounds like a wise idea, especially after the last few days. I'll go grab the paper and then make us some breakfast."

I pull myself out of the oversized armchair, wrap my winter robe around my body and put on my slippers. I grab my coffee before heading outside to the mailbox. I open the cottage door and step out quickly, trying not to let in too much of the cold morning air. I close the front door behind me, and I'm startled by flashes of light sputtering in my face. By the time I know what's happening, reporters are shouting at me with questions, shoving microphones in my face.

"How is Sister Maria doing?"

"What is her relationship with Office Laine?"

"Are you still a suspect in the dumpster murder case?"

Frozen on the small porch of the cottage, I silently stare expressionless at the new crews. I decide that today, I will not to run away from these people. They already have footage of me in my robe and house shoes so I might as well hold my ground and practice generosity.

"Grace and peace to you all this morning." I say with sarcasm and a crooked smile. I take a sip of coffee from my mug and hold my hand up as more cameras flash and add, "For the record. We have no comment."

I hold my mug out in front of me, part the sea of reporters, and walk along the sidewalk to the mailbox. Men and women follow me like excited sea lions, yapping more questions in my direction. Grabbing the newspaper and a few pieces of mail from the day before, I pretend as if no one is around me. I tuck the papers under my arm and make my way back to the cottage front door.

The crews follow me and stop just below the porch. I casually open the front door and head back inside.

I walk across the living room to the kitchenette and pour myself another cup of coffee. I look over at Maria, who is reading her romance novel, and I update her on the circus outside.

"FYI. There are at least fifteen reporters outside our front door and a photo of me in my robe will most likely end up in the comic section of Sunday's paper."

Maria puts down her book. "Reporters? Why on earth?"

I open the paper and see the scenes from yesterday outside the precinct on the front page. The larger of the two photos is Officer Laine standing heroically with his arm wrapped around a fragile looking Maria. The headline reads, *Noble Officer Rescues Kidnapped Priest*. The smaller photo at the bottom is me running down the sidewalk across the street. That headline reads, *Priest Murder Suspect On The Run*. Folding the paper, I toss it on the coffee table in front of Maria.

"Well, you know folks just love a classic tale about two catholic priests—one kidnapped and the other accused of murder. On the bright side, we might have a pretty good crowd at Sunday's mass."

She laughs and says, "Glad I've already decided to stay in for the day. Good luck on your run later. Let's hope those camera people are in worse shape than the ones yesterday. And if you're lucky, you might get to rededicate your life again at the nearby Baptist church."

Now it was my turn to laugh. "You know, some days, hell seems like a relaxing place."

I fix us both breakfast, scrambled eggs and hot sausage before I go to my room and work for several hours on John's eulogy. Sister Agatha is available at noon to see me so when eleven o'clock rolls around, I call Tony and ask him to come and hang out in the cottage with Maria. Maria says she's fine staying by herself until I get back but I'm uncomfortable leaving her alone—especially with the vultures swarming the place. Selfishly, I also don't want the distraction of worrying about Maria's wellbeing during my spiritual direction session.

Tony comes over right away and brings Sam, the cat, with him.

The animal's presence lifts Maria's spirits, which in turn affirms my instinct to call Tony. When they enter the cottage, Sam leaps from Tony's arms and gravitates immediately to Maria, who is on the couch. I watch with envy as Maria, without a word, woos the little creature to her. Sam leaps up into her lap and Maria rubs her fur while Tony and I sip coffee at the small dinette.

"How's she doing today?" Tony asks quietly while observing Maria and Sam on the couch.

I whisper, "She's okay. She said she slept well last night. We both stayed together in the living room."

Tony turns to me, and studies my face. "Yeu look as though yeu didn't sleep well."

I shrug off his comment. "After four cups of coffee, I was hoping the bags under my eyes would disappear."

His face contorts with concern. "More nightmares?"

The dream in all its pleasantries and horrors cause my eyes to turn down and I feel redness blushing my cheeks. "Yep, it was intense. But I'm going to see an old friend today who will help. How's the research going with Marcus? Any leads on the Laine family?"

"Uh, no, not yet. In all the public records, everythin' is squeaky clean like all the documents about the Laine family have been sanitized—as if they'd been scrubbed clean, or whitewashed in some way. Unfortunately, the records are all we've got to work with for now."

A thought hits me, and I remember Keith, the baby brother of the Laine clan.

"You know I might just have a lead. You remember that Baptist Church I ran into yesterday? Well, the pastor is Keith Laine, the baby brother of the family. He looks just like Officer Laine—tall, blond and handsome, but he's completely the opposite in spirit. I think I actually like Keith. He seems to have a level head, morals, integrity, and all that."

Tony eyebrows lifts and his back stiffens.

He says dryly, "Hmm. Okay. I'll go see him later today."

"Actually, it might be best if I go. We already have a connection through the funeral home down the street, and he might feel defensive if you showed up out of the blue, asking questions about his family. I'll go after I see Agatha and be back by two. You mind staying with Maria until then?"

Tony's face twists as if he's angry with my response. He stares at me, eyes sharp and intense.

"What's wrong? You look upset. If you can't stay that long, it's ok."

"No. That's not it." He says shortly and his face quickly shifts back to a half-hearted smile.

I realize that his sudden change of demeanor is not so much anger as it is jealousy. Tony's jealous of Keith and the possibility of going to see him. I decide to not beat around the bush. "Are you worried, even jealous, about me going to see Keith?"

"Yes." His smile buckles and his lips press together. "I don't like the thought of yeu being around a member of the Laine family."

"Why? Keith isn't like his brother. Don't worry about me. I'll be fine."

His voice is sharp and stern. "Don't tell me not to worry about yeu. I won't make the same mistake again. Not with yeu." After a long pause his voice softens. "I just don't trust the Laines, and right now yeu're, yeu're not at yeur best." Tony reaches across the table and touches the fingers of my right hand.

I turn to see if Maria's watching us. But the back of the couch faces us, and she's fully consumed by the presence of Sam.

I look up at Tony who softly strokes the skin around my knuckles.

His voice is low as he says. "Isobel, let me help yeu. I can show yeu how to use yeur créachta scáth, yeur shadow wound as a weapon for good."

I whisper intensely back at him, "What do you mean, use it for good? My scylla isn't good, she's a monster."

"Yeu musn't fear yeur monsters. Let me help yeu. Let me teach yeu the old ways, the ancient powers from long ago."

Hearing the couch shift under Maria's weight, I pull my hand back, and Tony's fingers fall on the table. The clock across the room tells me it's now half past eleven.

Giving Tony a curious look, I say rising to my feet, "Uh, let me think about it. For now, I need to go. Thanks for staying with Maria, and sorry about the reporters."

As I turn to walk towards the door, Tony, still seated, grabs my left hand.

His voice low again and deadly serious, "Isobel. Please. Let me show what I mean before yeu go see Keith. Will yeu come by the bar tonight? I have extra help coming so I'm free from bar-tending."

"Ok. Let me check with Maria later and see what her plans are—I make no promises, though."

He releases my hand and I say goodbye to Maria and Sam before swimming against the waves of reporters outside. I climb into the shelter of Merida and head across the Ohio River in search of ancient wisdom from Sister Agatha.

18: Courage

I've been told that during a winter long ago, sometime around the end of the nineteenth century, the Ohio River iced over, creating a frozen bypass for people to cross on foot between Kentucky and Indiana. To walk on a river a mile wide must've been an extraordinary experience, or absolutely terrifying.

Today, I take the second street bridge in my mini cooper, crossing over the murky waters below that mirror the gray skies above. The convent is only five miles into Indiana just past the little towns along the riverfront. I arrive at Sacred Heart, greeted by naked trees—bare in the winter winds. They look helpless and vulnerable along the narrow road leading deep into the property.

Sister Agatha, a ninety-two-year-old nun in full habit, waits for me on the front steps of the main building. A large wool shawl wrapped around her tiny frame, she hunches feebly over a wooden cane. I hurry out of the car and up the stone steps, concerned that she has already been standing for too long in the cold winter air.

I immediately open the front door for us and say, irritation in my voice, "Good God, Sister Agatha, you're going to freeze to death."

"Why is that?" She barks back. "Is it because I'm old and feeble?" She hobbles into the entry hall, and I follow behind. "At this point in life, I know it'll take more than pneumonia to kill me. And I don't need you, child, telling me when and how I'm going to die."

"Yes. Ma'am." I respond with a grin. "Won't happen again. I trust you'll die when you're good and ready."

Before my wit can inflate my ego, Sister Agatha whips her cane around her tiny body and wallops me in the leg.

"Ouch!" I cry in shock rubbing the side of my knee.

Without turning around, she laughs and continues leading me through the hallways. We enter a small square room with an old, floral loveseat adjacent to a green wingback chair. Sister Alex lowers her body into the chair and lays the cane down on the floor. I take off my boots and sit cross legged on the adjacent couch adjacent. A small table sits between us with a French press full of hot coffee beside two clay mugs.

I pour full cups for us both and inhale deeply the aroma of roasted java.

The room is plain. No art or decor adorn the walls. A small window on my right overlooks the graveyard where generations of faithful catholic nuns have been returned to the earth. My eyes move from the graveyard to the sister Agatha, and her eulogy begins forming in my mind.

As if hearing my thoughts, she says to me, "Bury me naked. I don't think these habits are biodegradable."

A hardy chuckle bellows out of me, and I respond in kind, "Only if we can keep the casket open throughout the service."

She winks at me then follows my right hand as I bring the coffee mug to my mouth. I respond to her already knowing her thoughts.

"It was wounded for a good cause. The knuckles, that is. However, the palm was cut—" I pause trying to find the words to describe the evening with Tony, which now seems like years ago—even though it has only been two days. Finally, I say, "It was cut by grief and anger."

She remains silent creating space for me and the spirit to respond to my words.

"Two nights ago, I found out how my mother really died. It was almost too much for me to bear."

I turn and look out the window at the graves of women. My eyes begin to burn but I resist the urge to cry.

"She was murdered. Burned alive."

My head turns back to Agatha who sits motionless. The only physical reaction to my words are her blazing, brown eyes. She stares so intensely back at me I can feel the heat of her gaze blistering my spirit. I cannot bear to see Agatha's scylla, to see the monster of the one woman still living who loves me like a mother. I fear her monster would devour me—take me down into a place I am not willing to go. My eyes break away from hers, and I stare into the black void of my coffee.

I take a deep breath and pause for a long moment. Agatha doesn't push, she simply lets her presence be present with me, whatever path I take. I begin again from another angle.

"My dreams are worse than ever. My body craves what I cannot have. My mind is scattered."

My eyes move from my black coffee to Agatha. Her regard is soft, which relaxes me, encouraging me to continue.

"The predator inside of me has finally surfaced. I fear that the monsters I have seen in my enemies these past fourteen years are simply mirrors of my own monster."

Silence fills the room. I stare out the window and sip my coffee.

I wonder aloud, "What if I'm not strong enough? What if Scylla consumes me? What if I become the very thing I have hated for so long?"

Tears well up in my eyes again. I turn to Sister Agatha, watch her sit in the stillness, drinking from her mug with a calm, casual demeanor. I continue letting my soul flow like running water beneath a frozen river.

"The past few days, I've been accused of murder, lusted consciously and unconsciously over a man who blames himself for my mother's murder. I punched a pig of a man, drank too much bourbon, and hid from reporters under a pew in a Baptist church."

Looking into my mug, I stare for a long while at my reflection in the dark surface.

Agatha breaks the silence. "Where have you experienced God?"

I hate this question. It always fills me with shame, and shame comes from the gut, the same place as compassion. Both compassion and shame twist my intestines, causing my stomach to turn over. They create a visceral reaction to an emotional state of being, a place where I feel the most out of control. Shame, like compassion, makes me sick.

I put my coffee down and answer with honesty, not for Agatha's sake, but for my own. "I don't know. I fear I'm no longer looking for God."

Agatha takes a breath and holds my words with me in silence. My eyes move to the left side of the room and thoughts pour out.

"I'm tired of looking for a God who's somewhere out there in the universe or trapped somewhere here, in my head."

I put my mug down on the coffee table and continue my rant.

"I need flesh. I need to feel. But the moment I let my feelings out, they betray me. They lead me to dark places, exposing my monster, and now that monster is loose. I feel her taking over, making me vulnerable to the world. I no longer trust myself and that scares me."

Blood pulses like acid, pounding vigorously against my forehead. I close my eyes; the fingers of my left hand rub my temples clockwise.

The voice of Agatha penetrates the darkness. "What is underneath your fear?"

"Fuck!" I scream into the dark caverns of my mind. Trying to hold the silence, my soul leans into the question. The answer comes in the form of a gentle whisper. "I'm afraid, afraid of losing control."

The next questions I hear seem to come from somewhere inside me. "What if you did lose control? What do you think would happen?"

My eyes open and focus on Agatha. "I would fall, fall down and never be able to pull myself up."

My breath is heavy and my voice rises to such intensity that I am now yelling. My mug somehow ends up back on the table in front me allowing my hands and arms to flare open as I scream out into the world.

"I would fail! Fail as a priest! Fail as a daughter! Fail so miserably that no one, not even Jesus Christ could save me." I gasp for air trying to pull myself together.

"Control," I say so softly I can barely hear my own voice. "Control is all I have. To give that up, would be the death of me."

Agatha remains quiet for several moments. Then she slowly places her coffee mug on the table and leans forward, placing her hands on her legs. Her head turns towards the window that overlooks the graveyard. She speaks without looking at me, her words penetrating my thoughts.

"Death is just the beginning. Those too afraid of dying are sadly, no longer living. Be brave, my daughter."

The lump grows in my throat, making it impossible to swallow. Tears form large pools in the bottom of my eyes, and I make the mistake of blinking. My eyelids are unable to contain the ocean of saltwater, causing a stream of tears to pour down my cheeks. My chest tightens. Agatha turns back to me, and for the first time today a smile spreads across her face.

I expect her to grab the box of Kleenex on the table behind her but she doesn't. She stares, smiling at me, watching the mess of tears and snot roll down my face and neck running into the white priestly collar. This time, I don't pull my eyes away from her gaze. She leans so close that I see a shadowy reflection of myself in her pupils. I stare long and hard at myself. Soon the monster I fear emerges from her eyes. At first, I think it's Agatha's Scylla but then I realize the monster is not coming out of her body—it's coming out of mine.

Through my peripheral vision, I see six tentacles swell into the room flaring wildly about, growing larger and larger. My body tenses as Scylla's dragon heads consumes the room surrounding us with dark clouds of static madness. Agatha holds my gaze, reaching out with one palm towards me open.

She calls out to me in a strong, sturdy voice over popping currents of electricity.

"Alex. You can do this. Take my hand. I'm not afraid of your monster."

My right hand reaches out to her, but one of Scylla's tentacles wraps around my wrist, tugging my arm away from her. The urge to give in to my monster's desire is strong, and I feel my spirit growing weaker. I resist the apathy growing in my gut, but other tentacles swing towards Agatha with teeth wide open. I instinctively swat it away with my left hand. Then my mind focuses, and my voice commands Scylla with authority.

"No! Agatha is my friend. She's trying to help."

At my command, all six of Scylla's tentacles freeze, refocusing their dragon heads in my direction. The room is suddenly still, and I say to myself and the monster, "I'm not afraid. We can work together."

The large tentacle wrapped around my right arm uncoils, and I reach out and grab Agatha's hand. Then, as if I had pressed a magic button in the dark chamber of my soul, I observe Scylla retract slowly back into my body through the reflection in Agatha's eyes. My eyes close, and I inhale deeply three times. Several long moments pass, and I open my eyes and see Agatha smiling, holding a box of Kleenex in front me.

I let go of her hand, take the box, and wipe my eyes and face.

She breaks the silence. "Thirty years old now, huh? Still a third my age."

I laugh and appreciate her not so subtle ways of letting me come up for air.

I reply with equal sarcasm. "Well, I know it was a century ago for you but what did you do when you turned thirty? Did you get drunk with a Scott, punch a man who grabbed your ass, and end up in the papers as a murder suspect?"

"Well, no." She says casually. "When I was thirty, I got drunk with a German. Back then I was a scientist, not a nun."

I toss the box of Kleenex over my shoulder and onto the cushion beside me. I stare at her in utter shock.

"What? How did I not know this? You were a scientist? Where? When?"

She leans over and slowly pours more coffee into our mugs. I reach out and grab my mug, and she leans back in her chair, holding hers with both hands. She's silent for a few moments, then she finally answers my question.

"I was living in Chicago, after migrating from Germany a decade earlier. My boss Albert took me out for drinks the night I turned thirty. German beer is better than Kentucky bourbon, but don't tell anyone around here I said that."

My face contorts in confusion. Something about her story is strange. I try to put the pieces together, working out the puzzle out loud.

"Chicago, you say? You were in Chicago sixty years ago as a scientist. Drinking with a German man named Albert? As in Albert Einstein?"

She sips her coffee and replies dryly. "Yes. He was my boss."

Her unenthused tone causes me to react. "Wait! Seriously? Did you work on the Manhattan Project?"

Agatha grins but remains silent. She sips her coffee as I stare at her wide eyed and perplexed. Knowing that I had probably been given too much information on the secret life of Sister

Agatha, I decide to ask her a round-about question.

"So, uh, what kind of scientist were you?"

"I was an astrophysicist. The universe and the science behind it all fascinated me. It was Einstein's theory of dark energy that brought me to America. Have you ever heard the term, Lambda?"

I shake my head as she continues.

"Lambda was Einstein's theory that the universe must have some anti-gravity energy that pushes molecules and particles away from each other. Where gravity pulls everything towards, dark energy pushes everything away. Now, Einstein ended up dismissing this theory before he died, but a scientist in the late nineties proved his theory was correct. There is indeed dark energy at work in the universe and it's pushing everything further apart, creating a darker, lonelier universe."

I chuckle to myself and say aloud, "I know exactly how the universe feels."

Agatha gives me a wry grin and I now realize why she shared this strange and personal story with me. She's still giving me spiritual direction when I thought the session ended with her handing me the box of Kleenex.

"Smooth. Very smooth," I say, smirking. "So, I or rather my monster is Lambda, the dark energy pushing away everyone in my life making my inner universe dark and lonely."

Instead of affirming my observations, she adds scientific perspective. "Lambda is not evil, it's simply one side of the coin. The other side is gravity, the general relativity of all things being pulled towards each other. I often have wondered—since we all come from stardust, and if the same particulars of the universe live within each of us, then the same universal energies do as well. We, like the universe, are in constant tension holding the pull of gravity, and the push of dark energy, inside of us."

"But if your theory is true, most people lean towards one side of the coin. Take Maria and me, for example. She woos the world and all its living creatures towards her, and I shoo every living thing away."

"Everything? Just a moment ago, you pulled me towards you and a few days ago, you pulled someone else as well."

I blush, averting my eyes at the thought of that someone else—Tony. My words come out raw and vulnerable. "My instincts seem to be betraying me for the first time in my life. I can't tell if my wounds are being reopened, or if something in my heart is warning me."

Agatha brings the question from earlier back to the surface. "Where have you experienced God?"

"Tony. I saw God in Tony two nights ago. He revealed the truth to me, not only about my mother, but about myself. He shined a light in me that illuminated a dark grief and hatred I had never found the courage to share with anyone. And instead of running to the hills, instead of allowing me to shoo him away, Tony stayed with me. He not only stood his ground, but he moved towards me, even when my monster, my dark energy, pushed him away. When he cleaned my wounds, Tony gently pulled me back, held my hand, kissed my cheek. My soul was exposed, and yet I felt whole again—if only for a moment."

Agatha smiles wide, leaning back in her chair, holding the mug of coffee. A long silence ensues, and then she places her cup on the table beside her and grabs an old, hardback book I hadn't noticed until now, sitting by the lamp. I worry that this book is an old Bible and Agatha was about to read some passage about celibacy to me, but then she extends the book to me.

I take it and look at the worn title on the spine. It reads, *The Wisdom of the Enneagram.*

"This book was given to me by my priest, as a gift for my thirtieth birthday. I've read it every year since then. I believe this might serve you—as it did me."

"Thanks." I say with gratitude. "So, what's it about?"

"It's about seeing the universe inside yourself. I'll leave it at that. If you'd like, we can discuss it when we meet again next month."

And with that, Agatha gradually pushes herself out of the chair, rising to her feet. Clasping her cane, she hobbles to the door.

I put my mug down, grab my coat, key and book, and follow Agatha unhurriedly to the front lobby.

19: Temperance

I return to my car and start the engine to get the heater going. The time on the dashboard reads 2:08. Those two hours felt like an eternity, and yet it seems as though I only arrived at Sacred Heart thirteen years ago. I check my phone and see that I have missed two calls—one around 12:15 PM from an unknown number that left a voicemail, and one from the funeral home around 1:15 PM. Plus, there are also half a dozen text messages waiting for my reply. I sit in the car while it warms up and listen to the voicemail. The sister of John Thompson, whose name I can't seem to remember, wants me to include a specific story about her brother in the eulogy during the funeral tomorrow. I decide to return her call when I get back to the cottage. Hopefully I'll remember her name. Then I call the funeral home to make sure nothing urgent is needed. A receptionist answers the phone.

"Barley Brother's Funeral Home, this is Joyce speaking. How can I help you?"

"Hello Joyce, this is Mother Alex, I'm returning a phone call from earlier, perhaps concerning John Thompson service tomorrow."

"Oh yes, Mother. Thank you for calling us back. Keith Laine needed to speak with you. Let me transfer you to his office."

"Thank you." I wait on the line for a few seconds until Keith's

218

voice greets me. His voice is calm, and yet I hear a twinge of urgency. "Mother Alex. Thank you for calling me back so quickly."

"Uh, no problem. Everything okay with Mr. Thompson?" I say with slight concern.

"Yes, however, since this is my first official service with you I'd like to discuss a few things before tomorrow. Could you come by this afternoon and meet with me for a few minutes?"

"Of course. I can be there in about thirty minutes. Will that work?"

"Yes, that'd be great. See you then."

I hang up the phone and look through the unread messages. Sent at 12:20 PM, the first message is from John's sister who of course didn't include her name.

MOTHER ALEX I'M SORRY TO BOTHER YOU AGAIN BUT DID YOU GET MY VOICEMAIL WITH THE STORY ABOUT JOHN? PLEASE CALL AND LET ME KNOW. OH BY THE WAY THIS IS JOHN'S SISTER.

The second message is from Maria describing her status:

ALEX. I'M FEELING A BIT MORE LIKE MYSELF. THE REPORTERS HAVE LEFT AND I SENT TONY BACK TO THE BAR. HE LEFT SAM WITH ME FOR COMPANY. SHE'S LIFTED MY MOOD SIGNIFICANTLY. DON'T WORRY ABOUT ME. DO WHAT YOU NEED TO DO TODAY.

I take a deep breath relieved to hear she's doing better. However, I'm annoyed with Tony for leaving her when I asked him specifically to stay with her. I check the last four messages and see that they are all from Tony. The first two were only minutes apart and the third and fourth messages were sent an hour later.

ISOBEL. DON'T BE ANGRY. MARIA ASKED ME TO LEAVE SO SHE COULD BE ALONE.

ALSO, I LEFT SAM WITH HER.

ISOBEL, PLEASE COME TO THE BAR TONIGHT. LET ME HELP YOU.
BEFORE YOU COME. DO SOME RESEARCH ON THE ENNEAGRAM. IT'LL HELP YOU BE MORE PREPARED FOR WHAT I'LL SHOW YOU LATER.

"The enneagram?" I say to myself reaching for the book Agatha gave me a few minutes earlier. I wonder about the coincidence—both Agatha and Tony both bringing to light the same topic. I open the old book, flip to the introduction, and read the first paragraph.

The wisdom of the enneagram is more than just a personality test or psychological approach to understanding self. The enneagram is rooted in ancient Babylonian astronomy and monastic mysticism dating back to fourth century desert fathers. To journey through the enneagram, one must be willing to face and befriend the monsters of one's soul. If and only then will the wisdom of the enneagram heal the wounds of one's soul.

The words send flashes of memories. I close my eyes and feel reality suspend. My thoughts leap from my broken painful childhood, grief over my mother's death, the first time I saw Scylla in the Baptist church, and the day I was brought here to live with the nuns. Sacred Heart is my home. These nuns are my mothers. I didn't realize until now how much Agatha means to me, how this place is the only home I knew, a place of sanctuary, a place of healing.

Startled by a sudden tapping on the window, I snap the book as my entire body leaps out of my skin. Sister Agatha is standing outside the car with her shawl wrapped around pressing her cane against my window. I manually roll down the window, but before I can chastise her about being out in the cold again she speaks up.

With a stern tone, she says, "Alex. Go away. You've spent enough time here. It's time for you to leave. Return to the world."

Then her stony expression changes and a slight smile turns up the corners of her mouth. Agatha reaches one knobby hand into the car touching my face. "But as you go, remember, you are a loved daughter of God."

And with those abrupt words of benediction, Agatha turns around and wobbles away. I roll the window up and sit in the car trying to process my feelings—feelings of rage, of grief, of deep pain that won't release their grip on me. I open the Enneagram book and return to the first page. At the bottom of the page, below the paragraph I read moments earlier, one lonely sentence stands out.

Death is only the beginning.

With these words I put the car in reverse, back out, and then head down the driveway. I notice on the way that the naked, bare trees I pitied before now appear strong and magnanimous against the winter winds.

20: Vulnerability

I call Maria to check in with her on my way back to the city. She's still on the couch binge watching chick flicks with Sam. I feel more comfortable about coming home later than I'd expected. I pull the car into the clergy parking spot in the lot behind Barley Brother's. The spot is designated specifically for clergy who need a quick getaway without getting stuck in funeral-home traffic. I hurry out of the car and make my way around the building to the front door—where I find Keith waiting for me outside on the steps.

I say sarcastically, "What's with everyone today, waiting outside in the cold for me to arrive?"

Keith smiles and replies without missing a beat. "Perhaps, it has something to do with our concerns for Louisville's latest murder suspect and most popular priest."

I laugh and reach out to shake his hand.

"Sorry, I didn't bring the paparazzi with me. I pray a photo op isn't why you called me here."

The smile on Keith's face fades and a look of sadness fills his eyes. He releases my hand and says so softly that I can barely make out the words above the wind. "Mother Alex, I pray that you know without a doubt that I'm nothing like my brothers."

I nod in acknowledgement, hoping for both our sakes that his words hold true.

He opens the front door and follows behind me as we enter. The receptionist is currently not at the welcome desk. I turn around to Keith to ask about her when I see Keith peeking out the blind of the nearby window.

Playfully, I say, "Still paranoid about the paparazzi, huh?"

His attention focused on the street outside, Keith says in the same low voice, "No. I regret that I was unable to be fully transparent with you on the phone. We don't have much time before they come."

Confused, I say, "Before who comes?"

Keith turns from the window and looks at me. "My brothers."

"Keith, why would your brothers come here?"

Before he can answer, the receptionist returns from the back room breathing heavily and with beads of sweat on her brow. No younger than fifty-five, I notice her aging hands have black smudges on them.

"Rev. Laine," she says intensely, addressing Keith as though I'm not present. "Everything is prepared as you requested. I'll signal you the moment your brothers arrive. At that point you should have about thirty seconds to get Mother Alex out."

My patience grows thin, and I voice my protest for being kept in the dark. "Out? Out of where? Keith, tell me what's going on."

Ignoring my questions, Keith keeps his focus on Joyce.

"Thanks. The boys should be here in less than five. I'll hurry." Turning towards me he grabs my arms firmly and says, "We must hurry. Trust me. I'll explain along the way."

This situation catches me off guard, and I hold back to look over at Joyce who moves to the window to watch the street as Keith did before.

"Alex, you must come with me now if you want more information."

My eyes move from Joyce at the window to Keith who, several inches taller, towers over me. I search his eyes, the same crisp blues eyes of his brother. I look for a sign, a mark of honor.

Keith releases my arm and stares back at me. He asks urgently, "What do you see?"

Without hesitation I say, "I see a good man."

Keith turns quickly and walks briskly out of the room. I follow close behind as we wind past several gathering rooms and offices towards the back of the building. We stop in front of dark wooden French doors. Keith opens them and goes inside the room, which is about the same size as the cottage living room and specifically laid out for small visitations. A large photo of John Thompson sits on an easel beside a table with a huge bouquet of yellow flowers and a beautiful, porcelain urn. Soft fabric chairs are spaced around the room for folks to gather in conversations about John's life. At the back end of the room, a small writer's desk sits against the wood paneled wall.

Keith moves swiftly across the room towards the desk and picks up a folder. "Alex, this is for you. It contains information about my family. I know you are working with the LCPD, and I believe this can help you."

"Keith," I say, still stunned at how fast-paced things are moving. "Why are you helping me? You know what I did to your father thirteen years ago. Why would you go against him and your brothers?"

"I was fifteen the day my father came home with the letter "A" carved into his forehead. I, like my older brothers, was furious that someone would scar our beloved father. Steve, along with Chris, Joe and Tim all wanted you dead that day, but I wanted to know why you would do such a thing. I asked my father several times and all he would say was that you were possessed by the devil, a witch who needed to be cleansed by fire. It wasn't until I was older, when I moved out of the house, that I started searching for better answers, answers to questions not only about my faith, but about my family. What I found out was too much to bear— the horror stories I discovered by tracing my family lineage of slave owners and corrupt pastors and politicians. I kept my research secret until my brother Steve discovered the files on our family that I had been gathering for years. He was enraged that I would betray our family name. I told him I was just curious and had no intentions of doing anything with the research. He didn't believe me and destroyed my computer and burned the information I'd collected. I was lucky he left me with only a black eye. That was also the year I secretly married my wife, a catholic. Both events together created a cavern between my brothers and me."

"Keith, I'm sorry about your estrangement with your family, I of all people, know the truth about your father, but why are you willing to risk bringing more trouble on yourself for me?"

He hands me the folder and says, "When you leave here you will understand. In the last few moments we have, I need you to know one thing. Your mother *knew* my father."

My head starts to spin as I grasp the folder with one hand, taking hold of the back of the wall nearby with the other.

"My mother? What do you mean she *knew* your father?"

"My father was in seminary with your father. He met your mother around the same time your father and mother started dating. The three of them were friends and stayed friends even after your parents were married. My father was jealous that your mother didn't choose him. Back then, your father pastored a church in a town close to our church. My father was the pastor at the Baptist church your aunt and uncle attended for twenty-five years. During that time, he must have raped over a hundred women ages fifteen to fifty. Alex, one of the innocent victims was your mother."

My chest constricts as my breathing grows heavy. Rage pulses through my veins as images flash of my mother being raped by the man I witnessed molesting a teenage girl in his office. The look on his face when I returned to his office with that sharp envelope opener. It makes sense. It was the look of pride. The look of a man who saw the daughter of my mother, the younger version of the woman he'd raped years earlier. My stomach churns, causing me to hunch over the back of the chair. Then suddenly classical music begins to play through the speakers in the corners of the ceiling.

Keith's head turns to the closed doors and says solemnly, "They're here. You must go. I wish I had more time to explain but my brothers somehow found out that I still held information about our father's past. It's no longer safe with me. They know you're here, they tapped my phone lines about a year ago to keep me under their watch."

"Keith, if they know I'm here, how the hell am I going to get out here?"

Keith races across the room towards the brick fireplace in the far corner, and says, "This house was built by the Barley family, before the Civil War. It was designed specifically for the underground railroad. This room has a secret passage that leads to the tunnels under the city."

Without further explanation he slides his hand under the mantel and presses a button hidden to the naked eye. The writer's desk beside me rattles and a hidden door pops open. The music in the speakers grows louder.

Keith shouts at me, "Leave now. Hurry. Pull the door closed behind you. Follow the passage. Someone will be waiting for you."

I waste no time asking more questions. I fling my body through the narrow door and pull it shut just as the music suddenly cuts out. I can hear the voices of men through the walls and strain my ears to listen. Keith greets his brothers, each by name, clueing me on who is in the room with him. His voice is calm and cool.

"Merry Christmas. Steve, Joe, Tim. Where's Chris? We can't have a family gathering without him."

I recognize the first voice speaking is Officer Laine.

"Hello baby brother. Chris is around, no need to worry. Now, where is she?"

"She? You must mean, Sara, well my wife is home with our baby girl."

A voice I don't recognize bellows out in annoyance. "No, you idiot."

Then there's a sudden commotion and the sound of a man groaning. I imagine the brothers giving Keith an uppercut to the gut.

"Where's the priest? Her car's out back. We know she's still here."

Keith's voice is weak and raspy making it difficult for me to hear his words.

"She's gone already. She left out the back ten minutes ago. Said something about walking home and getting her car later."

Steve's voice comes through the walls once again. "Sure. Sure. I hope for your sake you aren't lying. We'll just take the file and go."

Keith says, his voice stronger, "What file? You destroyed all the files two years ago."

Another clamor followed by a moan, indicates that Keith most likely took a hit to the face. Standing silently in the dark passageway my mind goes wild. I feel a violent urge to leap back through the door and break a chair over the head of one of Keith's monstrous brothers. But the file I clutch close to my chest keeps me from exposing my position. The information in this file must be of supreme importance to the Laine brothers.

Suddenly, to my horror, I hear metal cracking bone. Keith's screams fill the room.

One of the brothers laughs and says, "Still cries like a bitch. You always were a vulnerable shit. Come on, Keith boy, you don't need your left arm, you learned a long time ago how to use both hands."

The voice inside my head screams in rage, and I cover my mouth to keep from making any noise. To my relief, I hear a familiar, old voice. To my surprise, and perhaps to the surprise of the Laine brothers, Mr. Barley has entered the room.

He speaks in the tone of an angry father disciplining his sons, "Now boys. You must not behave like this in my house. Now get on, get on out of here before I make you!"

The brothers laugh at the old man, whom I envision is hunched over his wooden cane. But then the laughter stops at the sound of the hammer of a double barrel rifle pulling back.

I say to myself, "Holy shit. The old man has a rifle."

Then I hear the shuffling of several heavy footsteps. The brothers are moving toward the door, and Mr. Barley's voice comes through again, "Keith, I'm going to show your brothers out the door. I'll be back in a bit."

I hear the door close and wait several long moments. I strain my ears to make sure the room is clear. Slowly, I push the hidden door ajar and peek inside. I move silently into the room.

Keith sits in a wingback chair by the fireplace, grasping his left forearm. He sees me move towards him and shakes his head in disapproval. His face is contorted in agony. His eye is puffy and swollen, and most likely his arm is broken.

"Alex, you should be long gone by now." He says in a whisper. "My brothers are still in the building."

Kneeling in front of him, I squeeze his right hand and reply in a low voice, "I couldn't leave without making sure you'll be alright."

"My brothers were kind this time. It could've been worse. I'll be fine. But you won't be if you don't leave right now with the file."

"Okay. The file will be safe with me. I'll see you tomorrow at the service."

I rise to my feet, glide back across the room and through the secret door in the wall.

21: Love

I close the door. turn around and stare into darkness. After a few seconds my eyes adjust. The only light source is coming from the crack at the bottom of the hidden door leading back out into the room I just left. I dig in my coat pocket for my phone but frustratingly realize I left my cellular flashlight in the cup holder of the car. Feeling around the narrow closet space I now wish I had asked Keith more questions about how to descend down into the tunnels.

I don't see any doors along the walls that might lead to passageways. My foot taps on the floor and to my surprise a hollow noise rings below. I bend to my knees and feel around for a latch that might open a door. At the far end, there's a small, iron lever. I pull it up and toward my body—a small section of the floor opens. My body tenses against the walls, and I barely catch myself before falling straight down below. In the dim light, I recognize the outline of a ladder that descends to what must be the underground tunnels Keith spoke about.

I climb down the ladder and stand in a wider space. To my joy, I see a light flickering ahead. I cautiously make my way towards it, using the stone wall as my guide. I move forward a few dozen steps and come to an opening where a torch hangs on the wall burning bright. It's then that I remember the sweat on Joyce's brow and the black smudge on her hands. Keith must have asked her to prepare the passageway for me. I make a mental note to thank her tomorrow when I see her again.

I tuck the file Keith gave me into the waist of my pants, grab the heavy torch off the wall with both hands, and continue down the tunnel. The decline of the dirt floor is subtle, but I know that I'm descending further down into the underworld. The torch casts shadows along the walls giving the illusion of hellish creatures dancing around the passageway. Fear takes hold of me, but I quickly recall my own shadow creature, Scylla—the monster who once terrified me. Now, thanks to Sister Agatha, I know that I have power over her.

I check my watch. The hands read three fifteen in the afternoon. I keep moving forward, wondering anxiously where the tunnels lead.

Soon, in the distance, I see another light flicker farther down the tunnel. I have no idea who might be in the tunnels with me and remain silent as the light grows closer. I can't tell if it is moving towards me, or if it is standing still, but either way, my steps quicken as well as the beat of my heart. Several moments pass before I finally arrive at the light, only to discover another burning torch on the wall. My breath is heavy. Disappointment grows deep within my spirit. No one is waiting for me. No one is with me. I'm all alone.

I continue down into the darkness as I descend far below what must be civilization above. The journey through the tunnels is confusing, and I become disoriented. A few times I arrive at an opening that leads to the left or to the right. There are no markers to indicate which direction I'm heading, and so I simply choose to go right each time. After a few turns, I feel I must be moving in circles.

My mind fills with images of demons stretching out of the shadows and grabbing hold of me. At times, I increase my pace to a run with the hope of reaching my destination sooner. But then I become overwhelmed with despair and slow down to a walk again to save my strength.

Farther along, the walls seem to close in, and the passageway grows more narrow, which causes me to panic. I stop, take a few deep breaths, and tell myself to get a grip. My only choice is to move ahead.

Eventually, I come to a place where a stone wall has crumbled to a height of about three feet, and I am forced to climb through a narrow opening. Once again fear takes hold, and I envision the walls collapsing all around, crushing me.

I stop to catch my breath and settle my mind. I lean against the wall and shine the fading light of my torch down towards my wrist. The hands of my watch are stuck at three twenty-one. Not only am I alone, I have no sense of where, or for that matter, when I am. What I do know is that I'm trapped, frozen like my watch, suspended in time, imprisoned for eternity in the under-world. What irony—I stopped believing hell was a real place years ago, but no longer. At this very moment, I believe hell is a dark space beyond time, a narrow place where your nightmares come alive.

Fear paralyzes my body and I slide down the wall onto the hard, dirt floor. Terror rises with each breath and anger quickly follows, filling my heart with intense feelings of betrayal. Betrayal is my security blanket, a self-defense mechanism that protects me from risking deeper relationships with the ones I love. Sitting on the cold earth, in the dim light of despair, my thoughts wander into self-pity and paranoia.

I mumble to myself, "Keith betrayed me. He sent me down into hell to die. He lied. No one is here. No one is waiting for me. I should never have trusted him. Tony betrayed me. He said he would watch over Maria until I got back. He left her all alone, he left my mother alone. He let her die. How could I ever trust him again?"

Rage burns against my flesh causing tears to swell in my eyes. My deepest fears have come true, I've been betrayed, left alone and vulnerable by those I trust most. My boiling blood turns my brooding thoughts to the one person whom I wanted most to be with me in this hell of world. The person I needed now more than ever. The person who left me long ago. My mother.

She's somehow sitting right in front of me with her dark wavy hair, her blue eyes and pale skin. I reach out to her, but her ghost leaves me as quickly as she did twenty years ago. I scream in outrage at the top of my lungs. "You betrayed me! You forsaken me long ago to fight your battles, to fight the men you were too weak to stand up to. You lied to me! Mother, you've left me all alone to live—and now to die."

Hot, salty streams burn down my face and my wrathful words echo down throughout the passageway, only to be swallowed up by the darkness. I clench my fist into a tight ball, I feel the wounds of my right hand and then notice the light of my torch waning.

The dying light brings me back to reality, and I decide that if I am going to die in hell I might as well use the last bits of my light to see the contents of the file tucked tightly in the waist of my pants.

I pull out the envelope and open the seal. Dumping the contents on the floor, I shine the dimming light right above each item. There are several photos scattered on the ground and an old, pocket journal worn at the edges.

I examine the photos first and pick up one I recognize—my mother sitting at a bar smiling. She looks older than I remember her, and I soon realize why. My mother wasn't in an American bar, but a Scottish pub, and the reason I know this to be true is that I recognize the bartender. The bartender is a young man in his early twenties, standing six and half feet tall, wearing the same charming smile I've seen for the past five years. Tony leans against the bar, smiling at my mother. My heart rate steadies at the sight of my mother looking so happy and at peace.

I take a closer look at the other photos. I grab another photo off the ground and gasp in horror. My mother is tied with thick ropes to a large wooden cross staked into the ground. Her hands, feet and mouth are bound. Her dress is torn and bloody. Her eyes are wide with fear and rage. Quickly, I put the photos down, unable to bear looking at her so helpless and vulnerable. I shove all the photos back in the envelope and refuse to look at any more images of what must be her murder.

The light in my left hand flickers as it continues to fade. I pick up the journal and open it. Names and dates are written in orderly columns along the left side of each page and on the right, a location and description of each person has been written down.

Mary Helen Springer, December 12, 1987. Church office. Big breast. Moans like dog.

Stephanie Witt, January 20, 1988. Sanctuary balcony. Youthful. Tight between the legs.

Alex Henderson, March 9, 1988. Church office. Feisty. Large mouth. Soft lips.

I flip through the journal, glancing at page after page filled with the same disgusting activity log. My stomach growls reading the names. The earliest dates go as far back as 1975.

Searching between the sections dating between 1985 and 1990, I look for my mother's name. According to Keith's account her rape must have taken place sometime in the late eighties. After scrolling through several disturbing pages, I find my mother's name.

Sophia Charlotte Wayland, March 29, 1987. Good Friday. Drugged and willing.

Fury erupts like a volcano from my body and I scream at the top of my lungs. For a moment the walls spin and I almost pass out from the blood rushing to my head. However, I urge myself on and decide to plummet further into journal. I finally arrive at the last entry of the journal.

Emily McCall, January 7, 2007. Church Office. Pregnant. No condom needed.

This must be the teenage girl I caught Alan Laine raping in his office. Her name rings a bell in my brain. She's the same pregnant teenage girl he brought before the congregation. The date is the exact date I first saw Scylla emerge from his body during the church service. This journal is proof she was in his office, proof he raped her, proof of my innocence.

I search frantically on each page but there's no name anywhere in the journal that indicates the owner. The only marking I find is a symbol on the inside cover. It's the same symbol I saw branded on the neck of the murdered black man. The same symbol on the dagger in my dream. The same symbol Marcus confirmed from his detective work. The letters AM.

I have found a purpose, now, and a new will to carry on. I steel myself, refusing to let this journal die down here with me in my self pity. I place all the evidence back into the envelope and rise to my feet so quickly that the wind from my movement blows out the last light of the torch.

"Fuck!" I scream into the darkness.

And to my surprise the darkness answers.

"Isobel! Isobel!"

Turning to the voice in the darkness, I cry out. "Tony? Tony, is that you?"

Before the voice replies, I see a light shining ahead, radiating through the darkness.

"Yes! Stay where yeu are."

The light of his torch grows brighter and brighter as he draws closer. My heart leaps when his face peeps through the rubble mound that I climbed over earlier.

His light shines towards me illuminating his warm, charming grin. "'Ello, Isobel. I'm so glad I found yeu."

"Tony, you have no idea how good it is to see you. I somehow lost my way. If you get me out of this infernal place, I'll kiss you."

He stretches out his free hand, and I grab hold of it, gratefully.

I climb back over the collapsed wall and with enthusiasm, wrap my arms around Tony's neck.

He laughs and holds me tight. "Well, I was lookin' forward to that kiss but this will do."

Laughing, I look up at him and say, "I said, if you get me out of here. And right now, we're still stuck in hell."

"Well, okay, in that case let's get goin'."

Taking my left hand, he begins to guide me out of the tunnels.

As we walk along, I ask, "So, how did you know I was down here? Keith said someone was going to meet me, but I wasn't expecting that someone to be you."

"Well, I know yeu recommended that I not go see Keith until yeu had a chance to talk to him first. But I went ahead, anyway. Luckily, I caught him at church right before he left for the funeral home. We talked for about twenty minutes. I trusted yeur instincts about him and went ahead and told him everythin' I knew about his brother, about yeu and yeur mother. At first, he was shocked that I knew so much and wouldn't open up to me until I told him how I knew yeur mum. That's when he showed me the photos that I'm assumin' are in that envelope yeur hand."

"Yes, I saw the photo of you and my mom at the pub where you told me you first met her. The photo means that they were watching her well before you ever saw them."

"I know. Did you look at the other photos?"

My voice chokes up, "Only one. The one of her tied and still alive at the stake. I couldn't bear to see the others."

Tony stops walking and turns around to look at me. He presses my left hand to his chest through the opening of his button down shirt. His flesh is warm and welcoming to my cold, dead hand.

"Isobel. I'm so sorry. I should've noticed them watching her. I could've warned her. I should've—"

"Stop!"

To my own surprise a new feeling comes over me. I'm no longer angry at him for leaving Maria, for leaving my mother. In that moment, I can feel his pain, his shame, the burden of his guilt perhaps because it mirrors my own.

I stare into his eyes and say softly, my voice trembling. "Tony, please. Let go of your guilt. You've carried it long enough—just as I've carried my rage long enough. Let's stop wasting our energy to change the past—it's haunted us both long enough."

Tony stares at me, the light flickering around his watery, green eyes. I peer deep into the raging sea of grief that surrounds his pupils, and my eyes fill with tears.

Suddenly I see a dark creature emerge around the whites of his eyes. Then Tony's eyes flicker from side to side, and I realize my own Scylla is emerging. Our shadows on the walls mesh with those of our monsters. They grow larger and larger in the small space, and I feel Tony pull away, but I hold on. I grip his shirt, and tug him back, keeping our eyes locked.

I say to him, "It's okay. I'm not afraid."

Our swelling shadows consume the tunnel as well as the light from Tony's torch. Our bodies come together more and more tightly as our shadow creatures embrace. My hand glides up Tony's chest and around his neck. His hand wraps around my waist pulling me tight against him. Our bodies seem to merge as the room grows dark.

I feel Tony's heart beating like a steady drum against my chest as the light disappears. The space is now pitch black though I can feel the heat of the torch in Tony's hand. My cheek is pressed tightly against Tony's face

He whispers into my ear, "Isobel, yeu're different. Yeu've changed somehow."

I laugh and say, "You can thank the cranky, old nun I saw today."

Tony's lips softly caress my cheek, and my stomach flutters. I return the gesture, my lips exploring the bristles of his beard. Then to both our shock, I feel something growing hard against my inner thy.

Tony reacts with little embarrassment. "Well, that's our cue. We should probably get going."

I can't help but laugh. Our bodies naturally pull away and the dark mist lifts as our shadow creatures disappear. The light of the torch fills the space again, and I resist the urge to look down at Tony's pants.

"Uhh." I'm somewhat at a loss for words. "Sorry 'bout that," I say.

"Well, don't be. I'm not." He says with a wink. "Come on, let's get movin'."

Tony guides me once again, holding my hand, lighting the way. Along the path, he explains to me the strategy Keith had devised during their meeting earlier in the day. The plan was to allow Keith a few moments with me to explain the history between our families, and for him to give me the secret envelope of evidence. Keith knew that his brothers would be coming any day to bully him into giving over the journal and photos to them. Since his brother Steve was already after me, Keith thought it best for me to take them and escape through the tunnels where Tony would be waiting for me.

I tell Tony how the plan went down, leaving out no details—including Mr. Barley and his rifle and the beating that led to Keith's broken arm. I get to the part about me walking the tunnels and ask him, "So how is it that we missed one another in the tunnel? I thought you were supposed to be waiting for me."

"Sorry about that. I was delayed. Yeu see, once I knew Keith's brothers would be comin' for yeu, I went back to the precinct to update Marcus. Well, to update him and to ask him a favor."

"What did you ask him?"

"I asked him to watch over the cottage, knowing Maria is home alone and that one of the Laine brothers might come back for vengeance when they didn't find yeu."

Hearing his concern for Maria, I feel like a complete jerk for the thoughts and curse words I used against him earlier.

I squeeze Tony's hand and say gratefully, "Thanks. She means the world to me."

"I know." He replies looking ahead into the darkness. "I feel the same about yeu."

A smile spreads across my face, which is hidden in the shadows behind him. For the next hundred steps, we ascend in silence. I follow Tony along the winding passageway and wonder again where the tunnel will emerge.

Soon we come to a halt, and Tony's torch shines on a rod iron ladder dangling from the ceiling above.

"We're here. Right up there is the way out."

"Praise God almighty. Where are we exactly?"

"I'll let that part be a surprise." Tony replies, placing the torch on a nearby hook on the wall.

"Uh, okay then."

I grab hold of the rod iron ladder, and position my body to climb up and out. Tony taps my shoulder. I turn to him and see a wide, pearly smile.

"Isobel, yeu did promise me something if I got us out of here."

Grinning back I reply, "You're right and I'm certainly a woman of my word."

Without further hesitation I step towards him and thrust my lips against his mouth. Electricity streams out of my body and into his. His hands take hold of my face; his fingers comb through my hair. An intense, electric current pulses through our lips, and this time Tony is unwilling to let me go—he holds me tight.

I lean into his embrace and his mouth moves in and out of mine with fiery passion, intoxicating me with his taste. Our breathing is now the panting of wild animals as every inch of my body begins to crave him, wanting nothing more than to devour him.

Pushing him forcefully against the wall, I let the envelope drop to floor so that both my hands are free. I unbutton his shit and squeeze the hard muscles of his chest. His hands grip my butt pulling me up against him. His lips move down my neck but stop abruptly at my collar. I feel his body tense and his hands fall back against the wall, releasing their hold on me. My own hands pull away from his chest, and I step back suddenly embarrassed by my outburst. Bending down to my knees, I reach to out to pick up the fallen evidence.

Quietly, without glancing at Tony, I say, "Sorry 'bout that. I'm not sure what came over me."

He takes a deep breath and bends down in front of me. He touches my hot face with his cool hand and smiles unapologetically.

"Don't be. I'm not sorry at all."

Feeling free for the first time since I was sixteen, I smile back and move my lips inches away from his as I whisper with a slight growl in my voice, "You're right. What the hell."

Then I let go, letting the urges deep with me loose. My body flings forward and I ferociously kiss Tony—grab his face, bite his lips. He's caught off guard by the intensity and falls onto his back. My body is drunk with desire; I feel myself losing control. A black mist hovers over my thoughts, blood rushing out of my head and down below my belly. I can feel Tony's arms tense perhaps from fighting his own desires, but then I hear a voice somewhere in my head.

"Take him. Take all of him!"

My initial instinct agrees with the voice. I want Tony, all of him, every inch of his body. It's been thirteen years since I last kissed anyone and fourteen years since I've had sex. And teenage sex is not really sex, anyway. Right now, my body is hungry—starving sexually. I lean further, digging my hips harder into him, pinning him against the dirt floor. My hands move from his face, down the muscles of his chest and abdomen all the way to his pants. I feel him growing hard and grab hold. A moan groans from throat and his mouth pulls at my lips with pleasure.

The voice in my head cries out louder, like a bear roaring in a cave, "Take him! Take him, now!"

With both hands, I unbuckle his belt and begin unzipping his pants. Then like a bucket of cold water being dumped over my head, Tony stops my hands. He speaks the words I couldn't conjure for myself.

His voice is gentle, but firm as says, "No, Isobel. This, this doesn't feel right. Not here. Not now."

His words burn against my flesh like ice on fire. The truth sizzles against my lust, boiling my anger. The voice within me screams in defiance. I rise to my knees and grab my head in pain.

Tony sits up with concern. "Isobel, what's wrong?"

He reaches out to touch me. But the moment I feel his hands on my skin, the torment intensifies.

I pull away in agony, rise to my feet, press my fingers into my temples. I try desperately to release the pain as I say, "Tony, don't! Don't touch me!"

I turn my back to him; I feel the agony in my head simmer down.

"Isobel, I'm sorry. It's not that I don't want yeu, it's the fact that I want yeu so bad. But yeu were moving so fast, something just didn't feel right."

I put my palms on the stonewall in front of me and lean into it, fighting to take back my mind and body. Tony's right, something's wrong. Something dark and ferocious has awakened within me. I take a few deep breaths, and my stomach churns as I swallow the bile filling my throat. Anxiety and fear grip me, and I wonder, is this a different monster, or is it simply the old one playing new tricks? Maybe Scylla has evolved somehow and is fighting back with a new approach. She seems to use my body, my deep urges that I only let loose in dreams, as weapons against me.

"Shit!" I shout beating my palm against the stone. Without turning around, I say in frustration. "Tony. It's not you. You're right, though, more than I realized before. When you said that I'd changed. I've changed, and perhaps, not entirely for the better."

Tony steps closer to me and asks, concern in his voice, "What do yeu mean, not entirely for the better?"

I ignore his question, push myself up from the wall and say, urgently, "I need to get out of here before she comes back."

I turn towards the ladder and grab hold of the iron bars. As I ascend the stairway to heaven, Tony questions says, "She who? Who are yeu afraid of?"

I stop midway up the ladder and look down at him. My voice is low and deep when I answer him. "Me."

22: The Reformer

I get to the top of the ladder and push open what looks like the hatch to the deck of a submarine. I take another step up and stick my head through. At that moment, I'm not sure a breath of clean, fresh air ever felt so good.

A black mist lifts from my mind, and I pull myself up and out—into an unexpected, yet familiar room—the basement of St. Luke's. It's dark, damp, and freezing cold, but it's also an extraordinarily welcome sight.

I crawl the rest of the way out of the tunnel of hell on my hands and knees, roll on my back, and thankfully, praise the Lord.

I rise to my feet, and my heart slows down the steam engine of my body. Thankfully, I feel my old self returning. I walk around the friendly space beneath the sanctuary and my hormones settle down.

The dying light of day brings in a soft, illuminating glow through the dusty basement windows. An old, wooden door locked and secure sits adjacent to several bookshelves covered in old church documents and boxes full of God knows what. The room is hardly used by anyone except by me. In the middle hangs a large, worn punching bag I was given five years ago from a boxing club nearby.

Boxing is my saving grace. In the midst of leading a church full of stiff necked, stubborn children of God, I've found sanity and salvation in the basement, punching my frustrations away. At least three times a week, I come down here to pray with right hooks and uppercuts. The last time I was down here was right after a finance meeting that ended with someone saying, "if only our priest would bring in more young people we would have more money."

I give the punching bag a couple left jabs as Tony pulls himself out of the hidden hole in the ground.

Because of our recent encounter, I try to keep the conversation light.

"I had no idea there were secret tunnels underneath the city, let alone underneath my church. How did you find out about them?"

Wiping filthy hands on his jeans, Tony says, "It's a long story, but the short version is that I stumbled upon them about a year ago. Actually, Sam led me to them."

"Sam? Your cat?"

"Yes, yeu might not believe this but one of the entrances to the tunnel is located in my bar."

"Really? Is that what you wanted to show me later tonight?"

Tony looks out the window and answers, "Yes, but that's not all."

I wrap one arm around the punching bag as if I'm hugging an old pal, and he turns to me. Concern and worry wrinkle his forehead.

He says, "Isobel, I've much to show you. However, it's getting late and we should check on Maria."

Then I notice how comfortable Tony seems in this space and a thought crosses my mind. "Tony, uh, how many times have you used this tunnel door? Tony, have you been in my church before now?"

A devilish grin curls up the side of his face. Ignoring my question he says, "Maria is waiting." To my surprise, Tony pulls out a key and walks up the large wooden door and unlocks it.

"Hey," I say, and follow him. "How did you get a key to that door? How many times have you been here?"

To my irritation, Tony keeps walking, through the doorway, up the stairs and out a hidden door in the panel wall that leads to a small room called the sacristy. This room holds our clergy robes and vestals along with the tabernacle with elements of the Eucharist. I can hear him laughing ahead of me.

I hurry after him.

He opens another door leading into the narthex, the foyer outside of the sanctuary. We reach the side exit door of the Narthex that leads to the cottage fifty yards away.

I call out to him again before he opens the door. "Tony, answer me. Have you been spying on me?"

Tony swings around and faces me. "Twenty. I've been here twenty times. It took me several months to learn that the tunnels led here. The day I discovered this exit was on a Sunday mornin' several months ago. I popped out of the tunnel just in time to hear yeur sermon." Tony reaches out his hand to touch my face but stops himself. "Yeur words, yeur passion, they captivated me. So every Sunday since then, I journey through the tunnels and sit at the top of the stairs to hear yeur voice."

I look around the building, cautiously. I'm suddenly paranoid that some stray parishioner might see us.

I say, "Tony. You should've come in for the service."

"No." he says dryly, turning around towards the exit door. He pushes the door open, and he says, "I believe in yeu, but I don't believe in yeur God."

Stunned by his words, and the bitter wind blowing into the building, I stand frozen as I watch him walk out of the church. Then I snap out of it and hurry after him out the door toward the cottage.

We walk along the narrow sidewalk in single file, and I notice the wind picking up, pushing dark, gray clouds across the sky. I can feel intensity growing in the atmosphere and wonder if a storm is brewing north of us. The temperature has dropped at least ten degrees since I met Keith at the funeral home. The winter sun sets in Louisville around five thirty, which means I was in the tunnels roughly three and half hours. But it felt like a lifetime.

We reach the front door of the cottage, and I become aware of the hunger growls of my stomach. They're so loud I'm distracted from seeing a man walk up behind us. Without warning, I feel a large hand on my shoulder. An alarm goes off in me, and I pivot around, swinging. Marcus blocks my right hook with his left hand.

He laughs and says, "Good to see you, too, Alex. But next time, go for the gut with an undercut. It's harder to see that coming."

I smile, feeling a bit embarrassed but justified, nonetheless. "Well, after a day like mine, be glad I don't carry a gun."

Marcus laughs, glances over at Tony, and then pulls a chunk of mud out of my hair. "Well, by the looks of you both, it appears you've been wrestling trolls in a cave nearby."

For the first time since we came out of the tunnels, I look

down at my clothing. My black leather jacket, black shirt and pants are smeared with dirt and large patches of mud. I glance over at Tony, whose clothing is equally dirty and disheveled. I also notice that his shirt is still unbuttoned past his chest and his bottom lip is bleeding.

Tony winks at me and replies to Marcus' observations. "Well, yeu never know what yeu'll end doing with a Catholic Priest these days."

His comments aren't what I'm expecting, and I punch his arm hard in protest. "Jesus Christ, Tony. The Catholic Church doesn't need another sex scandal."

My words cause us all to laugh so hard that the front door opens wide and there stands Maria, staring at us.

"So, this is where the party is," Maria says. She hovers in the doorway, arms crossed, dressed in casual clothing—skinny jeans, chunky sweater and wool socks. Her hair is tied up in a large messy bun, and she also has on makeup and earrings.

She shivers and says, "Ya'll it's freezin' out here. Come inside for coffee and cake. Tony and Alex, please take off those nasty boots on the way in." With that, she swivels on her heels.

We follow her inside the cozy cottage. Tony and I kneel inside the door and remove our boots. The space is so narrow we end up face to face. He smiles flirtatiously at me with his sparkling, green eyes—I resist the urge to kiss him.

He seems to notice my painful scowl of self control and leans close to me. I feel his breath on my face as he whispers, "I feel the same way."

I snap back, "Good, so you know it isn't going to happen again."

"Yes." He says but then pauses to look across the room at the backs of Marcus and Maria in the kitchen before gently touching my face with the back of his hand.

"For now, that is."

At his words, my stomach growls loudly signaling me to change the subject. I stand up, and say to no one in particular, "Well, I'm starving and in need of a shower." Walking across the room towards Maria and Marcus, I add, under my breath, "A very cold shower."

Maria hands me a mug of hot coffee. "Thanks." I say and take a sip before asking, "How's your day been?"

"After a few hours, I got bored so I made tres leches!" She smiles and holds up a beautifully baked cake. "How was yours?"

I hesitate, take a bite of cake, and search for the words to sum up the entire afternoon. With a mouthful, I say, "Uh, enlightening. I think I'm going to go ahead and take that shower now."

Maria gives me a look that says, we'll talk later, and you'd better give me more than that. Then she turns to Marcus and continues a conversation they were having before I walked up.

With coffee in hand, I head to the shower. Tony watches me from the couch, petting Sam who's curled up in his lap. He smiles at me, and I smile back. As frustrated as the sexual parts of me are, the rational parts are grateful for his actions, or lack of actions in the tunnel. I would've gone all the way, and can easily imagine the layers of guilt I'd be feeling right now. Before I enter the bathroom, I raise my mug to him and nod. He covers his heart as he nods back.

I close the bathroom door and turn on the shower. I look at myself in the mirror as I undress. I pull off my jacket and my clergy collar, then remove my shirts, pants and socks. I lean against the sink to examine myself in the mirror. My hair is no longer red. It's brown from all the dirt and grime. My blotchy face has turned my skin even more dull and pale.

I study my reflection and notice how bright blue my eyes are in contrast to the brown dirt. I look deeper into my eyes and see that my pupils are dilated as though I've been taking drugs the past few hours. I wash my face in the sink and glance back up into the mirror.

To my horror, Scylla's out with all six grotesque heads staring back at me in the mirror. I yelp in shock and fall back on the toilet. Moments later there's a knock on the door. I hear Maria's voice on the other side of the door.

"Alex. you alright in there?"

I stand and look back into the mirror—only my reflection looks back. I say over the noise of the shower. "Yes, sorry 'bout that. There's a spider in here."

Maria snickers and says, "Well, whatever you do, don't eat it."

I take one more glance in the mirror and see that the pupils of my eyes are back to normal. I shake my head, finish undressing, and step into the shower.

The water is hot and soothing on my skin. It takes two shampoo attempts to clean my hair and half a bar of soap to wash everything else.

I linger for a long while, letting the hot water run over my body as my mind processes the tunnels and the intimate moments with Tony. I feel my body tense as I remember the taste of his lips, his hands squeezing my body. My mouth waters, stomach yearning with each thought.

Luckily, I have the wherewithal to turn the shower cold before my monster gets loose again. Like ice daggers on my skin, the water baptizes me back to my rational state. I continue thinking through the events in the tunnel trying to understand why and when Scylla turned against me. When I get to the part where I first kiss Tony, a terrible reality forces my body to jump out of the shower and into my bath robe. I pull the bathroom door wide open and race across the living room towards the front door.

Maria yells behind me, "For God's sake. What's going on?"

I put on my snow boots, hair dripping wet from my head, robe sticking to my body, and respond with haste, "I forgot something very important at church. I'll be right back."

Not until Marcus chimes in do I realize Tony isn't in the room. He says, "Tony, said the same thing five minutes ago."

Without another word, I fling my body out the front door and race down the sidewalk to the Narthex. I reach out for the handle, and the large metal door violently swings towards me. Everything goes dark.

For some strange reason, I'm now standing alone back in the tunnels again. There's a torch in my hand and my other hand holds the envelope with the journal and photos. The tunnel is freezing cold, much colder than I recall and the wind is gusting through the narrow passageway blowing my torch dimmer and dimmer. I kneel down with my back against the stone wall and open the envelope. Pulling out the journal, I flip through the pages, but each page is blank. No ledger, no names, no dates. Nothing. I begin to panic, and grab hold of the photos. They too are blank. No images of my mother at the pub or tied to the stake.

My voice cries out, "No, this can't be. No. No. No!" Then another gust of wind sails through the tunnel and blows out the fire of my torch. My body shivers uncontrollably in the freezing darkness.

I hear Tony's voice calling out, "Isobel. Isobel."

But there's no light anywhere to be seen. How can he find me in the dark without a light. I call after him, but my voice is faint. I try to stand up, but my legs are numb, paralyzed against the ice-cold stone ground. My head suddenly screams at me, pain pounding against my forehead.

Tony calls out again, his voice louder and stronger. "Wake up. Isobel. I'm here. Wake up!"

My eyes spring open and I turn my head to Tony who is kneeling over me—panic on his face. To my relief, I realize it was only a dream.

I sit up and ask, demandingly, "Where is it? Do you have the envelope?"

"Yes, I went back to get it. It was exactly where yeu dropped it earlier."

I sigh and close my eyes. "Thank you. It just hit me in the shower."

Tony grunts and says, "Uh, I can see that yeu literally jumped out of the shower."

Glancing down at my lower body, I see that not only am I lying on the freezing pavement of the sidewalk, but my robe is pushed up around my thighs exposing my bare legs. No wonder I thought I was paralyzed. My face flushes with embarrassment, and I pull my robe down and around my legs. I put my hands on the ground and push myself to my feet. The blood pounding in my head rushes to my freezing legs, and the world goes black again.

I wake up sometime later alone in my bedroom with an ice pack on my forehead.

I turn my head to the side, the ice pack slides off, and through the window, I notice the night sky. The lamp next to me shines on the envelope of evidence resting on the bedside table. I sit up slowly this time and pull the blanket off me. I'm still in my robe from earlier but someone has taken off my boots and replaced them with wool socks. Leaning on the edge of the bed with my head in my hands, I hear a knock at the door.

"I'm awake. You can come in."

The door opens slowly, and I expect Maria or Tony but it's Marcus who comes through the door.

He greets me. "Hey. How are you doing?"

"I'm okay. Confused a bit but okay. What exactly happened?"

Marcus pulls out the desk chair, slides it in front me and sits down. "According to Tony, right after Maria and I watched you run out of here like a madwoman, you reached the church door right as Tony was racing back to the cottage like a madman. The door swung open and hit you. You fell back and hit the back of your head on the sidewalk. You were knocked out, came to, and then you passed out again. That was when Tony picked you up and brought you inside. It all happened about two hours ago."

I rub the back of my head and feel a large, very sensitive bump. "Awesome. Just when I thought the day couldn't get any worse."

Marcus pulls out a bottle of aspirin and hands it to me. "Ya, Tony filled us in a bit about your afternoon. Tony and Maria have gone to the bar for dinner and drinks. I volunteered to wait until you were awake to take you back to your car. Also, Tony said you might have something to show me."

Marcus glances at the envelope on the side table.

I open the bottle, pop a couple of aspirin in my mouth, and then say, "Go head. Open it and see for yourself."

I swallow the pills and watch Marcus open the envelope and pull out the contents. He starts with the photos, flipping through each one with a neutral expression. Then he opens the journal and reads a few pages silently before looking up at me.

"I take it you've looked through the photos and journal for yourself and don't really need me to comment on them."

I nod in agreement having no desire to dive back into the range of emotions both sets of evidence would ignite.

I say, "What can we do with these?"

"Well, I'll need to examine both more fully before I draw any conclusions. But this could possibly crack our case wide open, at least we now have some hard evidence against the Laine family. But what we don't have is the connection between this symbol and the Laine family."

He points to the "AM" on the inside cover of the journal and says, "This symbol was discovered not only on the victim you found in the dumpster, it appeared in several places where murders took place during the past year. This symbol is the only link between all the victims and crime scenes. You know about the house that burned down with two black folks inside two days before Christmas?"

I nod and say, "Yes, it was in the newspaper on Christmas Eve. Maria thinks it was no accident."

"She's right. It wasn't an accident. This symbol was found on the necks of both victims. It was difficult to find since the bodies were burned so badly, but I knew where to look."

"Hmm. Then this explains the message on the bathroom mirror the day Maria was kidnapped. Whatever happened to that clue?"

Marcus shifts in his chair, hesitating before answering my question. "I erased it. I wouldn't normally have done such a thing but I had a hunch that there was leak in the investigation team, a spy feeding information to Officer Laine each step of the way. The message was only helpful for you and me and I didn't think it would help us find Maria."

"So, that's how Office Laine knew when and where we would be watching. It was all a set up from the beginning. I bet the rest of the Laine brothers were in on it too. Was the kidnapping all a charade to get back at me? To simply taint my reputation to the media?"

"Yes, and probably more so. Alex, I'm a reformer, a person who sees right and wrong around every corner. I've been keeping a critical eye on Officer Laine for quite some time. The chief and I think that all of it was a setup for something bigger to come. We think this group is planning something big, and they need a scapegoat, and the scapegoat could very well be you."

I remain silent, mentally digesting his insights. It wouldn't be the first time I was the scapegoat for this family's evil behavior. Maybe they're coming back to seal my coffin after they failed thirteen years ago.

After several moments of deep thought, I finally ask, "What do you need me to do?"

"Nothing. We need you to do nothing."

His response triggers my anger, especially since I'm already feeling helpless and useless.

I snap back at him. "Really? I can help. Look at the evidence I brought you. Why are ya'll shutting me out?"

"Alex, we aren't shutting you out. We just need you to lie low for a bit. You're drawing too much heat, and it's only going to get more dangerous for everyone. We also need you to stay away from the Laine family—even Keith."

My arms cross over my chest, and I fight the urge to argue with him. I know he's trying to protect me and all the hard work he's done on this case over the past year.

I respond coolly. "Okay, I can understand the laying low part, but I can't possibly stay away from Keith. I have a service at Barley Brother's Funeral Home tomorrow and he's the new owner."

"I see. Well, that's a problem. What time is the service?"

"Ten o'clock. Why?"

"Because I'll be coming. I'll be undercover as some distant relative."

"Well, you'll need to be an adopted cousin because this family is super white."

Marcus laughs and stands up. "Get dressed. I know you're hungry and probably could use a stiff drink."

"Yes to both. It won't take me long to get ready. I'll be out soon."

Marcus leaves the room, the envelope of evidence in hand. I close the door, and open my wardrobe. We priests don't own much, including many clothing options. I decide on non-clergy attire, and put on dark jeans, a forest green sweater, and my boots. I've had quite enough of my clergy collar for one day, and I'm currently off the clock anyway.

I step in front of the mirror on my wall and see the fiery chaos that is my hair. Sleeping on wet hair inevitably creates a wave of curls on one side and matted tangles on the other. I braid the knots of hair all back into a loose, low bun. The blotchy spots on the face from earlier are gone, and my skin is back to its normal pinkish pigment color.

I leave my bedroom and see Marcus waiting by the door with my cleaned, leather jacket in one hand and the envelope in the other.

"Ready?" He asks.

"Ya, let me just grab my keys and phone." I take my keys off the side table and search for a moment for my phone. "Oh, wait. My phone is still in my car."

Marcus hands me my coat. I wrap a large scarf around my neck, and we head out of the front door. As I close the door, I see Sam sleeping soundly in the oversized chair beside the window. For whatever reason, her presence in the cottage gives me a sense of peace.

23: The Helper

Marcus pulls into the back lot of Barley Brother's Funeral Home next to my car still parked in the clergy spot from earlier. He puts the car in park and I get out and head to the driver's side of the Mini Cooper. The gusts of the wind are fierce, forcing me to steady myself against the car. I pull the keys from my pocket and notice a white slip of paper stuck under the windshield wiper. I grab hold of it tightly, keeping the wind from carrying it away. One side is blank but the other side read, "Witches burn like niggers."

Marcus rolls down his window and yells above the noise of the wind.

"Alex, what is it?"

I walk over to him and hand him the note. I say, sarcastically, "Just another word of encouragement from our favorite family."

Marcus looks at the paper, and then opens the envelope of evidence. "Might be best to add to our collection, don't you think?"

"Fine with me. I was just going to blow my nose in it anyway. Are you coming to the bar for drinks?"

Marcus replies, "Not tonight. I need to get home to the family. See you in the morning."

"Family?" I say curiously. "I didn't realize you have a family."

"Yep. A wife and two kids," he responds casually.

"Thanks again for giving me a lift. Take good care of that." I add, pointing to the evidence, which seems to me a little too vulnerable sitting there all by itself.

Marcus hands the package to me and says, "Actually, I think it best for you to take it to Tony. It's not safe at police headquarters right now with Officer Laine and his crew lurking around. I also don't want to bring it home, or for you to leave it in the cottage. Tony will keep it safe and out of reach from the Laine clan."

I nod, take the evidence and return to my car. I unlock the door and sink inside the worn leather of the driver's seat. I start the car and wait for the heat to warm up the small space. The enneagram book from Sister Agatha lies face up on the passenger seat. I pick it up, turning to the first page. I read the same line from earlier today when I sat in the parking lot of Sacred Heart.

Death is only the beginning.

The words have new meaning in the light of my long afternoon. I think back to the tunnels, the pitch-black grave where I rested holding the evidence of my mother's rapist and murderers. I think about Tony, the moment we kissed, the moment my monster erupted out of me, wanting nothing more than to devour his being in every way. Gulping down the lust and power filling my throat, I remember that Tony asked me to read up on the Enneagram before coming over tonight. He said he wanted to show me something at the bar, something connected to the information in this book.

I hold the book to my chest and close my eyes, giving myself a brief moment with my desires. My heart begins to race at the thoughts of seeing Tony again. His emerald eyes. His tall, muscular stature. His warm hands. His soft lips. His hard body. Then suddenly a force awakens inside me snapping me back to reality.

My right hand punches my left palm and I chastise myself.

"Isobel, cut it out! You can do this! You can control Scylla. You have power over her. Remember Agatha. Remember the work you did today."

As I start the car, I look in the rearview mirror and see Marcus waiting patiently to make sure I get out of the parking lot safely. I wave at him casually, wondering how long he has been watching the madwoman staring back at me in the rearview mirror.

We exit the parking lot, pull out to the main road, then turn in different directions.

On the way to Tony's, I check my phone. There are a few text messages from the deacons about Sunday worship, and another two calls from John Thompson's sister, whose name I still can't remember.

I call her using my favorite greeting when I forget someone's name, "This is Mother Alex returning your call."

To my dismay she answers the phone and replies, "Oh Mother Alex, this is John's sister. Thanks for calling me back."

Of course. I can't catch a break today. The conversation takes up the five-minute travel time to Tony's. I'm still on the phone with her when I park the car. John's sister continues giving more details than necessary about her brother, their family, and how the holidays are just not the same anymore. I juggle the phone on my ear and stuff the evidence and enneagram book into my jacket as I say sympathetic words during the brief moments when she takes a breath. As I walk down the alleyway, I see a crowd gathered beside the dumpster taking selfies—which disturbs me on many levels.

I finally end the conversation saying, "Yes Ma'am, we will do his memory justice tomorrow. Peace of Christ to you."

Then I hurry past the groupies a bit disturbed but grateful I'm dressed in pedestrian clothing. I open the large metal door, and I'm greeted with a tidal wave of techno thumps mixed with pop music from the nineties. I squeeze past a few folks in the hallway and shove my way into the open room where over a hundred people are gathered—a crowd larger than I've ever seen in my pews on a Sunday morning. It's Friday night, and I figure the size of the crowd of mainly lesbians and gays is due to both family hangovers and the Christmas Eve murder.

The dance floor is packed to the brim, every table and chair is taken, and there's even overflow—people standing around full tables here and there. Across the room at the bar, I see Tony hustling about with two other bartenders. I notice Maria sitting at the far end with her back to me, her hair in a bun.

I work my way through the crowd, my long limbs weave between and around tables and chairs. Along the way, I unsuccessfully maneuver around a narrow passage between chairs and accidentally knock over a martini on one of the tables. To my horror, my clumsy actions upset a mammoth man with biceps the size of bourbon barrels. The ogre leaps out of his seat and towers over me. Attracting the attention of half the room, he shoves me back against a chair with his pot belly.

I now wish I was wearing my clergy collar because I assume this giant would consider my sanctity before choking the life out of me with his bear-like paws. I stand my ground, apologize for spilling the drink and offer to buy him another, but he doesn't hear me over the noise of the music and the bustling crowd. His face turns red, eyes bulge out of his head. I wonder to myself if he heard "fucking gay man" instead of "forgive me, man."

I try to squirm around his body, but his belly presses harder against me, and his claws grip around my shoulders pinning my arms downward. I lean my head back to keep my face from touching the chest hair hanging out of his half unbuttoned paisley shirt.

My fighting instincts are about to kick in when out of nowhere, an equally tall figure forces his body between us. Staring at the back of the mystery man's head, I hear the faint sound of a Scottish accent over the blaring music and then laughter roars out of the giant. The figure in front of me turns around and Tony's charming smile grins down at me. He winks and grabs my hand, pulls me through the crowd and back behind the bar to his bedroom/office.

I follow him willingly into the room and close the door behind us. The room is dark. The noise from outside buzzes through the door, but at least I can finally hear myself think. I lean my back against the wall, and catch my breath. I put one hand inside my jacket checking for the evidence as the other hand presses the aching bump on my forehead.

Tony speaks with intensity, "Yeu're like a magnet for madness, yeu know that. Out of all the martinis to knock over tonight, yeu knock over Baloo's."

I reply with amusement, keeping my eyes shut. "Baloo, like the bear from the jungle book. Of course, if the shoe fits, or in this case, the very large claw."

With a calmer tone, he says, "Yeu're lucky he thinks I'm cute or that would've ended up differently."

I smile at the image of Baloo and Tony as a couple and hear Tony step towards me. I hear the switch of a light and Tony's standing directly in front of me.

He looks at my forhead and says, "How's yeur head? I guess I should apologize for knocking yeu out earlier."

"It's okay. And yes, you should apologize."

Tony's hovers with a sympathetic smile and then gently removes my hand to look at the mutation growing out of my head. Before I can say anything, his lips press softly against the bruise on my forehead.

He says softly. "Isobel, I'm sorry. The last thing I would ever want is to harm yeu."

My stomach flutters at his touch and my heartbeat quickens as his scent fills my nostrils. Before Scylla can leap out like a jack in the box, I push him back slowly keeping him at arm's length.

I take a deep inhale and say, "Apology accepted. And unless you want a repeat from the tunnels, I suggest you keep your distance from me."

Tony laughs and touches the red wound on his lower lip. "How could I forgot? Yeu have a way of leavin' yeur mark."

I smile back at him and say, sympathetically, "Ya, well, sorry 'bout that."

"Don't be. Like I've said before." He steps closer towards me and adds, "I'm not."

Pushing him back again, I say sharply, "Well, maybe that's your problem. Lack of confession. I know a priest who could help you with that."

He crosses his arms pulling his flannel shirt tight over his chest. I gulp as he replies defiantly. "Do yeu now? And who might that be, yeu?"

"Hell no!" I say, reaching for the door sensing scylla churning in my gut. "Maria is way better in the confessional booth."

I pull the door open, exit the room, and make my way to Maria, who is having a cheerful conversation with a middle-aged woman who is clearly not interested in Maria's words. The volume in the club has decreased significantly, and I notice the DJ taking a break on one of the stools at the bar. I walk past him and catch Maria's eye. She jumps from her seat and gives me a big hug.

She cries out with enthusiasm, "Alex, you made it!"

Returning the hug, I give the older woman a look that says, "This is my lesbian, back off." The woman rolls her eyes, takes her drink and walks off.

Maria turns around and says with astonishment, "What happened to Erica? She was a real help in getting me another drink in the middle of this chaos."

I shrug innocently and spew out, "I don't think helping you get a drink was her true motivation."

Maria snaps back. "What do you mean? She saw me struggling and wanted to help."

"Ya, help you get into her pants."

"Come on!" Maria shouts. "Why do you always see the bad in everyone?"

"Yes. I can't help but see everyone's shadows," I say, and then signal one of the bartenders. No more stools are available, and so I continue standing as I give my observations to Maria. "That woman wanted you to have sex with her, that's why she was so helpful."

I lean against the bar and order the usual. Maria has already received her chicken salad and fries, and so I decide to sneak a few bites off her plate as I wait, hoping it will calm the beast growling in my belly.

Maria quickly changes the subject. "So Tony said you both had an eventful afternoon."

"Oh he did, did he?" I say, annoyed. "Let me get my drink and I'll tell you what I know."

Maria gives me a wry smile and takes a bite of her sandwich. My drink comes sooner than expected, which gives me no time at all to think through how to tell Maria about my day. After a couple sips of the bourbon, I decide to begin the story at the tunnels. I tell Maria about getting lost in the darkness and about reading through the evidence in the journal along with photos of my mother's murder. Maria is so taken back by the story of Tony and my mother and her horrible death that she is sobbing by the time I get to the part when my torch burns out. Worried that she's causing a scene, I quickly tell her that Tony found me and got me out of the tunnels.

I decide not to share intimate details, or anything about Scylla and her sexual revolution, but I confess that I kissed him right before we climbed out of the tunnel. Maria gives me a look of disapproval confirming my decision to not share more details. I try to explain my actions, over Maria's shoulder see Tony having a conversation with the DJ.

"Maria, I'm sorry. I was tired, vulnerable, and well, you know, a man that looks like Tony is hard not to kiss, especially when moments earlier you thought you were going to die."

Maria grabs my hands and says graciously. "It was a moment of weakness that could've easily led to a broken vow." She looks into my eyes for a long moment before adding. "My sister, you have committed no sin. Let go of your guilt. There is nothing to forgive."

I breathe deep, smile and say, "Thank you. I needed to hear that." I release her hands and take a gulp of bourbon.

"However," Maria says, playfully, "you need to know that for women like me, men that look like Tony are quite easy not to kiss."

The bourbon gets lodged in my throat when laughter erupts from me. It takes a huge effort not to spew it across the bar.

We laugh, we eat and we drink like old times. Over the past year, I've learned that Maria is an entertainer. She's a great story-teller and would make a hilarious comedian. She loves to have a good time and be around others who enjoy a good time as well. I normally stand back and listen and watch as she tells stories about her childhood in Texas. She's got some good ones, such as when she fell into a cactus bed, the time she faced killer rattlesnakes, and the many times she played with her brothers in the watering hole. A crowd normally surrounds her, but tonight I'm her audience of one.

After a while, Tony catches my attention from across the room. He signals for me to meet him. That's when I remember the enneagram book tucked inside my jacket, which must be connected to whatever he's about to show me.

I finish my meal and turn to Maria. "Tony wants to show me something here at the bar—something that has to do with my spiritual direction session today. Mind if I go talk with him a bit?"

Maria gives me her maternal look, and says, "Only if you promise not to kiss him."

I laugh and put my hand over my heart, which is conveniently blocked by the enneagram book. "You have my word. And you, don't you get into trouble while I'm gone."

She grins, and nods.

I slurp down the last bits of bourbon and start on my way across the room to Tony. This time I take a different path avoiding Baloo and his bear cubs—the long way around crowds of people—finally, I get to Tony.

He has to yell directly into my ear because the music has been cranked back up on the nearby dance floor. "We have to be careful to not draw attention. There's a hidden door at the far end of this wall. I asked the DJ to play somethin' that would get everyone's attention. Once he gives the signal, we need to move quickly."

Hoards of people are all around, many pushing right up against us. I wonder how in the world we're going to simply disappear without notice behind a hidden wall. But then the music suddenly stops, the room still with anticipation. Tony wraps his arm around my back, and I glance up at him questioningly. Then the DJ scratches a record and familiar opening words pierce the silence, "Bye, Bye, Bye—" The crowd screams with excitement and everyone moves away from the walls towards the dance floor.

Tony pulls me close to him and guides me along the wall so I don't get caught up in the wave of N'Sync fans. We stop at a column with pelicans carved into the crown molding at the top that's built into the wall. Tony pulls out a large iron key from his pocket and pushes it inside a keyhole hidden by the column's edge. A crack in the brick wall opens, revealing a five-foot door. Tony glances around the room. I watch his face as he makes sure no one is looking in our direction. He turns and give me a nod. I hunch over and slide through into a space behind the wall.

24: The Achiever

The dark closet-like room is the same size as the hidden space back at Barley Brother's. The light from the outer room helps me locate the walls and get my bearings before Tony squeezes his six-foot five body through the door and closes it behind him.

The room feels impossibly tiny—our bodies are scrunched together, his front side against my backside. It's dark, and there seems to be just enough room for me to turn around so that my face won't be pressed against the wall. I swivel in an about face and feel Tony's breath against my forehead. His hands seem to be digging around his jeans.

Then I feel something hard against my leg, and I blurt out, "Really, Tony? How about applying some control?"

Tony laughs, and to my relief switches on a flashlight. He holds it under our faces and says with a grin, "Oh, don't worry. I took care of that hours ago." He plants a quick kiss my on forehead and adds in a more serious tone, "Since yeu are the smaller of the two of us, yeu'll need to open the door under our feet. I'll push my body against the wall, hopefully givin' yeu enough room to pull the door up halfway. Then yeu'll need to maneuver up against me to get it up the rest of the way."

"Tony." I sigh. "Why do I think you planned this moment to be as awkward and intimate as possible?"

"Isobel, truly, I've done no such thing. But I won't say I'm not enjoyin' it either."

He chuckles, forces his body back against the wall, and shines the light on the floor. I see the handle, reach down and grab hold of it. I then swing one leg back towards Tony and lunge with the other to give me leverage and room. The trickiest part is getting the door completely open without falling in the hole. I turn my back to Tony, spread my long legs wide against the two walls and bend over. Tony holds my hips to keep my body from diving head-first into the tunnel below.

As my butt presses against him I remark sharply, "If I hear one word from your mouth in the next few moments, I will seriously consider never stepping foot in your bar again."

Tony remains silent, but I can feel the delight radiating off him. While balancing my body into Tony and using the walls to hold myself up, I somehow manage not only to open the small square door but also to keep us both from falling.

Tony takes my hands as I step on the ladder rails. Then he shines the light at the floor of the tunnel. I descend first, then down he comes.

We both have our feet planted firmly on the ground, and Tony breaks the silence. "Well done. Yeur quite—" He hesitates, choosing his words carefully. "Athletic. Yeu must get that from yeur father because yeur mum said she could barely walk straight without turnin' an ankle."

I laugh at the memory of my mother who would say all the time how clumsy she was. Tony, clearly pleased with my response adds, "She is why I brought you down here. I want to show yeu what I found early last year when I first started learning the tunnels."

He slips his palm into mine and leads me along the passageway. We follow the light of his flashlight through the tunnels about a quarter of a mile before we come to a large wooden door on the right side of the stone walls. Tony pulls out the same large iron key from before and opens the door before us. He walks through the doorway as though he has stepped through it a thousand times.

I stand in shock and awe by what I see. The room is significantly larger than I expected. The dimensions of the space are at least ten times the size of the cottage with torches burning bright every ten feet along the stone wall except for the furthest area of the room which remains in pitch black darkness. The ceiling cascades at least forty feet high with stalactites jetting down from above.

The cave must be connected somehow to cave systems under the city, and I think that perhaps it's connected to the Mega Caverns just north of here.

I walk inside and notice a path, a wooden deck of sorts that curves along the wall. It wraps all around the empty void at the far end of the cave. The deck forms a track with a circumference of half a football field, circling a stone island with a rushing river.

I make my way closer and observe Tony walking around the track towards a bridge at the far end of the room, which appears to be broken, or at the very least, useless. It rests against the wooden track where the river rushes under the earth into the darkness. I watch Tony with curiosity as he stops at the bridge and bends over the side. He reaches down into the running water and the bridge begins to creak and moan. Then magically it glides slowly across the top of the river, stopping at the edge of the island. Tony steps onto the bridge and strolls across.

I call out to him over the sound of the rapids. "This is incredible! How long do you think this place has been here?"

Tony smiles and hollers out, "I'm so glad yeu like it. From what I've gathered about the cave systems, Louisville's history and some markings here on the island, all this could be somewhere around three hundred yers old. I call it the Island of Essence."

"Wow. Simply amazing," I yell out. I decide to hold the rest of my questions about the cave and island, and I head there myself.

I race around the wooden track to the bridge and walk across cautiously, unsure how deep the rapids below might be. The bridge is sturdy and well made, considering it might've been constructed before the founders of the United States declared independence. I step onto the stone island and feel a hollowness underneath my feet, as though this ground might open up to another room or cavern below. This makes me a bit uneasy until I see Tony standing in front of me smiling with confidence.

He speaks in a reassuring tone. "I know, it's a weird feelin' when yeu step out here for the first time. Like the world might just open up beneath yeu. Don't be afraid, I've been out here a hundred times now and haven't died yet."

I saunter around the island in an effort to fully grasp the size of it in comparison to the grandeur of the cavern. The stone island is shaped in what appears to be a perfect circle. There are cracks, straight lines carved into the ground running at odd angles. A lip along the outer edge keeps the river splashing over into the circle, but it looks as though it would allow excess water to flow into the river.

I follow one of the lines that crosses over a third of the circle to a point, and then I cut across another third, which creates a triangle. For several minutes, I trace five lines with my steps, following each one to a point before pivoting to another line, which makes an odd shape that has seven sides. At first, the path felt random–the lines lead to several points at roughly forty-five-degree angles. Then, I see the last line leads back to Tony, who I now assume is standing at the head of the circle directly opposite the bridge at the other end of the island. I take another look and study the lines crossing each other and realize they come together at different points. Now I see it—the full image is finally clear to me. I pull out the Enneagram book tucked tightly into my leather jacket and see the same circle and lines on the front cover.

Looking up from the book, I exclaim, "This is an enneagram."

Tony comes beside me and says, "Yeu've done yeur homework."

Tony walks around the circle pointing to the lines on the stone floor. "Yes, this island is the symbol of the Enneagram. It is a sphere, a universal mandala. A symbol of unity, wholeness, and oneness. A triangle, rooted in the Law of Three. which was created to help us see beyond binaries and learn to live in harmony with the three forces. This is a hex, a figure symbolizing the Law of Seven, which teaches us that nothing is still or static—that the universe is always becoming something new."

"Okay. So, what does this symbol do? What is the purpose of the island?"

"The Enneagram guides us back to our original essence. I believe this Island was created for training."

"Training?" I say, and enthusiastically start punching the air.

"Like a training ring for one-on-one contact—sword fighting and all that."

"No, not that kind of training. I think it was for soul training—a place to harness the powers of the universe that live within yeurself. It's to teach us how to live and be as we were created to be." Standing almost directly in the middle of the island, he grins wide. "From what I've gathered about yeu and yeur personality, I figure it might be best for yeu to experience it first, before I explain any further. Come stand here in the middle."

I meet him in the middle of the symbol and notice a small ring in the very center of the circle. I stop right at the outer edge when he asks, "Also, how's yeur Latin?"

I reply, "Strange question. My Latin is kind of opposite of my golf game, below par."

Tony chuckles, positioning me into the small circle with two strong hands on my hips. He says, "Good enough. So, there's really only room in the circle for one person. Wait until I get to the bridge before you step into the ring."

Startled by the reality that I will soon be alone, experiencing whatever is to come, I look down at the small ring with trepidation, and say, "Tony, what will happen when I step inside?"

He says, "Also, let me hold yeur stuff. Yeu'll need to be mobile," Ignoring my question.

I hesitate, but then hand him the book and the envelope before removing my leather jacket. He turns and moves swiftly to the bridge.

Over his shoulder he says, "Trust me. All will be well."

He steps off the stone island and onto the bridge.

I stare at him, wondering which of us is more insane.

Tony yells out to me words that I'm assuming are supposed to be helpful.

"Isobel. Lead with yeur soul."

I mumble a quick pep talk to myself to bolster my courage, "Easy enough. Okay, Alex, you can do this. You've always been an overachiever. Just do it, lead with your soul." I step into the circle.

For a long moment, I stand, staring intently at the stone floor anxiously waiting for something to happen. I look back at Tony on the bridge and shout, sarcastically, "I think your training ring is broken."

Tony crosses his arms over his chest and gives me a look that says, "Oh yeu just wait."

I'm about to make another caustic comment about his sanity, of the lack thereof, when the island begins to quake. The circle beneath my feet shakes, then it separates from the island completely and begins to lower me below. I glance up and watch the ceiling move farther and farther away as I sink down into the earth.

The disc I'm now standing on begins to turn clockwise—slowly at first, but the speed increases. Faster and faster it goes, and I lose my bearings—except that I can see that the inner walls are now completely over my head.

At last, to my relief, the spinning slows down and gently comes to a stop. I am now totally disoriented, slightly dizzy, and at least ten feet below the surface of the island.

When the dizzy feeling subsides, I blink a few times and open my eyes. The torches from the cavern above provide only a small amount of light, so I pull out my phone from my back pocket to use as a flashlight.

I shine the light along the walls and discover nine Latin numbers engraved in numerical order, spaced equally apart all except the four and the five, which are placed at a wider distance from one another. Circling slowly, I count my way around the wall and end on the number nine. Below each number are words also written in Latin. I thank the nuns for forcing Latin on me during my exile at Sacred Heart. The Latin on the wall is hauntingly familiar making it easy to translate. I read each word aloud and say its English meaning.

"I. *Ira*. Anger. II. *Superbia*. Pride. III. *Dolo*. Deceit. IV. *Invidia*. Envy. V. *Avaritia*. Greed. VI. *Timor*. Fear. VII. *Gula*. Gluttony. VII. *Libidine*. Lust. IX. *Quod acedia*. Sloth."

Above numeral nine, more Latin words are engraved. ILLE AUTEM APERI MODO. I stumble through the translation of the phrase but figure out a rough English read, "One passion opens way."

One passion. I assume passion is synonymous with sin, which leads me back to the nine sins around the wall. Speaking aloud to myself, I work through the problem in an attempt to solve the puzzle.

"So, which passion do I choose? Tony said lead with yeur soul. So, which of these passions connects with my soul?"

I begin with pride. "Well, this one feels too obvious. I'm a prideful person."

Turning to deceit, I laugh out loud, "Certainly, not this one. Maria says I'm overly honest."

I make my way through envy and greed and decide that those aren't right either. When I get to fear, I pause saying to myself. "Before today, you would've said 'no way' but I am afraid, afraid of turning into the monster inside of me."

Thinking about Scylla reminds me of my spiritual direction session with Agatha. Sitting before her, looking out at the graveyard, holding in my monster, I knew I was afraid, afraid of letting Scylla loose on the ones I loved. I reach out and touch the numeral six with my palm. The island shakes again, and I brace myself against the walls expecting the spinning to start at any moment.

Instead, the numeral six sucks back into the wall and to my surprise freezing water begins pouring out of the opening, filling the small space. The water rises to my ankles before I have a chance to think. I quickly press my palm against the numeral seven nearby, hoping it might stop the water, but the same thing happens—a hole opens and freezing water rushes out like a fire hydrant.

Unwilling to risk trying more numbers I look around for anything that might help me escape. The water is halfway up my legs when I decide to try to shimmy myself up the wall. I immediately stretch out my long arms, place both hands on the wall in front of me, and push my back against the wall. I secure one of my knees on the wall and balance for a moment before lifting up the other one. I'm moving up slowly but slightly faster than the rising water, I crawl up towards the surface. After several minutes, I'm within a foot from the surface, and the water, which is still rising below, is now over halfway full.

The island shakes again. I brace myself and hope with everything in me that I do not fall into the ice bath below. I reach up to the surface just as the island begins to spin. This causes me to lose my grip and fall. My body cannonballs into the chilly pool and I sink deep into freezing water.

Seconds pass before I pop up for air in time to watch the walls descend back down to their normal position. The inner circle with me on it rises back to the surface, and this forces the water to rush up out and over the lip of the island.

Soaked to the bone, I sit with my knees pulled to my chest—chin quivering, body shaking. Fury and frustration pulse through my icy veins as Tony runs frantically to me.

I spew out, "Lead with your soul, my ass! Thanks for the heads up on the whole freezing water part!"

Tony squats down beside and says sympathetically. "Isobel. I truly didn't know that was going to happen. It's never done that with me."

Still sitting, I take off my boots and dump a puddle of water out of each. The thought of pouring them on Tony's head crosses my mind, but I decide I will need his shirt after I remove the layers of potential hyperthermia causing clothes from my skin. To ease my anger, I mock him with a very poor attempt at a Scottish accent.

"*Truly* yeu say. *Truly!* Yeu *truly* didn't know. One passion opens way. Well, how the hell was I supposed to know which passion to push. Anger. It was probably number fucking one!"

I peel off my socks as Tony continues his apology, "I've been in that thing several times now and never got wet. Yeu must have chosen the wrong passion. I thought yeu read the book on the enneagram and knew yeur number."

To his good fortune, wringing my socks kept my hands from ringing his neck.

"No, I did NOT choose the right passion. I picked fear which obviously is not my problem or passion or sin or whatever the hell it means. If murder was on the list, I would've chosen that. And when was I supposed to read the book? It was given to me by Agatha, today. Perhaps I could've found time at the funeral home before the Laine brothers showed up. No, maybe I should've taken a few more hours in the tunnel to read before my torch burned out. Maybe the two hours I spent unconscious from you knocking me out with my own bloody church door would've been better spent reading."

I rise to my feet, my body shaking uncontrollably. I turn around and pull my soaked, super absorbent sweater over my head, which causes my wet hair to dangle like dreads over my face.

I twist the water out the sweater and add with a shuddering jaw, "Tony, I'm going to need your shirt. I've got to get out these clothes off before my body temperature drops any lower."

Tony still doesn't respond.

"Tony, seriously. I'm not walking out of here naked."

I look over my bare shoulder at Tony who is staring intensely at my bare back. He moves towards me like a zombie and slowly unbuttons his flannel shirt. Afraid there might be a serious cut or scrape on my back, I spin my body around feeling my skin with my hands.

"Oh God, did I cut open my back? I don't see or feel any blood."

Tony puts both his hands on my shoulder and turns me around so that my back is towards him. His touch feels like a hot shower after playing in the snow all day.

He says softly, "No, Isobel, yeu aren't cut. It's yeur tattoo."

I feel embarrassed forgetting about the large ink work I had done when I was eighteen. It was a year after I caught Alan Laine with the teenage girl—a year after I was accused of attempted murder—and one year after I moved into a dorm at Sacred Heart. I researched the monster Scylla, the Greek monster my mother told me about as a child, the monster I see in the eyes of others, the same monster I now know lives within me.

"Scylla." I say shortly, my body shaking a bit less from Tony's warm blanket like hands on my arms. "Ya, I got her tattooed on back when I was eighteen."

Tony releases his right hand from skin and traces his fingers along my back outlining the six dragons heads of Scylla.

I feel insecure and fill the silence with words. "I'm still not quite sure why I decided to wear this monster permanently but then again, I was eighteen. I know. It's hideous."

After tracing each piece of the monster, he spreads his large palm over my back. The heat radiates out of his hand throughout my body and thousands of goosebumps pop all over my flesh.

"Isobel," he begins softly. "It's beautiful. Come here let me warm you up."

With one smooth motion he spins me around, pulls me close, and cradles my back. His shirt is fully unbuttoned, and I can't help but wrap my arms around his waist and press my body against his chest. He wraps his shirt around me like a jacket, which encloses me in his warm flesh. My cold, wet jeans keep my hormones locked down, which allows me simply to enjoy the heat of his skin, the tenderness of his touch, and the cozy womb of his affection.

Once my shivering stops, I release my grip and say with gratitude. "Thanks." I take a step back and add, "That was... efficient."

Tony laughs, takes off his shirt, and hands it to me. "Yeu're welcome my bonnie lass."

I blush, turn around, put on his shirt, and button it all the way up before removing my jeans, which are becoming stiff around my legs. My promise to Maria enters the forefront of my mind, and I chuckle to myself as I put on my leather jacket and pick up my wet clothes.

We start toward the bridge to the wooden track.

Tony asks, "What's so funny?"

"Well, I confessed to Maria earlier at the bar the whole tunnel incident."

"Yeu did? Yeu told her everythin'?"

"Well, no. I might've left out a few details here and there. I basically told her that I kissed you and—"

Tony interrupts, "And that yeu felt bad about it and needed to confess yeur sins." He steps in front of me, turns and stops me in my tracks. A scowl on his face, he says, "Is that right?"

My heart leaps into my throat. "Well, yes. I feel bad, and yes, for me it is a sin, or it could have led to a sin. But just because I feel bad doesn't mean I didn't love every moment of it."

His mouth breaks open into a wide grin. "Love. Yeu loved every moment?"

Caught off guard by my own words, I feel Scylla stirring in my stomach. "No, that's not what I meant." I say and step around him in an effort to reach the large wooden door.

Tony races ahead of me, beats me to the door, and blocks the way with his arm. "But that's what yeu said. Yeu must of meant it."

"Okay, you're right. I did mean it. And yes, I did love kissing you. Alright. Let's go."

He doesn't budge—stands firmly in front of the doorway. "So, tell why were yeu laughin' earlier?"

I sigh. "Because I promised Maria if I came down here with you, I wouldn't kiss you again. And now I have to explain why I'm soaking wet and all my clothes are off, why you're half naked, and why I'm wearing your shirt with nothing else on but my underwear. So, anyway, at least I figure, hey, I kept my promise."

Now Tony laughs. I push him aside from blocking the doorway and step into the dark tunnel.

Still cackling to himself, he pulls out his flashlight and says, "Come on. Let's get out here."

I follow him back through the tunnel and wonder about the logistics of walking into the bar with Tony, shirtless, and me, pantless.

We get to the ladder, but before we climb up to the tiny room, I make the best decision for both our sakes.

"Wait. Tony."

He turns around from the ladder and looks at me.

I squirm a bit in the light of his flashlight. "I've got a plan. You're going to leave me here and go up alone. I'm going to give your shirt back so you don't give Baloo the wrong message. Also, with your, uh, muscles, I mean, your build, you'll draw too much attention to the hidden door. If you'll bring me back one of your shirts, I can at least put on my boots and leather jacket and make this look like a flannel fashion statement."

Tony points the flashlight down on the ground, giving the tunnel a soft glow. He speaks slowly in a tone that suggests my plan is ridiculous and doesn't make sense. "So yeu're telling me, I'm goin' leave you down here all alone with nothin' on but yeur pretties. No, fuckin' way, lass."

"First of all, my pretties? What century are we in? Also, it's our best option."

He shakes his head in frustration. "No, it's not. That's a terrible idea. How about yeu go on up the ladder with yeur flannel fashion statement and I wait down here for yeu to bring me another shirt."

It never occurred to me for him to stay behind. It takes a moment or two for the idea to sink in, and Tony steps closer to me.

As if reading my mind, he says, "Yeu never thought of that, did yeu now? Yeu know why? Because yeu're always trying to be the hero. It must be tirin' for yeu feel you have to sacrifice yeurself for everyone else all the time."

Tony takes another step and stands inches from me. The glow of the light creates a sun-kissed bronze color on his skin and it chisels the outline of muscles from his pecks to his abdominals.

I gulp, and he adds, "Isobel, for once, let someone else take the punch."

A deep growl echoes in my gut. I put my hand over my stomach to silence the noise.

Tony smiles. "Hungry again?"

"Yes, but not for food. Yeu can't stand that close to me looking like that without… without" I hesitate trying to choose my words without sounding insane, but then another voice speaks so clearly I can't tell if it came from inside my head, or a few feet away.

"Without getting fucked!"

"Shut up!" I shout and shake my head. So much for not looking insane.

Tony takes a step back, and I keep my body from lurching towards him. "Is it safe to assume yeu weren't talkin' to me?"

I drop my wet clothes on the floor, and quickly put on my boots. "Safe. Not at all. And yes, I was not talking to you."

"Scylla? Yeu were talkin' to her?"

A growl comes out of my throat this time and echoes in the tunnel. "Yes. Earlier, you did call her beautiful. That probably didn't help."

I put my boots on, and push past Tony to the ladder. "Okay, let's go with your plan. I'll be back as soon as possible."

I grab hold of the iron steps and Tony comes around me with the flashlight in hand. He wedges his body in the tight space between the stone wall and iron ladder.

"Wait. Isobel. Are yeu goin' to be alright?"

"Yes, I just need to go before I hurt you." I climb two steps before Tony stops my hands on the bar. We now stand eye-to-eye, but I force myself to look away.

"Isobel, look at me."

I keep my head turned; Scylla screams in my head, "Look at him. Look at him!" My head turns against my will, and I shut my eyes. It takes all my willpower to keep my eyes closed and my body stoic.

"Isobel. I'm not afraid. She won't hurt me. Let me talk to her."

My eyes pop open. From the look on Tony's face, I can tell, my pupils are enlarged and Scylla is out.

Tony speaks in the language of his ancestors. Strength in his voice, Gaelic flows from his lips as he holds my gaze. Tears roll down my cheeks and I feel weak, but I dare not lose my grasp on the bars.

His sea green eyes burn bright. They blaze like fire into mine, and he whispers, "Bi bòidheach - bi nad charaid don uilebheist agad."

His words ease the tension in my body and I feel Scylla settling down as continues, "Leig le do chridhe fhosgladh - gràdh a-rithist is a-rithist. Sàbhalaidh do dhialas an saoghal."

My heartbeat slows to a steady pulse and the churning in my stomach stops completely. I close my eyes and inhale a long deep breath. Tony strokes the knuckles of my hands which cling tightly to the rail.

I open my eyes and say, "How'd you do that? What did you say?"

His hand moves from my knuckles to my face, stroking the line of my chin with his fingertips.

"I just told Scylla who's boss, that's all."

He winks at me playfully, but I know by the look in his eyes that he had spoken sacred words, evoking a power that exists beyond time.

I decide now is not the moment for a million questions. I reply, gratefully, "Well, whatever you said, thanks. I feel much better."

Moving my hand to the next iron rail above, I say in my best terminator impression, "I'll be back."

I ascend to the door above and to my surprise, Tony has the flashlight in his mouth and is climbing up the other side of the ladder.

"Tony, what are doing? You said you would wait down there?"

He mumbles with his mouth, "No reason to wait down there. I figure, after yeu go through the hidden door, I'll wait up inside the room. I also thought yeu would appreciate me not standin' at the bottom of the ladder lookin' up at yeur pretties."

I can't help but laugh at the word "pretties" as we ascend to the top. I stop at the end of the ladder and say to him, "True, I certainly wouldn't want you down there looking up at 'mi pretties'."

Tony hands me the flashlight, gives me a curious look, and says, "Also, yeu promised Maria yeu wouldn't kiss me, but I figure yeu never said anything about me not kissin' yeu."

Before I can protest, Tony wraps one large palm around my neck, leans his grinning face between the rails, and kisses me hard on the lips. My heartbeat quickens, but before I can react, he vanishes, sliding down the edge of the ladder to the floor like a fireman. I'm left stunned, clinging to an iron ladder.

It takes a moment, but I collect my wits, and yell down the ladder, "Cheap shot Tony. I'll get you back for that one."

Out of the darkness below, I hear him say, "I would be disappointed if you didn't."

I pull myself through the narrow door above and slip into the dark room. Before closing the hatch behind me, I leave the flashlight turned on and drop down into the tunnels.

I bellow out, "Heads up, Tony!"

A loud thud and a groan from below brings a smile to my face. I half-heartedly respond, "Sorry 'bout that!"

Coming from below, I realize a Scottish sailor has replaced Tony and is spewing profanity. I close the door and make my way back out to the bar wearing the sweet grin of vengeance.

25: The Individualist

The next three months are busy and extremely cold. Christmastide ends with snow showers and below zero temperatures. We have only a few weeks of ordinary time before the forty days of Lent and seven days of Holy Week begin with Passion Sunday and end with the arrival of Easter morning.

For three months, I do my best to find a steady rhythm of spiritual direction, enneagram study, and soul training on the Island of Essence while also juggling all the regular ongoing church work. Sundays are full of services and confessions. Our attendance increases dramatically with the publicity—and I recall the age-old public relations mantra, "I don't care what you say about me, just keep talking." Maria and I have made a big splash on social media: a priest as a murder suspect and a priest in training kidnapped and rescued by Louisville's newest police hero, Officer Laine.

My Mondays through Thursdays are spent with the usual priestly duties of hospital visitations, funeral and memorial services, church administration, committee meetings, Bible Studies and the mundane madness of everyday ministry needs such as toilets overflowing and boilers breaking down.

Detective Marcus is in attendance at every service I do at Barley Brother's Funeral Home to make sure Keith and I aren't harassed by members of the KKK. For quite some time, I don't notice anyone suspicious—it's not until after the fifth service when Marcus points out a man posing as a relative. One of Keith's three other older brothers, Joseph, Timothy and Christopher Laine consistently show up and sit on the back pew of the chapel during each service I conduct. I'm comforted that Keith's arm and face mend quickly, but I decide to keep my distance from him at the funeral home, hoping his brothers will leave him alone.

I stay busy, and Maria fills most of her time studying and preparing for her final priest exams, which are scheduled to take place the Monday following Easter. These tests will determine whether she can take her vows in December. She's already invited her family from Texas to come for Christmas, hoping that stepping into the role of priest might build a bridge back to her father.

One evening, I come home and find Maria on the couch, crying, after an upsetting phone call. Her mother told Maria that she won't travel to Kentucky without her father, and that her father has no interest in coming for Christmas.

I sit beside her, hold her close, and say, "Maria. You won't be alone when you take your vows. I'll be there. Tony will probably come—maybe even Marcus. I wish you'd been present when I took my vows because then all the family I will ever need would have been present."

Without a word, she tilts her lips to my forehead and kisses me with gratitude. I turn on a chick flick and pour us both a large pour of bourbon. We huddle together on the couch under a big quilt and spend the rest of the evening like sisters.

Even with all the chaotic affairs of clergy life, I somehow find time to focus on Enneagram work. In the early hours of the morning, I research and read anything and everything on the Enneagram including the book I received from Agatha. Considering my recent inner turmoil with Scylla I decide to see Agatha for spiritual direction every Friday and meet up with Tony on Friday nights for spiritual training at the island of Essence. My morning sessions with Agatha make my soul training with Tony easier in the evenings.

During spiritual direction, Agatha guides me through the work of self discovery and soul reflection of the enneagram readings. Each session begins with Agatha creating space for me to process my findings and to give time and energy for Scylla to emerge.

Typically within five minutes, Scylla enters the room with her normal intensity, but after several moments of holding Agatha's hand and breathing deeply, she settles down, letting her six tenacles float like seaweed around me. Agatha guides me, as Virgil did Dante, down into the seven layers of my childhood hell. When I'm with Agatha, I feel comfortable giving Scylla more freedom to come out, rather than trying, often regrettably, to stuff her in the closet of my soul. Even with Tony, Scylla becomes more cooperative.

* * *

After each hour with Agatha, I return to the cottage. In the monastic study of bedroom, I devour books about the ancient wisdom of the enneagram, which prepare me for my training in the evening.

My first few sessions with Tony are more challenging than I'd like to admit. It's as if I'm trying to find my sea legs on a ship in the middle of a storm. I struggle to choose my passion and to discover my deadly sin in the form of a Latin numeral in the inner circle. I know both Agatha and Tony have a good guess concerning which number I fall into, but it takes me all of January and half of February to locate my true passion.

After lengthy research, my knowledge of the Enneagram grows, and I begin understanding the three triads: the head, heart and gut. At first, I think I'm somewhere in the head triad, maybe a five —greed, or a seven—gluttony. From the ice bath of failure in the first round in the ring, I know I'm not a six—fear. But five—greed—is the passion of people who prefer observation and objectivity. They hoard both their energy and their time for the sake of learning and gathering as much information as possible. Agatha says these people are the Albert Einstein's and Stephen King's of the world. Considering my love of reading and learning along with my constant irritation with humanity, it seemed to me that five is a good guess, but this passion was painfully ruled out in the second round of training on the island. That night I pulled myself out of the inner ring before the spinning began.

This time, however, the island swirls me around on its surface like a merry-go-round with no handlebars, gravity flings my body, and plunges me down into the icy rapids. Luckily, Tony fishes me out before my body is pulled beneath the bridge and out into the underground rivers of the cave.

Later, at the bar, Tony informs me that he is five which explains how he managed to get into the ring without ever experiencing the water obstacle. Fives think and think and think before acting. He studied the enneagram for six months before stepping into the inner circle, and he knew exactly which passion to push.

I, on the other hand, learn through doing—act first, think later. I ask him what happens when your passion is chosen correctly.

He answers me with a beer in his hand and with the stubbornness of a catholic nun, "Isobel, the Island of Essence is about self-discovery, combining the study of psychology with the practice of spirituality. No one can tell yeu who you are, yeu must discover that truth from within. I do have a theory that the Island dishes out a different experience for each person—which means, I cannot answer yeur question."

Two Fridays later, my next attempt is number seven. Agatha leads me to believe this could be a good possibility, considering gluttony would fit well with my personality. I devour life with a gluttonous fervor and desire adventure coupled with high intensity.

Back down in the inner circle, I push "VII." Fortunately, I am prepared, dressed in quick-dry running clothes. The frigid water comes gushing out once again. I crawl out of the tunnel and hold on with all my strength to the edge of the inner circle, but the spinning is too intense, catapulting me back into the river.

Upon further reflection at the bar with Tony and after several glasses of bourbon, I'm not a seven at all. For one, people in this number are overly optimistic, constantly consuming positive energy and avoiding pain. I thrive on pain, plus stress and chaos wake me up, sharpen my senses and my physical abilities.

Friday nights when I'm not being washed out to sea by the Island of Essence, I explore the tunnel system beneath the city. For hours, Tony shows me the tunnels and where many of them lead. I learn the way to St Luke's and to the Barley Brother's Funeral Home. The passageway between the bar and church takes about thirty minutes, and it's twenty minutes from the church to the funeral home. Returning to the bar from the funeral home takes forty minutes, and along the way, we discover more tunnels leading to different locations around the city. I mark each ladder with a different ribbon to keep track of where each location is in relation to the world above.

As we navigate the tunnels, Tony tells me stories of Al Capone and other notorious bootleggers who would use the tunnels of Louisville to flee from authorities. Tony's bar was one of the central hangouts and a club for criminals like Capone.

In the dead of winter, I find myself running the tunnels like Capone. After half an hour with the punching bag beneath the sanctuary, I take the ladder down and run with a cave diver flashlight around my head.

One other Friday night in the tunnel systems, Tony takes me thirty minutes further west, past the funeral home. We stop at another iron ladder, which leads up and out to a dungeon-like basement right beneath Churchill Downs.

Under the cover of darkness, Tony and I sneak around the famous horse track, and I confess to him that I've spent my entire life in Kentucky and have never been to the Derby.

Back at the bar, Tony makes us both a mint julep and promises to take me to the Derby races in May.

I manage to keep my commitment to Maria during my time with Tony—the vow that I would not kiss him again. However, this doesn't keep Tony from kissing me. Tony seems to have a way of bending the rules, especially those that came from institutions like the Church. In no way does he feel that I am breaking any promises or vows if his lips initiated the kiss.

The nights of soul training in the ring consistently trigger the aggression of Scylla, which always leaves me on edge at the end of each session—my instincts raw and intense. My adrenaline escalates like electricity in the water as the rush of freezing river washes over me. I do my best not to devour Tony with brutal words or sexual hostility. I simply ignore him the moment I get out of the water and storm straight to the large wooden door.

I walk briskly down the tunnel and try desperately to calm down Scylla before returning to society. Tony keeps his distance, following a few feet behind me, and does not say a word. He knows that we will debrief later at the bar. When I reach the top of the steps, however, Tony is right there with me, looking into my eyes on the other side of the iron ladder.

He addresses Scylla floating around me and repeats the same Gaelic words, "Bi bòidheach - bi nad charaid don uilebheist agad. Leig le do chridhe fhosgladh - gràdh a-rithist is a-rithist. Sàbhalaidh do dhialas an saoghal. "

Those sacred words inevitably ease the fire in my body, settle my stomach, and Scylla retracts back into my flesh. Then Tony's warm hands take hold of my face, his sea green eyes peer into the wounds of my soul, and he speaks to me softly, saying, "Isobel, yeur passion will save the world."

Then his lips press against mine, firm and intoxicating. I keep my body stoic, clinging tightly to the rails, but the moment I motion to kiss him back he slides down the ladder, waiting for me to exit to the room above.

Tony pushes my vow to the limit until the night I break them. The night I discovered my passion.

* * *

To my surprise, after a few months Scylla is willing to work with me, responding to Agatha as she pokes and prods at the wounds formed by my father's physical abuse, my violent nature at school, and the Baptist pastors I listened to each Sunday. The hardest and deepest laceration always oozes towards the end of the session—my mother's disappearance and death, which remain tender and sore open wounds.

Agatha senses my pain and the tension in Scylla each time I say my mother's name aloud. But instead of coming at me directly, Agatha takes a different approach. One session she asked me to draw a picture of my mother on a piece of paper, and then to burn it over a candle. Another time, we walked through the graveyard of sisters just outside the room.

One Friday morning, Agatha and I sit with coffee in hand letting the silence fill the space. Before Scylla makes her debut, Agatha puts down her mug and removes her headdress. For thirteen years, I have never—not once—seen Sister Agatha's hair. To my surprise, her long, pure white, hair cascades down over her shoulders all the way down to her elbow. Without a word, she reaches into her habit and pulls out a large silver medallion, which is hanging on a chain around her neck. She unhooks the latch and holds out the round pendant in the palm of her hand. I choke on my coffee the moment I recognize the large symbol engraved in the middle. It's a swastika.

"Agatha," I say with equal parts anger and fear. "Why do you have the Nazi symbol around your neck?"

Agatha places the medallion on the coffee table in front of us. She says sternly, "Child, this is not a symbol of the Nazis. I, of all people, would know the difference." Her tone softens as she continues. "This is an ancient symbol, thousands and thousands of years old. The swastika is an Eastern symbol used by the Hindus and Buddhist, by the Ancient Greeks, and also the Druids and the Celts of Scotland.

My curiosity is aroused and lean towards her. She pauses to sip her coffee, and I pick up the necklace and examine it. The weight of it indicates it must be pure silver. I rub my thumb over the engraving and realize, to my embarrassment, that the direction of the lines are opposite those of the infamous symbol used by Hitler.

The symbol is surrounded by the Celtic knots. I flip the medallion over and see that the silver piece is composed of three layers that have been compressed together. With the pendant in my right palm, I turn the face like a dial, clockwise, and watch the lines of the swastika shift into another symbol, a pentagram.

I say, with sarcasm, "Well, this keeps getting better."

Agatha smiles and says, "Turn it clockwise."

I do as she says and twist the medallion to the right. The lines in the middle of the star rotate forming a symbol recently introduced to me, an enneagram.

I say, "Of course. Why not? This symbol pops up everywhere these days."

I look up at Agatha, several questions racing around my mind, but before I can ask any of them, she says, "This pendant was given to me for safekeeping thirteen years ago."

I sit up straight, confused by her words.

Agatha puts her coffee mug down and places both her hands over my right palm, which is holding her family heirloom. She stares at me with glistening eyes and continues, "Isobel, this medallion was your mother's. She sent it to Father Anderson a year before you came to live here at Sacred Heart."

I stand up and hover over her, and her words sink in. Scylla comes out, thrashing about like live electrical wires in the middle of a storm. The pendant burns like a hot coal in my hand, causing me to drop it on the rug. Agatha, who appears under hindered by my reaction, stares up at me from her chair, sympathy in her eyes.

I feel myself losing control and step around the coffee table towards the window. I stare out in the graveyard, inhale through my nose and exhale slowly out of my mouth. A full minute passes before I turn around and speak to Agatha.

My voice is low, almost a growl, "Why is it that the people I've known the longest, those few human beings in the world I trust, feel the necessity to keep information like this from me?"

Before Agatha can respond, I quickly add, "And if you ask me 'where do I see God?' I'll walk straight out that door and ring the neck of Father Anderson."

Agatha picks up the French press and pours more coffee in each of the two mugs on the table. She picks up her mug and motions for me to sit down. Begrudgingly, I move back to the couch, Scylla bouncing around me like untied shoelaces. Plopping like an angry child on the cushion, I grab my coffee and signal to Agatha to start talking.

She slowly brushes her long hair behind her and replies in a soft, neutral tone. "When Father Anderson brought you here, he gave me this necklace and a letter your mother wrote with specific instructions."

Agatha reaches over to the side table, pulls open a small drawer, and removes a white envelope. She turns, hands it to me, and says, "This was the letter that came with the pendant."

I put down my coffee and open the envelope. I find two hand-written letters, one addressed to Father Anderson and the other addressed to me. The first letter is short, only a third of a page. The date reads, October 31, 2010, a few months before her death.

Father Anderson,

I trust you know my daughter well. You have advocated for her when no else would and for that I trust you. Please give her this medallion and letter only when she is able to see her shadows. Thank you again for watching over Isobel. I'm eternally grateful.

Charlie Wayland

The second letter has the same date but is addressed to me.

My Darling Isobel,

I pray that when you read this forgiveness will brew in your heart. I'm sorry I left you so many years ago. I've alway been an individualist, unique and special, and my shadow is constantly pushing and pulling the ones I love. My emotions have often gotten the best of me, and now I've had watched you grow from a distance. I've found refuge here in the land of my people. My family in the highlands doesn't know that I've returned. I stay hidden in the shadows for my safety and most importantly yours. I've met a young lad at a nearby pub. He's a student at the school and the son of a preacher. I wish you could meet him. He's like you. He's not afraid of monsters. Know that I love you and that I'm proud of you. I know now my time here is short. I trust that one day I'll see you in the great mystery beyond, but until then, be brave—befriend your monster. Let your heart break open—love again and again. Your passion will save the world.

Life of my life, love of my love,

your Mom

P.S. This pendant was passed down from my great, great grandmother. I've been told she, too, had fiery hair.

A stream of tears cascades down my cheeks dripping down my neck to my lap. I remain hunched over reading the letter over and over. The pit in my gut expands, widening the cavern of my grief. Everything in my life is colliding, the past crashing into the present. Worlds separated by space and time are aligning. The mention of Tony and monsters. The acknowledgement of her coming death. The last line, the same words Tony speaks to me on my way out of the tunnels. "Your passion will save the world."

Holding the letter and the pendulum, I close my eyes and feel the strength of my mother, the presence of an ancient spirit. I take in a long, deep breath and exhale, and sit up straight. I look across the room at Agatha and speak with determination.

"I have more work to do."

* * *

That night of soul training on the Island, I stand once again in the inner circle, but this time, I wear my mother's medallion around my neck. After finishing the enneagram books, and after two months of training and spiritual direction, I eliminate the head triad; five, six and seven and the heart triad; two, three and four—pride, deceit and envy. With this knowledge, I focus on the gut triad; one, nine and eight—anger, apathy and lust. The gut triad or the instinctive triad should've been the place where I started—considering that every action, every decision and life choice I make comes from my gut.

Number one, the passion of anger is likely the best and obvious choice. Down in the inner circle, I push in the stone number

"I." To my dismay the water spills out of the gaping hole as it's done previously with numbers six, five and seven but this time instead of scrambling to the top, I try a new approach. I do nothing. I wait patiently and let the water fill up the narrow space. It takes every ounce of discipline I have to simply be, and to remain still as the icy baptistery fills up. The water rises up my legs, passes my shoulders and covers my head.

I'm submerged, holding back the tension of fight or flight. The water rises several feet above my head, and I float at the bottom, watching the waves splash up and over the top edge.

Like a scuba diver without an oxygen tank, I remind myself that the moment I climb out, the island will spin me out into the river. Tired of doing the same thing and expecting the same results, I hold my breath, waiting to see how the island will respond. My stubborn curiosity keeps me down in the well of the inner circle. Soon my head begins to pound, and my lungs burn, but I force my body to relax, expecting and hoping for another secret door to open, or for something miraculous to happen.

Time passes quickly and my body begins spazzing, forcing me to bail on the plan. I push hard off the bottom of the well but in my panic to get to the surface I knock my head against the stone wall, which not only delays my ascent, but I become disorientated.

My body sinks to the bottom, and I feel helpless. All strength and power leaves my body, and I begin to lose consciousness. I catch a glimpse a large snake swim past me, and part of my mind recognizes the creature as one of Scylla heads. It swims towards the wall and pushes the numeral "VIII."

Then the waters suddenly turn into a whirlpool, swirling me

around and around before shooting me up to the surface like a geyser, spitting me onto the island like Jonah and the great fish.

The world turns upside down and I find myself sitting on large stone steps. I glance around and notice the white columns of the Baptist Church, in which I grew up, the one from the photo Tony gave me. Then I see her, my mother looking up at me from the bottom of the steps. She smiles a wide smile. Her dark curls bounce in the breeze. Her arms stretch out towards me, her palms open. She repeats the last lines of the letter.

"Be brave, my daughter, befriend your monster. Let your heart break open. Love again and again. Your passion will save the world."

Then I feel a warm sensation of air filling my lungs and a startling jolt of electricity. I awake out of the darkness of my subconscious mind. I open my eyes and see Tony's face over me, his mouth against mine—his breath is giving me breath. His Scylla, six arm-like eels, extends out of his back digging straight into my ribs, jump starting my heart like a car engine.

Before he realizes I'm now conscious, I wrap one hand around his head and the other hand around his back and pull his chest to mine. Tony is caught completely off guard. He's paralyzed for a brief moment, which opens a window of opportunity. I swing my legs around his waist, twist my body over his, and flip up both in one smooth motion. Now straddling him, his waist between my legs, I look down at him with a wide smile.

I say with gratitude, "Thanks. That was exhilarating."

Tony's eyes grow wide and his eyebrows lift. He takes a deep breath, stares at me and says, "Yes, well, uh, yeu're certainly welcome."

He touches my face and concern floods his eyes. He pushes a wet strand of hair away. "Thought yeu were dead there for a moment."

I take hold of his warm hand, and say quietly, "I think I was, you know, dead, at least for a moment." My right hand touches his lips as I add, "But you, you saved me, Tony. You saved me with your Scylla."

Tony kisses my palm, and his eyes search mine. He says tenderly, "What else would I do? Isobel, I, yeu mean everything to me."

My stomach flutters at his words, and I don't know how to react. I glance back at the inner circle of the island and suddenly remember Scylla pushing the number eight.

I turn back to Tony exclaim, "You know what? I think my dying paid off. My passion is eight. At least that's the number Scylla pushed right before I passed out."

A grin spreads across Tony's face. "What is it? Did you know my number was eight this whole time?"

Before he answers, his left hand takes hold of the back of head and his right glides behind my back and flips his body over mine. The world spins and I find myself on my back once again looking up at Tony, as he straddles my body between his legs. Tony answers my question with his charming grin.

"Yes. I knew yeu were an eight the first day I met yeu five yers ago. And if yeur mother taught me anthin' it's that eights hate to be told what to do, let alone be controlled by someone else."

Squirming beneath him, I respond playfully, "So, you think you know everything about me, is that right?"

Before he can say anything more my right knee kicks up

against his back causing him to fall forward, giving me leverage to swing my body back on top of him.

Now pinned beneath my body, I grin victoriously at the startled Scot and add, "My mother was smaller than me, plus with these long legs I have about thirty pounds of extra leverage."

Tony grabs my hips, tilting me closer to him as says, "Yeu don't have to tell me. I'm fully aware of how yeu're different from yeur mum." His hands slide up my spine as he adds, "Yeu need to know, I was never attracted to yeur mum. She was brilliant, but she wasn't my type. I prefer tall, stubborn women."

My body hovers over his, my lips inches above his mouth, the taste of him beckoning me closer. Instead of kissing him, my hands find their way to buttons of his flannel shirt and my attention turns to the muscles of his chest. I glide fingers from his neck to his chest and slide all the way down to his stomach and the waist of his jeans. Tony's hand combs through the wet waves of my hair as my lower body leans against his. Tony removes my soaked, long sleeve shirt, pulling it up and over my head.

Now, wearing only a sports bra and running shorts, I feel his warm touch glide down my neck to my breast, where Tony's hand stops short. I look down at my chest with concern when I notice his attention is focused on the medallion.

Tony glances up at me, holding the pendant in his palm. He says "I know this necklace. It was your mother's. Where did you get it?"

I answer, my voice wavering, "My mother gave it to me."

"How is that possible? I was sure this was taken when she died or locked up with the other evidence."

I smile faintly as I answer him, "My mother mailed it to Father

Anderson for safe keeping only months before she died. She told him to wait until I could see my shadows before giving it to me. This morning, Agatha gave it to me along with a letter my mother wrote to me."

Tony wraps both his arms around me and pulls me down against him. I melt into his embrace and nestle my face in the bristles beneath his jawline. After a long moment, he lips press against my forehead and move gently down my cheek to the tender places of my neck. Tony's hands begin searching beneath the elastic band of my bra. Soon his large palm locates its destination, and he cups my breast—massages my flesh.

I let out a small groan of satisfaction. My hands pull at the button and zipper of his jeans, and Scylla unfolds herself from my body—she stretches out like wings. I raise up for a moment, press my hands against Tony, and close my eyes in concentration. Focusing my will, I slide back down into Tony's body, and the six arms of Scylla pierce his flesh.

Tony groans with pleasure as electricity zips through my body into his. I lower down to kiss his lips, but before my mouth touches his, his legs twist over my hips, flipping me onto my back. Somewhere in the movement, my bra disappears along with his shirt, and I lay naked, swollen breasts rising and falling beneath his chest. With one hand underneath my head, his other hand slides down my stomach over my hips beneath the fabric of my shorts.

My eyes snap shut with anticipation but before his fingers reach their destination an image of Maria staring at me suddenly flashes in my mind. My body convulses in alarm, and my forehead slams into Tony's face. Immediately his hand yanks out of my shorts, and pinches his nose. Tony groans in pain spitting out Gaelic words I don't understand, and by his tone, they are profane in nature. His words return to English as he looks down at me, confusion, and concern in his voice, "Isobel, yeu alright? What happened?"

I sit up, find my bra nearby, and pull it over my head before I answer, "Sorry. I...I... it was Maria, she...well. her face sorta jumped into my head."

Rubbing my temples with one hand, I give him a side grin, hoping to soften the blows to both his face and to his hormones. To my ease, Tony smiles, sitting back calmly on his heels.

He says, "Yeu know, the first few times yeu came into the bar, I thought yeu were a lesbian. The whole priest thing was hard enough but the thought of yeu not interested in men was fuckin' unbearable."

Laughing, I reply, "So how did you know I wasn't attracted to women?"

"Well, to be quite honest, I'm still not sure yeu aren't attracted to women, but I could tell by watching yeu over the years, how yeur energy shifts when yeu're sexually attracted to someone. I've only noticed it with men and with Maria."

The smile drops from my face, replaced with a sour look. I respond sharply to his observations. "What do you mean with Maria? Do you, do other people think we're together?"

"Don't get upset, Isobel. It's just an observation. And yes, the way yeu look at her, the way yeu watch over her with that ferocious protective stance. People sometimes think yeu're together. And yeu thinkin' about her with my hands all over yeu makes me think there is somethin' between yeu two."

I get to my feet and search for my wet shirt, hoping to leave this conversation behind as soon as possible. Tony stands up, puts on his flannel shirt and continues the conversation.

"Isobel, there's nothin' to be embarrassed about. It's okay if yeu like women and men. Nor am I not upset yeu were thinkin' about Maria, I just wish it wasn't while I was lyin' on top of yeu."

I put on my shirt, make my way across the bridge, and grab my bag of supplies, which includes a towel, change of clothes, keys and my cell phone. I walk along the wooden track to the door, and Tony follows close behind. We head out the door and down the tunnel. He keeps going on about me playing for both teams, and I try to ignore him as best I can. The only time I back down from a fight is when I'm embarrassed or caught off guard. At the moment, I'm both, which makes it impossible to process my feelings for both Maria and Tony. I search my mind for rational and objective answers, and by the time I get to the ladder I turn around to Tony with an answer.

"You're right. I have feelings for Maria. There's something about her that pulls at my gut. I want to protect her, to make sure she's safe, and I felt this way before she was taken at Christmas. I'd die for her, but just so you know I've never wanted her in my bed. Truly. Trust me, I've wrestled with my sexuality for a long time, hoping, wishing, even wanting desperately to be a lesbian, to stop being attracted to men. It would've saved me a whole lot of frustration and madness over the years. When I was a teenager, I kissed and fooled around with several girls trying to will my sexual desires in another direction, but it never worked. I knew by the age of eighteen that being a lesbian was against my nature. I was born a heterosexual woman, and there's nothing I can do about it."

Tony steps towards me and shines the light at our feet, which gives the tunnels a soft luminous glow. He is slow to respond—the tension settles before he speaks.

"Is that why yeu became a priest? So yeu wouldn't have to wrestle any more with yeur sexuality?"

His questions surprise me. No one has ever been so forthright with me on this topic. My response to why I became a priest is often a canned answer like, "to lead God's children into a place of healing and sacred community." But Tony, he sees through me, past my hard exterior somehow peering into my wounds without judgment, without accusation. Staring down at the ground I feel the beating of my heart—a heart that's vulnerable in the presence of Tony.

"Yes. I became a priest hoping it would kill my sexual desires—put to death my lust for intense human connection." Pulling at bits of stone at the nearby wall I add sheepishly, "But some parts of me won't die."

My words bring back the image of the number eight from the inner circle. I became vulnerable when I was submerged in the watery grave, embracing the possibility of death. That's the moment Scylla came out—when my true essence as an eight was revealed. Scylla saved me revealing my deepest passion.

I turn to the ladder with the bag over my shoulder and begin ascending the iron steps to the world above. Tony follows me along as usual on the other side. He meets me at the top, and I wait for his Gaelic benediction. But this time, Scylla is nowhere to be found.

He speaks to me and to me alone. "Isobel, Bi bòidheach. Be brave. Bi nad charaid don uilebheist agad. Befriend yeur monster."

My mother's words flowing out of Tony's mouth tears open my heart. Tears burn in my eyes, and I look away, embarrassed and angry.

His voice grows stronger, "Leig le do chridhe fhosgladh. Let yeur heart break open."

My chest tightens, making it difficult to break. I feel Scylla expanding out of me, and I suck in air through my nose, my hands grip the bars—my knuckles turn white.

Tony takes my face into his right palm, gently guiding my gaze back to him. He continues, his words, fierce with passion, "Gràdh a-rithist is a-rithist. Love again and again."

His emerald eyes glisten in the shadows of the tunnel. The calming seas of his emerald eyes lift from my soul the heavy burden of guilt and grief. My body becomes weightless, and I allow my heart to break open to him. I close my eyes and let go of the ladder completely, but instead of dropping down into the tunnel, I float across from Tony as Scylla's arms steady me in the air.

Tony smiles with wonder and speaks the last words of the letter, "Sàbhalaidh do dhialas an saoghal. Your passion will save the world."

The next moment, I grab Tony's face and kiss him hard on the lips. He leans into my mouth with delight, moving his lips firmly over mine. We kiss for several moments before he pauses, looking into my eyes with a very serious expression.

I say, "Tony, what is it?"

His eyes hold mine, and he says, "I've been wanting to say something to yeu for awhile."

He bites his bottom lip, and I feel my stomach flutter in anticipation of his next words. I'm unsure whether I'm ready to hear

Tony say what I think he is about to say. I grow nervous and sense the return of gravity. My hands release Tony's face, and I step back onto the ladder.

He continues saying, "Isobel, I need you to know that I lo—"

But before he can finish, Tony's interrupted by the ringing of my cell phone, which is in my backpack.

His face contorts and I say with relief, "Sorry. Hold that thought. I guess you can get cell service down here as long as you stand at the top of the ladder."

I reach into my bag and pull out the ringing phone.

"It's Marcus. I should probably answer it."

I answer the phone; Tony leans over and starts kissing my neck in protest.

"Hey Marcus." I greet him trying hard to hold a casual tone while gripping onto the phone and the iron rail as Tony's lips tickle my skin.

"Okay. We'll be back at the bar in a minute... Yes, I'm with Tony... Yes, I'll make sure he brings the evidence."

I hang up and say to Tony, "Thanks for making that conversation as awkward and difficult as possible."

Tony responds with more kisses on my neck and then says, "Yeur the one who answered the phone. Plus, I don't like it when other men interrupt me."

The thought of someone caring enough about me to be jealous makes my heart skip a beat. I grab hold of his shirt, and kiss him hard on the mouth for a long, sensuous moment.

I come up for air, slightly out of breath and say, "Tony, I never took you for a jealous man."

He gives me a wry smile adding, "There's a lot yeu don't know about me, my bonnie lass."

He kisses me again before turning around to the wall behind him. He pulls a stone loose and reaches his hand inside, retrieving the envelope with the pocket journal and photos that Keith Laine gave me almost two months ago now. I crawl up into the hidden room above, and Tony hands me the evidence before he follows me back into the world above.

26: The Investigator

Every Friday night at Ten o'clock sharp, Marcus arrives at the bar, and the three of us meet in Tony's backroom where we devote ourselves to the latest updates and discoveries concerning the investigation.

The journal is our holy grail, the key to bringing justice to the rape of innocent women over the past half century, and to hate crime murders that have taken place all across town—in addition, very likely, to the death of my mother. But building a case against Alan Laine and his sons turns out to be a slow process of in-depth research and thorough documentation. It would take a medieval monk less time to transcribe the entire Bible than it has been taking us to find the name linked to the initials AM.

We have been focusing on the Laine family and have learned that Pastor Alan Laine retired from his most recent church here in Louisville five years ago. He currently lives on the family farm just southwest of the city. Interestingly, his wife died suddenly in a car accident one year after I was accused of attempted murder.

Alan and his wife had four sons—no daughters. Each son is married with children, except for Steve, who is twice divorced. Each generation of Laines has had at least one Baptist pastor, the newest clergy member being Alan's fourth son, Keith.

The Laine farm has been in the family since the early nineteenth century. They currently breed million-dollar horses that race in the Kentucky Derby every year. Information has come to light that the Laine family were prominent slave owners who fought and supported the Confederacy during the Civil War. One night, Marcus enlightens us on a horrifying truth I was never taught as a child in public schools.

Sitting beside me at the bar, Marcus says, "After the Union victory, the Laine family, like many southern slaveholders, was paid reparations of three hundred dollars for each slave they owned. For the Laine clan that was the equivalent in today's economy of six thousand dollars per slave. The family had over two hundred slaves which means they received one hundred and twelve thousand dollars while their slaves were freed with empty pockets."

Stunned by this news I foolishly say, "Well, didn't each slave get a mule and an acre or something."

Marcus replies dryly, "In theory, but most local governments never followed through, and the federal government, including Johnson, who was president when the war ended and the presidents that came after him, never cared enough to enforce the policy. History books seem to leave out a lot of ugly truth. Like how George Washington's teeth, those pearly white teeth seen in paintings, came from the mouth of a living young, black man."

Trying to recover my pride I add, "That's terrible. I can't imagine living in that world two hundred years ago."

Marcus snaps back, "Oh, nothing has changed. The illusion of racism ending has been the greatest magic show the country has ever seen. If racism is dead, reparations from the government would've been made and ivory towers, like that damn Baptist seminary down the road, which were endowed by slave money, would have been torn down long ago."

I now understand why Marcus finds it ironic that the Laine family has burial plots near the great Muhammad Ali at Cave Hill Cemetery. Because of many conversations like this with Marcus, my eyes have been pried open with the pliers of truth—revealing how white I am and how ignorant my country apparently wants me to remain.

We have learned that several members of the Laine family were accused of being linked to brutal acts of violence and hate crimes against African Americans and other minorities during the course of over fifty years. There remains speculation that the Laines reformed, and currently run, the local branch of the Ku Klux Klan. However, no hard evidence has ever been brought forth, and to no one's surprise, not one individual from the Laine family lineage has ever been found guilty by the courts of hate crimes.

For months, we have searched through public records, police documents and even FBI files that we requested on each Laine member, but we are still unable to figure out the meaning of the letters, "AM." We have dug through and determined the initials of every person connected with the last name Laine going back two centuries, but the letters remain a mystery.

Since Christmas, the hate murders have increased dramatically across the city, averaging one a week. One time, a mentally ill white man shot a black man and woman in a grocery store. The national newspapers picked up the story, and the white man confessed to going first to a black church to kill them, but the doors were locked.

Toward the end of March, the hate crime killings stop, and I become optimistic. But Tony and Marcus both believe this is the calm before the storm, and that a larger, more deadly crime will soon occur.

It's Friday night before Psalm Sunday, the final week of March, and I enter the backroom to find Tony and Marcus sitting around the desk, peering over the pocket journal. Before leaving each night, Marcus spends time studying the contents of the journal away from any prying eyes at the police station. I close the door, and Tony hands me a glass of bourbon. I sit on the edge of Tony's bed, sipping my bourbon. Marcus turns to me, and with a straight face says, "Alex. What year were you born?"

I tilt my head to the side and say, "'91, Why?"

Tony shifts in his chair but holds his poker face as Marcus leans over and gives me the open journal. He says solemnly, "Look at the date beside your mother's name."

I take the notebook, hesitate, and glance over at Tony. His eyes narrow. Holding my breath, I read the entry.

Charlie Wayland, March 25, 1991. Good Friday. Drugged and willing.

The first and only time I read words was down in the tunnels right after Christmas. For whatever reason, I couldn't see back then the truth that now stabs my gut like a red-hot poker. I close my eyes and let the journal fall to the floor. My blood boils, my heart rhythm quickens, and my breathing increases. My hand shaking, I dump the rest of the bourbon down my throat. The intensity in my body grows, forcing me to stand. Both Tony and Marcus move towards me. Marcus reaches out to me first, but I push his hand away.

"I'm okay!" I shout louder than I intend. "I just...fuck. I need another drink."

With pursed lips, I hold up my empty glass, and storm out the door. I find a bottle of Angel's Envy on the shelf behind the bar, pour a shot and gulp it down. I begin to pour another as bourbon burns like fire down my throat into my belly. Tony comes up behind me and takes the bottle from my shaking hand, pouring us both shots. Without a word, I see the anger hovering like dark clouds in the whites of his eyes and good and well my own Scylla is brewing within me. We shoot back the bourbon, and I close my eyes as the wave of alcohol washes over me. My hands ball into tight fists, and I do everything I can to keep Scylla from letting her dragon heads loose to destroy everything and everyone around me.

Tony leans his head down beside my face and whispers the soothing sacred Gaelic words he spoke earlier in the tunnel.

"Bi bòidheach - bi nad charaid don uilebheist agad. Leig le do chridhe fhosgladh - gràdh a-rithist is a-rithist. Sàbhalaidh do dhialas an saoghal. "

My fingernails uncoil from my palms, and my hands open up. The seething rage in my bones moves into my eyes. Hot, salty tears stream down my face. Tony wraps his arms around me pulling me close. I bury my head into his chest and weep.

After several minutes, my anger subsides and I take a step back from Tony. He's wearing a tight white, tank top that pulls across the muscles of his chest and abdomen. He has removed his flannel shirt, shoes and socks in the back room because it was getting too hot. I stare way too long at his body and notice him watching me. He stands up straighter and steps towards me with a wry grin.

I'm slightly embarrassed and try to break the awkwardness I'm feeling with sarcasm. "Thanks John McClane. You always know how to rescue the damsel dangling in distress."

Tony's expression shifts to surprise. I explain the joke assuming he doesn't understand my reference. "You know, Die Hard. Bruce Willis saved his wife who's hanging out of the Nakatomi building."

Tony grabs both my arms and laughs way harder than I was expecting. Then he plants a wet kiss on the cheek and cries out with joy.

"Isobel, yeu're brilliant."

Even more confused, I rub the residue of his lips off my cheek, and I ask, "Thanks, but what on earth are you talking about?"

"McClane. The McLaine clan. The Laine family must be from Scottish or Irish descent. They likely removed the Mc like many immigrants did sometime in the eighteenth century."

My eyes widen, and we both race into the back room to tell Marcus.

* * *

Later that night, I find myself lying on the bed in the back-room, curled up against Tony as I try to recall how I got to his bed. A few faint images blur across my mind; the journal of evidence, Marcus sitting at the desk, and lots of bourbon. At some point in the night I remember Tony carried me from the bar to his bed. For a moment, I fear the worst—that I broke my vow of celibacy. I let out a sigh of relief when I notice that all my clothes are still on, all except my boots, which are on the floor by the door. The desk lamp is on across the room, providing enough light for me to look at the time on my watch. Four thirty in the morning.

"Shit," I whisper a little too loud.

Tony stirs, his arm, draped over my waist, pulls me deeper into him. At first, I think he's awake until I hear a snore rattle beside my ear.

Quietly, I slip out of bed and I look at my phone, seeing three missed calls from Maria. Fearing the walk of shame into the cottage, I begin formulating my excuse until I read a text from her.

YOU'RE PROBABLY BUSY OR ALREADY IN BED. NO WORRIES. ALL IS WELL AT THE HERMITAGE. SEE YOU TOMORROW NIGHT FOR DINNER.

I forgot that she's out of town at the hermitage across the river, studying for her final priest exams, which are coming up in two weeks. Sighing with relief, I grab my jacket and boots and tip toe towards the door. I slowly open it, and a loud creek pierces the silence.

"Isobel." Tony calls out to me. "Where're yeu goin'?"

I turn around and reply, "Uh. I'm going home to my own bed. Maria will be worried sick."

Tony sits up and says, "Yeu told me last night she's out of town and won't be back until tonight."

"I did? You're right. I forgot. She won't be home until dinner this evening."

My right hand rubs my forehead as I stare at the floor, feeling guilty for many things—including the lie I just told. Tony gets out of bed and comes to me wearing nothing but his sweatpants.

"Hey. There's nothin' to be ashamed about." His hand sweeps a strand of hair from my face and my eyes turn up to meet his.

"We didn't do anythin' but sleep. We both were too drunk to drive, and I would've made a bed out there in one of the booths, but yeu said yeu didn't want to be alone. I closed the bar around one and we both fell asleep after that."

The events of the evening return me when I see the journal lying open on the desk beside the photos of my mother's murder right next to an almost empty bottle of bourbon. I remember now that my mother was not only raped by Alan Laine, but nine months later, I was born. All the feelings come rushing back and salty tears form once again in the corner of my eyes. Sitting down at the desk, I rub my face with my hands. Soon, my eyes are drawn to the journal on the desk, which is open to the last entry.

Emily McCall, January 7, 2011. Church Office. Pregnant. No condom needed.

I had read this entry before, but this time the date catches my attention. Three photos of my mother sit beside the journal, the one on top is an image of her tied to a stake, flames burning beneath her, soon to consume her body. She's not screaming, crying or even fighting the ropes holding her prisoner. If anything, the look on her face is magnanimous, eyes blazing with power and passion, as if she's about to rise up out of the flames. The date and photo lying next to each bring a strange tingling curiosity at the forefront of mind.

"Tony?" I ask unsure of how to phrase my question. "When did my mother die? What was the date?"

Tony walks in front of me and says, "It was a few weeks after Christmas and New Year's. I'd have to check to make sure but I think it was around midnight on January 7, 2011. Why, what are yeu thinkin'?"

"The date of the last entry is the same date that my mother died. Not that there's any significance connection between these two events. However, that was also the same night I first saw Scylla in another person."

I stand up and hand him the photo of my mother and the journal, which is open to the last entry.

"You remember the story Maria told you about me finding Alan Laine with this pregnant teen."

Tony nods and gives me a confused look.

I continue on with my theory. "Well, hours before I caught him raping her in his office, I was in the church service where he shamed her before the congregation. During that time, I saw Alan's Scylla emerge. I had never thought about why Scylla showed up right then. There were several other moments the monster could have appeared. Why *then?* Why that moment?"

Tony's eyes move from the photo to the journal and back at me. "Yeu think there's a connection between yeur mother's death and yeur ability to see Scylla. What time was the church service?"

"It would've been around six o'clock, and with the time difference between Scotland and Kentucky, her death and the service took place at around the same time."

"That's a truly interesting revelation." Tony exclaims. He gets up and moves towards the desk. "I've never thought of such a connection, or that Scylla could be passed down from one generation. to the next."

Tony sits in the chair and places the journal and photo back on the desk. His eyes focus on the wooden planks of the floor.

I say, "Tony, when did you start seeing Scylla?"

He pauses for a long moment. The tension in the room shifts, and I sense Tony's pain as he hesitates. He keeps his gaze downward. "It was the night my father died. I was twenty-one, drinkin' at a pub. At first when I saw the shadow creature emerge from some guy pickin' a fight with me, I thought it was a delusion, and that I must be very, very drunk. But I soon learned that the monsters were real—as real as the people they come out of. It wasn't until yeur mother's murder that I started seein' my own shadow creature. Now, I wonder if my father saw them too, and his death passed the ancient power along to me."

Solemnly, I ask, "How did he die?"

"The Church killed him." He replies without missing a beat. "He was a Presbyterian pastor for the Church of Scotland. I'm an investigator by nature. I hang in the background and observe life. I watched my father and the non-stop, twenty-four-hour pace of running multiple parishes give him a massive heart attack. I found him in his home office one morning, lying on the floor dead."

Tony turns his eyes to wall as stands up. Then he pivots towards me and looks me in the eye. With tears of sorrow and rage he says, "I couldn't save him. There was nothin' I could do to bring him back. If only I had the power, I have today."

Tony grabs the bottle of bourbon from the desk and takes a large swig. I can see the clouds of Scylla forming a haze around his body, so I take the bottle of bourbon out of his hand. But instead of taking a drink, I put the bottle back on the desk. Turning to Tony, I place my hands on his bare chest, which is heaving with sorrow.

I close my eyes and evoke my own sacred words. "Tony, let it go. You've carried this burden long enough. Don't let your guilt have power over you."

His breathing slows along with the rhythm of his heart. He grabs hold of my hands, and I stare into his sea-green eyes, my palms flat against his flesh. Tony leans down to whisper the words interrupted by Marcus' phone call hours earlier, "Isobel, I love yeu." My breath stops short.

The last time I heard these words was long ago. They were said by the last person on earth I ever thought truly loved me, my mother. My mouth goes dry, and I swallow a large lump lodged like a giant pill in my throat. I step back, my hands drop, and I turn my face towards the door.

"Tony, I—" Tears fill my eyes with grief and my gut turns over with guilt. "I cannot return your love." I say, reaching down to grab my boots. But before I can flee Tony takes my arm.

"Isobel, it's okay," He pleads. "Please, for once in yeur life let someone love yeu just as yeu are, monsters and all."

I keep my eyes down, turn and look at the photos of my mother, helpless and vulnerable, beside the book of horrors. Tony reaches out to the desk and tucks the photos inside the pocket journal.

He says in a soft gentle voice, "Embrace yeur own wisdom. 'Let it go. Don't let yeur guilt have power of yeu.'"

I lean my head back, drop my boots to the floor, and take a deep breath. I let new air fill my lungs. tilt my head forward and breathe out. I study his body from his bare feet up to his furrowed brow.

Finally, I say with determination, "You're right. I need to let go." I push him backwards with both my hands on his bare chest. Tony stumbles to the edge of bed and watches me curiously.

He says cautiously, "Isobel. I didn't confess my love to yeu to simply get into yeur pants."

Standing in front of him, I pull off my clergy collar and untuck my shirt and say, "I know. If that was your intent, you would've done so earlier, when I was drunk."

I undo each button of my black shirt from my neck all the way down to my navel, remove the shirt, and toss it over the desk chair. Tony watches me in silence, and his eyes survey my body with wonder and awe. I turn around and feel his eyes follow my every move. I begin to unbutton my pants and feel his large hand rest softly on the tattoo along my spine. His fingertips outline the dragon heads of Scylla—I let my pants fall to the floor—and his fingers slither down my spine to the dimples below my waist.

Then Tony's grabs hold of my hips and twists me back around. With both hands, I nudge him down onto the bed, straddling my legs over his lap, lowering myself down onto him. My lips find his and the taste of his mouth soothes the last bits of painful memories lingering in my mind. I reach for the drawstring of his sweatpants, but he gently moves my hands to his lips, kissing each knuckle before placing them around his neck. He wraps one arm around my back, using his other hand to move us deeper into the bed.

Tony gently places me onto my back, resting my head against a pillow. His mouth begins at my lips, moving to my collarbone and then down to my breasts. A large strong hand undoes the clasp of my bra while the other pulls it smoothly away from my body. Tony's kisses caress each breast and his tongue circles around my nipples. My eyes squeeze shut as a tiny moan leaves my mouth encouraging him further.

Tony's tongue leaves my breast, sliding down the middle of my stomach, sailing gracefully over my navel. Both of my hands grip the bed sheets as his teeth tug at my underwear. With one hand, Tony glides his fingers up from my ankle to my knee and along the line of my leg. My hips rise in the air and with one fluid motion Tony pulls my pretties down my legs, past my feet.

Now, lying naked and exposed, I pull his face towards mine and say in a demanding tone, "I want you, Tony! All of you."

Tony smiles, kisses me tenderly, as says. "I want you, too. But tonight, Isobel, let me love yeu without givin' yeu more guilt to let go of later. Let me please yeu without yeu breakin' any of yeur vows."

Before I can protest, Tony glides his large fingers up the inside of my thigh, stroking my flesh along the way before penetrating the depths of my being. A groan of euphoria erupts from me, and my body convulses with pleasure. Tony draws every ounce of misery from my body, replacing it with several long satisfying moments of pure ecstasy.

My breath is heavy as both of his hands move back up my body wrapping around my back and neck, pulling me firmly against his bare chest. Cradled like a vulnerable creature in Tony's flesh, I fall asleep, feeling safe for the first time in decades, satisfied, and maybe even truly loved.

27: The Loyalist

The next six days sail by giving me little time to process, or rather to completely ignore the intimate night, naked in Tony's bed. An ice storm comes through on Saturday afternoon trapping Maria across the bridge in the hermitage until Sunday evening, leaving me to handle Saturday evening and Palm Sunday service without her. My workload also doubles at church with preparations for the high holy days of Maundy Thursday, Good Friday and Easter. The first four weekdays, I spend my mornings in hospital rooms and nursing homes giving the Eucharist to those unable to attend mass. The afternoons are consumed in the church building doing extra cleaning, setting up the sanctuary and writing homilies. After each twelve-hour day, I return to the cottage and plop down on the couch with a glass of bourbon neat, no rocks, and sit exhausted with Sam curled up in my lap.

In regards to Tony, I force myself to put all my feelings on hold, including guilt, shame and possibly love in order to get through my priestly responsibilities. Tony tries calling me twice during the week, but I keep ignoring him, hoping he'll know I need time to process, and as a pastor's kid, understand my extremely busy week. On the morning of Good Friday I receive a third text message from Tony which jars me back to last Saturday morning. My phone reads:

HELLO MY BONNIE LASS. WILL I SEE YOU TONIGHT AT OUR USUAL TIME?

My face blushes as butterflies fill my belly. I'm thankful I read the words in the privacy of my room away from Maria who would know the scandals of my heart. My mind returns to Tony's bed. Images flash of his bare body pressed against mine, and I experience the tingling sensations of his hands on my flesh, which return like phantom feelings along with the unforgettable last few moments being held in Tony's arms.

* * *

It's late morning and we both are cocooned together under the wool blankets of his twin bed, breast against breast, nestled like rabbits in winter, snugged tight in the heat of our bodies.

I feel Tony's lips press against my forehead as he says, "Good Mornin' my bonnie lass."

With my eyes still closed, I find his lips in the dark and respond with a gentle, slow kiss. Tony's arm wiggles out of the cocoon of blankets and turns on the lamp nearby. I bury my face in his chest and groan, "Oh God, what time in the morning is it anyway?"

I peak out into the room with one eye at the clock on the wall. To my dismay and no doubt Tony's, I leap out of bed in a panic and the cold stings our bodies.

"Shit!" I say scrambling to find my clothes. "I've got to get back to the cottage. I've got so much to do."

Tony laughs and watches me bounce about as I hurriedly dress.

He finally gets out of bed and says, "Come to bar, let me at least make yeu a cup of coffee before yeu leave."

I put on my boots, gulp down a hot cup of coffee at the bar, and give Tony, who's sitting unhurried and shirtless on a stool, a quick peck on the cheek.

"I must go." I say in a business-like tone. "It's a crazy week, but I promise to come back for more training Friday after our service."

I turn to leave, but Tony grabs my hand and pulls me into his body.

"Isobel," he replies with a deep Scottish accent. "If it'll be that long, m' love, I'll need a better kiss than that."

My face breaks into a side grin and the to-do lists of the week take a back seat for the next few moments. I drop my duffle bag of clothes so that both my hands are free to slide up his thighs, which are straddled around me. I move them up along the soft skin of his stomach, chest and neck. I grab hold of his rugged face and press my mouth against his, locking our lips in a passionate embrace. I feel Tony's large palms on my back move slowly down to my butt. He squeezes me tightly, pulls me deeper into him, forcing a soft moan to escape my lips. Then Tony grabs hold, lifting me up with his strong arms, and places me on his lap. My legs wrap around his waist as his kisses move down to the collar on my neck. As his hands reach for the top buttons of my blouse, my phone suddenly rings and a call from the church keeps us from returning to his bed.

* * *

Standing at the shut door of my bedroom, I'm unable to decide how best to respond to Tony's text. I put the phone in my back pocket, leave my bedroom and see Maria, dressed for the day, sitting with coffee and homemade blueberry muffins at the kitchen table.

She looks up from her book titled, *The Role of Priest in a Postmodern Church*, and asks, casually, "What's your schedule like today? Are you going to see Agatha and Tony as usual?"

I sit down in front of her, reach for the coffee and reply, "Not sure. I've been pretty wiped this week. Agatha told me last Friday that today wouldn't work for her. And Tony—" I pause and try my best to conceal any facial expression or extra voice inflection at the sound of his name. I haven't told Maria about last Saturday morning, nor have I said much about the last six weeks with Tony. After my night in bed with him, my broken promise to Maria seems the least important item in the confessional booth.

I stuff a chunk of hot muffin in my mouth and mumble casually, "He knows I'm busy today. So, what's your day like?"

Maria smirks—she can read me like the book in her hands. Graciously, she tells me about the last bits of studying she's doing for her final exams on Monday, thereby allowing me to change the subject. She offers to help me finish preparations for the Good Friday celebration of the Lord's Passion this evening, but I let her know I've already got everything in place, which will give me time to squeeze in a nap this afternoon after I finish the last few hospital visits of the week.

I finish breakfast, leave Maria to her studies, and go about the work of my day. To my disappointment, my afternoon nap is excommunicated from my schedule when a member has a massive heart attack after lunch. I meet the family at the hospital only moments before the man dies on the table in the emergency room. After several hours with the family, Maria takes over allowing me to rush back over to Saint Luke's at five thirty to finish last minute details for the service. The organist is already practicing and the deacons have finished the last minute set up for me. I hurry back to the tabernacle to prepare the host, the blessed sacrament of the body and blood of Christ. I grab the small pieces of crackers and scurry down the aisle of the sanctuary to the Lord's table.

I make it back to the narthex right at six o'clock when the doors open, just in time to greet people as they flow into the sanctuary and make their way into the pews. My church goers in general are loyalists. They want to believe in systems like church and government, and trust these institutions often with blind loyalty.

Five minutes before seven, Maria rushes through the doors of the Narthex and quickly moves into the sacristy to put on her robe and prepare for the processional. Moments later, the service begins. I take a deep breath and fill my lungs with the peace of Christ.

Robed in red with a gold stole draped around my neck, I enter the sanctuary with my palms pressed together in prayer and ask the parishioners to all stand. I progress up the long aisle in silence passing each pew slowly. Out of the corner of my eye, I see Keith Laine holding a two-year little girl. He's standing beside a tall, beautiful brown skinned woman. This is the first time they have come to St Luke's and the first time Keith, and I have acknowledged each other publicly since John Thompson's memorial service. Seeing his interracial family in my Catholic Church, I now know why the Southern Baptist Laine clan violently burned his branch from the family tree. He smiles at me, and I give him a slight head nod while holding my solemn appearance.

I arrive at the altar and prostrate my body across the floor. The silence is broken by the sound of people kneeling in the pews to pray.

After several long moments, I rise to my feet, address the church, and the parishioners all rise to their feet. I raise my outstretched hands into the air and give the invitation for all to join in prayer. The pianist plays and after several measures of introduction, I begin the prayers of people, lifting my voice through choral singing and chanting on behalf of the God's children before me. Then one of the ordained deacons leads the general intercession, after which we transition to the adoration of the Holy Cross.

Maria stands at the back of the sanctuary with a large wooden cross. I close my eyes and chant the ancient antiphons, *We adore the cross of Christ,* as Maria gives a choral response singing, *Come, let us adore.*

The people stand, Maria lifts the cross high and glides up the aisle to the altar. Moved by the sacred moment of carrying the cross, tears stream down her cheeks. I receive the burden of the cross, raise it high above the congregation and sing *Behold the wood of the cross, that hung the Savior of the world.* Once again Maria responds with *Come, let us adore.*

I lower the cross and two young altar helpers robed in white take hold of each wooden arm. I bend forward and kiss the cross of Christ. Maria follows behind along with all those present in the sanctuary. I stand by the cross and watch, as one by one elderly men and women, parents with small children including Keith, his wife and baby daughter, press their lips against the cross.

The line decreases to the last few folks, and I tilt my head to the side to see which parishioners are bringing up the rear. To my shock, standing behind an elderly woman hunched over a walk is a tall, muscular man, wearing blue jeans, a brown leather jacket over a green, flannel shirt. With a smirk smeared across his unshaved, rugged face, Tony waits his turn to kiss the cross.

I stare for a little too long as he draws near, mindful of the handful of people behind him. His emerald eyes fix on me, as he bends over and touches his lips to the cross—the same lips that still linger on my skin. He pauses momentarily as he passes me by, close enough to my body that his hand brushes against mine as he whispers faintly, "Isobel, m' love." Butterflies flutter in my gut, forcing me to take a deep breath, trying to settle Scylla pulsing through my veins.

The last few people pass through concluding the adoration of the Holy Cross. Maria and I pick up the cross, walk up the steps, and place it in front of the altar, which transitions us to Holy Communion.

Seeing the table, I suddenly realize that I have forgotten to fill the cup of Christ with wine. I turn to Maria, and with our backs to the congregation, I ask her to return to the tabernacle to get the wine.

Swiftly and gracefully, she walks down the side aisle back towards the narthex. As Maria approaches the doors, I notice a tall, white man with golden, wavy hair step out of the pew and follow her out. The lighting of the sanctuary is dim making it difficult to recognize the figure. Distracted by my error and with all eyes still fixed on me, the narthex doors close behind the man, and I am left with a nagging feeling that I choose to ignore. It's not until Maria does not return with the wine that a sense of worry twists in my gut.

Moving on with Holy Communion, I utter the holy words and serve each member the Eucharist without the blood of Christ. Soon Keith stands before me with his arms crossed over chest, signaling his refusal as a non-Catholic. When he bends forward, his golden, wavy hair falls in front of this eyes, and I freeze in horror.

Seeing my paralyzed state, Keith asks in low voice. "Mother Alex. What's wrong?"

My eyes scan the sanctuary for Maria who still hasn't returned from the narthex. I respond urgently, "Your brother Steve is here. He followed Maria out to the Narthex."

Keith immediately whispers in the ear of his wife, who is right behind him, and rushes down the aisle walking briskly back to the Narthex. Tony, standing at the end of the line, notices Keith leave abruptly and follows out the back of the sanctuary in the same abrupt manner. Keeping my eyes glued on the narthex doors, I continue passing out the body of Christ.

Ten minutes pass by before I conclude the service, bow before the altar, recess rather briskly, and return to the narthex.

I step into the large foyer and glance to my left and right out the exit doors. There are no signs of Maria, Tony or Keith. A wave of silent, solemn congregants flood into the space before I have a chance to look outside. To fulfill my priestly duties, I shake hands and give head nods, motioning people to hold the silence as they leave.

Ten minutes go by, and Keith's wife comes out of the sanctuary looking worried and confused, their sleeping daughter in her arms. I approach her and usher her into the sacristy, the small room where the tabernacle and clergy vestments are held.

I close the door behind us and speak in a calm pastoral tone, "Hi. I'm Mother Alex and you're Keith's wife and daughter."

Clutching her child close to her chest, she nods and replies, "Yes, this is Eva and my name is Raquel."

"It's nice to finally meet. I often work with Keith at Barley Brothers, but I'm sure you're wondering what happened during communion. Well, you see Keith's brother—" I hesitate since I don't know how much Raquel knows about her racist, violent in-laws. I don't want to worry her unnecessarily, but before I can continue, Raquel finishes my sentence. "Keith's brothers are white supremists, most likely running the local branch of the KKK. He told me you saw his brother Steve follow your colleague outside. You don't need to worry about protecting me with the hard truth. Keith and I keep no secrets, especially about our families."

Surprised and relieved by her direct approach, I say, "Good. Here's what I know. Maria was kidnapped three months ago, right after Christmas. Although we can't prove it yet, I know it was Steve and the other brothers. Also, the Laine family and I have a long, violent history."

"Yes," Raquel interrupts again. "When you were seventeen, you carved the letter 'A' on his father Alan's forehead after catching him raping a teenager girl. And his family most likely murdered your mother in Scotland."

"Wow. Y'all are serious about that whole no secrets thing aren't you."

"Deadly serious."

"Okay. Well, you're pretty much up to speed then. Why don't you and Eva wait here for a minute while I lock up the sanctuary and make sure everyone's out of the building before we make our next move. Just in case I don't return, let me show you another place to hide."

Raquel sits down on a bench beside the robes and shifts Eva to her lap. I walk over to the far wood paneled wall and push a small section of the molding with two hands. A door springs open revealing the entrance to the basement below, where my punching bag is as well as the entrance to the tunnels that Tony showed me months ago.

Raquel's large hazel eyes glare at me with grave concern. Eva begins to cry and without hesitation, Raquel unbuttons her blouse and pulls out her left breast. Eva latches on to her nipple and Raquel rises to her feet. I smile, impressed and reassured by her confidence. She stands eye to eye with me, breastfeeding her child with one hand and grabbing hold of my shoulder with the other.

"Thank you, Mother Alex, but if you don't return in ten minutes, I'm calling Detective Clay."

I give her an affirming nod and think to myself, "This is my kind of woman."

Exiting the sacristy, I hurry across the narthex to the exit door that leads to the parking lot. There's only one car left, a burgundy dodge minivan that I assume is Raquel's. I close the door, walk across to the other side of the Narthex and peer out the window towards the cottage. The lights are on inside. Just as I begin to open the door, I see two familiar husky men walking around the cottage towards the church.

I whip around, out of view, and hope they didn't see me. Thinking quickly about my next move, I fly through the doors of the sanctuary, race down the middle aisle and up the steps to the Lord's table. The outside doors to the narthex slam close and I leap off the chancel, slipping behind the organ as the doors of the sanctuary bang open against the door stops. A male voice echoes through the silence.

"Mother Alex. We know you're still here. Don't worry. We haven't come for you this time. We just want the nigger woman and the baby."

Crouching down on my knees, my heart pounds in my chest, pulsing angry venom through my veins. I take a deep breath and decide that whatever my next move is, it must be to protect Raquel and Eva. Several scenarios play out in my mind like reels on a projector.

Option one: I fight them here and now, but the likelihood of them carrying a gun is high and they'd probably wouldn't blink twice at putting a bullet in my head.

Option two: I run out the back door and get help. But I'd be leaving Raquel and Eva alone to whatever these sick bastards want with them. This leaves me with option three. Convince them to take me instead.

Before I reveal myself to the Laine boys, I pull out my phone and message Marcus.

ST LUKES. LAINE KLAN HERE. R & E IN SACRISTY.

I turn off the phone, dump it in a nearby plant, stand up tall, and walk slowly around the organ to make my presence known.

"Well, well." I say, voice steady and confident. "It's none other than the racist, cowardly Laine boys."

The two Laine brothers, Paul and Joe are halfway down the aisle when they see me.

"You know, y'all really need to get a day job." I continue in an agonizing tone as I work my way down the side aisle. "Perhaps, some therapy or maybe just a padded room. Prison is probably the best option for murdering kidnappers like you. Don't worry the police will be here any minute."

They stand at the other end of the wooden pews and watch me. Then they both pull out handguns from behind their backs.

"We should've taken care of you a long time ago. What makes you think we won't kill you right here and now?"

Keeping my poker face, I say with a smirk. "Because, your father, whatever slimy hole he's living in, would be disappointed in his loyal sons, for not bringing him the one woman who brought him to his knees thirteen years ago. How's his face looking these days?"

Paul's face turns red, and I can see it swell with fury. He lifts his gun and screams with rage. I duck behind a pew as several bullets come my way. Chips of wood from the pew splinter into the air. The firing stops and Joe, irritated with his younger brother, says, "She's right! We can't shoot her. Paw wouldn't want it. Besides, she deserves to burn like her mother."

He continues his taunt as they make their way towards me, shuffling their large bodies between the pews. "I want to hear her scream like her whore mother. And did she scream and moan as those flames consumed her naked body. Hmmm. What a waist. She was a hot piece of ass."

My eyes narrow with rage and an electric current buzzes through body, raising the hairs on my skin. I feel Scylla growing out of me as the brothers make their way closer to me, moaning sexual torments. By the time they reach my end of the pew, I spring to my feet, Scylla is out with all six slithering arms poised like cobras ready to strike.

Standing still, giving the appearance of paralysis, I realize neither brother has the ability to see the monster posed for attack, which gives me the advantage of surprise.

Unaware of the monster in front of them, Joe steps within arms reach. Scylla whips two of her heads wrapping around his wrist and the dragon mouths latch onto this arm. Joe tries to raise the gun with his hand, but his hand is shackled. Shock and confusion spread across his face, and his hand shakes violently, forcing him to drop the gun. Following Scylla's lead, I give Joe a solid right hook to the face, which causes him to fall back into the pew.

Paul, observing his older brother with frustration, quickly steps over and lunges towards me. But Scylla swings another arm like a lasso, wraps a noose around his neck, and drags him over the back of the pews headfirst into a kneeling bench.

Joe pulls himself up, face bloody, fists in fighting position. I cross my arms with a wide smile and let Scylla loose. Two tentacles rope around his waist and pull him towards me. A second before Joe slams into me, I step to the side just in time for his body to crash into the brick wall behind me. Laughing in amusement I give Scylla a double high five.

I applaud her saying, "Well, done! We've done some good work these past few months."

Then suddenly all six heads of Scylla twist around in the direction behind me. Before I can react, a pain shoots into the back of my head and the world goes dark.

28: The Enthusiast

Sometime later, I open my eyes and see only darkness. My head thumps like a bass drum in my ears. After several blinks, a faint light flickers in the distance along a wall, which helps me orient myself to the surroundings. My body sits on a cold, stone floor still wrapped in the red robe from the service earlier. There are shackles digging into my wrists and around my ankles just above my oxford shoes. I sit up slowly and search the dimly lit space. Stalagmites protrude like daggers nearby, and I realize I'm beneath the earth, most likely in one of the caves under the city.

A few feet away on my right, two figures are huddled together. One person appears to be sitting cross legged on a pile of cloth, and the other is curled in a heap, half of their body hidden under something black. Squinting, I adjust my eyes and recognize the wavy, long hair of a woman. Maria, wearing the black clergy robe, is unconscious beside a person so bloody I can barely make out his face, let alone who he is.

"Alex, it's Keith," he says in a raspy, hoarse voice. He coughs and clutches his side. "Where's my family?"

I scoot closer to him across the cold stone as far as my chains will allow. I speak in a low voice, unsure who might be listening.

"They're safe. Trust me. I hid them away before your brothers came inside the church."

"Thank you, Alex." He says gratefully. "I owe you my life."

Looking down I notice the area beneath him I once thought was a blanket of sorts is actually his legs twisted and mangled into a heap of broken, bloody bones. I swallow a lump of bile filling my throat.

"Keith, you...uh." I find my pastoral neutral voice. "My friend, you're in bad shape."

He smiles at me, white teeth flashing against the red blood of his lips.

"Ya, don't worry. I'm an enthusiast. I have the ability to ignore pain," he says with a slight chuckle. "My brothers jumped me in the parking lot when I followed Steve. They tossed me in a van with Maria. Along the way they drugged her with some sort of injection, then they broke my legs the moment they dumped us down here." Keith holds two fingers to Maria's neck and sighs.

"Maria's hasn't been doing well. I'm not sure what drugs they gave her, but her pulse has been dropping dangerously low. She needs a doctor."

"Shit." I say under my breath, searching around for any tool that might work to remove my shackles. "We've got to get out here. Where's Tony? I saw him follow you out of the sanctuary."

"I don't know. He went out the opposite door towards the cottage. That was the last time I saw him."

I'm about to ask more questions, when I hear footsteps. They grow louder coming in our direction. I scoot back against a nearby boulder as four figures step into view. Each one is dressed in white robes, heads covered with tall, white hoods that drape over their faces. As the figures come closer, red patches with a white "Xs" that cover the right side of their chests gleam in the flickering light of the torches two of them carry.

Silently they march towards us. Two of them grab hold of my arms, and another takes out a key and releases the chains binding my feet to the ground. My hands still shackled together, they force me to my feet. I hear the bottom of my robe tear as I stand up. I decide that any effort to free myself won't help anyone at the moment, and I restrain myself from kicking the one with a key in the crotch and giving the figure to my left a two-fisted uppercut.

I turn to the right and watch the fourth figure pick Maria off the floor and intentionally step on the mangle legs of Keith in the process. Keith grits his teeth, grunts, but doesn't give them the satisfaction of crying out in pain.

The figure carrying Maria steps in place behind me and my entourage. Her body draped in black lies limp like a doll across the white sleeves of the white supremist. The two figures who grip my arms pull me forward, and I feel the barrel of a gun press against my back.

Then the charming voice of Officer Laine whispers directly into my right ear. "Control your monster or I'll put three bullets in your back."

At his words, I bite my tongue, and remain calm and silent as the gun digs deeper into my spine.

We follow a path along the wall for several minutes. Torches burn every ten feet on my left as pure darkness creates an endless void on my right.

Thoughts race through my mind as I process the current reality of this dismal situation. I know the white robes and hoods are not a good sign. These men are preparing for a ceremony of sorts that will certainly end with violence and death, most likely the death of Maria. I glance behind at Maria and realize that if anyone is watching us, it would appear from a distance that I'm leading this processional. The sleeves of my red robe cover the shackles on my wrist which have forced my palms together in a position of prayer. The two men have pushed me slightly in front of them. Officer Laine is directly behind me with the gun that no one a few feet away would notice. Everyone is wearing masks except for Maria and me, but she currently has the role of the lamb on the way to be slaughtered, and I am the priest at the altar.

Evil outcomes circle like vultures in my mind. I know without a shadow of doubt that I'm being set up. They're going to pin whatever happens next on me. At this point, I prefer dying especially if that means Maria will live.

We stop abruptly and my prophetic vision begins to play out. Torches burn in the distance, but it's difficult to make out the shapes in the darkness. Then a camera flashes somewhere in the cave, illuminating the room with a burst of light. When my eyes finally adjust back to the darkness, we move closer to the burning torches.

A dozen white robes and hoods come into view. The Ku Klux Klan forms a wide circle around an old, wooden altar stained with layers of crimson. On both sides of the altars stand an American flag stands tall and a Christian flag. There's a large cross behind the altar and another masked figure standing more than six feet tall beside the altar. He lifts his hands into the air and a horrifying voice cries out, sending shockwaves of memories that whip me back thirteen years. The last Baptist service I attended, the old Baptist church where the pregnant teenage girl was shamed by the red-faced, rapist preacher.

Alan Laine's voice penetrates the darkness piercing my ears with every word. "Tonight, God demands justice. God is angry! Tonight, He demands a sacrifice, a cleansing of sins. Brothers, I bring forth two sinners, two heathen lesbians, a whoring witch and a dirty, illegal Mexican. They've been living in sin and their sinfulness has been allowed to continue for too long. They must pay for their sins, be cleansed and made pure by blood and fire! Bring the sinners to the altar!"

Rage bursts through my body and I lunge forward screaming. But before I can kick the men holding me, Officer Laine digs his gun deeper into my back.

He barks behind me, "Don't even try it, bitch. It's time for you to pay for your sins."

The large claws gripping my arms squeeze them tighter and yank me into the circle of the Ku Klux Klan. Maria's helpless body is placed like a doll on the altar, her face falling limp to one side. Alan Laine steps up to the altar and pulls out a dagger with a wooden handle. I thrash in fury.

"No! Leave her alone. Kill me instead. She's done nothing wrong. I'm the one you want!"

Alan laughs with the same chuckle I heard the night I attacked him in his church office right before I carved his face with the letter opener. His eyes burn red through the small slits in his hood—they look like the eyes of a demon. His hatred grows as his Scylla expands and dragons emerge through smoke from his body.

He growls at me and says, "Witch, the time for your judgment will come soon enough."

He takes the knife and cuts Maria's black robe down the middle exposing her clergy clothes—a black skirt and blouse. He rips the robe from her body and tears away her skirt and blouse, which leaves her body bare on the altar. I squirm violently against the men holding me as Alan cuts off her bra and underwear. But then a blow against the back of my head brings me to my knees, blurring my vision.

I shake my head, and blink myself back to reality. Officer Laine steps around and gives his gun to the man on my right who instantly presses it against the temple of my forehead. Officer Laine squats down in front of me, staring at me through the slits of his hood. His hazel blue eyes grow narrow, and I watch the storm brewing in his pupils. He peels back his hood revealing the wide teeth of a wolf about to devour its prey, licking his lips only inches from mine.

He whispers in a tone that sounds inhuman, "I'm going to enjoy this even more, knowing you'll be watching."

Anger washes over me, clouding my mind. I bite at him, barely missing his mouth. His large palm reacts with a powerful slap across my face, which causes my lip to burst open. He grabs my jaw and holds my face still as he slides his tongue across my mouth to taste my blood—then he smiles.

Officer Todd Laine stands upright again and covers his face. My head is now at the height of his waist. I watch as he pulls his robe up and unbuckles his belt. At the sight of him unzipping his pants, I expect I will be the target of whatever dehumanizing sexual dominance act comes next, but I see I'm wrong when he turns and makes his way to the altar. Stunned by the pain in my head and horror filling my gut, I observe him prowl around the blood-stained table where an unconscious Maria lies naked and exposed to the evil closing in all around. Officer Laine removes his boots, his pants and his briefs before he climbs onto the altar and positions himself directly over Maria's body.

My eyes shoot a dagger Alan Laine, the father of this wicked boy—the seed of this sick, sinful creature.

Alan raises his hands into the air and speaks with supreme authority, blessing Officer Laine's actions to come, "In the name of God, my son, remove the sins of this woman, cleanse her soul with your seed of purity."

Officer Laine crouches over Maria, his white robe draping over her body. My eyes snap shut with horror as my body retreats inward—my worst nightmare about to unfold. Stomach churning, I swallow a large clump of bile rising from my gut and then force my eyes open again. I refuse to be blind and instead choose to be fully present to witness the evil before me—I am unwilling to allow Maria to suffer alone.

Office Laine begins thrusting himself into Maria, penetrating her again and again. I watch in horror—and it seems time has been suspended, this dimension of reality has become warped, I am in a black hole that is comsuming all goodness, all love in the world.

My hands in chains, my body kneeling, I watch helplessly as the rape continues of my colleague, my friend, my beloved sister. Officer Laine's Scylla emerges with fury, ferocious dragon heads flinging out from his hunched back as he continues forcing himself into her repeatedly. Sharp teeth bite at Maria's body and snap across her chest. The only saving grace is that she remains unconscious, asleep to reality. Tears stream down my cheeks like burning acid, and my heart cries out to God for salvation.

The voices of the men around me penetrate my prayers. I watch them behave like fans cheering during the final minutes of a Friday night football game as their team's quarterback throws a long pass that's caught, advancing the ball toward what will be the winning score.

Officer Laine increases his motion, he grips the sides of the altar and thrusts harder and harder into Maria's tiny body. I stare at the demon drenched in white, devouring the innocent, beloved child of God.

Finally, after long agonizing moments, Officer Laine finishes his religious rite of passage. The smell of blood and semen fills the air as he wipes the rabid foam from the corners of his mouth. He hops off the table and puts on his jeans and boots and takes his place in the inner circle. The other robed men congratulate him, give him high fives and pat him on the shoulders.

Alan Laine steps back up to the altar and I feel the paternal pride radiating out of him. "Well done, my son," Alan cries out in the direction of Officer Todd Laine. "You are a righteous man of God."

Alan's attention turns to the ravaged woman before him. "God, our father," he prays with power and conviction. "Your child has been purified. We now free her from her sinful body, in your mercy receive her soul this day."

With both hands wrapped around the dagger, he raises the weapon above his head, holding the sharp weapon directly over Maria's bare chest.

29: The Challenger

I lurch forward in fury, the gun pressing hard into my temple, and I think through my next move. I've also known that I was a challenger, but I never dreamed I would one day challenge the man who raped my mother, the man who I now know is my father. Right before Alan lowers the knife I scream.

"Father, stop!" My cries echo through the cave, my voice pierces the darkness.

Alan Laine freezes, hands high above his head. The tension in the space intensifies as all attention focuses on Alan and the gun at my temple lowers. Rising slowly to my feet, I continue talking buying more time, time for the universe to work a miracle, perhaps time enough for God—wherever the fuck she is—to throw me a hale Mary.

"Yes, Alan." I declare with conviction. "My mother was Sophia Charlotte Wayland. The night you rape her, March 27, 1991, she conceived me. I am Isobel Alexandria Wayland. You are my father."

To my surprise, one of the white men steps out of order, fumbling with confusion towards the altar. He cries out demandingly and points to me.

"Alan, is this true? You told me Charlie was whoring herself around town, cursing men with witches' poison. You told me she drugged you that night."

I take a step back stunned and bewildered. It's my father's voice. My thoughts scramble together. My father or whoever I once thought was my father is here, is present in the room—a member of the KKK. How can this be? How did I not know?

The white-robed man beside Alan raises his voice louder, "I called her a liar when she said you raped her. I trusted your word. I believed you when you said that you would never betray our friendship."

Alan lowers the dagger to his side and turns to the man questioning him. In a casual tone, Alan replies, "She's lying, Joe. Don't let her deceive you. She's just like her witch of a mother."

No longer able to remain silent, I address the man who raised me from birth, who beat me in the name of God everyday after my mother supposedly died. The same father who forsook me at fifteen, the man I haven't said one word to since I walked out of his home with a duffle bag in one hand and a fist full of hatred in the other.

"I'm not lying." My voice shakes at first but steadies as I focus my ferity.

"I have proof. This son of bitch kept a journal for decades documenting everything he did." Speaking now to all the men in the room I add, "The journal was given to me by his youngest son, a Baptist pastor, a man of God who refuses the wicked ways of white supremacy. A true man of God who has been broken and bruised by the hands of his brothers. Keith Laine discovered his father's sinfulness. If you don't believe me, believe him. All the women, all the innocent girls Reverend Alan Laine raped for years—I know their names. They know his face. I will find each and everyone of them."

Turning my eyes back to Alan, I feel the inferno of hell boiling in my blood. I speak with all power and authority bestowed upon me as a priestess of the mighty high.

I scream, "Alan Laine, you will pay for your sins!" and move towards the altar. Scylla billows out of my back in the hurricane winds building around me. "Your evil acts against God and against the children of God have come into the light. You stand accused before God. You cannot hide in the darkness any longer."

Out of the corner of my eye, I notice that my Scylla no longer has six heads. The reptilian tentacles have merged forming two large dragon wings humming behind me. I glance down at my feet, as Scylla lifts me off the ground. I hover a foot in the air and raise my hands, turn my palms towards the heavens and a halo of blue flames radiates from my flesh.

"Alan Laine, you cannot flee God's justice," I proclaim in low growl. "You will burn for your wickedness."

Then the voice of Officer Laine's bellows in the distance, "Shoot her! For Christ's sake, kill the witch."

I hear men gasping and moving chaotically around, but I hold the tension, and remain in my meditative state. Nearby a gun goes off, but one of Scylla's dragon scaled wings reacts like a shield to deflect the shot. The bullet bounces back, and I hear a man groan in pain.

Confident and determined now, I close my eyes and will Scylla to take us to Maria. I float towards the altar, and Officer Todd flings his body in front of me. His Scylla is raging—all six heads bite wildly at me. I drop to the ground, and my Scylla transforms back into six fierce dragon heads. Then our Scylla's collide like sea monsters warring on the waves of the ocean. Officer Laine and I box in the ring, surrounded by a dozen snarling jaws snapping at one another. I block a right hook with my forearm and swing my shackled hands up slamming two fist into his jawline. Blood splatters from his cheek bones where the shackles cut open a piece of flesh. I grin with pleasure, but my enthusiasm ends when Officer Todd gives a powerful uppercut to my gut. I fall back slightly and barely block the next punch to my face.

Out of the corner of my eye, I see Alan running in white angelic robs towards me, directly behind Officer Todd. Before I can redirect Scylla, he grabs the chain between my hands and jerks me down onto my stomach. I catch myself with my elbows keeping my face smashing against the stone floor. My Scylla fully occupied, Officer Todd kicks me in the ribs, knocking the wind out of me. I gasp for air—strength now leaving me. My Scylla, yelping like a wounded dog, retreats into my body. Office Todd six heads wrap around me, constricting my body now crouched in pain on the stone ground. Alan, still holding my chains, yanks me onto my belly and drags me across the cold floor toward the wooden cross at the other end of the circle.

Yelling out like a mad man, Alan defends himself before his followers, "She's a lying bitch! I've done nothing wrong. Remember she's the sinner, the lesbian witch. You just witnessed her power, the evilness that we must destroy. Scripture demands justice against women like her! It's time for her to burn like her mother."

The men circle back together and clap their hands in approval. Lifting me off the ground by my hair, Alan shoves my body against the vertical beam of the cross. His hand grips my neck pinning me against the wood. My heels rise off the ground, and I struggle to breathe.

He turns his head and calls out demandingly, "Joe, bring me the ropes and the gasoline. It's time to cleanse this witch's soul with the fires of hell."

Out of the corner of my eye, I notice Joe hesitate for a moment and then pull out a large bundle of rope from beneath his robe. My stomach churns at the sickening reality that the man who raised me came prepared to murder me. Joe strolls up to Alan still clutching me against the cross. He picks up a canister of gasoline beside one of the legs of the altar. I squirm, trying to take in more oxygen as my head begins to spin.

Alan extends his left hand to the thick, braided rope but Joe pulls back. Alan's grip on my neck loosens slightly, dropping me back onto my heels, which gives my lungs a few seconds of reprieve.

He turns to Joe and says coolly, "Joe, we've been friends forever. Trust me. She's lying. I would never have done that to you. Now, give me the rope."

I listen to the men argue, and a movement along the path in the distance catches my eye. Alan and Joe continue arguing about my mother and their history, and I watch Tony creep silently in the shadows behind the circle of white men.

Looking down at Joe, hooded and robed, I notice he's significantly shorter than me, with a smaller frame and petite build. Then my eyes turn to Alan, a tall muscular frame, well over six feet. If my memory serves me, Alan has similar fiery red hair and cold blue eyes to mine.

I think back to the ten years I watched Joe with my mother. I never saw him hit her or abuse her in any way. I wonder if the truth of my real father was what haunted her and caused her to flee. I wonder what lie Alan told Joe after my mother tried to tell her husband about the rape. I turn to Joe and plead with him.

"Father, you forsook me long ago, but I know you loved my mother. I beg you, please, do not listen to this lying piece of shit. He's made a fool of you, has deceived you, and turned you against your true love."

Alan's grip tightens again, but I'm determined to keep speaking until my final breath.

"Joe, he was jealous of you. He stole her from you long ago because she chose you. Don't let him win again."

Joe takes a step closer to Alan and for a moment I think he's about to hand over the ropes, but then he turns to me.

Looking me in the eyes, he speaks to Alan in a tone loud enough for all the men to hear, "I always wondered why you never wanted our children to play together, why you never came to our house, why Charlie was always—always different around you. I refused to believe the truth about what happened twenty years ago, the night before she disappeared. You're right. She is a witch."

Joe turns his attention away from me and looks at Alan, "But you, you are something worse."

Then to my surprise, and by the gasp of the men in the room, to the shock of everyone, Joe rips the white hood off Alan's head. The claws around my throat release as the face of the leader of Ku Klux Klan is exposed. The man before me wears the face of a Hollywood actor who refuses to age. The scar on his forehead is completely gone along with any wrinkle or expression. Alan Laine has clearly undergone multiple skin grafts and surgeries to remove any traces of the mark I left with a letter opener thirteen years ago. His youthful face is frozen in place, Botox creating the look of a forty-year-old politician. His thick, strawberry blonde hair is speckled with white, and his blue, gray eyes stare into mine only a few feet away. A wide, victorious smile spreads across his face.

"Oh Alex, you look disappointed," Alan says in response to my dumbfounded gaze.

"Thanks to you, I no longer age." He strokes his face with pleasure and turns to Joe who has taken a step towards me. "I look better than ever. Now, we look more like father and daughter."

Joe screams out in rage, "You son of a bitch!" Then he flings the rope at Alan who gets tangled in it for a moment, giving Joe enough time to give Alan a right hook and punch to the gut. Joe's sudden aggression against the leader of the KKK triggers commotion among the bystanders.

Alan stumbles back, bent over at the waist, and Officer Laine tackles Joe, which takes him to the ground right in front of me. Tony leaps out of the darkness like a grizzly bear tackling the man who shot at me earlier. The gun falls to the ground. Tony retrieves the weapon quickly while keeping his large, muscular frame on top of the man.

I hurl myself onto Alan and reach for the knife still in his left hand. My hands are still shackled, and it's impossible for me to get any physical leverage on his large body. After a few moments, he manages to flip me over onto my back and pin me between his legs. He holds the sharp dagger's edge against my neck.

Alan calls out to Tony, "If you want her alive, drop the gun."

Tony responds coolly, "You're mistaken, I have a gun, yeu have a knife. Drop the knife or this man's dies."

Alan keeps his eyes focused on me, and I watch an evil grin form on his face—a smile I've often seen mirrored on Officer Laine.

Alan flips the dagger in his hands and responds to Tony's demand saying, "Kill him, I have three more sons."

Then speaking to me in a low growl he says under his breath, "Hold still my child."

Grabbing my face, he forces my cheek to the side where I see Tony pressing the gun against the back of the head of the man he sits upon. The sudden change of expression on Tony's face sends a shock wave of fear through my body. Alan holds my face to the ground with his forearm using his free hand to pull off my clergy collar, exposing a large portion of my neckline. Pain pierces my skin as I feel the sharp tip of the knife dig into my flesh. I scream in anger, kicking my legs under him.

Tony shouts, "Stop! Stop! What about this? Yeu said this journal didn't exist and yet, here it is."

Alan stops carving into my neck and looks over at Tony who pulls out the journal from his back pocket waving it in the air. Tears swell in my eyes as I stare helplessly at Tony.

Tony says calmly to Alan, "Come on. Let's trade. The journal for both women."

I feel Alan's body freeze, and he removes his arm from my face.

Somewhere nearby, I hear Joe blubbers out. "It is true! You son of bitch, you raped my wife."

Alan roars out, "Shut the fuck up, Joe! So what, I slept with your wife. She was a witch and whore, anyway."

A few feet away, Joe manages to break free from Officer Laine.

He lunges in hellbent fury towards Alan. Joe stumbles and kicks the can of gasoline, which sprays gasoline over Alan's white robe.

Alan twists his body towards Joe. He swiftly removes the knife from my neck and plunges it into the chest of his attacker.

I cry out in horror as Joe gasps for air. Crimson red seeps across the white robe, and Joe collapses over me, face down, pinning me deeper into the cold stone earth. My chained hands feel the warm, sticky blood pouring out of Joe and over my chest. It mixes with my own blood that's now running down my neck. I lie helpless and horrified under the dead body of the man I once called Dad.

Alan wipes the dagger on the back of Joe's white robe, and I hear the men around the circle stir with anger and anxiety. Some even call Alan a traitor and a false prophet. I turn my head and watch blurry white robes disappear into darkness, fleeing down the paths and out of the cave.

Officer Laine's voice calls after them, "Cowards! We know who you are. You're the traitors!"

With Alan and his boys distracted by the scene of white men fleeing into darkness, Tony seizes the opportunity. He moves swiftly behind Alan and presses the gun against his forehead.

"Yeu sick bastard. Drop the knife and get off of her."

Alan's face contorts into red rage. His lips tighten as he rises to his feet, up and off of my body. I painfully push Joe's limp body off my chest. I feel dizzy, and take in several deep breaths, allowing oxygen to fill my lungs.

I'm slow to get up, and feel that I might pass out. I push myself to my knees. Officer Laine grabs the knife off the ground, throws himself on top of me, and my body is pinned once again under a rapist.

My reflex action kicks in instantly when I see the dagger plunging down on me. One of the arms of my Scylla slows Officer's Todd's attack, giving me a split second to catch his wrist before the sharp tip reaches my face.

I struggle for a moment against the brute strength of Officer Laine when the gun fires and Officer Laine jerks to the left in pain. The knife falls to the ground as he grabs his right shoulder.

Without hesitation, I thrust both fists into his genitals. A yelp of pain erupts from him, and he falls to the side of my body. I flip back, rolling over my left shoulder in order to get to my feet as quickly as possible.

Alan rushes towards me and a gun goes off again. He groans, grabs his leg and falls to the ground, cursing.

Behind me, Tony yells, "Isobel, get Maria and get out of here."

I grab the knife off the ground and leap onto Officer Todd who is still groaning with pain. I slip my hand up his white robe, pressing the knife against his swelling genitals. "Give me the keys, or I'll make sure your raping days end here and now."

Officer Laine reaches into his robe and pulls out the keys. I grab them and make my way to Maria while Tony commands the rest of the Laine clan to back away. I quickly unshackle my wrists and cover Maria's body with her torn black robe. Her face is pale and her body cold as ice. I rip off my blood-soaked robe. Tony side steps towards me, keeping his gun pointed at the Laine clan.

He says in a low voice, "Isobel, get Maria out of here."

"Tony, I'm not leaving you alone, one of you against five of them."

He says, "Don't worry, I've got a plan."

I grab his free hand squeezing it firmly in mine saying,

"Promise me you won't do anything stupid, like get yourself killed."

He turns his head to me and grins. "I promise, my bonnie lass."

I let go of Tony, scoop Maria into my arms and race down the path, following the light of the torches. I make my way back to the area of the cave I woke up in less than an hour ago where I find Keith in the same position, crippled and half dead.

Looking down at his twisted legs, I shake my head and say, "Keith, we need to get you out of here."

For a split second I consider the possibility of leaving him for the sake of Maria's life, but I'm freed from the horrible decision when Tony comes running up to us.

"Isobel, we've got to hurry, I could only stall them for a few moments."

"Can you carry Keith?"

"Yes." Tony hesitates before picking Keith off the floor. "Sorry, lad. This is goin' hurt like hell."

I glance down at Maria's face and to my horror, her skin is as white mine and her lips are turning blue. Panic fills me, and I turn to Tony who is squatting down to pick up Keith.

"We must hurry. Maria isn't breathing. Do you know the way to Island from here?"

Keith grunts, grabbing clumsily onto Tony's neck with one hand while holding Tony's gun with the other.

Tony lifts his body off the guard with both arms and says, "Yes, the fastest way is to take a left and follow the torches to the tunnels. I'll follow behind yeu. Keith, you cover my back."

I take off down the path to the left, trusting my legs to carry both Maria and me at the quickest pace possible. Soon I see the entrance to the tunnels, but I also hear the voices of men running up behind us. Two gunshots go off.

Tony's words of encouragement let me know he's not far behind me, "We're alright, keep movin'. We will lose them in the tunnels."

We reach the tunnels and Tony asks Keith to get the flashlight out of his chest pocket. Tony places the flashlight in his mouth and takes the lead. His pace is almost a sprint forcing me to run like I've never run before. I follow close behind him, weaving through the maze of dark shadows. After ten minutes of sprinting, my chest burns along with the aching muscles of my arms and legs. To my relief we pass the ladder leading up to Tony's bar and I know we're only minutes away from the Island.

Tony picks up speed, and I force my body to do the same. We arrive at the large wooden door and Tony, showing no signs of fatigue, sets Keith gently down on the ground. He pulls out the iron key from his back pockets and unlocks the door.

Heavily winded, I hear the sound of the river rushing around the island. I glance down at Maria's lifeless body cradled in my arms. Tears fill my eyes, worry constricts my chest. Tony hands cup my face and my eyes meet his. I swallow a large lump as his words settle the acid bubbling in my belly.

"Isobel. All will be well."

30: The Peacemaker

Tony takes Maria from my arms, and we race around the wooden deck to the bridge. Reaching down into the rapids, I pull the hidden lever that swings the bridge into place. We cross over the waters to the Island of Essence.

Tony places Marie's limp, pale body in the center. I stare at him with pleading eyes and ask, "Can you save her like you saved me?"

Tony shakes his head. "No, I can't. In order to bring someone back, yeu must love them, love them beyond yourself. I do not love her the way I love yeu." Then he takes my hands into his and says, "But I believe you can, Isobel. I know yeu love her more than yeu love yourself. Bring forth Scylla. Use your power to save Maria."

Salty tears flood into my eyes. "Tony, I'm not strong enough. I can't save her. I'm too broken, too angry, too selfish to love anyone like that."

Tony says, "I believe in yeu. It's time for yeu to believe in yeur-self." He rises to his feet and once again repeats the sacred Gaelic words, "Tha i na h-uabhasach brèagha, Iseabail, a 'bhana-bhuid-seach gheal. Tha neart a 'sruthadh tro na h-uighean. You are the great, great granddaughter of the white witch, Isobella. The power that ran through her veins runs through yeurs."

I grab hold of his hand and beg, "Tony, please stay with me."

"I love yeu, Isobel. Be who yeu were created to be." He releases my hand, walks away, and crosses back over the bridge.

As the bridge separates from the island, he cries out to me, "Lead with your soul! Let go, Isobel!"

I look down at Maria's lifeless body and my mind fills with images of Officer Laine pounding his flesh into her. I fall over her body, weep, and pull her close to me. "Maria, I'm so sorry." I cry out, rise to my knees, suck in gobs of air and snot through my nose. "I'm so sorry. I failed you. You've always been the peacemaker in my life. I need you! Please wake up! Maria, I love you."

The island begins to quake, and I realize Maria and I are in the inner circle. Slowly, we both are lowered to the bottom. Below the island, I stare at the walls engraved with Latin numerals. My eye remains on the number eight, and I remember the night I almost drowned.

I take a deep breath, let go of my guilt, my shame, my fear and my anger. I let go of rage—all the hateful rage towards Alan Laine, my father. I let go of my rage towards Officer Laine and Steve, the rapists of my friend, and my half brothers. I let go of it all and trust the monster within me to save the one I love.

Helplessly holding Maria in my arms, I reach out and push "VIII."

Rather than water gushing into the inner circle a blast of blinding light beams through the hole. Then the other eight Latin numbers sink into the wall, one after the other, beginning with number nine and moving clockwise to number seven.

Light beams through each opening illuminating the small space with a wave of dazzling brilliance, forcing my eyes to close.

Now I feel Scylla emerge from my body. Electricity pulses across my skin, and my head begins to spin, or perhaps it's the island that's spinning—I do not know. I keep my eyes shut and will my spirit to let go.

Moments pass, I barely open my eyes to watch Scylla's dark clouds of dragon heads dig into Maria's body like six conduits of electrical currents. I feel the pulsing rhythm of my heart jolt life back into Maria.

I rest my head on Maria's chest and search for signs of life.

Seconds pass like centuries across time as I wait.

Now I hear a voice praying aloud, "Our Father, who art in heaven, hallowed be thy name." As the words flow, I realize they are coming from my lips. Then I see her, a white witch standing in dark woods. Her eyes are closed, and her hands are clasped as she prays the ancient words along with me.

"Thy kingdom come thy will be done on earth as it is heaven."

The young woman, pale as the midnight moon, has the wings of a dragon. She slowly rises off the forest floor into the air as our voices carry towards heaven, "Give us this day, our daily bread and forgive us our debts—"

She has a heavy Scottish accent and her fiery hair wafts in the wind as her flesh begins to blaze with blue flames. Our voices grow louder together, "Lead us not into temptation—"

Then I feel it, a faint beat thump in Maria's chest. Then another thump. Then another.

My eyes burst open, and I realize I'm floating in the air, holding Maria against my chest. Scylla's tentacles have once again mutated into dragon wings, and we hover above the Island of Essence.

Maria gasps for air, takes in a deep breath to fill her lungs, and life rises and falls in her chest. I look down at her face.

Her eyes open just long enough for her to finish the prayer. "Deliver us from evil," she mumbles in a raspy voice. She gives me an enchanting smile before falling unconscious again.

I pull her body close to my chest as Scylla slowly lowers us back down to the island floor.

My heels return to the ground, and I look up and see Tony, standing in front of me, his eyes are awestruck with wonder and tears roll down into the bristles of his beard. He gently takes Maria from me and cradles her like a small child in his long, muscular arms.

He smiles at her with gratitude and relief for the miracle he witnessed. My arms fall limp to the side as they finally acknowledge their fatigue. I close my eyes, inhale deeply, and then exhale the weight of the world from the bottom of my lungs. My mouth splits open into a wide smile and my gaze returns to Tony and Maria. Reaching with both my hands, I wipe away the streaks of tears from Tony's face.

He leans down close to me, eyes sparkling with the light of torch fire burning all around us, and he kisses me deeply, which sends a small burst of electric currents through my weary body.

After a long moment, his lips release their hold.

My hands still cup his neck and cheeks, and we declare together in pronounced agreement, "Amen."

Epilogue: Life

Following Maria's resurrection on the Island of Essence, Tony and I somehow managed to get both Maria and Keith up the ladder and through the narrow space into Tony's bar. Thanks to Marcus and Raquel, two ambulances were waiting in the alley.

Upon arrival at the hospital, Keith was immediately taken away for surgery. The surgeons weren't hopeful at first, but because of miraculously skilled hands, coupled with recent scientific advancements, we received good news. Following nine hours of piecing his bones back together with screws and rods, the doctor informed us that he will most likely walk again with the help of a cane.

Keith's legs were, of course, a shock to the medical staff, but Marie's toxicology report was downright flabbergasting. With the amount of blood loss and large dose Gamma-hydroxybutyric acid, the doctors were amazed she wasn't dead on arrival. She remained in a coma, however, and none of her physicians said they could be sure if or when she would awake. Some said it might be hours and others said it could be months.

I remained at her bedside only leaving during the times I was needed at St Luke's for Saturday evening mass and Easter morning services. Police officers stood guard twenty-four seven outside the hospital rooms of both Keith and Maria.

Tony stood guard over me as well, never letting me out of his sight. I caught small doses of slumber on the sofa in Maria's room and would wake up to Tony's warm hand resting gently on my back like a blanket over my chilled body.

* * *

Back on Saturday morning following the events of Good Friday in the tunnels and caverns below the city, I woke up abruptly from a deep and dreamless sleep. I was slightly disoriented when I found Tony next to me on the sofa. He kissed me on the forehead and handed me a hot cup of coffee.

Gratefully, I sat up and sipped the coffee in silence, then I turned to him and searched his intense, alert eyes. Thousands of unanswered questions washed over me, but he didn't wait for me to ask, apparently knowing full well the first question on my mind. His voice steady, Tony explained his role in the events that unfolded after he followed Keith out of the sanctuary.

He said, "By the time Keith and I got to the lobby, Maria was nowhere to be found. Keith ran outside to the parkin' lot and around to the cottage. I decided to check the sacristy and the basement area that leads to the tunnels, thinking maybe Maria was able to hide there. But once I discovered both spaces were empty, I hurried to find Keith. When I stepped outside, I saw a van screechin' out of the lot onto the street. I jumped in my car and followed them to Cave Hill Cemetery.

"The grounds are closed after dark, but someone opened the gate for the van, which trapped me on the outside. I had to park the car and climb the fence.

"By the time I found their location, the van was empty, but I saw white cloaks disappearing into a crypt nearby. Having studied the tunnels for so long, I knew one of them led somewhere beneath the cemetery. Once all the white cloaked men had vanished, I slipped into the crypt and followed their trail of torch light.

"I lost them for a while because I was trying to keep my distance as I wound around the tunnels. But then I heard Keith screaming in pain and followed his cries to their location. Four men were still beating him when I arrived, and I knew then I couldn't get them both out on my own. Wastin' no time, I raced back through the tunnels to the bar and called Marcus. By that time he had received your message, but he arrived at the church after they had taken yeu in Keith's van. I knew time was short, and it would be impossible to explain to Marcus how to find the KKK group down in the tunnels. I told him to have two ambulances ready in the alley hoping I'd be able to get everyone out alive. I grabbed a few supplies and headed back into the tunnels. By the time I made it to the place I last saw Keith and Maria, Keith informed me that they had taken Maria and yeu to the ceremony. I made it to yeu the moment yeur shadow creature morphed into dragon wings. Isobel, when yeu took flight, when yeu bursted into blue flames. I knew yeu were a warrior sent from heaven."

Tony ended his story there, knowing we both remembered clearly the events that followed. I decided I'd received enough answers for the time being and so I lifted my face up to his and returned his kiss.

* * *

Tony was vigilant watching over me all weekend. He drove me to and from the hospital, checked rooms and closets in the cottage before I entered, and stood in the back of the sanctuary during services and even when I was sitting on the toilet or taking a shower. The only time he left my side was when I asked to be alone with Maria. But even then, he leaned against the door. For quite some time, I never once witnessed Tony asleep, and I began to wonder how little I knew about him. Even for his size and build he seemed to have superhuman strength. I remembered how he'd sprinted effortlessly with Keith's two hundred thirty pounds of dead weight. He wasn't even out of breath or winded when we arrived at the island.

Late Saturday night after mass, we snuck in a bottle of bourbon and Sam the cat into Maria's room. While sipping on our second pour of Angels Envy, I asked Tony what happened after I ran off with Maria's body.

He said, "I had the gun in one hand knowing I had less than a handful of bullets against five men. So I used the journal as leverage. Holding the gun pointed at the three unwounded Laine men, I stood next to one of the torches on the wall. I told them I would burn the journal if they didn't follow us. Alan was leaning against the altar trying to keep the blood from his bullet wound from bleeding when he agreed to my terms. With nothing else to use as leverage I held the journal over the fire. Once the evidence caught fire, I walked over to Alan and tossed the burning journal down to him. His robe covered with gasoline caught fire more quickly than I had imagined. By the time his sons reach him, his body was fully engulfed in flames. I knew I had only minutes to spare, which hopefully would give us just enough time to escape."

I smiled at Tony, and raised my glass to him, and then we both gulped down the rest of our bourbon.

* * *

It is now Sunday evening, and Tony and I are in Maria's room, hoping and praying for a miracle. Through the window I notice that the sun is beginning to set, when my attention is drawn away to Maria who is in the bed, still unconscious. To my delight, I see movement—Maria has begun to stir. A few seconds pass, her eyes pop open, and she asks where the heck she is.

I tell her, and it soon is apparent, perhaps due to the effects of the date-rape drug, that she remembers none of the events of Good Friday, including her death and resurrection.

This news hits me with mixed emotions. I'm relieved that she doesn't seem to suffer any painful memories, but I'm burdened by the reality that I will have to explain—and therefore to relive the horror of what happened to her. I know that watching her experience the shame and grief is going to be almost too much for me to bear.

Nevertheless, I proceed.

Tony, overwhelmed by what I am recounting, leaves the room when I reach the part about her rape on the altar by Officer Laine. He had told me the day before that he arrived at the KKK ceremony just when I stopped Alan Laine from plunging the dagger into Maria.

Following long minutes of weeping together through the details of that evil night, I decide to skip over the part where she died as well as her resurrection on the Island of Essence. But when Tony comes back into the room thirty minutes later, he spoils my plans.

Handing Maria more Kleenexes, Tony tries to cheer her up by asking, "So how'd you feel about the part when you died and came back to life?"

Maria's face contorts with confusion and she whips her head around to me, sitting on the other side of the bed.

She cries, "Died? I died? Alex, you forgot to tell me that small bit of information."

I glare at Tony whose eyes are wide with surprise and embarrassment.

"Maria, I'm sorry." I begin, apologetically, and I turn my eyes to the tile floor. "I just didn't have it in me to tell you yet about that. It was hard enough giving details about everything else, and I just didn't want to relive one of the worst moments of my life."

Maria takes hold of my hands and says, softly, "It's okay. I understand. Tony, could you tell me this part of the story?"

Tony agrees, and I rise to my feet, a wave of more tears burning in my eyes. I leave both Maria and Tony alone and exit the room in search of fresh air and more coffee.

On my way to the cafeteria, one of the police officers named Mike, who rotates on guard watch at Maria's room, follows me into the elevator. I greet with a smile as the doors closed behind him.

"Hi Officer Mike, are you on Sister Maria duty tonight?" I ask in a friendly voice.

He responds in a flat tone, keeping his expression neutral and his eyes forward. "No, Mother. I've been given a different assignment."

"Oh." I reply, caught off guard by his stern disposition. "Well, I hope it's got nothing to do with me."

Mike remains silent, and the tension in the small space elevates as we descend to the first floor. I step off the elevator and head in the direction of the cafeteria.

Officer Mike follows a few steps behind me the entire way through the hospital corridors. I offer to buy him coffee and he declines with a simple head shake. He escorts me all the way back up to the eighth floor and then watches me return to Maria's room.

That night as I close my eyes to sleep, I wonder about Officer's Mike's strange behavior, but soon enough, I'm engulfed weight of exhaustion.

* * *

It's now Monday morning, Tony and I are sitting on the sofa that I'd been sleeping on in the hospital room for the past three nights. We watch Maria scarf down a stack of syrup drenched pancakes, and laugh as Tony tells dirty Scottish jokes with a thick accent.

There is a knock at the door and Marcus walks into the room with a handful of documents, today's newspaper on top. He had told Tony and me shortly after we arrived at the hospital that he would have to keep his distance while he investigated the events of Good Friday with his team. So when he pulls the short doctor's stool in front of us we are anxious to hear the details of the investigation. Marcus sits down and takes his time before beginning.

"Early Saturday morning, my team and I went to the location Tony gave us, and we swept the entire cave but found little to no evidence. There was no trace of the KKK or anything you described to me, Tony. The place was obviously wiped clean, too clean. The smell of bleach was strong."

Anger erupts from me. "Marcus, how is that possible? There should have been blood everywhere. What about the body of Joseph Wayland?"

Marcus turns his eyes down to the stack of papers in his hand. He pauses for a long moment and then takes a deep breath. "Last night someone found his body. It was in the dumpster behind St Luke's."

"What?" I exclaim with confusion. "Why would they dump his body there?"

"Alex, it gets worse." Marcus says, soberly. "The letter 'A' was carved into his forehead."

I leap to my feet—rage blurring across my vision. "What?! Of course it was!"

"Alex, I'm sorry. We've kept this story from the press as long as possible, but it's worse than we could have ever imagined. They have a photo of you, Alex. It's on the front page of today's paper."

I snatch the newspaper from Marcus and unfold it wildly. My hands shake as I stare at the same image that prophetically flashed before my eyes as I led the caravan of KKK members to the altar down in the caves.

The large black and white photo is blurry but not distorted enough to reveal my face clearly. The shackles on my hands are hidden by my sleeves and the three men in white capes and hoods stand slightly behind me. The tag line in large block letters reads:

CATHOLIC PRIEST, LEADS KKK, MURDERS FATHER ON GOOD FRIDAY.

My mouth hangs open and I'm too stunned to notice Tony standing right in front of me. He gently takes the paper from my hands and pulls me into his chest.

He says, "Marcus, the police can't possibly take this seriously. This is slander."

Marcus stands up and shakes his head. "The photo was dropped anonymously on a flash drive, and the only evidence we have against the Laine family is you both claiming to fight Rev. Alan Laine and his sons. But now it's not enough to counter the evidence against Alex. This morning the cottage was searched. Alex's red clergy robe was found in the washing machine with traces of Joseph Wayland's blood."

My head swirls taking in all the lies against me. I push away from Tony and ask urgently. "What about Officer Laine? Where is he and his father who we know has severe burns?"

"We called Officer Laine. According to him and a few eyewitnesses, he's been on leave with his family down in Paducah on their family farm for the past week. Yes, Alan Laine does has severe burns on his hands and neck but they are claiming it was from grease fire in their kitchen on Saturday morning"

"Alright, Marcus," I say dejectedly. "What does this mean? What happens now?"

Marcus pulls out his cuffs and walks towards me. Before I can react Tony steps in front me with his arms crossed.

"Marcus. Yeu can't be serious. Yeur really going to arrest her, here and now."

"I'm sorry but I have no choice. You're fortunate the officers outside like you or else this would be more painful."

I put my hand on Tony's shoulder and add gravely, "It's okay. He's right."

I extend my hands in front of me, and Marcus gently places the handcuffs around my bruised, raw wrists.

"Tony, I have a plan." Marcus says, encouragingly. "Alex has a very good lawyer. She won't go to prison. We've arranged for her to be placed on house arrest until trial but we have to take her downtown first and get her prints."

Before Tony can protest again, there's a knock at the door. The attending physician enters the room and closes the door behind him. Completely ignoring the three us including me in handcuffs standing tensely at the end of the bed, the doctor moves straight to Maria. Holding a file in one hand, he looks down at her solemnly.

Maria, wipes tears from her eyes, and pushes the tray of half eaten breakfast to the side. She asks the doctor in a trembling voice, "What is it? What's wrong?"

He glances around the room at our faces and begins, apologetically, "I'm sorry to intrude but I felt this news couldn't wait."

Turning back to Maria he continues, "Maria, your blood work has shown unusual results. We've run multiple tests these past twenty-four hours."

He hesitates, apparently trying to figure out his next words.

Maria chimes impatiently. "Cancer? Infection? STD? What is it?"

The room goes still. Tony and Marcus stand like granite statues. I walk over to Maria's side and grab hold of her shoulder with cuffed hands.

Instead of reading the results, the doctor gives a piece of paper to Maria. She reads it silently, her mouth falls open and another tear rolls down her cheek.

"Mary, mother of Jesus. I'm pregnant."

TO BE CONTINUED

About the Author

E. E. Whitaker lives in Louisville, Kentucky. She is a Baptist pastor and seminary teacher who has been serving churches for more than fifteen years. She holds a Master of Divinity and is finishing her Ph.D. work in Amsterdam. When's she's not preaching, teaching and traveling the world, she's walking her Labrador Lucy. You can often find her in a local cigar lounge playing chess and enjoying a glass of bourbon with a mild cigar.

Check out her website, www.eewhitaker.com, and join the mailing list for updates about speaking events and book release dates for the sequel.

Follow her on Instagram @eewhitaker and her Facebook page, E.E.Whitaker

Email the author at info@eewhitaker.com